A COMMON READER
Pleasantville, New York

THE GLASS NIGHT

John de Falbe was born in 1963. He is
married and lives in London, where he is
a director of John Sandoe (Books) Ltd,
an independent bookshop in Chelsea.
The Glass Night is his first novel.

The Glass Night

John de Falbe

The Cuckoo Press

THE GLASS NIGHT

First published in 1995 by
The Cuckoo Press
10, Blacklands Terrace, London SW3 2SR

A CIP catalogue reference for this book
is available from the British Library

ISBN 0 9524501 0 0

Book designed by Fenella Willis

Typeset by Disc To Print (London) Ltd

Printed in Great Britain by
BPC Paperbacks Ltd
A member of
The British Printing Company Ltd

For Nell

1

Listen – do you remember when you came in late one night during the summer and made love with Kate in the sitting-room? Perhaps it was a regular tryst, in which case I don't know how the occasion itself is coloured in your mind. I can't reach it except by a date: the day of Percy's funeral, six weeks and three days before Kate's fall.

I was there.

I let myself in with Tilda's key and went out to the balcony. It was such a warm, clear evening that it seemed a pity to sit inside. I had brought with me four bottles of wine, token thanks in advance for having me to stay, and I decided to fetch a glass and settle myself in the armchair where I could enjoy the freak caress of the night as I waited for you. The curtains were drawn across the balcony windows, and it was soon dark. The lights of the City running off to the horizon found a reflection within me: my thoughts wandered as memories were teased to the surface, and I don't know how long it was before I realized you were home.

Didn't you get my message on your answer-phone? Don't you pay any attention to your father?

You weren't alone. It surprises me that you didn't come outside together on such a beautiful night – what's the balcony for? But I understand that its appeal would be muted by the urgency of sexual desire. And so I was there, quietly admiring the view, when suddenly I became aware that you and Kate were making love indoors, scarcely four metres away. What could I do?

1

If I made my presence known, besides spoiling your pleasure I would cruelly embarrass all three of us, and I could hardly add, 'But don't mind me, carry on!' If I stayed where I was and you came out later, flushed with the heat of one another's body, and found me, how would you avoid the feeling that you had been spied on? You would shudder, and your saliva would turn sour. How would I explain my silence? You would think I witnessed the scene with sweaty, perverted relish. Since I didn't reveal myself at once, the awkwardness of doing so increased as your amorous enterprise proceeded. Clearly you didn't expect me to be there, and my failure to hear your entrance seemed a feeble, irrelevant excuse. Are you so accustomed to your sister's absence at night that you just assumed she wouldn't be there?

In the end I settled myself in such a way that I could pretend, if you found me, that I was asleep. Supposing you came out to the balcony after making love, you would find your old man quietly snoring in a chair, an empty bottle of wine beside him. I hoped the spectacle wouldn't be too embarrassing for Kate: she has a lively sense of the ridiculous, and I imagined she might appreciate the situation. If you didn't discover me until you pulled back the curtains in the morning, or saw my overnight bag at last (how did you fail to see it when you came in?), then, similarly, there would be little cause for embarrassment – except, perhaps, for you, Jake, on behalf of your thirsty father, who had sat out all night on your balcony without announcing himself. My only anxiety was that it should suddenly turn cold. Was I a coward? I prefer to think I was prudent.

As I sat in that chair, trying not to hear my son making love indoors, I was sharply affected. Not by the arthritic fist of my disapproval, for I'm not so severe; but by the thought that for me, Dan Flasch, to be seated in that chair on that balcony overlooking the East End of London, aged 53, while my son made love inside, was a miracle. That afternoon I had watched Percy being lowered into his grave near his home in Croydon, while my wife Ruth was at home in Coventry waiting for our daughter, who didn't turn up. Who could have predicted all this? And who knows where you and your children – if you have any – will be thirty years from now? In the same way, when I glance at what the future holds, I find I can only conceive a safe delivery as miraculous.

Where was Tilda, by the way? With that Jon, I'll bet. It was bad of her not to phone. If Mum had known she wasn't coming, she would have come with me to Percy's funeral. Instead she stayed at home waiting, letting her blood curdle with worry.

As the light of dawn grew into the sky I had a strange experience. Against the dim silvery-blue of the dawn, I suddenly saw two vertical lines, as if etched on glass, and below them I could clearly see the gutters and aerials of a shoddy housing estate and the ribs of the warehouse roofs. As I wondered what the lines were, I realized that they were no longer simple lines but several parallel ones which quickly acquired the shape of a tower, and then the appearance of a horizontal line removed all doubt that this was the tower of a church. Yet it had no substance: the colour between the lines was identical to that of the sky – as if, as I said, it was etched on glass. Then it seemed to thicken, as if the glass was replaced while I blinked with a panel of pale, translucent alabaster. Very rapidly now it gathered body from the light and I saw that it was a dirty, if handsome, white stone church – I discovered later that it was Hawksmoor's Church of St Anne in Limehouse. But it seemed as if a miracle had occurred: at first no trace of it existed on what had seemed to be a clear sky, then for an instant it was a quality of the sky itself, a strange translucence without relation to the buildings beneath, then it separated itself from the light and became matter. (With such talk of miracles you must think I've suddenly gone senile. What will you think, then, when I say that the moment of watching that church appear in the dawn was like seeing the hand of God?)

I admit, I was surprised the other day when you asked me for an account of myself. After falling three floors from your balcony to the pavement, Kate is in a coma. On top of this, you are tormented by the memory of your recent argument with her, and the wanton intake of drugs which those tests have revealed in her bloodstream. Nobody suggests that she jumped, but it's possible that you're wretchedly afraid of the suspicion that you were instrumental in the disaster. And all of a sudden you want to get immersed in the reedy waters of family history! But why must you dissipate like this the precious sources of attention and sympathy which have risen so abruptly in you? I suppose the violence of the previous week has given way to an eerie calm as you wait for Kate's awakening. Looking at her expressionless face reminds you that, submerged beneath the blank surfaces of our lives, are stories, like dark crystals, which tell us what we are and what we will be. Unable to reverse what has happened or to define it until the future is behind you, you're locked in limbo, as in the waist of an hourglass.

I can imagine you standing on the balcony, howling with rage into the night: 'WHY HAS THIS HAPPENED?' and 'WHAT SHOULD I DO?' You wonder if she will ever regain consciousness and, if she does, will she recover completely? The fall, and much else, may be erased from her mind. What would a partial recovery be like? What of her other injuries? For the present your girlfriend is out of action, outside time. Your life has changed too, albeit less dramatically than hers, and it will continue to change according to her recovery, in ways that are now unfathomable. Fate has struck a senseless, malevolent blow, and you wonder both how to reorientate yourself towards it and what it would feel like to do so.

You asked me: 'How do you learn to adapt yourself?'

'To what?' I said.

'To whatever happens. I don't know. I mean, how did you ever – cope?'

'With what?'

4

'With your life, Dad! For Christ's sake, with your past! You know what I mean. Tell me how you made it fit!'

What followed was a very peculiar feeling for me. As you remember, we were speaking on the phone. Luke was at home, and Tilda – without Jon, for a change – and, of course, Mum. We had finished supper, and we were chatting in the sitting-room. It was only two days after Kate's fall so, not surprisingly, our conversation had turned to her repeatedly during the evening. When I answered the phone you launched into your questions without any preamble. You had come from trying to visit Kate – once again, you hadn't been admitted – and your voice was loud and agitated. The others realized it was you and they hushed, anxious to glean whatever they could about Kate from my side of the conversation. Tilda's eyes were round and vast with anticipation and she fiddled with her earring as she listened. Luke picked at the loose threads in the torn knee of his jeans. Mum was holding her coffee mug near her throat as if the action of picking it up or putting it down was suspended. She smiled – maybe to encourage me to relax – and then she bit on her lower lip as if to restrain her concern. They couldn't hear your question, but imagine my sense of vertigo as I tried to justify myself so baldly in front of my wife and children. Meanwhile I could picture you alone in your hangar-like flat, desperately waiting for my response.

I think I said you shouldn't suppose I had all the answers. It was feeble and I knew it at the time but, watched by Mum and Tilda and Luke, I couldn't manage any better. I failed you. But I want to return to your question now and treat it with the seriousness you deserve. I want to make amends if I can. So how did I learn to adapt myself? How did I make my past fit (if I did)?

You know the main facts about my past, but now you sense that they might have been otherwise. Everything is always conditional on what went before, and you want to know the kind of stories I've composed for myself so that I can recognize and secure myself in the present. For though you see we emerge from the past blindly, as from a chrysalis, you also feel and want to believe that there's a direction, and you want to see this accounted for. How, for example, did I ever come to marry my foster-sister?

Naturally, in my own mind my past isn't simple, and never was. It has always been variously coloured and has acquired different shadings as I have aged. What seemed to be an unimportant episode was transformed by a later event into a memory charged with significance; what seemed important was forgotten. Objects and circumstantial fact survive like talismans from regions in time and space where memory cannot reach. So I have my mother's letters to Tilly, and her ring; I know that Julius had beautiful, long-fingered hands, and that he and Barba had only one opportunity. I know something about the war and about Coventry, and I can piece things together; I can imagine what might have happened. Like the great stone mullions of the windows in Gothic cathedrals, the war conferred on us its own dynamic and structure. Now our lives are like the brittle plate-glass surfaces of skyscrapers, marked only by what they reflect; for where memory dominates invention the material is more fragile, sharper, tauter, more austere, more tense.

Incidentally, you were gone when I came back inside the flat. I had the impression that you never knew I was there. Or did you discover me asleep and leave in embarrassment, not wishing to face me? Didn't you notice when you came in that the door wasn't double-locked? Perhaps your argument with Kate sprang from the shame of discovering me. Perhaps I, unwittingly, was responsible for her fall.

2

Crammed inside a sealed box-car like pickled walnuts in a jar, my parents may have sensed in my flight with Tilly a swaddled beat of hope. Perhaps they even said it was a miracle.

Your great-aunt Tilly's view was certainly different. For the rest of her life she was niggled by the thought that she hadn't done enough: that somehow she might have saved the whole of my family instead of just me. I wasn't aware of this self-reproach until about 1959, when we were sheltering from the grim heat beneath the awning on her lonely balcony in Jeddah, smoking and sipping sweet tea. She had paid for my trip. It was my twenty-first birthday present, she said, although she had already given me one. I stayed for three days and she hardly drew breath. I'd seen so little of her in recent years that I was dismayed to find on my arrival a rather brassy middle-aged woman with a tight mask of make-up and a pinched look at the corners of her mouth. It was a relief to see her loosening up as we talked – and that was why she had asked me. She felt that my shoulders were at last broad enough to assume some of the weight of my past. I'd always known the outline, of course, and, as any child would, I had constantly elaborated on it in my imagination. But it wasn't until then that I knew the full story, nor how the episode still haunted Tilly.

I shall try to reconstruct it.

★

The train stopped again and Tilly looked out of the window. Across some waste ground she saw a large illuminated swastika banner undulating from the eaves of a customs shed. Among the accusing beams of searchlights the border guards were stark and glinting; guns snuggled firmly and gracefully against their greatcoats as if they were accustomed to use. Beneath the engulfing steel helmets their faces looked pale but alert, and the tramp of jackboots was like the muffled ticking of a clock.

Suddenly the door of Tilly's compartment was thrown open. She was alone, and she turned quickly, bracing herself. Two huge soldiers entered, filling the awkward space and compressing it with stifling militant efficiency. The first carried no gun. He had a fleshy face and dark, probing eyes. The second was much younger. His gun was slung casually at his waist and he seemed to be smiling at Tilly, pushing forward his heavy jaw.

'Luggage!' said the first, and he rapped the luggage-rack impatiently. In their black leather gloves, his fingers looked like steel claws.

Tilly opened her suitcase on the seat beside her and, as he searched through her underwear and clothes, she was conscious of the younger one's eyes goading her into embarrassment. She refused to meet them, and watched impassively as her possessions were inspected. Then the first soldier straightened up again and demanded her passport. As she dropped it into his outstretched hand she felt as if she was not only showing him her travel permit but exposing her whole life, together with the motives for her journey, for the grace of his approval. He looked at her photograph and then closely at her, as if he was holding her chin between thumb and forefinger. His eyes dropped as he flipped the pages to find her visa, then he slammed it shut with a snap of his fingers and handed it back to her.

As the two guards turned round noisily to leave the compartment, Tilly remembered that her visa would be invalid unless stamped. 'But what about the stamp?' she said.

The guard stopped, and turned. He peered at her with undisguised contempt, but said nothing.

'The stamp,' she repeated nervously, making the appropriate motion against her passport with her other hand.

Still the guard didn't speak, but stared as if intrigued by her stupidity. She wondered what she had done wrong: was she in trouble already, before she'd even got into the country? Suddenly she was afraid. Then the guard relaxed his pose. 'We are customs control. Passport control is coming,' he said, jerking his thumb over his shoulder.

A few minutes later the passport official arrived, also accompanied by a guard. As he studied her passport he said, 'Why have you come to Germany?'

His eyes were suddenly focussed intently on hers, as if he could read there the letter her husband had received from his friend Frank Foley at the embassy in Berlin: *'The best thing your wife can do is urge them to leave... even go to Germany herself... but it would certainly be dangerous...'*

'Tourist,' she said, and swallowed.

'You have chosen a surprising time to come sightseeing in Germany,' he observed politely.

Although acutely aware that she was being tested, Tilly didn't know how to respond, and she shrugged.

The man was still as he watched her, and she shuddered as if his hands were closing on her shoulders. Then he drew his stamp from his pocket, applied it to her passport and handed back the precious document. 'Have a pleasant trip,' he said, and departed.

Tilly took a dark blue scarf from her bag and tied it tightly under her chin, then she switched off the light and settled herself into the corner. She was perturbed by the guards' unnecessarily aggressive manners, and for a moment she thought fondly of the polite ticket-collector on the train from London. What would it be like to live among such people, as Esther and her family did? And they were Jewish! Once again she involuntarily recalled Captain Foley's letter: *'There is no doubt that the Nazis intend to get rid of all the Jews, and any that don't leave will be murdered. The Nazis may dissemble to ease their task, but they are not embarrassed by it... If your wife's friend's parents-in-law have already been arrested then it's to be assumed that they are already dead... The Jews themselves don't really seem to believe what's happening. (It's not surprising. It defies the imagination.) Times will be hard, they think, and people may be killed – but we will survive. However, if the Nazis have the power to prevent it, they will not. And nothing opposes that power...'*

The country outside was illuminated in places by thin swathes of moonlight: when Tilly opened her eyes they appeared as rippling metallic gleams through the slit at the edge of the drawn curtain. She couldn't see where she was going: lulled by the train's monotonous rattle, she felt as if she were being sucked into an encircling darkness in which, though mobile, she was suddenly and brutally alone. Until now she had cheerfully disregarded any murmurs of alarm about travelling alone in Germany because there was such a clear goal: she hadn't seen Esther for over ten years, nor had she met any of her children, and she had only met Jakob very briefly. But now she was painfully aware of how little she knew.

Suppose Captain Foley was right?

Once she had been able to picture Esther's life. She remembered going to a party with Esther when she first met her long ago in Zurich and everybody, not just Esther, spoke to her in English. The women told funny stories and the men laughed; there were surfaces of polished brass and chrome. They went to an exhibition of Modern Art where Esther knew lots of people; they visited a friend of hers, a Russian emigré who smoked cigarettes in an ebony holder and talked to them in exotically accented English about psychoanalysis. She had another opportunity to witness Esther's life-style at Esther's wedding to Jakob Flasch three years later, when she danced with a charming Viennese doctor. It was utterly different from what she was used to at home in Coventry, and she loved it. Esther's letters were exuberant with her new life when she first went to live with Jakob in Berlin, and Tilly had an impression of hectic activity and glamour. When the letters grew shorter after Esther's first child was born, Tilly wasn't surprised, but they had never picked up again. On the contrary, after they moved to Hamburg they got even thinner and peculiarly empty of any news. Tilly had tried to encourage her but without effect. She wondered if Esther had simply lost interest in her remote English friend, but when she gloomily cut back her own flow of letters Esther pleaded with her to resume her efforts. Nowadays, for three good letters she received on average about one meagre postcard in return. It was only from loyalty to the friendship she had once had with Esther that she continued, and from the vague sense that something was wrong. Now it occurred to Tilly that this sense had probably sustained her more than she was aware, and she was afraid. She knew nothing of Esther's life. She wasn't travelling to a friend's cosy hearth: she was travelling into the unknown; she felt unequal to the task she had set herself and acutely vulnerable. Folding her arms, she tried to go back to sleep, but thoughts of what she might encounter continued to jostle against each other in her mind. She imagined herself in the station in Hamburg and stumbling through the city's streets, conspicuously ignorant, obviously a stranger. She felt vividly the harshness and tension about her, but the physical aspects of these remained unknown. While she was at home she had been looking forward so much to seeing Esther and her family, but now she only felt trepidation. She remembered Esther's last card: *'Tilly, why are you coming to Hamburg? If it is to visit us, it is mad. Don't come. It is not safe. If you're coming anyway, it is still mad. I would like nothing better than to see you – but still, it is not safe.'*

It seemed to Tilly as though she failed to sleep at all, but from time to time she awoke with the sensation of a bruised hip as the train lurched over an uneven set of points. And at last she realized with surprise that the train was stationary, and the corridor was full of people hustling to descend. Rubbing her eyes, she pulled aside the curtain and saw the crowd streaming down the platform. Her pulse quickened as she buttoned up her overcoat and prepared to join them.

Tilly was aware of bundles being handed to and fro, of luggage being stacked hurriedly on the platform amid the belching steam and the roar of engines, and of people shouting in the full vowels and explosive consonants of German. With only one small suitcase and no companions she didn't need to engage a porter or to speak with anyone else. She glanced about the cavernous hall for the exit and the taxi-rank. Huge swastikas were suspended from the roof. Wherever she looked she saw soldiers pacing up and down, sternly watching, but as she made her way through the confused throng of travellers she tried to resist the impulse to look about her. Without breaking her step, she joined the queue waiting outside for taxis. In front of her stood a large blonde woman dressed in a magnificent fur coat, who shuffled her feet impatiently and repeatedly looked at those around her, as if it was their fault that she was kept waiting. To nobody in particular she said: 'It's a disgrace to be kept waiting like this!'

Tilly looked up without thinking, only to find that the woman was looking directly at her.

'I don't know why we put up with it,' she continued. 'I shall speak to the authorities.'

The woman hadn't taken her eyes from Tilly, and now a gap had opened between her and the rest of the queue. 'But look,' said Tilly, 'Taxis are coming.'

'You are foreign?'

'Yes.'

'Where from?'

'England.'

In the same way as the soldiers, the woman glared as if to impress her superiority on Tilly. Then she moved forwards and waited in the queue with her back turned like a granite bulwark.

When Tilly's turn came, she gave the driver the address of her hotel in Neustadt. Only when she was seated comfortably in the back did she allow herself to look around. It was still only eight o'clock, but the streets were already bristling with activity. The trams were full, shops were opening with a clatter of released shutters and bicycles bumped over the cobbled streets. Tilly perceived an air of prosperity, not so much in the stately old red brick buildings, but in the neat clothes and the confidence with which people seemed to be moving. She saw all sorts of uniforms, but there were fewer soldiers than she had expected. A woman with an already plump shopping-bag was haggling with a man selling fresh fish from a barrow and Tilly twisted her head to watch the mime until the taxi turned the corner. Despite the swastikas, like a rash on the city's skin, it seemed that the reports and her fears of conditions in Germany were exaggerated, and only the sight of a beggar being pushed rudely away from a butcher's doorway disturbed this thought.

Delivered safely to her hotel, Tilly checked herself in and was taken to her room. She felt foreign. Everything was slightly different from what she was used to: the bed was made in a different way, the furniture was rather heavy, the taps a different shape, and the unfamiliar tangy smell, though by no means unpleasant, was distinct. Tilly opened the window and looked outside, with her elbows resting on the wide marble sill. Like the hotel, the buildings on the other side of the street were well-kept blocks built around the middle of the last century. The ground floors housed shops and offices but, so far as she could see, the upper floors were mostly apartments. The swastikas couldn't be ignored, but they seemed unconnected with the busy street below, where she was again surprised by the impression of orderly, unruffled affluence. The shop windows looked as if customers were expected, the pedestrians had an air of purpose and industry that was familiar to her from

Coventry; laughter could be heard, and commands: but Tilly sensed that the people of Hamburg were concerned above all with the state of their accounts.

She had chosen this hotel because of its proximity to the Flasches' flat. It wouldn't take more than five minutes to reach them, which meant that if she was ready to go out in twenty minutes she could be with them in less than half an hour. But now that there were no further obstacles, her eagerness suddenly drained from her. Instead of rushing along to Esther, she ran a bath. Jakob would probably be at work, and the older children would have gone to school. Perhaps Esther had taken them to school herself, in which case she too might not be there; and she might go shopping before coming home. The possibility of finding nobody there hadn't occurred to Tilly before, and now the idea gave a discreet lift to her mood, for which she immediately felt savage shame. As before on the train, her sense of foreboding directed her mind back over the years of her curious relationship with Esther. It had begun when her father asked her to go with him on a business trip to Zurich in 1926. He was taking up an offer from Esther's father to visit his workshop, an offer which had been made before the Great War when Herr Mackstein was making a tour of English watchmakers. He had since gone into compasses, which was why Mr Shearer was interested: with the decline of watchmaking in Coventry he was turning his attention to other precision instruments.

Lying back in the hot water, Tilly wondered if she was supposed to have understood a lot more from Esther's letters. Had she been very blind? But she had been busy herself! She had moved to London, she had got married; she had a demanding job. For this trip she had asked for a month's leave, just in case, which was the longest holiday she had taken for years – probably since Esther visited her in England before her own marriage, and they went to Brighton. She had been working in the bank in the High Street then. It seemed like such a long time ago, and it was – ten years. Her honeymoon in St Ives with Percy was less than three weeks because they both had to go back to work. It was a pity that Esther and Jakob hadn't been able to come to the wedding – but then Tilly remembered a conversation she had had with her sister Barbara the day before the ceremony.

Barbara was to be chief bridesmaid and she still hadn't done the hem of her dress, so Tilly was fixing it up with pins while her sister stood in front of a mirror winding a crimson velvet ribbon round her finger. Barbara's soft skin and the gentle curves of her face gave her an air of sweet compliance, which was belied by the surreptitious sparkle in her brown eyes and the fact that she hadn't finished her own dress yet.

'Whatever happened to those German friends of yours?' Barbara asked, twisting herself round at the waist to look down at Tilly.

Tilly was irritated by having to do this job herself at such a late stage. And, though she admitted it to nobody, she was nervous about getting married. Now she frowned, unable for a moment to think who her sister meant. 'Oh, you mean Esther?' she said suddenly.

'Yes.'

'Why do you ask?'

'I heard something on the wireless about the Jews in Germany and it made me think of them. Do you still hear from her? You were good friends with her, weren't you?'

'I get a letter occasionally. I don't think they're having an easy time,' Tilly had said unsteadily, and added: 'It all seems very far away.'

Tilly raised one hand to pick the dirt of travel from beneath the rims of her nails, and as she disturbed the water she was startled to find that it was getting cold. It was strange to think that Esther had ever seemed so distant. And how had she become so close again that she undertook this blind mission of help? Wasn't it only because she had come to believe that

Esther needed her in some way? And with sudden clarity Tilly realized that it was this as yet undefined need which had brought her here.

Shivering, she got out of the bath and dried herself briskly, chafing her skin as if in self-rebuke. What if Esther really was out? What if she and her family had gone somewhere? Or been 'taken away', in the sinister phrase Esther had used about her own parents? What if she had come too late? And she dressed herself with preposterous haste, as if by doing so she could forestall their departure.

After years of wondering about Esther and her family, Tilly was on the point of seeing them for herself: and suddenly the threat facing them seemed claustrophobic and immediate, as if it was closing in on them from the opposite direction at the same rate as her own approach. She wanted to run to keep ahead of it. It was difficult to see what that threat might be as she walked unnoticed and unchallenged down the street, but she was so anxious now that she paid very little heed to her surroundings. She knew that she had only to turn right out of the hotel door, take the second turning on the right and then the third left, and she would be there. She didn't have to raise her eyes from the ground. But at the last corner Tilly was instantly aware that she was entering a different kind of street. The hum of sound and motion which had absorbed her suddenly vanished: ahead was a narrow, shabby street in which the sound of her own footsteps was unmistakable. Tilly looked up to see the numbers on the doors. From the names beside the bells it was evident that the houses were subdivided into smaller units; everywhere the brickwork needed pointing, and the upper stories cast a gloomy shadow over the street. A child came out of one of the houses dressed in a tatty black jacket and trousers which were much too big for him. His grey face consisted of separated hollows, and his dilapidated shoes were held together with string. He was followed quickly by a woman in a shawl. As Tilly passed them they gave her a look which she immediately described to herself as furtive. And then with a shock she realized that they were Jews.

The recognition terrified Tilly, and she remembered her father's words when she expressed surprise at hearing that Esther's family was Jewish. It was when she was with him in Zurich. 'What did you think they were? Polynesian?' he had said.

The fury that she had felt then resurfaced now as an abrupt panic, as if she had dived into the sea to show that she didn't mind getting wet, forgetting that the sea had a mighty current and she wasn't a strong swimmer. And as she pressed on a bell marked 'Flasch' she had to fight back a shrieked warning within her to hurry away. Why couldn't she be satisfied with knowing that they were alive? What business was it of hers? And anyway, if that was the condition to which they were reduced, what could she hope to achieve?

She pressed the bell again, and a window opened above her. 'Who is it?' a voice called.

Tilly stepped back into the street. Overhead, a gaunt, grey-haired woman was holding a window open, looking at her suspiciously. Suddenly her lips parted, her eyes widened, and a smile like morning light spread across her face. 'Why, Tilly! You are a miracle!'

While your grandmother hurried to let her in, Tilly had a moment to compose herself after the shock of her friend's appearance. Grey-haired at the age of thirty! Last time she'd seen her, her hair had been long and black and sleek. Her full, sensual face had lost all its flesh and become a thin, beaky structure, all bones and eyes.

As they embraced each other, Tilly felt through Esther's thick jersey how thin she was, and her own body suddenly seemed lush and well-fed to the point of deformity; and she found that she was weeping – whether from delight at seeing Esther after so long or from sorrow at her transformation, she didn't know.

'Tilly, Tilly...! Well!' said Esther, releasing herself so that she could step back and look at Tilly. 'Why these tears? Well...! But you are lovelier than ever! You've changed your hair!' At their last meeting she had persuaded Tilly to have her white-blonde hair bobbed. Now it was gathered in a tidy coil at the back of her head, which suited her better. The bob had looked self-conscious on her, exactly as if someone had persuaded her to do it against her better judgement; while gathering her hair back suited her wide cheekbones and wide-set eyes. It occurred to Esther that Tilly might be considered beautiful, despite her clothes, which were as drab and ill-cut as ever.

Esther closed the door and took Tilly's hand again, then she turned and led her into a dark hallway which smelled of decayed wood. 'But I'm afraid you will find me much changed,' she said, flicking her fingers across her face. 'Never mind.'

Still holding Esther's hand, Tilly followed her up the creaking wooden stairs. She didn't know what to say. The answer to the question 'How are you?' was everywhere so manifest that to ask seemed ludicrous; and insulting, for the contrast with her own circumstances and those of Esther's former life was startling. So she said nothing and allowed herself to be led silently upwards, past closed doors with pieces of paper bearing the names of the occupants pinned to them and, in the shabby passages outside, several pairs of old boots. On the third floor they came to an open door which cast a shaft of light across the landing, revealing the bare boards and a gash in the wall's crumbling plaster where the banister had been torn away. Esther stood aside and ushered Tilly into the room.

It was larger than she expected, and lighter. As she turned towards the window, two white-haired people stood up, whom Tilly recognized as Esther's parents.

'Good gracious!' she said in confusion, 'What a surprise!'

Herr Mackstein's face was heavily lined now, but from the way in which he approached to greet her, his hand reaching out and his head thrust forward, she could see that he had lost none of his quickness. His wife was much slower than Tilly remembered: she seemed tired and, while her smile indicated genuine pleasure, it was no more than a sad flicker. In her arms she held a baby – me – wrapped in a blanket, and behind her were two small, dark boys. Each one was holding onto the back of a chair, and now they watched Tilly with stretched, solemn eyes.

'Tilly, it is a joy to see you!' said Herr Mackstein, clasping her right hand between both of his. Then he threw out an arm towards his wife. 'Come, my dear. Tilly, you remember my wife?'

Frau Mackstein extended some fingers, which Tilly shook awkwardly. 'It's a little difficult,' she apologized, indicating the baby. 'You are most welcome.'

'This is Daniel,' said Esther, stroking the baby's hair. On his face there was a slight rash. 'He's been a bit ill – haven't you, little one? Come, boys,' she said, turning and bending at the waist, reaching out with both hands. 'So here's my friend Tilly, who you thought didn't exist. Come and say hello.' Still eyeing Tilly uncertainly, each of the little boys took one of their mother's hands and edged forwards. Jakob, the taller of the two, had a pointed chin; Abel, though younger and shorter, looked stronger.

Tilly kneeled down and put an arm round each of them. 'I've heard so much about you,' she said in her hesitant German, 'I feel as if I know you. I've wanted so much to meet you!' And she kissed them gently on the forehead, eliciting for the first time cautious smiles.

'Now, Tilly, do take off your coat,' said Herr Mackstein. 'Please, let me take your coat. And some coffee – Esther! What are you thinking of? Give poor Tilly some coffee!'

As he said this Tilly stood up, and she saw Frau Mackstein cast a look at her husband which, though she couldn't interpret it, she knew she wasn't meant to see. But Herr Mackstein either missed it or was too excited to pay any attention. He had removed a coat on the back of the door from its hanger and was now ceremoniously hanging Tilly's on it instead, smoothing down the collar.

'And how was your journey, Tilly?' Herr Mackstein continued. 'When did you arrive? Only just this morning? Then you've come straight here without even stopping to catch up on a little sleep! You must be exhausted! But it wasn't too uncomfortable, I hope? Good. Things are a little cock-eyed for us here at the moment, but at least the trains are running properly...' As he spoke he pulled up the armchair for Tilly to sit in, then a rocking-chair for his wife, while organizing Jakob and Abel with nods and quick movements of his wrists to bring up other chairs for himself and Esther.

After a moment Esther returned with a mug of hot black coffee which she presented to Tilly. Tilly sipped it slowly, enjoying the bitter taste and the warmth of the liquid as it travelled down her throat.

'And how is life in London? You are married now, I think...?' said Herr Mackstein.

Tilly wondered if he disapproved of her coming on her own. 'Yes, it's a shame Percy couldn't come,' she said. 'He's an architect. He just couldn't get away.' It wasn't true, but she wasn't going to admit that Percy had wanted to come and she had insisted on being alone.

'Well, it's a pity. What is he like?'

Tilly laughed. 'Well, he's tall. But he doesn't stoop, like some tall people.'

'Like a true Englishman, he carries himself straight.'

She laughed again. 'He's kind... What else? Oh dear, how do you describe your own husband? He's perfect, of course!'

They were all delighted by Tilly's confusion. She had blushed to the roots of her hair, which suggested to them better than any words that she loved him, which was what they wanted to hear.

'You must be missing him,' said Frau Mackstein.

'I've only been away twenty-four hours,' said Tilly, 'but I suppose I am missing him, yes.'

'Maybe we'll meet him another time. And your parents, are they well?' said Herr Mackstein.

'Yes, they're pretty well. They send their regards, by the way. I don't see them as often as I should.'

'You are young, you are busy,' said Frau Mackstein.

Her husband sighed. 'I remember when you came to Zurich with your father,' he said. 'He enjoyed seeing my workshop, I think. He spent hours there looking at everything and talking, and abandoned you to Esther.'

'It was wonderful. I think I grew up faster there in a week than in a year in Coventry.'

'Tilly!' Esther cried. 'You make it sound as if I corrupted you!'

'Oh dear, no,' said Tilly, laughing. 'But there were cafés, other languages, things you don't get in Coventry. People talking about books and ideas as if they mattered. But – goodness me! Are none of you having any coffee?' she said, suddenly realizing that nobody else had a mug.

'No, no,' said Herr Mackstein. 'We've all had our coffee.'

'I thought the English always drank tea,' said his wife.

'Drink up, Tilly, and don't pay any attention to Mother,' said Esther. 'It's good for you.'

Tilly felt slightly uneasy. 'And what about Jakob?' she asked. 'How's he?'

'He's at work at the moment,' Esther said.

'Jakob is very well,' said Herr Mackstein. 'He is very well.'

'Papa, that's not quite true, you know it's not. He's been having rather bad pain with his back lately,' she explained to Tilly.

'Backs can be such trouble,' Frau Mackstein observed. 'When one's back is healthy, one takes it for granted, but as soon as something goes wrong with it one realizes how much one uses it...'

'Quite so,' said Herr Mackstein. 'And one abuses it, what's more, when it's healthy...'

Esther quickly interrupted and invited her to look around the flat. 'And you, Jakob and Abel, you must begin your lessons.'

'I don't like mathematics,' said Abel.

It surprised Tilly that the boys were being taught at home by their grandfather, and she wondered if the prohibitions imposed on Jews extended to school. 'But mathematics are fun!' she said, as she followed Esther into the passage outside.

'That's our living room in there,' said Esther, 'And there's a small kitchen beside it. We're lucky because we also have three rooms upstairs, which we use as bedrooms.'

The bedrooms were small. They were sparsely furnished, clean, and, if not exactly tidy, then at least ordered. Some clothes were draped over a piece of slate leaning against a wall, and next to a pile of books by the skirting-board stood a pair of cut-glass decanters. Despite the few visible relics of a more gilded life, it was plainly the home of a poor family. Tilly thought of the glittering crystal and the splendid clothes everyone was wearing at Esther's wedding party, and she shuddered: while she had been steadily building up her life in the blessed safety of England, Esther's world had been falling apart. It was impossible to admire Esther's home, for it represented nothing but loss. Moreover, Esther must have a good idea of what she would think, and she wouldn't expect compliments. Tilly had stayed with her in Zurich, after all; and though Esther said that her family wasn't rich, she had seen for herself on her visit to Coventry that Tilly wasn't accustomed to any display of wealth. So Tilly kept silent until, sitting on the grey blanket which covered Esther and Jakob's iron-framed bed, she had an opportunity to speak with Esther directly and alone.

'Esther, I don't have to tell you how lovely it is to see you – to see you all. And it's lovely to be greeted as if nothing in the world is amiss. But please, let's be honest. You know why I've come, and you also know that all this... this dreadful business is distant from me, by chance, and I don't understand it very well. But if I'm to be any help then we must all stop being so proud and try to put our heads together a bit... There, I've said my speech!'

Esther sat on the bed beside Tilly and took her pink hand, examining it as if it was detached. It was bizarre to hear Tilly summing up so much so briskly, and then dismissing everything that made it all so complicated. Perhaps she really didn't understand. From someone else it might seem insulting, or silly, but, though the ease with which Tilly came to the point might be thought a little ridiculous, it was also a relief. And the straightforward sympathy was certainly refreshing. It was reassuring too to find that she still felt the same instinctive trust in Tilly that she had always felt before. 'Of course, Tilly, you're right. I must try to explain. But it isn't easy. You see, it's difficult for us to see clearly ourselves.'

Beginning with her move to Berlin ten years ago, Esther gradually unfolded the events leading to the present, and it seemed to Tilly as if a landscape was being provided for the obscure colours and shapes that had emerged before from letters. Jakob was a well-to-do Berliner who, like Esther, wasn't a practising Jew. For a time they thrived in spite of occasional harassment, but the freak weed of anti-Semitism soon strangled all other aspects of their lives. They were openly insulted, they were refused service in shops – in a series of quick blows their status was undermined until suddenly they were not only not protected by the law but actively attacked by it. A crime against a Jew was no longer a crime but an act for congratulation. Even before this was openly stated by the authorities, they had lost their house and all their possessions. 'But *all*, Tilly, *all* our possessions, except for what we were wearing. Luckily Jakob had some money in his pocket and we managed to get to Hamburg, although he was in terrible pain. I think I told you that much – I wanted to tell you something about it, you see, but it was hard to know where to start. There was no point in telling you all our troubles: they're all the same – no, they are not the same, but they come from the same thing, a sort of approved madness. And to go on about it seemed to be giving in to something, like admitting it was real. Not that it wasn't real – it is still horrifyingly real! But taking the trouble to tell you about it was like saying it had a right to exist, do you understand? And then I was a bit afraid. There were rumours of bad things happening to Jews with friends abroad. So I was careful for a while, and then I took courage again. And of course it grew quite difficult to know what to say to you: I was – and am – so dominated by the immediate circumstances of life here, from which I'd kept you apart. I wanted to keep you apart too, Tilly. You reminded me that civilized people somewhere still led a civilized life, untouched by all this... It may be hard for you to appreciate this, but it was very valuable to me. I can't begin to tell you how much strength I've gained from your letters. And so, here you find us... without coffee – yes, but I'm very pleased to give it to you rather than Mother; the children having lessons at home; Jakob finding work only with very great difficulty – now he is shovelling coal near the Port. Yes, that's why his back is bad. It is a problem. But still we act for you as if everything is all right. I myself believe it a bit. One gets used to it, you see, in a strange way. The children have known nothing else. And, although we don't always know where tomorrow's supper will come from, we believe it will be all right, because it's very hard to believe that this thing can continue for long. The Nazis can rob us and make us work, but we will outlast them. Jakob's parents were taken after Kristallnacht, it's true, but they behaved unwisely in the circumstances... We don't know what's happened to them, but thousands of others have been released unharmed so there's no good reason to think they won't come back.'

Remembering Captain Foley's remarks, Tilly wondered if Esther really believed what she had just said. 'And what about your parents? Why did they come?' she asked.

'To persuade us to go to Switzerland. But we can't, because of Jakob's parents.'

'And now?'

'What do you mean, 'now'?'

'I mean... Well, the fact is that they haven't come back yet. How long are you going to wait? Don't you ever think of going to Switzerland while... while it's still possible?'

'We've talked about it. For the moment the answer is 'no.' We're going to wait until the end of June, and if they still haven't come back then perhaps we will go. If you, like my parents, were hoping to persuade us to go sooner, then I'm afraid you will not succeed, Tilly.'

'I see.'

'I wish I could persuade my parents of that. Incidentally,' Esther added, 'What do you mean by 'while it's still possible'?'

Tilly looked away from Esther and pressed her free hand into her lap. 'I've been in touch with a friend of Percy's,' she said, 'who works in the British Embassy in Berlin. He spends all his time giving out visas. He says the Nazis intend to kill every Jew they can lay their hands on.'

Esther hesitated. Then she said, 'Nonsense. They may make us work for them, which won't be a holiday, but they won't kill us. How could they?'

Tilly shrugged helplessly. Then the suspicion suddenly came to her that they understood different things by Esther's last question. At first Tilly thought she was alluding to the psychological difficulty; now she wondered if she wasn't referring to the physical logistics of so vast a task. Her mind froze in outraged incomprehension at the idea of a massacre. She hadn't considered how it might be accomplished if embarked upon. That Esther might already be thinking in these terms frightened Tilly. 'I don't know,' she said, 'But I understand that that's their intention. And I don't see why you should run the risk.'

'It's not a game of poker, Tilly...'

'But it's you who's playing poker! You're gambling that nothing will happen before the end of June!'

'This is our home, Tilly! What would we do over there – in Switzerland, America, England? This is our country too, not just the Nazis'!'

'But you're not even German, you're Swiss!'

'I am German. My parents are also German although they have lived in Switzerland for some years.'

'A moment ago you were saying that you won't leave because of Jakob's parents. Now you're saying it's because it's your home.'

'I said – if they come back, then we probably will go. But the point is that emigrating isn't just moving sideways on a chessboard; it's like trying to play chess on a draughts-board.'

'It seems crazy to me, Esther. What will you do?'

'We'll carry on, as we have for the last few years.'

'If you survive.'

Although Tilly's words were unambiguous, they sounded glib to Esther, as if Tilly didn't fully understand their implication because privately she didn't doubt that they would survive. This imminent slaughter was an event without substance to her, as if she was playing with the idea. For all her candour, she didn't believe that it could happen.

'You're trying to scare me, Tilly. But I'm scared much more convincingly every time I walk into the street. You needn't waste your breath.'

Esther's reasons for not leaving the country shifted in and out of Tilly's focus. They seemed foolish, and she was uncertain whether Esther believed in them either. She seemed to have built them into a wall about herself which, though ramshackle, she sensed was also impregnable. Yet she couldn't blithely accept this and go away. She continued to press Esther, despite the rebuffs, always conscious that whatever she said was already intimately known to Esther. She tried to find out if the rest of her family viewed matters in the same way, and as she did so she felt that she was insinuating unpleasantly that Esther wasn't giving the others the opportunity to state their own views. Esther insisted that they had discussed it repeatedly; and Tilly had no choice but to concede. Who, after all, was she to doubt it? Should anything happen to Esther and her family she would never forgive herself for not trying harder, but she couldn't go on saying that they were wrong to run the risk.

She was twisting her wedding-ring. A strand of honey-coloured hair lay against her cheek, stuck there by a silent tear. 'This is awful, Esther. I feel like the Devil, trying to shake your resolve. And it's only for my own peace of mind that I can't leave a stone unturned.'

Esther touched Tilly's soft cheek with her thumb. 'Don't be so hard on yourself, Tilly. You're right to challenge me. And you have a right to your peace of mind.'

They sat for several moments in silence. Tilly wanted to repeat for the last time her offer of help, but it seemed shrill and futile now. It was difficult to know how to continue their conversation. Changing the subject artificially would be repulsive.

'There is one thing you might be able to do for us though, Tilly,' said Esther gently, as if she had been waiting for just such a lull.

Tilly turned quickly, and wondered how she hadn't noticed before how long Esther's eyelashes were. 'What?' she said.

'You must promise to say if you don't want to do it. And I mean that seriously.'

Esther waited, her fist closed on a fold in her skirt, and only when Tilly nodded in acknowledgement did she continue:

'At the beginning – do you remember? – I said that you would find us behaving as if everything is more normal than it obviously is. Well, one thing I can't trick myself about is Daniel. He suffers from vitamin-deficiency. I can't get the right food for him, and he will get seriously ill if he's exposed to this for much longer. You asked how you could help, and here's the answer: could you – would you – look after him for a short time in England? Until we join you, or come to fetch him? Assuming it's possible to leave Germany with him. Please, don't be afraid to say no. I know it's a lot to ask.'

*

Early the following morning Tilly boarded the train for Berlin. They had all said that she should act at once because the separation would be more difficult if delayed, and Tilly inferred that her continued presence might also endanger them and jeopardize her chances of success. So when she returned to her hotel she telephoned Captain Foley in Berlin and briefly explained her intentions. He replied that a visa could be given immediately for the child if she applied for it in person.

Although Tilly was ready to do anything within her power, when she offered to help she had imagined it in terms of a specific and finite action. In one way Esther's request demanded less of her than she was prepared to give, for instead of helping the whole family she would be devoting her efforts to just one of them, a baby. On reflection, Tilly realized that she had hoped for nothing less than a magical relief of the entire family's plight, as if by her presence alone she would procure their safety; and then her life would go on as before. Beside this fantasy, the proposal that she take Daniel away appeared more modest and better suited to her abilities. But she quickly saw that it required a much profounder commitment, which she hadn't conceived of making. For how long would Daniel be with her? At least two months, and then...? Tilly wondered if Esther really didn't fear that the separation might be permanent, but was strenuously denying the possibility to avoid pain. It was as if the only reason for her leaving with Daniel was the stated one – his frail health.

Yet as she turned over the explanations in the privacy of her hotel room, they still seemed unconvincing. Why did they have to turn to her for this? It would surely be more obvious for the Macksteins to take Daniel to Switzerland. They had thanked her for agreeing to help and apologized repeatedly for the nuisance, as if it was unnecessary, and yet there seemed no question of their performing the service in her place. Tilly didn't ask directly why this option wasn't followed, because she feared it would display a lack of willingness on her part, which she didn't feel. And she sensed that they were staying because they still hoped to persuade Esther and Jakob to leave with the children sooner. It was as if each one of them acknowledged that the danger to the others was immediate and severe, but was unable to relate it to themself and act upon it. The only one who did what they all agreed was the sensible thing to do was me – and I, as a baby, had to do what I was told. It was an imposition, said Herr Mackstein, and Tilly was a saint to accept the burden – but the baby would be off her hands in no time. Did he believe this? If he really thought that the gesture was unwarranted by the situation, why was he so anxious to get the others out fast?

Tilly would be wholly responsible for Daniel; all a mother's duties would be hers, although she wasn't a mother. Telling herself that it wouldn't be for more than three months, she accepted this. After all, the Flasches were living in the danger zone and they were optimistic, so why shouldn't she be so herself? Likewise they must be more aware of the true nature of the dangers than Captain Foley, so why should she pay more attention to his melodramatic announcements than to them? There was every reason to hope for a speedy reunion, and in the meantime it would surely be rewarding to look after Daniel. It wasn't a responsibility to accept lightly, but it didn't occur to her to decline it; it was even a little flattering to be entrusted for so long with a friend's child. And having agreed, she concentrated on fulfilling the first part of her mission as efficiently as possible.

Leaning back in her seat with her eyes closed as the train clanked out of Hamburg, she thought of her husband, as she had done many times in the last few hours. She couldn't refuse to take the baby – but what would Percy think? She was confident that he would agree that her decision was right, but he still wouldn't exactly welcome it. She would just have to trust him to support her in this, as he had in so many other things. He had mentioned his friend in the Berlin embassy out of the blue, as if the Flasches' predicament hadn't registered with him at all. Although he knew of their importance to his wife, he hadn't met them, and it was only Tilly's extreme distress one evening, as she told him how she had received no answer to two letters which she had particularly asked to be acknowledged, that made him suddenly say: 'I'll write to my old friend Frank, in the embassy there. If there's anything you can do, he's the chap who'll know.' Captain Foley's answer had come without delay, and Percy was at first dismayed to find that – albeit unofficially – he recommended that Tilly go to Germany herself. He said: *'Not going would incur no criticism; going would be widely condemned as foolish. I know all this, but you asked for my frank opinion of what she could possibly do to help, and there it is.'*

The same day, Tilly had secured leave from work for a month in April and then gone home to write to Esther and Captain Foley. She announced her decision to Percy on his return from work while they were standing in the hall. He paused before replying, nodding slowly. Then he said, 'Of course, you know I can't let you go.'

Tilly stepped back from him, taking her hands from his shoulders. 'What?' she said.

'I said, 'Of course, I can't let you go.''

'Percy! Don't be so pompous! How will you stop me from going?'

'If you must go, then I'll come with you.' He took hold of her raised hand.

'For heaven's sake, Percy!' Tilly cried. But she replaced her hands lightly on his forearms and said, 'Let's go out, sit down, and talk it over sensibly.'

At an hotel nearby they ate a light supper, and they each drank a glass of port afterwards. By their return, Tilly had persuaded her husband that there was no point to his going. She would be weighed down, she said, by the feeling that she was dragging him into something which wasn't his problem. He said that if it was her business then it was also his: he wouldn't resent it. 'I know that you wouldn't resent it,' said Tilly, 'But that's not the point. I would spend more time worrying about you than about Esther and her family. Knowing that you were safe at home would be much more useful.' In the end he conceded, but on the condition that she liaise with Captain Foley.

In such a situation, some men would have bullied her or taken over the enterprise as their own, but Percy wasn't like that. He had respected her decision even though he didn't much like it. It was the same after they were married. Her parents were shocked that she returned to work. Apparently they thought she should devote all her energy to pampering her husband and scrubbing the floors of their house in St John's Wood. But Percy had supported her: for as long as they had no children, he said, there was no reason for her not to work if that was what she wanted to do.

It was strange thinking about their wedding. It seemed to belong to another life. Not only was it remote from her present circumstances, huddled in the corner of a railway carriage in Germany, but also it happened before she even knew Percy very well. She had no good reason to suppose that he would be so supportive, only a dumb belief. It was an act of faith. And even then it was confused, as far as her parents were concerned, because he wasn't a Methodist. The wedding was celebrated in the local Methodist church in Coventry, and she was driven from the house in Craven Street in an open carriage. Opposite her on the way to the church sat her father, proud and a little nervous in his grey top hat and tailcoat. Conscientiously, he tucked a rug under Tilly's knees: although the day was bright and clear as polished brass, it had turned out cold. The carriage halted outside and Tilly's stomach hopped within her, grinding against her heart. Mr Shearer smiled and pressed her fingers as he descended. She cautiously extended one foot in its delicate ivory satin shoe, and as she stepped down she took her father's proffered arm, dimly aware of his other hand lifting the train of her dress so that it didn't catch on anything. With her finger-tips resting in the crook of his elbow she went forwards, and was startled by a sudden whoosh of joy like a flight of birds from a tree.

The reception was held in the Central Methodist Hall, but instead of going there directly the carriage detoured through the centre of the city. Tilly felt giddy riding through the famil-iar streets in such pomp with Percy. When much younger she had frequently imagined herself getting married in Coventry, but she had thought of it only in terms of her wedding-dress and the church, with the city in the background like stage scenery. Now she found herself passing right along Market Street in the old medieval quarter, through the heart of the city. It was narrow, and if she reached out she could almost touch the flaking walls, shake hands with Mr Frome the butcher or buy a couple of crisp round cabbages at the greengrocer's while she introduced her husband. It smelt of age, and bustle, and home; people pointed at them and grinned knowingly. As they approached Holy Trinity Church they passed Owen Owen, the huge new department store where in the last few days she had spent so much money, and now the ground rose more sharply towards the stolid mass of the church itself. Not far beyond it was the cathedral. It was hidden from view now, but the spire was visible like a suspended mirage above the church; then it vanished as they double-backed down Hertford Street.

Tilly's thoughts returned to Percy and the baby. How could he gladly assume the role of father to a baby whose parents he hadn't even met? The child was sickly, moreover: how difficult would he actually be? Or would he be perfectly healthy as soon as his diet improved, as Esther said? Fuzzily, half-asleep, Tilly wondered if she would manage to continue her job. Perhaps there was some kind of organization which could look after Daniel during the day. Would he be classed as a refugee? Perhaps a nanny would be the answer, but how could they afford to pay her? (Whatever was she thinking of? It would only be for a couple of months, they said.) Would she and Percy be able to go out alone in the evenings? Were he their own baby, they would have had months to prepare themselves for the change, and they would have been glad of it: but this was so sudden! How could she expect Percy to be happy with the arrangement she was forcing upon him? And what would her own family say? Even if Percy believed that she had taken the only possible path, her parents would surely insist that she had gone too far, that there must have been another way to help.

Her father's attitude towards the Macksteins had always been strange. When she went to Zurich with him he had seemed quite happy looking at Herr Mackstein's workshop and talking business, and he had taken Tilly so that she could 'see a bit of life that wasn't available in Coventry'. But when a few months later she had suggested that she might go to some kind of finishing school there, he was furious. He said he didn't want her picking up any more Continental ways, and he wasn't going to chuck away money to deprave his own daughter. It was unclear what he meant by this, but he was evidently serious about it because he didn't even help her with the cost of the fare to go to Esther's wedding, as she had anticipated he might.

Suddenly Tilly was aware of a disturbance in the neighbouring compartment. A violent bump made the thin wall behind her head tremble, and she heard the harsh jabs of male shouts. 'How dare you sit here, Jew?' – 'Filth!' – 'What do you mean by sitting on this train?' – 'Papers!' – 'Taking away space from Germans!' – 'Jewish swine!' – 'Out!'

The short, slashing utterances were accompanied by blows which sounded like kicks. Tilly opened her eyes and saw the backs of two or three soldiers straining to get into the other compartment. From the noise and the different voices, there must be several soldiers in there already. They must be drunk, she thought. And was the victim alone? Quickly Tilly closed her eyes again. The uproar grew, and it was plain that the man was being savagely attacked. She could hear him begging them to take his money, his ring, anything in his possession – but please! to let him be. 'Yes yes, we'll have them, won't we boys?' Howls of pain merged with the laughter, so that at moments it was eerily hard to separate them. 'This is what we do to Jews we find on trains!' – 'This!' – 'And this!' Was there blood, Tilly wondered? With so much beating he must be badly injured by now, maybe unconscious. Weren't there any police on the train? Tilly felt herself shaking. She was only five feet away, separated by a seat and a wall that would probably yield to one punch from these thugs. She sat with her arms folded, as if trying to hold herself together, trying to appear oblivious. She wondered if she had been noticed, or if she was being watched even now, but she didn't dare open her eyes. Even the sound of her breathing seemed likely to provoke their attention. 'And now,' said one of the assailants, 'What shall we do with the little bastard? What shall we do with you?' He kicked, and Tilly heard a grating laugh followed by a strange, rasping groan like creaking wood. 'Out of the window!' – 'Yes! Out of the window with the Jew!' – 'Let's throw him out of the window!' they all shouted excitedly. And Tilly heard them clambering over each other as they struggled towards the open window, and then with a cheer they dropped him. For an instant Tilly opened her eyes, and she glimpsed a messy heap tumble away from the hurrying train. She suddenly felt hot. In her pocket was a birth certificate with the word 'JUDEN'. She felt sick. Sweat seemed to be oozing from her thighs, and a drop trickled down between her breasts to her stomach. She breathed deeply, struggling for control of herself. Then she heard the soldiers moving off down the corridor and her terror subsided into a tight clot of revulsion and fear in the centre of her stomach.

The episode lasted barely five minutes, but it brought into vivid focus Tilly's task during the hours that followed. Many people must have been aware of what happened, like herself, but none had made even the slightest gesture of disapproval. It could have been Esther! Or Jakob, or Esther's parents, or children... And if it was discovered that she was helping Jews, perhaps she would be treated in the same way too! How had she been so blind? she wondered. How had she been so blind for so long? Even though she knew that the Nazis victimized Jews – people talked about it, after all, and condemned it – even though she knew about it in a general way, the implications hadn't sunk in. But how was it possible to fail to understand something so monstrous? She thought back to the early Thirties, when German politics and the plight of European Jewry had been remote from her life in Coventry. She knew now that Hitler had outlawed all political parties other than the Nazis as far back as July 1933, but the significance of this act hadn't impinged on her then, nor did it register when a month later he was absolute dictator. She had a disturbing picture of brown-shirted thugs, who seemed to behave unusually brutally towards defenceless citizens, but when she tried to relate these louts to their victims the picture faded. What had the Jews done to deserve such treatment? Nothing, so far as she knew. Why, then, had the attacks been made? This sort of thing didn't happen of its own accord. In Coventry, it was inconceivable. No glimmer of justification had occurred to her, and so she assumed that the reports were misleading. They lacked something that reached into her own experience and engaged her with the words. And why hadn't her friendship with Esther operated on her in this way? Wasn't that a sufficient personal link? Or was it precisely that link which had prevented her from understanding? And suddenly she realized that it was the children who had made her underestimate the force of the threat. She had always thought that if things were so bad then they wouldn't have children – and yet here was Daniel, born in 1938!

In the taxi she stared out of the window, but she saw only a blur of grand streets festooned with swastikas and swarming with people in uniform. She resisted the temptation to look around and pick out details, forcing her eyes to glaze over. Instead she started to think chaotically about the invasion of the Sudetenland and then strove against the savage images that it prompted. The sense that she must remain aloof in order to succeed, as if the surroundings had nothing to do with her, worked in her as an imperative. She couldn't afford to be moved by anything she saw, and the only way to secure this detachment was to notice nothing.

'I've come to see Captain Foley. He's expecting me,' said Tilly on her arrival at the Embassy. A telephone call was made, and after waiting for a minute or two she was conducted up a wide flight of stairs darkened by portraits of British men, and along a passage to his office. 'Come in,' a voice called, and she entered. Another door in the wall to her right was half-open and, as Captain Foley approached her with outstretched hand, Tilly guessed that he had just this moment come into the office himself. He was tall and slightly stooping, with neatly cut black hair and a moustache. His face was puffy, with red blotches slanting beneath his eyes from his nose, which made him look pitifully tired.

'Tilly Henderson? Delighted to meet you,' he said, pressing her hand. 'Please...' As she sat down in the chair he indicated, he took his seat behind the desk. On the wall beyond him Tilly was pleased to see a picture of the King.

Captain Foley asked how she had been managing so far, and she told him of her friends' living conditions, and of her conversation with Esther; it took her aback when he said that they sounded much better off than most Jews. Briskly but calmly, she explained how she had encouraged the whole family to leave, but in the end her own ignorance demanded that she stop trying to tell them what to do, and accept their own assessment of their situation graciously. To demonstrate the depth of her own stupidity, she mentioned her shock at the incident on the train.

'It isn't stupid to be shocked,' said Captain Foley. 'When such things cease to shock, then it is stupid. Terrifyingly stupid. All the same,' he added, 'You were right to pretend indifference, even though it's a sad and rather frightening thing to hear oneself say so.'

Not wishing to waste Captain Foley's time, as soon as she could do so politely Tilly brought up the object of her visit and put the relevant papers on the desk. He glanced through them, nodded, and then reached for two forms which they filled in together. When these were done he gathered them up. 'If you'll excuse me for a moment,' he said, 'I'll take them next door. Can I offer you a cup of something?'

He returned a minute later bearing two cups of strong coffee, and resumed his place opposite her. 'It's a major responsibility you're taking on,' he said. 'I know that these are good friends of yours, but I do hope you haven't been forced into the decision against your will?'

'Of course not,' Tilly answered at once.

'Good. I didn't think so. Nonetheless, the circumstances are so bleak here that one forgets all too easily that one has one's own life to return to.'

'It's true – I haven't thought very much about how I'll cope with him at home.'

Captain Foley paused, watching her, as if waiting to see if she would retract or amend her words. But she was silent, absently inspecting her fingers.

'You ought to,' he said. 'You should realize, even if they don't admit it, that it may be for much longer than two or three months. In short, you may find that you have an orphan on your hands.'

'I know. The Flasches imagine that they'll collect him soon. That's what they say, anyway, and I hope they're right. But I think they suspect it may be much longer. Thinking about it on the train here, I caught myself assuming it would be permanent.'

Captain Foley leaned back in his chair. 'I'm afraid you're right to assume that. And will you be able to look after the child yourself? I could give you the names of a couple of organizations who might help.'

'I see no reason why I shouldn't look after him myself.'

'What about Percy?'

'Yes. I haven't told him yet.'

'You haven't told him? Don't you think you should?'

'Of course, I will. I wanted to get everything sorted out first and present it to him as something settled: otherwise he would worry, and so would I. And for the moment that sort of worry would be a hindrance. I know it will be difficult for him, but I don't believe he'll think I've done wrong. You know him — what do you think?'

He smiled as she turned the question on him. 'It's several years since I've seen Percy, as you know. But I think you're probably right, yes. Now, I'll go and get those documents.'

While he was out of the room, Tilly suddenly realized that he had been interviewing her: surreptitiously, he had been trying to find out if she appreciated the significance of what she was doing. She was indignant. Did he really think she was being wholly irresponsible? What if he wasn't satisfied with her answers? Would he stop her taking Daniel? She didn't think he would. His demeanour suggested that one thing mattered to him above all else — to get Jews out of the country. And she contented herself with the thought that it was for Percy's sake that he wished to reassure himself: he wouldn't stop her, but he wanted her to understand.

The documents had been prepared, and as Captain Foley handed them to her he said, 'Best of luck!' His eyes looked tired and swollen. 'Anything else I can do? Is the baby going to be all right travelling?'

'Yes,' she said. 'I can buy food which is forbidden them, after all. But thank you, all the same.'

Then he escorted her down to the entrance. A taxi was called and Captain Foley took his leave, apologizing for not seeing her back onto the train.

It was late when Tilly arrived in Hamburg. Tired but pleased to have accomplished her business in Berlin, she returned directly to her hotel and went to bed. Now all she had to do was to collect the baby and leave the country as fast and unobtrusively as possible.

She could see no reason why she shouldn't catch a train the following night, and she proposed this when she visited Esther in the morning. Esther and her parents approved her intention to leave soon, but they advised her to go by boat instead of by train. She might not like travelling by boat, but the Port was nearby, and as soon as she was on the boat she would, in effect, be out of the country: in this way she could avoid a long journey through the heart of Germany. And so, without wasting time, Tilly went to the Ländungsbrücken to buy tickets for the ferry.

There was a queue at the ticket office, which built up behind her as fast as it melted away in front. When she reached the window she bought tickets for the eight o'clock boat, and was dismayed to hear the impudent excitement in her voice. Behind the metal grille over the counter, the man's eyes shrivelled with suspicion, and she heard the shuffling of feet: fear fluttered its wings inside her. It must have been plain to everyone that her only concern was to get out of Germany. But let them think what they like, Tilly thought, she wasn't doing anything wrong. Why should she be embarrassed about wanting to leave the country?

On her way back to Esther's flat she went shopping. She had come out with a list of things to buy, and now she walked through the Port Quarter and the Fish Market looking for the shops that Esther had recommended to her. Notices were fixed to the doors of most of them saying 'JEWS NOT SERVED HERE', or 'JEWS AND DOGS KEEP OUT!' Quietly, Tilly filled her bag with prunes and apples, eggs, meat, milk and some very expensive spinach. Then she bought some extra things which weren't on her list, for which they thanked her profusely when she got back. She had only bought a few groceries, but they told her she was a fairy godmother.

Tilly's appearance in Hamburg had given the Flasches a glimpse of normality, but her imminent departure now emphasized their isolation. Their mood during the day was subdued and became increasingly tense as Esther told Tilly in detail about Daniel. Tilly had changed nappies before, but now that she would have to do it regularly she felt that she had to learn all over again. She would have to do it properly, taking care of sores and knowing exactly how to cope when travelling. But it seemed that nappies were the least of her cares. While she prepared food for Daniel and filled a bag with his things, Esther explained to Tilly about Daniel's sleeping and eating habits, his likes and dislikes; his digestion; his temperament on waking and his drift into tears when tired. And, above all, she had to know about the symptoms of his deficiencies, what to do if he suddenly seemed very slow or if he started itching. Daniel slept for three hours during the afternoon, but when he was awake Tilly held him on her lap, touching him and letting him touch her. She was conscious of the pain this caused Esther, who must have been longing to hold her child herself on this last day with him, but it was so clearly vital that Daniel accustom himself to Tilly at once, before she took him away, that she made no move to surrender him to his mother. Whenever Esther did take Daniel for a moment, he seemed interested not in her but in the ring on the middle finger of her right hand, three tiny emeralds set in a gold band.

As the day wore on, Tilly ached to be gone. She didn't know

whether she would see Esther again; nor did Daniel's family know whether they would see him or Tilly again.

'Where is Daniel going, Mummy?' said Abel.

'He's going away with Tilly.'

'But where?'

When Tilly saw the confusion and alarm in Jakob's and Abel's eyes, she felt as if she was kidnapping Daniel, and every minute that she spent with the family made her feel uncomfortable. The air was clammy with suppressed fears and unvoiced grief. A word out of place, Tilly thought, would transform the studied calm which surrounded her into a torrent of sadness. But still, they wouldn't be letting her take Daniel away unless they were sure that he had no chance of survival in the present circumstances. While she felt that she was abandoning the Flasches to their death, Tilly knew that in their view she was abducting Daniel from certain death to life – and leaving them in the same uncertainty in which she found them.

Jakob, my father, returned to the flat. His fingers, like birds' feet, were hooked over the back of a chair; he was bent with exhaustion and the pain in his back.

'Why don't you come with us to the Port?' Tilly asked.

'Look at me, Tilly. Look at my nose,' he said.

Jakob's nose was like the Tower of Lebanon, a majestic curved flag of his Jewishness. 'I assure you, you'll be better off without me,' he said.

'I'm sorry, I didn't think,' said Tilly, and she blushed.

At last it was time to go, and without fuss Tilly said goodbye to the boys and to Esther's parents. Then she hugged Jakob and Esther, put on her coat, and picked up Daniel, her suitcase and her travelling bag. She had turned to go down the stairs when Esther suddenly stopped her. 'Wait, Tilly, just one more thing!' she cried. Lungeing forward, she slipped her emerald ring into Tilly's pocket and kissed Daniel on the forehead for the last time. Then she turned round, and as Tilly walked downstairs she heard the door of the apartment close.

At the bottom step Tilly paused. 'Are you ready then?' she said to Daniel brightly. He was heavy, and she settled him higher up against her shoulder before walking out into the street. She wanted to weep. For the first time she felt the weight of his complete dependence.

By the time she reached the tram stop from where she could go directly to the harbour, her arm was aching. Putting her case on the pavement, she moved him to her other arm. His nose was running and she reached into her pocket for a handkerchief to wipe it. He resisted, jerking his head back with a cross whimper. 'Hey, hey,' she said, 'It's good for you.' He cried out as she tried again, and more fluid came out of his nose. Hastily Tilly wiped it away and stuffed the handkerchief back into her pocket, then she held him in both arms and rocked him a little. 'Don't cry, little one, don't cry, Daniel,' she murmured softly. It was strange to think that such a tiny nose could have so much muck in it.

'So, are you comfortable?' she said when she was seated on the tram with Daniel in her lap, snug against her stomach. 'It's all a bit much to take in, isn't it? Here you are on a tram with a strange woman, and you haven't a clue where we're going. But don't worry, we'll get used to each other soon enough. Let's hope you'll like where we're going. Have you ever been on a tram before? I wonder. Look at all the people out of the window, and the houses as we rattle past... Then we're going on a boat, where you'll be able to sleep quite comfortably, I hope. Poor dear, you can't understand a thing I'm saying...' Daniel watched Tilly's lips as she chatted, as if fascinated by the shapes she was making and the strange sounds that emerged. Seeing that he enjoyed it, Tilly continued uttering whatever came into her head rather than falling silent, and she found it comforting. His open appreciation encouraged and sustained her: considering her enterprise with detachment, she was nervous, as if observing herself as a child trying to find her way home in the dark.

The sight of the boat waiting at the waterside immediately made her feel safer. Daniel was enjoying himself too: he was so good and quiet. Whoever said that babies cry all the time? It was going to be no trouble at all taking him back with her. Looking across the Elbe at the ghostly shapes of the blacked-out docks, Tilly saw the cranes in the moonlight, glistening streaks across the dark sky, and the angles of the ships winked at her gently. On the quay, the phalanxes of huge warehouses marched into the darkness, presiding over the sprawl of fences, winches and stacks of goods and mocking her naïveté with their solid, impenetrable self-importance. Occasional hooded lights cast faint trapezoid shadows in great strides across the open spaces. As her eyes grew accustomed to the shades and shapes she saw that the docks stretched far away in every direction. Many more ships lay at anchor here than she had originally thought, and from the flickering pin-heads of light she judged that people must be busy on many of them.

A steep gangplank took them from the wharf to the murky deck, and Tilly found the way to their cabin.

Stepping over the high threshold, her neck and arms and shoulders aching from Daniel's weight, Tilly saw the bunk and suddenly felt exhausted. With a final thrust of effort she fed and washed Daniel. Then she ate an apple and lay straight down to sleep.

The boat was only five minutes from the quay when Tilly was woken by Daniel's crying. She drew him to her side, thinking that he would soon go back to sleep if he could feel her warmth. But he didn't: he continued to cry with increasing violence, pushing his hands into Tilly's flesh at first and then rolling on his back and yelling. Tilly cuddled him and talked to him, she tried to give him some milk, checked his nappies (they were clean); she offered him a spoonful of stewed apple. Still he wouldn't be hushed, and she remembered his cotton rabbit and his scrap of blanket which Esther had insisted she take. She reached into her bag and gave them to him. Daniel clutched them tightly, chewing on them and making them sodden with tears and saliva. He wouldn't let them go, but still he wouldn't stop crying. He had been so good earlier on: what was wrong now? It was as if he knew he mustn't cry until they were safe and, now that they were, he was doing so with desperate energy, raging at being taken from his mother, raging at being taken from his home, raging at being on a boat in the North Sea with an unknown woman whose language was incomprehensible, raging at his own helplessness. And it made Tilly want to cry too. 'I know, I know,' she said, 'You want your mother. So do I, Daniel darling, but she can't be here. I'm taking you so that you can be well, so that you can live. Don't cry. I'm trying to do the best I can.' Little beast, she thought, she deserved some sleep too; if he could cry like this, there couldn't be much wrong with him.

When Daniel finally went back to sleep, Tilly looked at her watch and saw that it was six o'clock. She settled her head on her pillow with relief and instantly dropped off. An hour later she was awake again. Daniel was howling furiously. Tilly sleepily changed his foul-smelling nappy, fumbling with the pins, and for a moment Daniel was quiet. But no sooner had she turned out the light than he was violently sick.

Tilly was beginning to get alarmed. The boat was rolling a little – anyone could be seasick. But this sustained crying suggested that something serious was wrong. She thought back to all that Esther had told her, but nothing seemed to account for it. She dragged her memory for all that she had ever heard about babies' ailments, but could think of nothing which might explain what was happening. And there was nothing she could do, nobody she could ask. Increasingly tired, worried and lonely, Tilly tried to nurse Daniel's unknown malady with nothing but patience and sympathy. Daniel remained implacable: with occasional pauses just long enough for Tilly to consider relaxing, he cried all the way to Hull.

When she stepped onto the quay, drained and appalled by

the night, a miracle seemed to occur, for he suddenly stopped. Then he smiled and pulled her hair vigorously, as if to draw her attention to a spectacle which shouldn't be missed for the world.

3

I thought Kate would look waxen against the white sheets, her pale skin stiff and thick, the colour of sour milk. I imagined that her inert body would seem dead, her presence spectral, as if her mind had been knocked from her as easily as a walnut from its shell.

I had, of course, written to her parents after the accident, expressing my horror and offering my help in whatever ways they might find useful. It was a difficult letter to write because of the danger of referring to Kate as if she were dead – but then, not having seen Kate myself, it seemed as if she was indeed dead, for the idea of a tragic accident implied to me a violent end to what had gone before, instead of the sudden opening of a struggle, which this is. Anyway, either I achieved some delicacy or, considering their affection for you, they overlooked my clumsiness, because a fortnight or so later I received a very generous and admirably calm response from Mrs L. As you suggested, I had asked her whether I and the rest of your family would be welcome at Kate's bedside, and she answered that, in due course, we would. They had been advised by the doctors that Kate should not be allowed visitors until her condition was 'stable', but thereafter anyone known and liked by her might sit and talk, or read aloud: it's thought possible, apparently, that she will be roused by these familiar sounds at the touchlines of her consciousness.

You complained before of the desperate suspense when, knowing that Kate was badly injured, you weren't allowed to see her. To be told that, after falling three floors from a balcony, someone is severely concussed and their leg is broken in four places, is like having a bright light suddenly directed at your face from the darkness and then switched off: when it's gone you have the impression of glare, not of illumination. I too wanted to see Kate for myself, to absorb what this clinical description meant in relation to her. I'd heard that her fall was broken by the brick wall beneath the balcony – as if she tripped in her flight – and I gather that this probably saved her from worse injury; which, when the comparison is a coma, can only mean death. But I was still anxious to see her for myself.

Mum had been the previous day, so I went on my own. As you know, she has been jumpy since Tilda's startling announcement that she is pregnant. Not surprisingly, she found it frustrating trying to sustain a monologue for more than a few minutes without any reaction from Kate at all, or hope of any. She was tired before she went, and she returned depressed by a sense of her own inadequacy. Because she wished it so fervently, I think she half-expected Kate to come round as she was speaking, and was unduly distressed when this didn't occur. So, forewarned, I took with me the pages you've just read.

While reading them aloud to Kate, I found myself changing words which I thought she wouldn't like and leaving out phrases which might upset her – I completely skipped the passage about the assault of the Jew on the train, for example. It wasn't at all like reading to blankness: from her impenetrable unconsciousness she was influencing me. I don't mean to imply any mysterious telepathic communication, I simply observe that I adapted my reading for Kate's benefit. And, suddenly aware of her obscure power over me, I had the strange sense that what I was reading, which I had thought to be outside memory's grasp, was not the passive object of my will but was endowed with its own transforming activity. It was dynamic, it had light of its own, like a stained glass window which depends for its fulfilment both on the movement of light without and on the viewer within. This is true whether the colours lead lyrically into each other, with perhaps a naturalistic picture on the glass, or whether they abut harshly – red against purple, or blue – in an abstract pattern. The glass mediates between the light and the eye; it filters the light, so that what we suppose to be uniformly bright sunlight is reformed by the window in a sequence of coloured pools and shafts across the room or hall. A story mediates with the past just as the stained glass filters the light, and the listener (counterpart to the perceiving eye) makes his or her way around the story according to taste and capacity – and the properties of the light. The body of glass and colour is manipulated to explore and establish relationships with light. And light, they used to say, is the source of all life; we originate from light. Although infinite itself, light's yield is finite. But as we know, it can be seen through an indefinite number of lenses; it can do, and be made to do, the most astounding things.

You've seen Kate yourself several times now, there's no need for me to describe how she was. I knew what to expect too – that her leg was mending satisfactorily, that her head was shaved, exposing the bruises spreading up from above the right temple to the top of her head – but I was still shaken by the physical confrontation. While she knew nothing of the thick plaster-cast around her leg, I was intensely aware that it was *her* leg whose fractured bones now lay, so fragile, in the hoist. I was surprised that the bandages had been removed from her head and, seeing the purplish, yellow-grey lesions clustered round the stitched-up wound, I experienced a painful constriction in my chest, as if until then I hadn't understood the shattering-force of the impact. From where I sat on the other side of her bed, however, the injuries weren't so noticeable, and I became conscious of her stillness. But it was a strange, brittle stillness. You see the folded cavity of her ear and the lobe's curve against the pillow, and you wonder if she hears; the tip of her slightly pointed nose faintly twitches from time to time as if responding to a fleeting scent; the lashes of her closed eyes flicker, as if the pupils have contracted beneath the eyelids; her lips suddenly quiver, as if stirred by a word down in her throat. I held her hand, pressing her slender fingers against mine, touching the trim nails and the smooth little knuckles: the gentle warmth in her palm held the promise of pressure. In the same way, if the light behind a stained glass window remained constant, the stillness would be uncanny but you'd know the sun was there.

Having told you the story of my origins, I wonder if you have ever speculated about Mum's? Over the years, she and I have concocted a version which I always supposed would remain private, but it seems appropriate now to share it with you.

4

Towards the evening, Barbara started to feel dizzy. Sitting on her bed for a moment, her nail file idle, she imagined her head as a house in which all the skylights were propped open: through them could be seen clusters of fiery stars. A couple of the girls at work were down with the 'flu last week. To get ill now, just when Julius was coming home on leave and she had three days off in a row, counting the weekend, would be cruel luck: she might as well tie some stones to her feet and jump into the Sherborne – although to drown there, it was true, would be a surprising achievement. She'd end up only twisting her ankle and wrecking her shoes. If she chose the Sherborne to drown in, it could only be because she didn't actually want to drown – so she might as well wear Wellington boots for the occasion. Perhaps the water would slop over the top in icy shafts to her ankles and she would catch pneumonia.

Then she remembered that she hadn't eaten anything all day. She hadn't wanted to. It wasn't surprising that she felt a little odd: she had been looking forward to this evening for weeks, for months.

The fourteenth of November nineteen hundred and forty, Julius Gallagher comes home to Coventry on leave; he comes to Craven Street, to the Shearer household. Barbara could picture the neighbours watching Julius at the door, Mrs Pearson pulling a lopsided, well!-I've-seen-it-all-now! face, pushing out her rampart bosom beneath her checked housecoat, then catching Elsie's eyes across the fence. 'I say, Elsie, isn't that that scapegrace Julius Gallagher? What's he doing knocking on the Shearers' door? It can't be for Miss Tilly, she's in London, married I'm told. Must be for Barbara. Don't tell me she's stepping out with that Gallagher fellow, her grandfather would have a fit if he knew, him in his brown boots!' And yes, it was Julius, Corporal Julius Gallagher.

She had expected to see him at the end of August; she had booked tickets for *Gone With The Wind* at the Rex Cinema. But his leave was cancelled at the last moment for some reason, or so he claimed, and anyway the cinema was destroyed the previous day in an air raid. It was in May that she had seen him last, when they went dancing every night of the week except for one. They went to the Rex, with its aviary of tropical birds and real Wurlitzer; they went to the Rialto Casino Ballroom where the Gaiety Dance Band was playing; and he took her to the Magnet Club. All her friends were jealous because the illuminated fountain was on that night, and also the special lighting system which could be programmed for the dances. (The waltz, in pastel shades, lasted more than half an hour.) Billy Monk's New Rhythm Band was playing too. Where else had they gone? To the Savoy, of course! How could she forget? They won the quickstep competition! It was dancing which had first brought them together, if you didn't count the Methodist dos. They first noticed one another at the Connor's New Year dance. He was mostly with Belle Howarth. Julius made the best of it but it was obvious to anyone that Julius was a natural while Belle wasn't much of a dancer. Barbara could see that she kept on hesitating. People asked, 'Wherever did he learn to dance like that?' Jane Blythe said he used to go to Orme's and to Professor Daniel's, but he denied it. He said he learned the same way he learned to turn a cartwheel, you either had it in you or you didn't. But she didn't believe it: somewhere, he had been taught how to foxtrot, and to quickstep and to tango and to waltz. She'd been dancing that night mostly with Pete Hyman, and occasionally with Joe, who was home on leave, Lieutenant Joe Dodds MC. Pete was a good dancer, but he was past forty, and Joe – he wasn't bad, but he wasn't good enough for her. She remembered going past Julius and Belle in the waltz and catching his eye. He winked at her, and she knew that he realized she was a better dancer than Belle. It wouldn't have been right to wink back, especially with Joe watching her as if his life depended on it, but she smiled. And ten minutes later he came up and cut in on Peter – 'Do you mind, old boy?' – knowing that Barbara didn't mind, already taking her hand.

Since alcohol wasn't available in the ballrooms, the men tended to go to the pub before a dance. Barbara would come along at eight o'clock with her friends, and half an hour later Julius would arrive with the other men, who were always a bit tipsy – she could tell because their sense of rhythm was fuddled. But Julius's breath didn't smell and he never appeared to be in the least drunk, even though his friends swore he always drank just as much as them in spite of being a Methodist. It was the custom for the men to have a second handkerchief, which they held in their right hand when they danced so that they didn't soil their partner's dress or touch any exposed skin. But Julius didn't bother with this. At first, Barbara was a little shocked, but he didn't care. He said it was daft, and told her to look at all the men with their silly handkerchiefs: didn't they ever wash their hands? Were all the girls so afraid of being touched? If so, why was it more agreeable to be grasped with a piece of sweaty cloth? They must spend all their time thinking about that instead of enjoying the dance. Barbara could feel his fingers against her back, firm and alive: it wasn't just his feet that danced, every muscle in his body joined in and a handkerchief between herself and his hand would have been as intrusive as a boxing glove.

She leaned back against the bed's buttoned headboard and recalled the swish of her dress following her as they turned.

When her friends saw her dancing with him time after time,

they realized that something had started and they told her, at every opportunity, to be cautious. He was a rascal, they said, who couldn't settle down and always made trouble. As a woman you couldn't afford to trust him, and probably not as a man either – just think of his father, who died of drink, and let that be a lesson if nothing else was. If he didn't dance with a handkerchief it was because he wanted – well, wasn't it obvious? Barbara ought to insist that he hold one, and look out for herself. A girl couldn't be too careful with a man like that. But Julius was three inches taller than most of the other men, he had lovely hands and he was lively. In all the warnings she received, Barbara detected a note of envy. There were jokes about his eyebrows, which were said to be like little squirrels' tails, and about his hair because it wouldn't lie flat against his scalp. They said that he was a hooligan, and Rose Evans said that if that was what the hair on his head was like, his 'other' hair was probably like pine needles. But Rose Evans would have given her buck teeth to find out.

Barbara stepped across the room and reached into the cupboard for her sling-back dancing shoes. They were old and rather scuffed, and she wondered if instead she ought to take the grey satin ones with the T-bar and buckle. They weren't quite so good for dancing, but they were smarter and she enjoyed wearing them. Once again, she thought of her grandfather, one of the last of the old school of watchmakers. Earlsdon was part of Coventry now, but when his father had gone to live there it was a separate village, whose residents believed themselves superior to those living in the city itself. They were richer, and they liked to demonstrate it. Take their Sunday boots: since it was known that they wore black boots to work in, when they wore brown boots on Sundays it advertized that they owned two pairs. Eventually their old attitudes and labour-intensive techniques proved incompetent and, in the late attempt to compete with the Prescot craftsmen, Mr Shearer had joined the syndicate of Coventry manufacturers

who formed the Coventry Watch Movement Manufacturing
Company. They bought new premises in Spon Street, where
many operations could be performed under a single roof, hoping thereby to save the time and expense of outworkers.
Barbara remembered the sheets of metal in the corner of the
workshop and the men on their stools with their white aprons
pinned to the benches to catch anything that fell. As a girl, she
had marvelled at the tiny pieces of machinery and the delicate
pincers and tweezers in those large, rough hands, from which
emerged the intricate movement of the watch. But the company still failed to compete – as her father had long predicted
– and all that survived of old Shearer's heyday was his boots and
his attitude towards the world. 'He is a lout, Barbara,' he had
said of Julius; 'his father worked with bicycles!'

Barbara was fond of her grandfather, but he couldn't be
expected to see reason; his opinion didn't matter. Her parents'
case was different. She didn't like to think of them sharing her
grandfather's prejudices. After all, her father had long ago distanced himself from the family business. It was his younger
brother David who now sat in the Spon Street office in the
chair once occupied by their father. Yet, moulded by a tena-
cious Methodism, her father was zealous in his duties both
towards his family and his craft. Home and business were not
clearly divided in his life. The house in Craven Street was adjacent to the workshops and he expected his family to take an
interest, which was why he had taken Tilly to Zurich. Barbara
wanted Julius to recognize that her parents were kind people
and to like them. And she was convinced that if her parents
would only admit the evidence supplied by their eyes then they
would all get along very well together. At a bazaar in the
Methodist Central Hall, Julius had once set up a stall,
uninvited, on the pavement, where he sold puppets of
Coventry dignitaries which he had made himself. She was only
ten at the time, but she clearly recalled the bald pink cotton
pate of her grandfather with the bulging button eyes and the

thick, indignant lips. She stuck her tongue out at Julius because everyone else was cross with him, but secretly she found it funny. 'How dare you bring that insolent rubbish here?' said her father. Julius spun a coin in the air and caught it with a slap on the back of his hand. 'Heads or tails?' he had said with a laugh. Barbara giggled suddenly at the memory of his imitation of Alderman Figg at the inauguration ceremony in Trinity Street three years ago. Some way down the street, Julius had started to copy him, chin up, tapping his imaginary lectern, clipping his words and, with a little exaggeration, making him seem harmless and ridiculous. She was standing nearby with Tilly, and they were both aching with squeezed-in laughter, trying not to catch their parents' eyes. Many of those who laughed openly joined in furiously condemning him afterwards for his disrespect. Barbara saw that he enjoyed making a scandal but, though she didn't expect to persuade her grand-father, she thought her parents ought to be able to see that he was neither a lout nor a fool.

Until this year, Barbara had known Julius's mother much better than she had known him. While her wayward son's attendance at church and Methodist dos was erratic, Mrs Gallagher was to be seen at the same place in church every Sunday, intent on her prayer-book, increasingly crabbed and myopic, the hair curling down from under her hat growing greyer over the years. And at every charity bazaar in Coventry that Barbara had ever been to, there was Mrs Gallagher at her stall of homemade marmalade. Among the many jars there was always a special one of whisky marmalade. It always stood in the same place, and nobody ever bought it. Whether it was the same jar every year was avidly debated – nobody ever dared ask her – but it was generally agreed to be a formidable brew. People joked that she had killed her husband with it, but she went on producing it undaunted. Her embarrassment at her son's indiscretions was evident in her pouting, tightly closed lips, and a look of kindled ferocity which terrified Barbara as a child: but if Mrs Gallagher heard anyone criticize Julius, she defended him with the vehemence of a dog whose tail has been trodden on, and rebuked him when she thought they were alone. That time with the puppets, she hadn't hesitated to point out that he had sold all his wares and also handed in all his takings – unlike some others she could mention... Barbara's parents said that she was a good soul really and you had to feel sorry for her. But Barbara didn't feel sorry for her at all: she liked her.

When Julius's leave was cancelled in August, Mr Shearer offered little consolation. Since the news of his son-in-law Percy's disappearance on some mission, he was inclined to regard any able-bodied soldier on leave as a layabout. 'I am sorry, Barbara,' he said, puckering his brow. 'Isn't there someone else who can take you to the Rex?'

'What about Stanley Stevens?' said Mrs Shearer. 'I've heard he's home.'

'On crutches. It's not so good dancing with someone on crutches.'

'Barbara!' Mrs Shearer paused, and then said, 'I hope it's not because of something he's done that his leave's cancelled?'

Barbara suspected her mother of hoping precisely that it was because of something he'd done, but she herself didn't know. There was only a telegram, which gave no explanation: 'LEAVE CANCELLED. NEXT DANCE STILL MINE?'

She had danced on several occasions since May but none of them were significant for her, which her parents realized quite well. When she told them some weeks later that she would be going to the Savoy with Julius, she knew from their strained faces that they saw her pleasure and didn't welcome it. Her mother sighed and said that she must ask her father. Mr Shearer groaned and touched his ear petulantly. 'I do wish you would abandon this idea. There is more to life than dancing, after all,' he said. 'I know you're keen to go and so I shan't stop you: but I want to see him. He's to come to the house to collect you, and I want to know what time you'll be back.'

In private, Mrs Shearer said to her husband that she could see that Julius was attractive in a wild sort of way; but they agreed that they didn't like the direction in which it all seemed to be heading. How did you stop a daughter from following such a path? Tilly had never presented them with a problem like this. Could they forbid Barbara to see him? In the past, it would have been possible. 'But in the past,' said Mr Shearer, 'a young man wouldn't have got away with that sort of behaviour. He would have been horsewhipped and packed off to the colonies.' Neither of them disliked Julius, but it was impossible to believe that he could provide a respectable home for Barbara if, God forbid, it ended in marriage. They couldn't deny that he was lively but they had hoped for a candidate with more solid accomplishments.

'You should have a word with him when they come back,' said Mrs Shearer.

'When they come back, do you think? Wouldn't it be much better to make it clear from the outset?'

'Do it when they come back. She's been working flat out and has looked forward to it so, and he's been fighting, after all. It would be a shame to spoil their evening.'

'Perhaps when he picks her up I'll just mention that I want to have a little chat with him later.'

'I'll have a nice pot of tea ready for when he comes. Be friendly.'

'Of course.'

At exactly quarter to seven, the doorbell broke into song. Mr Shearer answered it. 'Good evening, Julius.'

'Good evening, sir.'

'Come in, come in.' As he stepped aside to let Julius in, he noticed that it was still extraordinarily light outside, although it was an hour since black-out.

'Barbara! Julius is here!' Mr Shearer called up the stairs.

'I'll be down in a minute, in an instant, in a minute!'

Glancing in the direction of her voice, Julius smiled, revealing his white teeth.

'Come through, my wife will give you some tea while you're waiting,' said Mr Shearer, and ushered Julius through the door to his right, where Mrs Shearer was rising from her chair to greet him.

Julius unconsciously stooped so that he wouldn't bump his head, and then straightened. He stood at ease, cap in hand: the proportions of the room seemed diminished by his broad frame, yet he looked balanced and nimble. On the mantelpiece stood a wireless; a clock hung on the wall above, and a wood fire burned tamely in the grate beneath.

'Mrs Shearer – how do you do?' he said, stepping forward.

His smile unnerved her: his lips seemed to be pulled back at the corners, leaving a bare white rectangle. Deep crescent furrows appeared at the edges of his mouth.

'Hello Julius. How nice to see you. I'm very well, thank you. And yourself?'

'All the better for being here. All the better for being here, Mrs Shearer,' he said buoyantly. 'As you know, it's nothing but beer and skittles in the army, which gets on top of one. It's nice to come home and rest the right arm.'

Mrs Shearer laughed. She couldn't abide soldiers on leave who were solemn: they made her think of stuffed marrows. 'We know how hard you all work,' she said, 'but we don't slouch around at home, either.'

Julius looked quickly over his left shoulder, then over his right. 'Show me the man who says you do...'

'Sit down, Julius,' said Mrs Shearer, laughing again, and he moved into the chair behind him. Beside his pristine uniform and his dark hair which was slicked flat against his scalp, the maroon upholstery of the chairs looked suddenly worn and faded.

Barbara's footsteps on the stairs were heard, and they all raised their heads towards the door. Julius stood up and approached her as she entered. With a grin he took her hand and kissed it; behind his back, Mr Shearer scowled.

Barbara was wearing a dark blue polka-dot dress with a halter neck, reaching just below her knees. She had a string of pearls round her neck and little pearl studs in her ears. A blush swelled from her throat to her face, disappearing into the blonde hair rolled tidily about her head. She touched one of her puffed shoulders and blinked. 'Hello Julius,' she said.

'Hello Barbara!' he answered. 'Have you got your dancing shoes?'

Looking at her feet, her blush immediately revived. She was wearing brown walking-shoes, with socks over her stockings. 'Yes,' she said, 'it does look odd, doesn't it? I thought I'd put my proper shoes on when I get there, so I don't ruin them walking.'

'Never know what you're walking on in the black-out, eh? The voice of reason. How silly of me! Have you got a spare pair of Wellington boots?'

'Oh, Julius!' said Barbara.

'It sounds rather sensible, Barbara dear,' Mr Shearer announced. 'I'm sure I can find Julius a pair of boots...'

Julius turned in astonishment. 'Oh no, really! How kind of you! There's really no need.'

'No trouble at all,' said Mr Shearer, moving towards the door.

'Dad, he was joking, he doesn't want any of your boots!' said Barbara.

Mr Shearer's eyebrows twitched uncertainly, and then he smiled. 'Oh, my mistake,' he said, and looked hard at the teapot on the low table by the fire.

'I'm so sorry, will you have a cup of tea before you go, you two?' Mrs Shearer asked.

Barbara refused. They ought to be getting along soon, she said, and steered the meeting to a conclusion.

'You'll bring her back by half-past eleven then, will you?'

Mr Shearer said to Julius when Barbara went to fetch her coat and her purse. 'I wondered if we might have a little chat then?'

'Of course. Anything particular?'

Mr Shearer hadn't anticipated a question in response. 'No, no, nothing particular,' he said in his confusion.

'Are you ready, Julius?' Barbara asked.

Mrs Shearer kissed her daughter on the cheek. 'Now, you just enjoy yourself, dear,' she said.

'And if the sirens go, mind you get her safely to a proper air-raid shelter,' said Mr Shearer as they went out of the door. 'I'm relying on you to look after her, Julius.' And he made a mental note to offer Julius a cigar on his return. Julius made him feel old.

Giving Julius the parcel containing her shoes to carry, Barbara linked her arm in his and they turned down the hill towards Spon End. Suddenly, they were shy of each other. High above the city a few barrage balloons stood out as blocks of shadow against the mottled sky. The night was coloured, as if magnesium fuses had been ignited beyond the horizon and the moon was drawing the wisps of smoke and vapour to itself, white and green and orange teasing and tempering the darkness. Their steps rang in the silence against the glinting pavement, as if they were walking alone in an empty church which was vibrant with overlaid shadows and sparring echoes.

'Your father,' said Julius, 'thinks that nothing will come of this.'

Barbara was startled. 'What do you mean?'

'He said he wants to have a word with me when we get back. I suppose it's to tell me nothing should come of it. And if he thinks that, then he probably thinks nothing will come of it. Finish: finished: nothing. Simple as that, he thinks.'

Barbara's wrist shifted in the crook of his arm. She sensed a weightiness in his words which made her tremble. 'If he's right,' she said, 'there would be a lot fewer marriages. Happy ones, as well as unhappy ones.'

'And a lot more bastard children.'

The slums of Spon End smelt faintly, as if the low houses were built in a field of mud and rotting grass. Barbara didn't feel afraid here – she had passed through these streets most days of her life and she knew there was nothing to fear. But they were animated, nonetheless, as if from the hole left by an uprooted cobblestone a germ might emerge, or as if the damp creeping through the plaster and piercing the brickwork all around was wilfully malignant. A cat slipped into an alley on her right, back arched, waiting.

'Gold Flake tobacco: for a smooth and mellow aroma,' she said, reading the advertisement on the side of the railway viaduct. 'I don't know why, but I always say it to myself when I go under the bridge,' she added. It was nice having Julius beside her: she could admit such a thing without feeling silly.

'So advertizing works on you?'

'Oh no. I've never bought any of the tobacco.'

'But you noticed the advert.'

'I'm not blind.'

Julius pressed her arm against his ribs. Secluded in the deep shadow under the bridge, he would have kissed the girl at his side, but it didn't feel appropriate to kiss Barbara. She would probably resist his casual fumblings, and if she didn't then she would be mysteriously diminished in his eyes. He told himself that this was because he respected her, and wondered if he should ask her to marry him. But how did you decide that sort of thing? Her father had implied that they had reached a point which demanded a decision – which was right, except that Julius didn't intend the decision to be taken for him. He might be prompted to decide, but the direction was for him and Barbara to choose. He had been suspicious of soldiers who returned from leave married: why the hurry? Wasn't it unfair on the girl when he might be killed before seeing her again, leaving her a widow, perhaps a mother – and so young? But now he, too, was acquainted with the urgency. He wasn't going to die, nor did she think he was going to die, but he had seen soldiers losing their girl by failing to act. He was going away again soon, and he didn't want to lose her. A lot could happen in the months of his absence, and he might return to find her swept from his reach by someone else. Either he must resign himself to this possibility, or protect himself by securing her: he must make up his mind.

A man rattled slowly past them on a bicycle, crouched over his handlebars as if braced against some unseen menace. A flat cap was pushed down onto his head.

'Wasn't that Alf Summers?' said Julius. 'He didn't recognize me.'

'He probably wasn't wearing his spectacles. He's always losing them, and he's more short-sighted than ever. It's a wonder he can see to ride a bicycle at all.'

Behind them they heard a clatter, then an oath. They turned and saw the man pick himself from the ground and slap the dirt from his trousers. Then he swung his leg doggedly back over his bicycle and rode on.

Julius and Barbara laughed quietly, and as they followed the road round into Upper Spon Street they chatted about the war. On either side, the eerie light of the moon made the faded whitewash between the beams of the ancient wooden houses gleam, and the diamond panes of the mullioned windows twinkled silvery-blue like fishscales. Even the mortar in the brick topshops seemed to glitter, disporting its impurities. Julius looked up and saw three stars in a tight triangle, which quickly became the three golden balls over a pawn shop.

Suddenly the tranquil darkness was ripped through by the swooping wail of the air-raid siren. Barbara's stomach heaved with the familiar sick wrench, the feeling of being transformed instantly from a woman into a rabbit fleeing in terror for the nearest hole. The air was suddenly alive with the sound of banging doors and the street, which a second ago had been almost deserted, was suddenly full of people leaving it.

She was aware of Julius tugging her arm and she followed without thinking, gladly. They had only just entered Spon Street and already the sinister roar of aeroplanes could be heard. She looked up briefly: the sky was filled with them, she had never seen so many. How was it big enough to contain so many of those huge machines? She could see the bombs falling, like ink spattered across the stained sky. Then came the whistles and the first explosions: the world juddered, and they were running frantically. A fountain of red flames soared from a yard on her right with a greedy, scattered crash.

'Julius! Where are we going?' Barbara shouted.

'My house!'

It was only just around the corner in Norfolk Street, but there were public shelters in Spon Street. 'No!' she yelled, pulling her hand free.

'Where then? Quick! We must...'

His words disappeared beneath an explosion and the crackling rush of flames which leaped above the roofs to their right with billowing, abrasive smoke, and they could see solid objects being hurled high into the air. A jet of sparks jumped clear of the houses beside them, fireworks out of control. The stench and heat of destruction made Barbara and Julius stagger sideways: they saw in one another's wide white eyes their own horror, and then they ran towards the house.

Julius grabbed the door handle, expecting to enter without pausing on the doorstep. But it was locked, and the resistance to his momentum temporarily stunned him, while Barbara crashed against him from behind. 'I've got the keys! Don't worry, I've got the keys, I must have the keys!' he shouted, but his words were lost in the pandemonium.

As he hunted for them with shaking fingers, Barbara looked away. Between the siren and the first bombs (if any bombs came) there was always time to reach a proper shelter. However, not only had this raid started earlier than usual, but, hardly five minutes after the siren had begun, the flare of several conflagrations besides the one in Spon Street could be seen. The sky jerked and bloomed with orange, as if the firmament itself had cracked and let the stars loose upon the world.

The door opened and Julius groped on the table inside for matches. A candle in an old bedtime holder with a handle stood ready.

'You shouldn't light a candle,' said Barbara.

'Why ever not?'

Seeing that the black-out curtains weren't closed, she made to draw them against the gathering storm, but Julius stopped her. 'It's a bit late to worry about the black-out now,' he said. 'Anyway, I haven't brought you here to sit in the front room and wait for the ceiling to fall in on us.' He cupped his hand round the candle and told her to open the door of the cupboard under the stairs. It would protect them as well as anywhere else, he said. Ducking as she stepped inside, for a moment she thought of resisting. Shouldn't they try to get to a proper shelter? But he was following, and in the soft candlelight she saw that the cramped space was neatly arranged as a shelter. The sloping ceiling was reinforced with robust-looking planks. On the floor was a mattress with blankets and pillows; and on a low shelf stood a little primus stove and a kettle, some spare candles, tins of food and some bottles. Barbara had heard it said that the space beneath the stairs made an adequate shelter from anything but a direct hit: certainly it looked safe, and whoever had fitted it out considered it to be so.

As Julius knelt down to put the candle on the shelf, Barbara turned in the tight space to pull off her coat and momentarily brushed his head with her thigh. Abruptly, she moved away, hitting her head. 'Ouch!' she said. She lowered herself onto the mattress, twisting herself so that she was sitting against the wall with her knees hunched up: Julius saw her dress stretch tight across the curve of her hip. She smiled, the shadow twitching at the edge of her face so that her lips glistened. 'I love those Wee Willie Winkie candlesticks,' she said.

'Why don't you take off your shoes?' said Julius. 'I'm going to take mine off, if you don't mind.'

'Good idea!' said Barbara, as if she would never have thought of it herself.

Although Julius tried to concentrate on removing his own shoes, he sensed her feet wriggling free and her arms reaching forwards, pressing her breasts together, and he endeavoured to ignore the stirring in his crotch. Taking her shoes, he placed them on the mat outside next to his own, then shut the door.

'Have you still got my other shoes?'

'Yes, they're outside. In the living-room, I mean. I put them down to light the candle.'

Barbara nodded. 'My sister Tilly bought them for me before the war in Covent Garden.'

'Did she? I thought they sold flowers and veg in Covent Garden.'

'They do. And shoes. Nothing else, though.'

'Ah.'

Sitting near Barbara on the mattress with the prospect of an hour or two of complete privacy, Julius tingled with sudden, glowing consciousness of his good fortune. Thirty-one years old, veteran of many amorous opportunities – some engineered, some unexpected – but in the present circumstances he felt coy. He wanted Barbara too much to achieve the lightness of tone and touch that generally won him favours. If he advanced now and she rejected him he would be trapped with the twin shame of failure and abused advantage.

He smiled at her with restraint. 'I hope you're not too uncomfortable,' he said, indicating with a wave of the hand that she should take a blanket and pillow if she wished. Then he settled back firmly against the wall, his knees raised and feet wedged against the door opposite. She was facing him in a similar position, a little to one side. If he reached out, he would be able to touch her legs; if he moved his foot a few inches, he could touch her hip.

Barbara thanked him; she said she was comfortable.

It occurred to Julius that they would get cramp after twenty minutes and would have to move. She must realize this too, he thought. She must think he'd brought her here on purpose, having deliberately arranged the air raid – not that she seemed perturbed.

'I fixed it up for my mother last year,' he explained, patting the strengthening beams. 'Lately she's taken to trekking every evening to my sister's and her husband, out to Coundon, because she gets lonely on her own here. But I thought she would be here tonight because of me being home...'

Barbara laughed. The idea of Julius fixing up this den for his mother and the thought of her moving about on her own here, amused her. 'Well, I suppose that's lucky for us,' she said, and immediately regretted it, for he was looking at her with strange severity. 'I mean, it really would be even more, it would be very cramped with three of us in here, and of course she'll be much safer in Coundon than here with us,' she said quickly, and caught her breath.

Julius's skin prickled. 'Yes,' he agreed. 'There's more room without her.' Although they weren't touching, they were so close that they felt the warmth of one another's bodies. Each had an intimation of what the other would smell like if they leaned across, what the nape of the neck would feel like, what they would taste like.

Barbara averted her eyes and looked down at the sheet beneath her legs. She wanted to be close to him and feel him along her spread length. But she knew it wouldn't stop there; that he would expect things to follow. And though, despite her inexperience, she imagined that she would enjoy the consequences, she felt that she didn't want them – or ought not to want them.

Clasping her hands around her shins, Barbara rested her chin on her knees. There had been a brief lull in the attack, but now she could hear the screams of falling bombs and the searing cracks of explosions. There seemed to be so many that it was difficult to isolate the sounds. It was a continuous chaos of noise underpinned by the drone of the aeroplanes. No raid she had previously experienced came near to matching this one in violence, and she wondered what was happening to the city. She imagined burning streets and a vivid orange glow: were they aiming to flatten the whole city, to annihilate the entire population? Or were they mainly hitting the factories? She thought of the Daimler factory in Radford, near where they were supposed to be dancing this evening, and of the churches. Were they being destroyed too? In her mind, Holy Trinity Church was gathered into a massive jagged ball and hurled into the cathedral, levelling it to the ground. The blasts that she heard were accompanied by mental pictures of buildings leaping into the air and then crumpling into huge piles of flaming rubble. In Broadgate she saw Whitfield's collapse; Flinn the jeweller was a furnace; like a wounded animal, Hayward's lumbered to the ground; and Newton's, the draper where she had bought the stockings she was wearing now, burst outwards, sending a wave of heat into the shops opposite. As she counted her way from Broadgate into the High Street, picking off a building for each blast, she told herself that she was exaggerating, it couldn't be so bad. But, from the noise, it must be quite as bad – what else was happening out there? The city was being pulverized. People must be dying everywhere, lacerated by shards of glass and terribly burnt; shelters must be full of people in agony, crushed by beams, trapped. When would it be their turn, to be plucked out and scattered in ten thousand directions? The soles of Barbara's feet tingled. She could feel the tears running down her face and her shoulders shook uncontrollably.

Pale and sweating, Julius watched her. He saw her mouth open, but couldn't hear what she said: she seemed rather to be crying out. Pushing himself away from the wall, he turned and drew her to himself. Her head came gratefully to his shoulder, and her quivering became a convulsive sobbing. Burying his lithe left hand in the hair at her neck, he stroked her nape with his left thumb, while his right thumb rolled gently down her spine to the small of her back, where his index finger took over and slowly returned to the hollow between her shoulder-blades. Beneath the rhythm of his fingers, he felt the crisis of her fear gradually ebb as she relaxed against him, and her hand unclenched on his chest.

The noise hadn't abated. When she thought about it, Barbara felt no safer, but she was calmer. Close to Julius, she was no longer lonely in her fear, and this in itself soothed it. A finger joined his thumb on her neck and she felt them separate and draw together again, spreading outwards the point of calm created by his thumb. Beside the firm pressure on her back, she felt two other fingertips glancing against her and slowly, very slowly, their pressure increased until three fingers were moving in a strong, stately dance across her back. Despite the mayhem outside, shapes were being fashioned on her back, patiently, luxuriously. She could feel Julius's fingers searching out the knotted muscles; instead of pouncing on them, he stalked them, circling, feinting, dancing away the pockets of fear. His fingers were enjoying the movement itself, the controlled pace and the pattern: instead of rushing to get somewhere else, they dwelt within their activity. And slowly, slowly, so slowly that she had to concentrate closely to notice the process, his fingers continued to move outwards, always withdrawing afterwards, as if to consolidate the ground already claimed. It seemed as if he must have touched every inch of her back many times, but still he was finding new, untamed points, as if something under her skin was communicating itself to his fingers which he interpreted and knew how to answer.

'Are you imagining places being blown up?' he said, and he felt her stiffen in his arms.

Her head moved against his chest, nodding, and with the tip of his thumb he followed the trace of a tear to her temple, then slowly travelled down among the tiny hairs in front of her ear.

From her jawbone she felt him pursue an arc to her throat, and then smoothly reverse in a matching arc to the tendon at the side of her neck, and then back to her nape. It seemed the line was there, waiting for him to find it.

As if a hailstorm had become a shower of meteorites, the onslaught was renewed with stupefying violence.

'It must be a huge torch by now. They can see exactly where to drop their bombs. If we live to the end, we'll find nothing but ruins.'

He thought she hadn't heard him, but he spoke louder than he intended for she replied: 'Try not to think about it.' And her hand opened flat on his chest: three furtive fingers slipped under his jacket to his sternum, where they lay quite still, like a tactile shaft of light across a ballroom from a single half-open shutter.

His thumb slipped to her neck now. Slowly it worked its way back to her jaw and throat where it was joined by the index finger; gently the dance regained her chin and the fourth finger brushed against her mouth. When his middle finger touched her lips, she parted them and caught the tip between her teeth, where she held it for a moment, suspended, feeling the crevice at the nail with her tongue, before slowly releasing it.

Barbara twisted herself round, stretching her legs into the depths of the cupboard so that she was looking up at Julius, her head cradled in his left arm. When he leaned forward to kiss her, her hand came to rest on the back of his neck and she raised her head to meet his lips.

Suddenly the candle sputtered, and she drew away from him.

'I want to see you, Julius,' she said.

'I'll put in another one.'

Barbara sat up, releasing him to attend to it while she quickly checked some of her hair-grips in the darkness. The new candle flared into life and her feet were thrown into abrupt, clumsy relief against the end of the cupboard.

She expected Julius to settle back into the same place. But he was finding it uncomfortable and, moving his hands to indicate the length of the cupboard, he proposed that they lie down. Barbara nodded: it would be much more sensible to lie down – although she must be careful not to let this imply her surrender. If they were going to be trapped there for several hours, as the sustained barrage suggested, then they might as well make themselves comfortable.

They lay on their sides, facing each other in the narrow space. Julius put his hand to her neck and she matched his movement. For several minutes, their eyes roamed each other's faces in the soft candlelight; then their mouths joined again and they kissed patiently, with relish.

Julius slipped his left arm under her head so that his hand was free to move on her neck; led by a knuckle, his right hand wandered slowly down again to the base of her spine. He retraced the movement with his fingertips and then repeated it more slowly and firmly with his knuckle. Barbara was kissing him with enthusiasm, but he found to his surprise that her body was rigid, earnestly refusing to yield the gap between them. He opened his eyes, but seeing that she was watching him he closed them at once. While his fingers roved over her back, Barbara's hand never moved from his neck and her body remained tense and separate: only her mouth was mobile and giving. And the noise of the raid continued without interruption, as if they were shut in a box which was anchored in the eye of a tornado.

Without warning, Barbara drew away from him. 'This is appalling!' she cried, and tears started from her eyes. 'I don't understand how we haven't been smashed to smithereens!' And suddenly she was against him, trembling, her head pressed against his chest.

Julius's hands began again to travel over her back, and she felt the panic being squeezed out of her, drop by drop. And as she calmed down, warm and grateful beneath his generous caress, she became aware of his prick hard against her hip, and she wondered why she had been so anxious to avoid it. It was exciting, and why shouldn't he enjoy himself? Nobody could expect the noise of the world being destroyed to encourage her to be scrupulous in her conduct.

As his prick heaved against his trousers, Julius began to long for the end of the air raid if only because he could then take Barbara home and end his excruciating frustration. He glanced surreptitiously over her shoulder at his watch and discovered to his surprise that it was already half-past ten. Would they never run out of bombs? But then he felt Barbara shift against him and her hand alighted on his waist. Softly, but unmistakably, she caressed him, and he forgot his discomfort.

His fingers ran slowly down her side, then he spread his hand flat and felt the sharp rise and smooth curve of her hip. For the first time he didn't break the line but allowed himself to continue as far as he could reach on her thigh: and she didn't resist: instead, her fingers crept up to his chest and round to his back. Barbara felt his surprise and enjoyed it, but still she wondered how far she should allow him to go. His hand now was following the contours of her bottom, and he lifted her up towards him so that she found she was kissing him again. She felt his thumb moving firmly and gracefully down her spine, and all of a sudden she was greedy for him. Her hand moved swiftly to the back of his head and she pressed herself tight against him. But then his hand became someone else's. It sauntered jauntily to her knee and snatched at her dress and, before she had fully realized what was happening, it dived beneath her clothes like a hysterical glove puppet. She was offended and pulled away abruptly.

Julius shut his eyes, furious with himself. He had painstakingly built up her trust and then with one false, impatient, clumsy grab, spoiled everything. He wanted to tell her that he hadn't meant it, he'd made a mistake. When everything outside was being laid waste with unremitting ferocity, he didn't want to ruin it inside...

Then he realized that her hand was still on him. He opened his eyes and blinked, and saw that she was smiling at him curiously. A crease like the closed wings of a moth quivered between her eyebrows; her nose seemed to be clenched and her lips were set in reproof: but still the shallow dimples either side of her mouth betrayed a smile. Gently, slowly, he must start all over again.

He kissed her on the forehead and drew her head against his chest. The knuckle of his index finger was against her nape and, with his thumb and middle finger, he gently massaged the muscles around the base of her neck. After a few minutes he tentatively eased his other thumb down her arched spine to the small of her back and ascended again with the tip of his forefinger. For a moment he felt her tense, but she didn't stop him, and as his fingers began their slow gyrations across her back he felt her relax once more. Swivelling on his knuckles, kneading with his thumb, brushing with the tips of his fingers, he caressed her back until his fingers ached and he thought her flesh must be bruised. At last he paused, with the heel of his hand at the small of her back and the tip of his middle finger low down on her spine, while the middle finger of his other hand slipped round her neck and pressed beneath her jaw so that she raised her face to him. She smiled, and they kissed, and he felt her fingers stir once more between his shoulder-blades like an opening flower.

As his hand again sought her hip and buttocks, she shifted herself up higher without waiting for him to lift her. She moved carefully so that she didn't hurt his prick, and when she pressed against him again she could feel it jutting against her abdomen. Although it was at this stage that he had upset her earlier, she acquiesced to it now with confidence – indeed, she initiated it herself. For no reason that she could name, she suddenly trusted him to behave and not to blunder foolishly about her body. She kissed his chin and his nose, she kissed a circle around his face and then his eyes. On her right calf she felt one of his fingers tracing tiny circles, as if he was trying to count the number of stitches in her stocking. With ineffable slowness the finger climbed to the back of her knee, then descended. Feeling him strain to reach her ankle, she drew up her leg so that he could follow the arch of her foot, and then he circled the ankle between two fingers.

As his finger rose to the back of her knee again, Barbara felt as if she was floating in a delicate mist: she was distantly but intimately aware of another finger lazily duplicating the path on her other leg. An enchanting warmth enveloped her, and she ran the tip of her tongue to and fro along Julius's upper lip.

His hand slowly mounted to her kneecaps, and with the tip of his fourth finger he touched the inside of her thigh. She remained quite still, but he could feel her skin hot and breathing beneath his touch, her pores reaching for him. For several minutes his fingers dawdled above her knees. Unless she moved, his hand was prevented from intruding any further under her dress because the fabric was stretched across her knees and tucked beneath her. So he lingered, descended to her shins, to her ankles, then returned to her knees and waited, marking time with twin circles on each leg.

Barbara raised herself an inch and he plucked free the trapped dress with the back of his thumb. Almost nonchalantly, as if describing a high water mark, he drew a line above her knee, and then his hand slipped down again to her calves. Then, with the same compelling patience as before, his fingers climbed to her knees and to her thighs. Gently, agonizingly, his fingers performed their almost motionless spirals, and his touch became ever lighter until he was scarcely touching her at all but ruffling the air, like a butterfly walking on tiptoe at the top of her leg. And suddenly he felt the tiny cliff that marked the edge of her stocking: his thumb and index finger spread along it, exploring; then returned, while his index finger probed beneath her knickers, hovering over the bare skin.

He parted her lips with his tongue and the tip of hers

emerged and quickly touched the inside of his upper lip, then withdrew, and he followed it back between her lips, savouring her breath. He half-unhitched her right stocking from its suspender, then languidly switched to her left leg and released the other accessible clip. Now her underwear was loose, and his fingers made her damp hair quiver as they circled across the fabric. She felt the warm ball of his thumb low down above her pelvis and sensed his index finger reach out, poised like a bird: an involuntary spasm thrust her up to meet him.

Julius pushed aside the crotch of her knickers and it felt as if he had drawn his fingertip through a bowl of lightly whipped cream with a wild strawberry afloat on the surface.

Suddenly the noise slackened. They looked at each other, so still that they could feel the cadences of each other's blood. There was no doubt that the level had dropped.

'Do you think it's over?' Barbara whispered.

'Ssh.'

It grew no quieter. It was louder, then louder still, and suddenly the inferno was grating their ears again. Julius saw the expectancy drain from Barbara's eyes, and she looked dazed. She kissed him once on the lips, and then on his neck. Then she scrambled up and sat astride his legs. As she wrestled with his buttons, the clawing ache in his genitals became so vicious that he thought he would vomit. At last his trousers sprang apart, and an inane grin of relief spread across his face. Gingerly, Barbara pulled at the waistband of his underpants and reached inside. He felt her fingers skate along his unleashed prick and then tenderly cup his shifting, splitting testicles. Rising to her knees, she grasped his trousers: by a judicious combination of lifting on his part and tugging on hers, he was divested of them. When the same was done with his underpants, she hastily removed her stockings and then turned her back to him indicating that he should unhook her dress; she wriggled, and it slipped to the floor. Free of it, while he quietly took off his socks, she undid all his shirt buttons and pulled the shirt from his shoulders to his elbows. He shook it to the ground, and was naked.

Clothed only in her underwear, Barbara suddenly lay down again, with her left leg bent and the foot flat on the ground. Julius kissed her knee. On her other side, his legs were extended, but he had raised himself high above her on his braced left arm. She brought her hand up lazily and touched the channel of hair on his stomach. With his right hand he traced the outline of her face and then his thumb and middle finger followed her collarbones to her throat. She watched him: he wasn't looking into her eyes: he was absorbed in the passage of his fingers, and she felt them circle first one breast and then the other, so that her nipples buzzed. Extending her arm, she felt his groin's rough hair and smiled at the recollection of Rose Evans suggesting it would feel like pine needles. She pulled gently at one of the tight curls and then wrapped her fingers round his penis; she could feel it pulsing. Without releasing it, she turned her hand round and felt the loose hood of skin at its head between her thumb and forefinger. Then she let go and spread her fingers in the hair of his chest, just as he was spreading his fingers across her flat stomach.

With a flurry of urgent twisting, Barbara stripped, and suddenly Julius's left arm bent and he crouched over her. Her hand slipped to his shoulder and the back of his neck, then she sucked in her breath sharply as his tongue slowly crossed her waist and circled her navel. When she put her hand on the back of his head she felt actively connected with the sensation on her skin. At the same time she felt incapable of moving, pinned by the tiny pressure of his tongue as if it was a huge weight. Her belly was aflame and she had to fight the urge to press his face against it. His hand was following the curved bone of her hip now, while his tongue flicked lower with tiny jabs that made her catch her breath. His free hand was playing on her upright thigh; she felt the fingers slide down towards her buttock and she gasped, incredulous at the blaze in her body. Beneath his touch every part of her was endowed with a life of its own.

Lifting herself on one elbow, she drew his head upwards and kissed him. Their lips parted, and his right hand moved across her breasts and then firmly down to her waist; then, as they lowered themselves to the floor, she felt his fingers high on her inner thighs. Amazed at her own audacity, she opened her legs. There was an insistent presence at her vagina, and then it wasn't his fingers any more because his hand was touching her face. She shut her eyes tight, suddenly terrified that it would hurt. But as he pushed gently into her she found that even the mild pain was a fulfilment, and she opened her eyes again and smiled, welcoming him. For a moment she wanted just to enjoy his still presence deep inside her, and she held him tight both with her arms and with her legs.

'Barbara, are you safe?' Julius suddenly asked.

'What – what do you mean?' she gasped.

Julius's body went rigid. 'The – the time-of-the-month,' he stammered.

'Oh, well I wasn't yesterday and I am tomorrow, and I think I probably am today,' she said breathlessly.

'What?'

'Safe.'

'Oh. I see. So you are?'

'But maybe you'd better not do it in me though.'

Julius was confused. 'What? I'm already in you!'

'I mean, have your what-you-m'-call-it in me, your... your climax.'

As they began to move together in rhythm, he felt Barbara's surging delight engulf the currents of his dismay. He could feel her pelvis moving underneath him, and his thrusts became stronger, and deeper, and her hips rose to meet him each time. They settled down, goggling at the raw pleasure of their fuck-ing, which made them laugh. Suddenly he felt her writhe, and she cried out. He reached down and put his hand low under-neath her buttocks and thrust slowly, encouraging her to work herself against him: and he felt his own orgasm approaching. In the guttering candlelight he saw the rampant pleasure in her face and silently cursed the need to withdraw.

Suddenly there was a noise outside like the slamming of a thousand doors, and Barbara clutched Julius tight.

On the brink of orgasm, just as the tip of his prick was due to emerge and throw his seed away, Julius was propelled so vigorously into her that their bellies slapped together and his face struck the pillow beside her head. The surprise was too much, and he spurted lushly into her.

The blast subsided. Astonished to find himself still alive and their shelter intact, Julius raised himself on one elbow. Barbara was smiling, her eyes half-closed: she moved her hips and clenched the muscles of her vagina, and he knew that she realized exactly what had happened.

'We're alive,' she murmured, 'We're still alive.'

Kissing her eyelids, he felt her lips touch his chin and again he felt movements below, urging him. Their mouths met in a warm, glad kiss; discovering with intense satisfaction that he was erect, he began slowly to move in and out of her. Adjusting to his rhythm, she thrust herself forward to receive him, grinding against him so that she felt him sink tight within and against her. Their pace quickened, and slowed, and quickened again; and still they kissed, until suddenly her breathing staggered and her mouth broke away. She shuddered and pushed her hips hard towards him, and she gaped at him in astonishment. His prick felt numb and he was conscious of sweat streaming over his body as he bore into her, coaxing her to orgasm. Her body arched with the strength of panic and he rammed himself into her repeatedly, quick and hard. She juddered, and her fingers snatched wildly at the blanket. Agitated by her movement, the candle-flame buckled and flared. Julius saw that her throat was dappled with sweat.

As her breathing calmed, the air raid gradually invaded Barbara's consciousness again.

They held each other close in the dark, listening to the sounds of the bombardment. Heralded by chilling shrieks, the bombs pounded relentlessly into the city. When they fell nearby, or with particular violence, the individual explosions reached the couple like bolts of thunder in a storm; and above it all, like a hellish wind, was the sinister growl of the aeroplanes. Having no idea of the anatomy of havoc, Barbara and Julius imagined the city laid waste, a nightmare landscape illuminated by the glare of the moon and the flames of its own ruin. If by a freak omission they came out unscathed, theirs would surely be the only surviving building, and it was hard to conceive of anything alive in the wreckage.

Barbara's fingers played idly in the hair on Julius's chest. They had been silent for a long time when she said, 'All night, I've been thinking of my parents and relatives, and my friends.'

'Not all night. For a minute or two, you weren't.'

'Apart from then.' She chuckled, and kissed him softly, before continuing: 'I think some people would be shocked at us. Not just because of doing it, but because of doing it in this... when all around, people are dying — because they must be dying. Maybe my parents are dead. I keep thinking that.'

'You don't feel as if you've betrayed them...?'

'That's just it. I don't think what we've done is wrong.'

'I'm glad of that.'

'What do you think?'

'I think you're the Eighth Wonder of the World. Perhaps the Seven of the old world have been destroyed. Then you'll be the First and Only Wonder of the new...' His hand pressed more firmly, emphasizing his words, and she responded by rubbing her knee across his thighs.

'Will you think the same if you find you're pregnant? Assuming we're still alive?' he asked after a few minutes.

She didn't answer immediately, and Julius was afraid he had upset her. Then she said:

'I'll wash myself. But I think I would feel the same.'

'Good.'

'Good? That I'll wash, or that I'd feel the same?'

'Both. I think it would be sensible to wash. But I want to marry you anyway.'

He felt Barbara's body suddenly vivid against him, alert, as if listening for echoes of his words. Then she lifted her head, and her thigh was across his hips; she stretched, and he felt her lips close warmly against his own.

*

When Barbara awoke, her ears were buzzing. Silence draped the air like a shroud.

She nudged Julius. He groaned and, opening his eyes, realized from the stunning quiet that it was over.

'I'll go and have a look outside,' he said.

'I must wash, Julius. Wait for me, please.'

'I'll only be gone a moment. Find out if the all-clear has gone. I'll be back before you're dressed,' he promised.

Fumbling behind him, he lit a candle.

Barbara sat up and pulled at her clothes, which were crammed into a heap by their feet. 'Look at my dress...!'

'Everyone else will be in whatever they were in when it started. If there is anyone else.'

For a moment, the events of the night seemed distant, like the afterglow of a foul nightmare, but she couldn't ignore them any more than she could pretend that nothing had happened with Julius; and the night's terror revived in her. 'If there is anyone else,' she repeated.

Struggling into his creased uniform, Julius looked at his watch: it was half-past six. When he pushed open the cupboard door it was still dark. Between the candle and the pale moonlight the air writhed, like a blanket lifted at the edges by a gust of wind, and he found that his shoes were covered with a layer of coarse dust. After pointing out to Barbara the way to the bathroom, he kicked aside the glass of broken window-panes and opened the front door.

Julius put his hand to his nose, assaulted by the stench of the burning city. In spite of the light drizzle, fires raged across the first glimmers of the waxy dawn. With surprise, for he half-expected to see nothing but a smoking plain, he noted that the street was still standing. But, as he began to look around, the sight of the debris welded him to the doorstep. Dust and glass covered every surface like a mysteriously shredded membrane. In front of him lay a mangled bicycle, and in the half-light he saw that the whole street was littered with unfamiliar shapes, a riot of broken, dangling telephone wires and gutters. Further down the street there was a burst house: he could see the glint of flames in the smoke-filled rooms and hear the rustle of the sagging joists. Several people were moving about in front of it, and Julius was about to go over and talk to them when he heard someone approaching from the other direction.

The man nodded at Julius as he drew level. His face was black with soot, and one leg of his otherwise smart trousers was split from top to bottom.

'Has the all-clear gone?' Julius asked.

'Went half an hour ago,' he answered, ''cept the sirens are out so no one could hear it.'

Julius returned indoors. Barbara was weeping as she pulled on her stockings.

'There's no water,' she said.

'Maybe your parents still have water.'

She stood up and fastened her dress, then smoothed it with the flat of her hand. 'Julius, I hope they're all right. I looked out of the window upstairs. The whole city's on fire.'

From the window she had looked left towards the city centre. Where there should have been tightly packed roofs she saw instead angular, unrecognizable outcrops of masonry jutting from a rubble-gorged battlefield seething with smoke and flames. The market tower still stood, solitary in a shattered landscape where the buildings had once clustered about it. A view of Holy Trinity Church in the distance had been blasted open. On all sides, balloons of fire bucked against the fading sky, turning it a dull orange. Ahead, hardly two hundred yards away, Spon Street was burning; while beyond it to the right was Earlsdon and her home. The bombs looked to have been scattered more thinly there, but still she could see scarlet plumes and a tattered pall of smoke above.

Julius held up Barbara's coat so that she could slip into it easily. Then, with the package containing her shoes in one hand, he took her arm and they went into the street. She felt sore between her legs, and kept her eyes on the pitted ground; she didn't want to look at anyone. It would be easy to slip and get hurt on the shifting surface of broken tiles and glass. The acrid smell scorched her nostrils as she thought of home, but she couldn't form a picture in her mind of what might be waiting for her in Craven Street. She was grateful to Julius for not speaking.

It was light when they came down into Upper Spon Street, but instead of the fresh chill of dawn they felt the hot, stale breath of destruction. They stopped for a moment, staring at the gutted, sizzling cottages on both sides of the street. In some places, surviving possessions had been hurriedly thrown into heaps outside, and there were clusters of people. As Julius and Barbara approached they realized that these groups had formed around injured people. Further down, a man was clumsily laying a woman down on her back. Barbara wondered why, for it must be so uncomfortable and cold in the rain: then she saw that the woman's clothes were crimson with blood and understood that she was dead. Entering Spon Street, they were halted by the smell of roast meat. The front of a butcher's shop had been blown out. From a beam protruding into the empty space like a stripped bone swung a single, smouldering pig. The other side of the street was still blazing fiercely, watched by a group of children who were sitting on top of a large heap of furniture and boxes. All over the ground were filthy scraps of food and ashes. Some men wearing helmets were keeping people away from the grocer's, and above the crackle of the flames Julius could hear tins exploding. In a spitting furnace of sparks, an upstairs wall slowly slumped into the wreckage, opening a bathroom to the gaze of the onlookers. On the ripped pavement, Julius saw the twisted till, its drawer hanging out like a blistered tongue.

They were going in the wrong direction. Just as, without discussing it, they had come this way, now they turned and went back. There was a gap where a house should have been. The building adjoining it looked as if an almighty sword had cleaved it from top to bottom. A bed with a purple eiderdown clung to the sliced floor and, on the other side, close to where it was severed, clothes could be seen hanging on the wall where a wardrobe had been torn away leaving the contents intact. The top of a broken staircase reached like a talon into the void. Seeing the smouldering, tangled rubbish beneath, Barbara shuddered, wondering what had become of the people who lived there.

Ankle deep in the fragments of their city, she and Julius struggled past the blackened shell of the school into Spon End.

'Is this what he meant by 'We will fight them in the streets'?' he said suddenly.

'Do you call this fighting?'

'The Germans haven't got rid of us yet!'

The crunch of the glass under their feet was joined by the sound of metal against metal. There was a hollow thump as Julius kicked a saucepan. The street was strewn with the contents of a kitchen: bent cutlery and melted copper jelly moulds were scattered about as if they had dropped from the sky. A big tin washtub blocked their way and Julius pushed it aside with his foot. Immediately, they both jumped back, startled by a dog which was sheltering behind the tub. Disturbed, it stumbled clumsily to its feet. Some chewed carrion was dragging from its frothy red lips. Julius saw exposed bone and vomited. The dog had an injured leg, and as it limped away whatever it had in its mouth bumped rhythmically on the ground.

Barbara waited. She felt her stomach rise and bile welled from the inside of her cheeks, but she didn't think of anything to say. Fleetingly, she remembered the feel of Julius's hands on her body.

'You all right, Miss? He all right, is he?'

Barbara looked up. In front of her stood a warden whose face was encrusted with different substances of various shades and textures. His eyes glittered against this astonishing dirt.

'Yes, thank you,' she said.

'You sure he doesn't need help, Miss? He doesn't look too well to me.'

'He's fine.'

'If he's injured then...'

'He's all right, I said! Leave us alone, please...!'

The warden backed away, touching his hat ironically. 'Have it your own way then, Miss,' he said, and walked on.

Julius had recovered from his nausea now, and they passed under the railway bridge. On the other side they had to clamber over a web of wires which seemed related in some way to the garage on the corner. It smelt of gas. There was a crater in the road, with a car up-ended in it. And as they neared Craven Street, Barbara felt her heart like a jackhammer against her ribs.

On turning the corner, they came face to face with Mrs Pearson, who lived on the other side of the street. She was puffing; blotches of exhaustion and anxiety bloomed on her plump, veined cheeks. On seeing Barbara she gaped and then uttered a heavy sigh of relief that threw her shoulders forward.

'Oh, my! Thank the Lord you're safe, Barbara, at least!' she cried. 'I was just coming to look for a warden myself.' She looked at Julius doubtfully.

'Why? Whatever do you mean, Mrs Pearson?'

'Oh dear, I thought you knew, I thought you must've been in there!'

Barbara looked over Mrs Pearson's shoulder, then dodged beyond and began awkwardly, breathlessly, to run. Julius stumbled up the hill beside her and Mrs Pearson followed, her chest heaving.

Dense smoke billowed from the upper windows of Barbara's home; flames curled around the gutters. A knot of people stood arguing in the street. Barbara looked for her parents among them, but they weren't there. She heard Mrs Pearson shout behind them: 'Here's Barbara!' and the people turned towards her.

'Where are my parents?'

For an instant, everyone was quiet. A series of distinct cracks could be heard from the burning house.

'Where are they?' Barbara cried.

They all began to talk at once. Nobody knew: nobody had seen them in an air-raid shelter or coming out of the house. Were they in Earlsdon Street with her uncle and grandfather? Someone had gone to find them. They didn't realize that the house had been hit, it just started burning furiously half an hour ago. There was no water, there were no firemen...

Suddenly Julius left the group and ran towards the house.

'Julius!' Barbara shouted, 'Julius! No!'

Other voices joined in urging him to come away, but he didn't notice them. Pulling a handkerchief from his pocket to shield his nose from the peppery smoke, he tried the door handle. It wasn't locked, but the door wouldn't open more than a crack. He kicked it violently: it shuddered, and he heard something give; he kicked again and, as it opened, a cloud of smoke rolled out at him. He crouched and scuttled forward, trying to keep below the thickest of the smoke. Pausing, he saw the wreckage around the stairs, where the blast had occurred, and sticking out of it he saw legs. Already beginning to choke, he returned to the door and stood coughing just beyond the threshold, preparing himself to go back in; he heard people shouting at him, but he paid no attention.

With one foot inside, he hesitated. He felt nervous now, whereas before he had responded unthinkingly. Something felt odd, but he was uncertain whether the difference was in the burning house or in his perception of it.

Framed in the doorway, Julius couldn't see that the entire ceiling was buckling. Only at the last moment did he hear the deeper whisperings above the clamour of the flames. Raising his arms to shield his head, he spun round, but before he could escape something knocked him to the ground. And at that instant a beam smashed onto his foot.

He didn't move.

Barbara screamed. She tried to run forward, but she was held back. 'Julius! Move! Get up, Julius! Julius!' she yelled, straining against unknown arms.

Julius lay still, stunned by the pain in his foot. Then he felt the heat scorching his face, and he tugged. Finding that he was trapped, he thrashed like a hand trying to free itself of a wasp; through his panic he could feel the bones in his foot splintering.

Although enjoying its new freedom with a fierce roar, the fire hadn't yet reached Julius. Seeing his convulsions, two men rushed forwards. He saw the muscles in their arms swell and the sweat break out on their red faces as they heaved at the beam. It shifted, and he cried out in agony. They grabbed him under each arm, and as they pulled him clear he could feel the sharp rubble tearing through his trousers into his flesh.

Barbara was kneeling beside his shoulder, touching his face.

'I'm all right,' he said, and his lips cracked as he smiled. 'But my foot...'

'Your foot will mend, won't it? Won't it?'

'It'll mend. I hope it'll mend... but...' As he spoke, his mind stirred and he remembered that there was a reason for the pain. 'Barbara,' he said, raising himself on one elbow beneath her protesting hand. 'Your parents, Barbara...'

He felt the pressure leave her fingers. 'Are they in there?'

'Yes.'

Barbara closed her eyes.

Suddenly a new, aggressive voice rose above the surrounding noises. 'Barbara? Where's Barbara? Barbara? Ah! There you are! What's happening here?'

Barbara looked up and saw her uncle David standing officiously over her.

With a quick glance he inspected Julius, noticing his injured foot and Barbara's hand on his chest. He recognized him. 'What's this fool been playing at? Are they in there?' he said, before she could answer.

'Yes.'

'Oh Lord!'

As her uncle moved away, shouting at people to do this, ordering them to bring that, Barbara felt a thick, heavy swipe of exhaustion descend on her. It seemed to touch her all over, from the sockets of her itching eyes to her scratched insteps. At the same time, a fist of grief unfurled, pushing at her inside: she shivered, and silently she wept.

5

When I last went to visit Kate, I found you sitting on one of those plastic chairs with splayed metal legs in the corridor, where the bright, blank light is like an idiot's leer. You were leaning forward with your elbows on your knees, tie loosely dangling, your fingers fanned out in your hair as if in mute, exhausted defence against an unseen predator. And the realization comes again that you are bound to this black-edged uncertainty by your own proud decision to stay with her. You blink – 'Can I go through with this?' – and shudder at your frail resolve. Indeed, it's Kate who fell, not you. Appalled that you could play even for an instant with the idea of abandoning her, you rage bleakly at yourself; then you turn your mind and you will away your health, once again, to her...

She lies there, tranquil and young, a gift at the end of your fingertips, but a husk, an image.

Does she know what happened? Is she in pain?

WHERE IS SHE?

Can she dream?

Unable to see beyond the frontiers of her consciousness, you go back to the places you knew together. Perhaps to last summer, when she came on holiday with us – to the sun high in a benign blue sky; it dips and collapses against the hard rim of the sea, spilling its ichorous gore across the horizon – will she remember it? In the late afternoon one day, there was a breeze on the beach and we played an erratic game of frisbee. We had to chase the gusts, and once you rudely tried to confuse her:

'Kate! Hey! Your bikini's coming off!' In her moment of self-consciousness, you plucked the frisbee from the air just ahead of her. A strand of salty hair between her teeth as she splashes from the sea, the sand in her navel when she lies on her back, her tongue catching on her chin the dripped juice of a tomato; the idle saunter down the stony track from the house to the beach, scratching her ankles on the sturdy thistles; breakfast on the verandah, where flat-stomached Tilda already suns herself; Luke, still wet after his early swim, is consuming inadvisable quantities of fresh white bread and Mum is reading... Will Kate recall these things? She emerges from her bedroom after you, her knuckles pressed into her eyes, and we talk about the dawn, which none of us saw.

'Jake, my dear!'

Your head jolts up at my greeting, your hands are suspended in a gesture of supplication. They relax to your sides when you begin to rise, but at the pressure of my hand on your shoulder you sink into the chair again. Your face is puffy and tired, pale beneath the stubble on your cheeks and blotchy under your eyes. I nod towards the little room where Kate lies spliced into a machine.

'Come out for a breather?'

'It's so frustrating! What's the point of talking to her when she can't hear? She'd hate that horrible room! They put her there because she doesn't know where she is! And there's no point bringing flowers because she can't see them!'

You jut your chin, defying tears. I sense you caressing the overhang of shelved intentions – marriage, perhaps? No, laments won't reach her. Talk to her of what is hidden.

'Go back in,' I said. 'Tell her about yourself. I'm sure she'd like it.'

Tell her, if you like, about your mother, who is indebted for her existence to a German bomb. But it was more than just Mum who was conceived in that raid. It was a home, a form of life, without which our lives are unimaginable and the idea of them is meaningless. No wonder we made up stories. And if you tell Kate this, tell her also about Julius and Barbara, your grandparents.

And tell her about Germany. I think you must have been about six when we went to live there. Tilda was four and Luke two, both of them young enough to pick up the language effortlessly. But you couldn't get the hang of it, Jake. I remember how you watched, amazed and wistful, as Tilda yapped questions in shops and responded obligingly to the instructions of the lady who looked after you during the day. Thinking you'd quickly learn, we sent you to school, where you bitterly resented your dislocation. 'I don't think German wants me to learn it,' you said grimly one day, as if you would be locked out of the language for ever. But you did learn, and you're the only one of us who can still speak it, apart from Mum.

I was going to read to Kate again, but because in the end I only had a few minutes with her, I chatted about our time in Germany. I had a commission in Frankfurt and was due to go alone for a few months, but then Mum unexpectedly landed a two-year contract with the Technical Institute there, so we upped and went together. My German was rudimentary; Mum, diligent and quick as ever, was much better equipped. But it wasn't the language I talked to Kate about.

I found myself describing the window I went there to make – do you remember it, Jake? It was 82 feet wide and 31 feet high, the entire façade of the hall of a new bank. It was a lucky coup for me because all the best stained glass was being done in Germany at that time and it gave me a chance to prove myself in the front rank. But I hadn't actually done anything like it before – I don't know why they trusted me. It was very challenging, not only because of the sheer size but also because, where most stained glass is intended to be seen only from inside a building, here I had to attend equally to the internal and to the external aspects of the design and work with a complete double perspective. This didn't greatly affect the construction of the leadwork – there were other problems there – but it mattered very much to the two swathes of colour in the window. For these areas I used 'flashed' glass, which, as you know, has a separate layer of colour that can be acid-etched back on both surfaces through different shades to the clear 'antique' beneath; and I used silverstain. Judging the shades of etching and silverstaining is tricky when you're trying to achieve a consistent movement of colour over a wide expanse, but success really relies on the firing. The difficulty on this project was managing to do what I wanted on each side of the glass without ruining what was on the other. I was about to describe the firing to Kate as 'a very delicate act of balancing light', but then I glimpsed something in her motionless face – a crack in the glass – and I said 'time' instead: and yes, it seems now as if the past and future were grinding against each other as I treated the flashed glass, and I was turning time inside out.

Having called Tilda's boyfriend Jon ever since she has known him, Mum has suddenly taken to calling him Joe, and Tilda is doing the same. Why, for heaven's sake? Tomorrow Tilda is taking him to see Kate. Luke believes they will get married, after all.

Poor Kate.

6

Barbara and Tilly stared silently from the West Door. The cathedral's blackened walls were no more than a containing fence for the rubble, breached at intervals where the tracery was ripped from the windows. Among huge chunks of hideously fractured masonry lay the smashed ribs of the vault: in places, the collapsed roof was heaped higher than Tilly's head. Shrivelled pieces of lead curled among the ruins like split veins; exposed along the spines of ancient beams staggered broken columns of square-headed nails. Fragments of glass littered the ashes and the air still churned with grit.

The tower alone survived, a gesticulating limb, abandoned and stranded; the spire pierced the heavens like a disembodied shriek.

It was hard to recall the cathedral's solemn, well-ordered majesty. It would never be the same again; what had been was utterly gone, and considering the present in the image of the past seemed grotesquely silly.

Scrambling through to Priory Row, they continued on their way to visit Julius in hospital. Bicycles were useless because it was impossible to go twenty yards along the shattered streets without getting a puncture. But they were glad of the walk: since Tilly's arrival the previous day, they had scarcely been left alone together for more than five minutes. It was a relief to be out of the house.

As soon as she heard about the air raid, Tilly had attempted to telephone her parents, but twenty-four hours passed before she established contact with her uncle David and learned of her parents' death. On the Tuesday following the raid she managed to reach Coventry herself, together with Daniel, and she went straight to the Earlsdon Avenue house, where Barbara had been taken in. Although she had read about the attack and even seen photographs, Tilly felt strangely detached. Only when she was actually confronted with the ruined city did she feel the enormity of the disaster. Travelling from the station to the house in Earlsdon, the fact of her parents' death burst like an abscess within her and suddenly she felt dreadfully alone, as if waking to find herself in a story without a method of telling it or the means to understand it. Percy was fighting far away; he didn't even know what had happened. Perhaps he too was dead? She hugged Daniel to her side and thought of poor Barbara. How was she coping? Having witnessed the terrible events, she must surely feel the loss with even greater intimacy and violence.

A temporary mortuary had been set up for the emergency in Gas Street and, from the night of the raid itself to that day, some four hundred bodies had been brought there. Of these, about half were so badly mutilated that relatives couldn't identify them with any degree of certainty. In view of this, and of the numbers involved, it was announced that a mass funeral would be held on the Wednesday; and it was clear that another would have to be held for those still being discovered in the ruins. Private funerals weren't absolutely forbidden, but obstacles – or so it seemed to David and his father – were deliberately set in the path of those wishing to bury their dead in their own way. By acceding to the authorities' intention, Barbara was compounding these difficulties; and she was proving incomprehensibly obstinate. Although David repeatedly insisted that there was no question of her or Tilly paying for their parents' funeral, for he would be quite happy to foot the bill, she still wouldn't withdraw her signature and allow him to reclaim the bodies (which were too badly burned, in any case, to be recognizable).

With Daniel asleep against her shoulder, Tilly stood in front of the marble mantelpiece and listened to the men. She had never wholly trusted her uncle David. Looking at him now, she was disgusted by the way his shapeless nose emerged from his fleshy face, like a huge wart. Was it because she was supposed to be clever that he had always resented her? From the way he ordered his wife Sarah about, it was plain that he didn't like women to have their own views. Or was it simply because he was childless?

Barbara sat silently in an armchair, examining her fingers with indifference.

'What does it matter? They're dead!' Tilly cried. Then she dropped her voice for fear of waking Daniel: 'Isn't it bad enough that they're dead, without arguing over the funeral?'

'Matilda,' said her grandfather in his shaky voice, 'You and Barbara are deeply upset. Of course you are. So am I; so is David. But it's still necessary to be clear-headed, even in moments of grief. It's not simply a matter of how your parents died, but of how they lived. They were valued members of the community, Methodists...'

'There will be a Minister at the funeral, Grandad,' Barbara interrupted.

'It isn't the same,' said David, rising from his chair. 'Don't you understand?'

'They should be buried in a manner worthy of their life,' resumed old Mr Shearer, his wrists trembling in agitation on the silver knob of his Guilds walking-stick.

Barbara stood up. 'This is unbearable. You think they're too good to be buried at a mass funeral. What's so wrong with being killed in an air raid?'

'Quite. Must we drag delusions of civic grandeur into it?' Tilly murmured.

David disliked Tilly's haughty tone but he didn't know how to tackle it. He looked towards his wife for support, then at his father. 'I don't understand what's got into you two, I really don't! First you go and take in a little German boy,' he said, stabbing the air with his forefinger and thumb pressed together like an awl; then, turning to Barbara, 'And now you go and hitch yourself up to that Julius Gallagher behind everyone's backs! And to cap it all you won't even allow us to bury your poor parents properly!'

Mr Shearer sniffed. 'Now David, that's a bit harsh, in the circumstances.'

Knowing nothing of Barbara's engagement, Tilly looked inquisitively at her sister, her mouth curving in a refulgent smile. Barbara caught her lower lip between her teeth and nodded, whereupon Tilly put her free arm tightly round her sister's neck and kissed her. And suddenly Barbara began to weep convulsively against Tilly's shoulder. Tilly gently stroked Barbara's hair, her eyes clamped shut. She wanted to cry herself but she knew that to do so before the men would be a mistake. They didn't belong in the private domain of her sorrow. Feeling the tears through her blouse, she became aware of the pressure Barbara must have been under from their uncle and grandfather since the raid. She stroked the back of her sister's neck softly.

Woken by the sudden commotion, Daniel prodded the strange head at Tilly's other shoulder. His movement emphasized his weight and Tilly wanted to put him down. He drew in his breath and she was afraid he would cry: but he merely sighed, and pulled at the loose filaments of Barbara's hair until she raised her head to him.

Aunt Sarah said they were all tired.

'We must let them have their way,' old Mr Shearer said to David when his grand-daughters went to bed. But even as he uttered these words of resignation, his eyes reddened at the corrosive sadness which prompted them.

The violent deaths of his son and daughter-in-law were cruel enough, but the ban on giving them what Mr Shearer deemed to be a proper burial released in him an ungovernable wave of bitterness. It wasn't the idea itself of a mass funeral that appalled him so: the Great War had made everyone familiar with them and he accepted the practice without demur. Although none of his family fell in that first orgy of killing, he'd known scores of men who never returned. But, however terrible their deaths, they were trained, paid men who fell in combat: some were buried in mass graves, but even so they were soldiers buried as soldiers. Now civilians had been killed directly by the enemy, including women and children. Mr Shearer didn't doubt their courage, indeed he knew of many feats of conspicuous bravery during the raid – there was the Reverend Clitheroe, who saved Holy Trinity Church, of which he was the vicar, by his tireless energy; throughout the city the firemen worked heroically, despite the lack of water, and many were killed; everyone had a story to tell; even Julius Gallagher, it had to be said, acted courageously. Nobody disputed their valour, but the dead were not soldiers, after all, and had never claimed to be. Of course, they all knew of the dangers of air raids: slaughter had come from the air before November 14th, but then the unlucky victims were buried in accordance with their station in life. In the city of Coventry, a great many people were engaged in war work. His son David occupied a senior post in the Hawker-Siddeley aero-engine factory; his dead son John had made compasses. They took pride in their work and, as their father, and as a citizen of Coventry, he was proud of them. It seemed to Mr Shearer that his son and daughter-in-law were being buried as if they were soldiers *de facto*: and – though he would never admit it, for he respected the armed forces as much as the next man – he perceived such a burial as an insult.

'It's one thing for the enemy to kill civilians indiscriminately,' he remarked to David, 'but not allowing the dead to have civilian funerals is like saying the enemy has a right to treat civilians as combatants.'

Mr Shearer was aware that the task of burying all the dead privately in a city ravaged by bombs would be extremely complicated and, after a lifetime's experience of manufacturing and business, he recognized the value of simplifying logistics where possible. But there were occasions when it was necessary to accept difficulties without question, when the pursuit of ease was a shirking of responsibility, a form of faint-heartedness. Burying your dead was a supreme example of such an occasion. Your dead were your past; without them, you would be nothing. A funeral was an end, but not only an end: it gave form to mourning, but it was also an expression of continuity. This mass funeral was a tearing away of forms, a disavowal of which he could never approve, and he was dismayed that the Emergency Committee could even contemplate it.

'We should bury our dead properly!' he said, and David nodded his agreement.

Barbara's and Tilly's response shocked him, thereby exacerbating his own acute grief. Where did their attitude come from? They seemed not to care! Yet they weren't heartless girls – far from it. He had ascribed it in Barbara to immaturity and thought he could disabuse her, but when Tilly unexpectedly took her sister's side his explanation suddenly ceased to satisfy him. Nor could he convince himself that their understanding was clouded by the crushing events. Something was irredeemably absent in them. He might lament this, but forcing them to admit something which they apparently lacked the sensitivity ever to feel would cut them off and heighten their sorrow at a time when they ought to be comforting each other in the grief that they all shared. When he heard David speaking to Barbara and Tilly, it sounded like bullying, and with horror he realized that his son's words echoed his own: David's only seemed harsher because of his priggish dislike of Julius and his contempt for the poor infant Daniel. While Mr Shearer didn't exactly disagree with his son's opinions on these matters, he didn't consider himself entitled to pass judgement with such assurance. Indeed, he was instinctively inclined to sympathize with his grand-daughters – and, consequently, with Julius and Daniel. For in David's efforts to secure a private funeral for his brother and sister-in-law he detected a discordant, self-righteous desire to spite his nieces, as if venting his grief on them. And so Mr Shearer called off the harassment. 'We must let them have their own way,' he said morosely, and stared at his gleaming black shoes, which seemed far too large, as if unable to understand how he came to be wearing them.

Barbara entered Tilly's room and waited until she and Daniel were ready so that they could all go down to breakfast toge-ther. Recalling David's remarks of the previous evening, they agreed that he could only have said them with intent to wound; and their grandfather, by allowing them to go unchallenged, had showed that he was in sympathy with them.

In the cold dining-room they found the men already eating their toast and marmalade, while Sarah lingered in the kitchen waiting for the kettle to boil again.

'Good morning, girls. A bit of a holiday is it, Barbara?' said David, looking at his watch.

'Good morning,' Tilly answered. Barbara didn't respond. Her uncle knew she'd been told not to go into work because of the raid; but he had never taken her job seriously anyway.

'Say good morning, Daniel,' said Tilly.

Daniel turned his black eyes in terror from David to old Mr Shearer. He opened his lips but no sound emerged. The table was a huge unassailable expanse at chin-height. Beyond it, the adults were severe and imposing.

'Say good morning,' Tilly repeated softly, as she tried to settle him in a position where she could help him.

'G' mor',' he said. He was rigid, except for his trembling

lower lip. Tilly could see that in a moment he would cry out plaintively. Putting her arms around him from behind, she diverted his attention to the boiled egg that she was mashing in a bowl.

'And what will you two be up to this morning?' asked Mr Shearer. 'I dare say you've a lot to talk about.'

'We're going to the hospital,' said Barbara.

There was silence for a moment, which neither Barbara nor Tilly condescended to disturb. If mentioning Julius embarrassed or displeased the men, then it was their responsibility to avoid the subject.

'And will you be taking Daniel?' asked Mr Shearer.

'I don't see why not,' Tilly replied.

'The streets are hard going.'

The funeral was set for the afternoon and Barbara intended taking her sister to meet Julius in the morning. Much to Tilly's surprise, when the men had left the house Barbara followed Mr Shearer in advising her to leave Daniel behind.

'He'll be perfectly all right here, after all,' she said, 'and the streets will be very difficult for him.'

'He'd need to be carried most of the way, I think,' said Sarah. 'He'll be quite safe with me. You needn't worry, Tilly.'

After the thinly veiled antipathy towards her and Daniel, Tilly rebelled against leaving him alone in this house. But she had no wish to carry him for miles through the bombed streets, and Sarah's awkward smile allayed her suspicions. Instead of relief, however, she felt disappointment, as if it were she who was being abandoned.

Turning the corner into Much Park Street, Tilly reached out and steadied herself on a stump of wood sticking from the rubble. A passage had been cleared through the choked streets, but it was still necessary to keep a wary eye on the ground. The surfaces were broken with craters and cracks and several times she had stumbled on loose pieces of masonry.

'It's all so extraordinary, Barbara, it's hard to take in. I hope you're doing the right thing,' she said. 'It'll be interesting meeting him again.'

As they walked, Barbara had been telling her sister about her own particular experience of the air raid. She was uneasy at times, for her good luck felt like a betrayal of her dead parents and all the other dead and bereaved people, as if to feel anything but grief after the tragedy was disrespectful; and so to her own distress was coupled the guilt of unworthiness. But the very differences between the two events sharpened them, for as her mind switched from one to the other her emotions were always fresh, so that she might suddenly weep when a moment before she had felt feverishly happy. The contrasts clarified the focus. She knew that others saw and would continue to see her involvement with Julius as an aberration prompted by circumstances, and that the marriage would appear to them as one of expedience.

'But I wanted to marry him before all this happened,' she explained. 'I don't expect people like Uncle David to believe that, but I want you to believe it, Tilly. I know a lot of people don't like him, but I couldn't care less. I love him – and why shouldn't I love him now? You'll see, Tilly, you'll like him very much yourself, whatever you thought about him before, from a distance.'

Tilly remembered Julius, and she was sceptical of his virtues. She didn't question Barbara's feeling for him, but she had yet to see any proof that he returned it. Of course he was attractive – she had once felt a brief passion for him herself – but wasn't he a notorious deceiver? Didn't he always lead women on, and then dump them? Thus far her memory served her, but no further: although she could think of no actual instances, she was sure that he was a betrayer. However, despite her wariness on her sister's behalf, Tilly didn't voice her suspicions, for she recognized that Barbara might actually be a better judge of her own felicity; and she suspected that behind her own anxiety lurked resentment at Barbara's unexpected happiness. Tilly perceived the strength that she derived from this happiness and, even if it was no more than a temporary diversion which might incur its own burden of sadness, she couldn't begrudge her the comfort it offered now. Nor did she want to feel anxious: in spite of her mistrust of Julius, she found herself fervently hoping that Barbara was justified in her faith, for in the glow of her sister's happiness she might find solace for herself.

Several times their route was diverted because of demolition works. 'Not this way, ladies,' a soldier said as they tried to take a short-cut made by a German bomb. 'I'm afraid it's not safe.' He smiled, and beyond him they saw a group of soldiers dismantling the enfeebled structures. From time to time they jumped at the rumble of an explosion and saw the dust of the dynamite's blast rising in a cloud above the roofs.

When eventually they reached the hospital, the nurse refused at first to admit them. 'Anyone would think this was a clubhouse,' she grumbled. 'Besides, Corporal Gallagher has been operated on this morning. His mother is with him now and he's not in a condition to have more than one visitor after his anaesthetic.'

'Operated on?' Barbara repeated. Had she forgotten about this operation? Surely not! No, being unexpected, there must have been complications to his injury. In great agitation she explained that she was Julius's fiancée, and only then did the nurse let them through.

Julius lay on his back, asleep, his nose tilted towards the ceiling. Although his leg was in a hoist, from his serenity it looked as if he'd been put there for comfort's sake. He was snoring.

On a chair by the bed, Mrs Gallagher was knitting a khaki stocking. 'Ah, so you've come, have you, Barbara?' she said. 'Brought your sister too? Well, well, quite a little party we are. Pull yourself up a chair.' She raised her head now with a smile that revealed a depleted set of teeth, and pointed at two folding chairs by the door. 'Brought any grapes?'

'I haven't seen any grapes to buy, Mrs Gallagher,' said Barbara.

'Nor have I. Not for ages, I haven't. I just thought it would've been nice, that's all.' And she yanked vigorously on her wool.

Tilly leaned forward while removing her gloves. 'Hello, Mrs Gallagher,' she said, 'Barbara told me about the engagement... I'm so glad.'

'If you are, you'll be the first of your lot who is,' Mrs Gallagher retorted. 'But we don't mind about that, do we Barbara? Anyway – if that's so, Tilly, then I'm glad, and I'll take the opportunity of offering my condolences for your parents. Though I don't think it was mutual, I always did think they were fine people – examples to us all, I dare say. It's a sorry business,' Mrs Gallagher concluded.

'And what about Julius?' said Barbara. 'Is he all right? What's this about another op?'

'Yes. They took him in again first thing this morning. It's the something-fibber wasn't right, and now they say it never will be.'

'Never will be?'

'No. He's going to have a limp, Barbara. But what does a limp matter if you can sleep soundly?' And she winked at Barbara, directing her attention towards her son's tranquillity.

Tilly was astonished at the conversation's sanguine tone. 'Will it... will it be a bad limp?' she asked nervously.

Suddenly Julius coughed. His eyes opened, and in the swimming haze ahead he recognized Tilly. ''Lo, Tilly,' he said. Then his eyes closed again and his snoring resumed.

'It's just the anaesthetic, dear, don't take any notice of him,' said Mrs Gallagher, seeing Tilly's surprise.

For a moment they sat in silence, watching Julius as he slept. His hair was pushed into a tuft on top of his head.

It occurred to Barbara that she would never dance with

Julius again. She would always be quicker. He might limp, and perhaps suffer pain, for the rest of his life.

Just a week ago, everything had been so different. Now her future lay snoring, with his leg in the air. A week ago, this was not her future. Were it not for his interference, she thought, she probably would have died with her parents. It might have been better so. For an instant, she resented him.

'And how's life treating you then, Tilly?' Mrs Gallagher asked. 'You're in London now, Barbara tells me, married, and looking after a little boy?'

'Yes, that's right, Mrs Gallagher. My husband's away... And yes, I'm looking after – well, bringing up, I suppose I should say – Daniel. Trying to work at the same time isn't always easy, but life isn't easy for anyone at the moment, is it? I can't complain.'

'No. You've seen yourself what it's like up here. We always thought we had it comfy here in Coventry, compared with you lot in London – not that you'd catch anyone admitting it, mind – but it seems we've been caught napping, eh?' Mrs Gallagher seemed to have finished, but suddenly she added, as if it was an afterthought: 'And Daniel, the little boy, isn't he German?'

'Yes,' said Tilly.

'I suppose that makes for some problems, does it?'

Tilly was surprised by Mrs Gallagher's directness. 'Yes. Occasionally people are nasty,' she answered.

'Especially Uncle David,' said Barbara. 'Even Grandad.'

'Oh dear, now that's a shame,' Mrs Gallagher rejoined. 'Aren't people funny sometimes? There's no telling. You just bring him along to me if it gets tricky.' With her brows drawn together and her lips firmly shut, she reminded Tilly of those times at the charity bazaars when she had robustly defied the taunts and continued selling her whisky marmalade.

Suddenly Julius stirred again. 'I've got myself a blighty one, Barbara,' he said clearly. 'What about that?' His lips split into a broad smile and then he immediately went back to sleep.

Barbara wondered if he would be discharged now from active service. It was better, perhaps, to have a husband with a limp than a husband who might at any moment be dead. He might even be allowed to live in Coventry and work.

At last Tilly said that they ought to be getting back: they must get ready for the funeral. 'I want to leave plenty of time, because of Daniel,' she said.

'I'm sure I'll see you soon, Mrs Gallagher,' said Barbara as she put on her coat.

'Oh, you'll see me this afternoon if you want to. I'll be going along to the funeral myself,' she answered.

Beneath an ashen sky a large crowd trudged in a thick, uneven line up the cemetery's gravel path and over the grass to the graveside. Nobody spoke. The rasp of the gravel was like an echo of the familiar crunch of glass and rubble. The mourners were all dressed in black; only the glitter on a few uniforms and the wreaths which they all carried provided any colour.

Tilly held Daniel's hand. He walked sturdily, clutching a small bunch of flowers. A black cap with ear-flaps was fastened on his head, and each time he looked up furtively at the adults' faces it loosened itself a little more. Barbara had put it on for him and he had taken advantage of her inexperience by telling her that it wasn't supposed to be tight.

In front of them marched David and old Mr Shearer, their black overcoats reaching almost to the same point above their ankles. Mr Shearer encouraged his grand-daughters to come abreast, or even go ahead, but Barbara and Tilly said they were comfortable where they were. He thought it would be unkind to insist, and thereafter neither he nor David turned round, so that their stalwart figures formed a block in front of the girls, their lips shut tight as vices and their eyes fixed, like marbles. Barbara saw Mrs Gallagher standing alone on the fringe of the crowd, and she beckoned her forward and linked arms with her. David Shearer realized that Mrs Gallagher had been brought into their family group behind his back and was incensed by Barbara's lack of tact. But he had no wish to match her unpleasant behaviour by remonstrating, and he determined to endure the intrusion with fortitude. Barbara, after all, was still in shock.

The people in front reached the graveside, and Tilly and Barbara halted. They couldn't see it, but they could smell the disturbed earth in the grinning, coffin-filled trench. In the background Tilly saw a mechanical digger, and suddenly she started to weep.

Bending down, she picked Daniel up. Once in her arms he began to plug and scour his eyes with his small fists as if something was irritating them, and his flowers waved to and fro across his face.

'What is it, Daniel?' she whispered.

Daniel shook his head.

She pulled one of his arms aside to examine his eye. It was red from the rubbing, but through her own tears she could see nothing wrong. With his free hand he touched her cheek, and she felt a damp chrysanthemum brush her eyelid.

Barbara's hand was on her waist; she too was weeping freely. 'What's up with Daniel?' she asked.

'I think he's got a bit of grit in his eye.'

'Nonsense, Tilly dear, how can you tell?' Mrs Gallagher interposed. 'He's just trying not to cry, aren't you, dearie?'

He let go a tight-chested sob and stared at Mrs Gallagher. Then he looked between the heads in front towards the graveside. The hand in which he was holding the flowers was pressed against Tilly's neck, reminding her of his own unrecorded bereavement.

Some priest was speaking; now the Bishop stepped forward, and then ministers from the Free Church. Neither Barbara nor Tilly followed what was said. The wind plucked capriciously at the prayers, allowing only thin snatches to reach them. As in a dream, they were aware of themselves attending this funeral, but it felt as if they had stumbled into it by mistake, as if it had nothing to do with their own parents' death. They were weeping, but Tilly was thinking of Daniel's wrench from his family as she held him close, while Barbara couldn't stop thinking of Julius.

At last the funeral was over. The crowd shifted and the Mayor led the mourners around the long graves. Over every second coffin was draped a Union Jack. Some had labels with names attached to them, but most were illegible – either because of the slight drizzle or, Barbara speculated, because of blood-stains.

She looked along the ranks of coffins, which were already covered in a rumpled layer of flowers. 'Where shall I throw my wreath?' she said.

'I don't know,' said Tilly.

They watched other people peer into the trenches, searching for a sign, and then hopelessly sling down their wreaths.

'Just throw it anywhere,' said Tilly.

Barbara tossed it. It landed with a thud on the exposed edge of a coffin and slipped down to the earth.

'Throw in your flowers, Daniel,' said Tilly. 'Look, Barbara's thrown hers.'

Daniel looked from one sister to the other, as if making sure that they were watching him. Then, swaying from Tilly's embrace, he cast his flowers into the air. Slowly they fluttered down into the damp grave.

*

In the months following her parents' death, Tilly used to rise reluctantly in the morning, hugging the blankets' darkness around her in mute defence of the sealed world of her dreams. But at last she would obey the clock and briskly prepare herself for work before dressing Daniel. After breakfast she strapped him into the little seat fixed over the back wheel of her bicycle and took him to the Miss Cowleys' nursery near Regent's Park, where she left him; then she cycled for twenty minutes in the opposite direction, hoping to be at her desk by half-past eight. Sometimes she was late because the road was damaged by bombs and temporarily closed: she became adept at repairing punctures. Dismantling the wheel, finding the hole and patching it could be done, if she was lucky, within five minutes. She would arrive at work with grimy hands, and even after washing them an obstinate crescent of oil would remain under each fingernail. In the office she was always busy and, as her responsibilities increased, she became impatient with mistakes made by other people. She was good at her job and she knew it, and she expected others to match her. Although she was allowed to leave earlier, it was often nearly half-past seven when she collected Daniel from the venerable Cowley sisters and took him home. Then she fed him, bathed him in water heated on the stove in two large aluminium pans and read to him before tucking him into bed. Friends sometimes visited but usually she was grateful to be alone, for she was tired; tired, it seemed, beyond the feeble redemption of sleep. Yet, chastened daily by the sight of duty being done, she recoiled from the very idea of exhaustion: so her alarm bell smashed through the night's brittle shelter and, aching, she began again.

She devoted her Sundays, and the occasional weekday afternoons that were vouchsafed her, to Daniel. If it rained she played with him alone at home. If the weather allowed, they went together to the park, where he made her play with worms and feed his breakfast to the lean-necked swans; or they visited her friend Bridget Tripp in Kensington, who had two small children and a garden with a bird-table.

For several months she heard nothing of Percy. To begin with she didn't worry much – such silences, she knew, weren't uncommon. She didn't like to add her woe to the clamour of the pale wives importuning the regiment for news. But when two more hooded months followed the misery of her parents' funeral, she asked for just a word – and was told not to worry: he was safe. Two months elapsed before she asked again, and then she was informed that his whereabouts weren't actually known but there was no cause for anxiety. She pondered this, her mind a riot of interpretations, for another month. Did it mean that they simply had no confirmation of his death? Or was it a way of telling her that he was engaged on some secret enterprise? There were certain things one didn't ask; but it was odd that they didn't know. Was he 'missing, presumed dead'? If so, she wanted to know. And so she inquired again and was told that he was indeed missing and that it must now be assumed, regrettably, that he was dead. Nonetheless, they urged her not to give up hope. People often turned up; after all, this was war.

Tilly wasn't sure that she had much hope left to renounce. What sort of hope, she wondered, did they imagine was available to her? Hope for a miracle? It was better, surely, to acknowledge his death and learn to live with it as with a foul new cellmate in prison – except that there was nothing definite to which she could respond, no shape, no time; it was a death only by default. Could she announce, today, that he was dead? Or should she wait until next week? At what point could she permit herself to grieve? If not now, why then begin next week, next month? And so she remained silent, gnawed by loneliness and a sorrow that didn't seem ripe for expression.

And then, quite suddenly, the miracle seemed to happen, for just as she was beginning to acknowledge her widowhood, just after she had told Barbara and scented the comfort of grief, she received a terse message to the effect that Percy was alive and well in a prison camp in Moravia.

As if released from a magnetic field, Tilly was suddenly able to make plans for herself. While it was very much to be hoped that he would at last return in good health, it was virtually certain that he wouldn't do so before the end of the war – and with no prospect of it ending soon, it was pointless for Tilly to behave as if he might come back any day. Whether the war lasted two years or ten, she could contribute substantially more if she wasn't diverted by her role as a housewife. She reached this conclusion and then wondered in what way her position as Percy's wife had encumbered her until now. Her immediate circumstances hadn't changed but she realized now that she had always been detached from them: although enjoying her work, she had felt the focus of her life to be elsewhere, as yet unseen.

It was July 1941 and she hadn't heard from Esther since the postcards that arrived in the first month after she left her in Hamburg two and a half years previously. Tilly had never pretended to Daniel that she was his mother but, as the months passed and her fear for his family grew, she spoke about them less. Daniel's reunion with them was not only no closer but also less likely as rumours of the fate of Jews in Germany filtered through. Even if they emerged from the war alive, Daniel's first language would be English and he would have been brought up as an English boy: his experiences would differ so utterly from his family's, and continue to ramify so divergently, that he was probably already distanced from them for ever. Starting with the outbreak of war, Tilly had gradually accepted that all responsibility for his future lay with her, and she must therefore do her utmost on his behalf. And she did so unshadowed by resentment, for she had no children of her own. As awareness of her task sharpened, however, she doubted more and more that she was doing the best for him. It couldn't be good for him to be in London, spending each day at a nursery and then having only herself to turn to as a mother. The roof she provided was fragile, the love she gave was hungry and fickle. He ought to be with a family in a proper home, not with a lonely, busy woman. She thought of giving up her work, but she didn't want to; and in any case, she told herself, it would solve nothing because she still lacked a suitable home for him. And so she let everything drift on as it was.

One frosty Sunday afternoon in autumn, when the crisp leaves glistened underfoot like flakes of quartz, she went to see Bridget when her husband was at home on leave. Squadron Leader Alec Tripp was pleased to be at home and his family were evidently overjoyed to see him. While Alison, who was six, elaborately displayed the different clothes in which she dressed her dolls, her pride-bloated younger brother Harry showed his father how expertly he could jump up and down – first of all on the spot, then in zigzags across the room. He accompanied his movements with frenzied shouting, so that his father had to tell him to pipe down. For a few minutes he was quiet, sitting beside his father on the sofa, but then he tumbled again, determined to hop all the way to the dining-room door. Meanwhile Bridget produced a cake which she had made herself with carefully hoarded sugar and butter, refilled the willow-patterned teacups and listened with delight to her husband's tales of the RAF. He described the satisfaction of seeing a Heinkel spinning to earth with a plume of black smoke; he told the story about the wing-commander grounded for being drunk after shooting down two Messerschmidts, and how he then got wounded; and he told them about their celebrations after a triumphant attack on enemy bombers.

Tilly didn't understand why she was invited. Didn't they want to be alone together while he was on leave? As she watched the small family enjoying themselves, she was acutely aware of the contrast with her own situation. It was nearly eighteen months now since she had seen Percy, and the idea of him coming home was suspended in a mist of unreality. Even if he were able to come, it was impossible to believe that they would be able to chatter so blithely. She had once looked at Moravia on a map and it was like a headlong confrontation with the gulf that must have opened between them. It didn't occur to Tilly that such a gulf might exist between Bridget and

Alec, which her own presence was disguising. She only saw that they seemed to be happy, which made her suffer; and, remembering the RAF's failure to intercept the raid on Coventry, she wasn't much amused by Alec's yarns. But even as she despised herself for reacting so bitterly, she was seized by the thought that Bridget was deliberately, cruelly parading her handsome husband and her good fortune to Tilly, whom she knew to be alone.

Daniel was reluctant to leave Tilly, and he sat on her lap fiddling with two little mahogany blocks. From time to time she put him on the floor and encouraged him to play with Harry's bricks which were strewn across the carpet, but he was intimidated by Harry's zest and soon made his way back to Tilly's side. When he did so, Tilly relented. He was subject to periods of brooding silence – 'fits of melancholy' was her phrase for them. These upset her because she ascribed them vaguely to his upheaval from his parents: she longed to reach into his obscure sorrow and relieve him, but still she didn't know how to. From his behaviour now she judged him to be on the brink of this melancholy and was anxious to preserve him from it. She was pleased to see that Harry also seemed eager to draw Daniel out. He was an agreeable boy – she had often thought so – and if he was somewhat over-excited now, then it was only to be expected.

Stretching out his hand, Harry persuaded Daniel to join him in his games. They would see who could jump the highest, he said. When the older, taller boy predictably proved the victor in this contest, Daniel was in no way abashed. Falling onto the floor afforded him unexpected amusement and they did this together several times to the great satisfaction of both. Then Harry suggested that they play aeroplanes.

'I'm the English one! You're the German!' cried Harry. And when, to his surprise, he saw that Daniel accepted the part assigned to him, he spread out his arms and launched himself into the attack.

Daniel knew that he was a German, so he levelled his arms as Harry had done and braced himself. When Harry knocked him over, Daniel picked himself up at once and prepared for a counter-attack. With bent head and outstretched arms he stumbled across the carpet and struck Harry in the chest. Harry fell over backwards and hit his head on a table-leg.

He yelled, and Bridget hurried across the room to her son.

'Daniel! What do you think you're doing?' Tilly cried, grabbing his arm. 'You must look what you're doing!'

'Tilly, don't be hard on him,' said Alec. 'It wasn't his fault. Harry had it coming.'

The fall had frightened Tilly, and now she was embarrassed. 'No, but he should have taken more care,' she said. 'You must be more careful, Daniel,' she repeated, and settled him firmly on her lap.

Having watched the incident in silence, Alison now laid aside her doll and stood up in the middle of the floor in front of her father. Her hands were by her sides and her hair was tied in pert bunches behind her ears. 'Daddy,' she said, 'why is Daniel allowed to hurt Harry? He's a German, and the Germans are our enemies!'

'Alison!' said Bridget.

'That is a mistake, Alison,' said Alec, 'and I don't want to hear you making it again. It's the country we're at war with, not the people. You should behave to Daniel as you would to anybody else.'

It was fortunate, Tilly reflected later, that the scene had occurred among sympathetic people. It could so easily have been otherwise, and would probably happen frequently in various forms as Daniel came into more contact with other children. He couldn't be expected to understand his unusual circumstances; nor could other children. Blinded by zealous, infantile patriotism, they would hold his German birth against him if they knew about it. Tilly could encourage him to be quiet about it as he grew older but he should never feel ashamed of it. She must act decisively and exclusively for the benefit of his future by nurturing in him a warm sense of his own normality, so that he could meet challenges with confidence. In her present situation, she could not do this. She felt that she was living on the margins of life, and the pleasure she derived from him seemed to be a selfish one snatched at the cost of his childhood.

Her discontent was exposed and clarified by Barbara's resolve. Since the raid, Tilly had been to Coventry at least once a month with Daniel, and during her first few visits she concentrated on supporting her sister. But on August 18th Barbara had given birth to a girl, who was christened Ruth; and when, soon afterwards, Barbara's strength returned, Tilly found herself looking forward to visiting her sister for her own sake. In Barbara's new home she found a warmth and a depth which her own life lacked.

It hadn't been an easy year for Barbara. Invalided out of the army, Julius had been keen to marry her as soon as he came out of hospital. But she told him to wait. It seemed improper to get married so soon after her parents were buried, and she was so confused by sorrow and the pace of events that she doubted her ability to make a sensible decision. Her head ached, and she was dogged by a persistent urge to sleep. Returning from work to her uncle's house in Earlsdon Avenue, she could think only of closing her eyes and forgetting; the effort of rising in the morning was like trying to crawl from beneath a crushing weight. At night she dreamed of her parents and the air raid, and she woke feeling that she had betrayed them with Julius and that to marry him now, conscious of their disapproval, was a further insult to their memory. When she discovered that she was pregnant, her first response was that she must get an abortion.

But the next Sunday morning, as if an idea had insinuated itself mysteriously and taken root during her sleep, she awoke with the budding thought that she should marry Julius and have the baby. Her former qualms vanished, and now she saw that her parents' terrible death was separate from the question of her marriage. Her life was her own, and should not be lived in the shadow of their death. If their attitude to Julius hadn't swayed her feelings towards him previously, why should it be relevant now? Convinced, Barbara risked the contemptuous disapproval of her uncle and grandfather and married Julius.

Moving into Norfolk Street was a happy occasion. She felt welcomed by her mother-in-law, who also lived there for the time being, and loved by Julius. One day they were moving things from the attic in order to get at the roof to repair the bomb damage at last, when Julius said that one of the boxes contained papers of his father's and, thinking that his wife might be interested, he extracted some for her to inspect.

Among them was an advertisement for the sale of new shares on the amalgamation of Rudge and Whitworth, the company his father had worked for. '*During the past season the Rudge and the Whitworth cycles have attained the very first position in the Racing World. Their success has been simply phenomenal, more World Records and Wins of really first-class events having been secured than upon any other mounts. The following marvellous performances amply justify this statement:– ... One identical machine, weighing rather less than 25lbs., was used in all three events; yet, notwithstanding the terrific speed at which it was driven, it required neither repair nor adjustment.*' It was bizarre to think that a town could be transformed by something so mundane as the bicycle, but Barbara knew that such had been the case in Coventry, and this new link with the city's past confirmed and invigorated her in her new situation. Some of the papers were just quaint, however, in particular a pamphlet apparently written by Julius's father in 1917. The title and author were proclaimed in bold type on a pale blue cover. **Why the Earth is Flat by Jonas Gallagher**. Inside were several diagrams of bi-planes with dotted lines extending from their bellies to potato-shaped bombs. In the surrounding text, Mr Gallagher argued that the new aeroplanes would be unable to drop bombs accurately if the surface of the earth were curved. 'Manifestly,' however, they were capable of 'masterly precision'. Ergo the earth was flat.

Barbara was pleased with her new home but, as her pregnancy advanced and the baby writhed behind her stretched skin, she found that the frame in which she had enclosed the memory of her parents would no longer contain it, as if the material, after all, was liquid. Though believing it to be unjustified, the guilt of betrayal weighed heavily, and her growing stomach seemed like the physical burden of her crime. Her feet dragged as she trudged around the small house in her slippers, snapping and wheedling at Julius as if trying to justify her misplaced remorse; then she would lie with her hands across her face feeling the baby shift inside her, consumed by a torpor in which the only recognizable wish was that her heart would cease. Julius was obviously mad, as it seemed his father had also been. To judge from Mrs Gallagher's example, a touch of eccentricity was useful in a marriage with a madman. But Barbara didn't think she had the energy for all that now. She wanted Julius's patience to buckle, as if her guilt would find release through the valve of his cracked virtue. Whenever she walked in the city, gasping with the awkwardness of her own shape, she was stunned freshly by its battered, misshapen condition. On the one night when everyone in the city was shuddering with fear under the deluge of bombs, she had indulged herself: as a punishment, she had conceived. She dreaded having the baby.

But at last her time came, and Ruth was born safely. For a time Barbara's joy was kept buoyant by the currents of Julius's delight, but it was soon deflated by exhaustion; for though Mrs Gallagher helped as much as she could, Barbara found herself constantly hurrying and struggling to adapt herself to Ruth's peremptory demands. Sleep was possible only when Ruth permitted; eating was perfunctory, a necessary function; leisure was a matter of nostalgia.

But gradually, as she allowed herself to relax, she learned to balance in her new routine. Recognizing that their daughter had endowed their life together with a meaning outside themselves which reached into the future, Julius and Barbara were able to enjoy themselves in comfort. Barbara's cloud of fatigue dispersed and the guilt which had oppressed her for so long also withdrew.

Emerging from the trenches of her depression, Barbara at last became aware of the sadness and restlessness in Tilly's life. She brought out her father-in-law's pamphlet to cheer her up. 'I'm married to a madman's son,' she said. Tilly laughed, and in her laughter ran a thread of wistfulness. It was plain to Barbara that her sister missed Coventry.

★

It was Christmas Eve. Throughout the city the ruins were covered with a thick layer of snow which bound them together on the surface into strange, undulating shapes. The flattened space of the market and Broad Street was a lattice of gentle ridges and dimples, with outcrops of tin shacks like a rash of the pox. Inside the cathedral the piles of rubble were frozen into banks like petrified undergrowth.

Shortly before darkness, Tilly arrived with Daniel in Norfolk Street to spend the holiday with her sister's family. Uncle David had asked her to come to Earlsdon Avenue but, to his chagrin, she declined. She had agreed long ago to be with Barbara, she said, and reneging now would certainly disappoint her. When David objected that it was silly for them all to cram themselves into the little house in Norfolk Street when there were empty rooms in his house, she replied that it would be very cosy. As a compromise, the Norfolk Street party agreed to have Christmas dinner itself at Earlsdon Avenue.

Nor was it only with her own comfort in mind that Tilly

insisted on staying in Norfolk Street. Barbara had made it plain how much she looked forward to having Tilly and Daniel; like her sister, she was eager to enjoy Christmas without the baleful gaze of Earlsdon Avenue upon them. Possessing now a degree of equanimity which she hadn't felt since before the air raid and her parents' death, she was concerned above all for Julius's well-being. She was happy with him and, though she didn't quite see why not, it seemed that he wasn't disappointed in her. For he too had been caught up in a never-imagined sequence of events, and his life had changed beyond recognition. After his discharge from the army he had gone back to the Daimler factory where he used to work and, from being an unmarried soldier, he was transformed within two months into a limping civilian engineer with a pregnant wife who took upon her own shoulders the weight of her parents' death. He had behaved decisively, accepting responsibility and switching adeptly to the changing circumstances. Barbara recognized that such a rearrangement of his life couldn't have been easy and it was partly in deference to him that she wanted to preserve him, as far as was possible, from Christmas in Earlsdon Avenue. The tranquillity wrested from chaos – the bud of pleasure at last discovered in their own family – felt vulnerable because of its novelty, and she found that her duty lay in nurturing this bud rather than falling in with her uncle's wishes. But she was eager for Tilly's and Daniel's arrival: it would be fun having another baby in the house, and it was an age since she had spent time light-heartedly with her sister.

Julius had just put some fresh coals on the fire. As the flames curled around them and blazed upwards, a warm light danced through the blacked-out living-room. In the alcove to the left of the chimney-breast stood a Christmas tree with several candles glimmering softly among its branches. Now Julius sat in his deep armchair with his foot on a cushioned stool, clasped his long fingers behind his head against the antimacassar and stretched. His knuckles cracked loudly, and he closed his eyes and grinned with satisfaction so that his teeth glistened in the firelight.

Mrs Gallagher's shoulders twitched. She was sitting in the chair opposite, her head bent over a thick sock that she was knitting. 'Julius, how many times have I told you it gives me the shivers when you do that?' she said.

'I never counted. If I had a farthing each time, I'd be a rich man.'

Between them, but a little further from the fire, Barbara was sitting on the floor with Ruth propped between her legs. Clothed in layers of white, Ruth probed the beginnings of her tight yellow curls with one hand while, with the other, she clutched a blue cotton stuffed rabbit whose ear she was sucking mechanically. Her attention alternated between the fire and the illuminated tree, and from time to time she jabbed the air excitedly, as if discovering something in the flickering light. 'Aa!' she cried, inviting the adults to witness it.

There was a sharp knock on the door.

'There they are!' said Julius; and he swung his leg from the stool, raised himself onto his good foot and lurched across the room.

'Tilly!' he said as he opened the door, 'Come on in! Welcome, welcome! Let me take your bags.'

Tilly was wearing a small black hat with a strip of net which half-covered her face. After greeting Julius, she pulled out a pin and removed the hat. Her blonde hair was held up with carefully placed grips, leaving her neck bare. She was smiling, and now she reached down to Daniel's shoulders and steered him towards Barbara, who was standing with Ruth in her arms. The two sisters kissed in haste, for Daniel was already straining up towards Ruth. 'Hallo Barba, is that Ruth?' he demanded. 'Is that baby Ruth?'

'Yes, Daniel.' And Barbara sat down on a chair so that he could have a better view of Ruth, while Tilly said hello to Mrs Gallagher and Julius closed the door and hauled the bags upstairs.

Daniel was used to visiting Coventry with Tilly. Barbara and Julius were familiar figures to him by now, and even for several weeks before her arrival Ruth had been the object of his intense curiosity. It seemed extraordinary to him that Barbara's world could be transformed by the addition of a baby. Her life seemed fixed, and it was disconcerting to learn that something altogether new might appear in it. At first he behaved as if it was utterly ridiculous. Only by repeatedly talking about it with Tilly did he get used to the idea: then he was delighted by the miraculous emergence of something from nothing. Now he stood on the tips of his toes and, leaning against Barbara's legs, scrutinized the baby on her lap. His eyes swivelled up in wonder towards Barbara and then returned to Ruth. Timidly, he took hold of one of her tiny hands. His own seemed huge in comparison and he looked up again at Barbara to make sure she appreciated this phenomenon.

'What do you think of her then, Daniel?' Barbara asked.

In his enchantment, Daniel didn't know what to say. But then he suddenly wrinkled up his nose as a familiar, stifling smell rose from the placid baby's nappies. 'I think she's done something,' he said, and hurriedly backed away, giggling.

Barbara sniffed. 'Oh Ruth! How could you! What a way to act in front of Daniel! And you were only changed half an hour ago!'

As Barbara left to attend to Ruth, Julius entered the room bearing two bottles. 'You'll have to forgive our Ruth, Daniel old chap. Babies don't have quite so much control as the rest of us. But she'll learn – you'll see. At least, let's hope so, eh?' he said, and winked.

'Julius! That's enough now! Don't tease the child,' said Mrs Gallagher.

Daniel squeezed his stomach, laughing as if the exquisite joke was too much to bear. Then his hands flew to his buttocks and he jumped across to the armchair and fell against it. 'Maybe she'll never learn!' he squealed. 'Maybe when she's as old as me, even when she's as old as you Julius, she'll still...' The thought of what she might still be doing at such an advanced age sent him into another fit of giggles and he buried his face in a cushion.

'Daniel, whatever's got into you?' said Tilly, who had watched the proceedings uncertainly – amused, but thinking that she ought to reprimand him for his vulgarity.

'That's the spirit, old chap,' said Julius, placing his bottles carefully on a side-table. 'I know, it's that chair – it always gives me the giggles too.'

'You do encourage them so!' said Mrs Gallagher. 'It's not right.'

'Now, talking of encouraging,' said Julius, turning to Tilly, 'Mother knows a thing or two about that. She's managed to lay her hands on a couple of bottles of stout. I know it's not what Society recommends, but will you have a drop all the same?'

Tilly said that she would, since it was Christmas, and so he filled four glasses. After handing one to Tilly he gave one to his mother, who inspected it critically before sipping. Then he took his own and returned to his chair, where Daniel still had his face thrust against the cushion.

'Excuse me, it's my turn now,' he said. Stooping, he put one arm round Daniel's waist and lifted him up. Suddenly Daniel found himself deposited on Julius's stool, and Julius was reclining in his chair. 'I bet you couldn't do that, could you?' he said.

Daniel shrieked at this hilarious suggestion, and then turned towards Tilly with his eyes stretched wide and his lips pinched together as if they might burst open again, appealing to her to witness just how extraordinary Julius was.

'Isn't he funny?' said Tilly, enjoying the unusual sensation of leaning back in a comfortable chair with a glass of stout. 'You shouldn't take any notice of him, you know.'

Julius drew a box of Chesterfields from his pocket, tapped one of the cigarettes on the packet and placed it between his still smiling lips. After lighting it, he cast the match into the fire with a flourish.

When Barbara returned she handed Ruth to Julius and then sat on the arm of his chair with her stout. With one hand Julius rocked the baby, while his other manipulated his cigarette for Daniel's entertainment, flicking it over his fingers. His mother watched and listened with grumpy contentment, pausing regularly from her knitting to bring her glass to her lips and drink, each time making an identical little gurgle, like a drain.

Presently Tilly and Barbara took the babies away. While Barbara put Ruth to bed, Tilly gave Daniel his supper; and when he was in bed Barbara read him the story of the Three Wise Men bringing their gifts to the infant Jesus. Afterwards, Barbara asked Tilly if it was all right to read him this story, because she knew that Jews did things differently. Tilly said she didn't know exactly, but it was a nice story, and he liked it – so where was the harm?

When they came back downstairs, Julius and his mother had finished preparing the supper. The table was laid and they all sat down to eat. There was pea soup followed by rabbit, which Julius had obtained from a colleague at work, an ingenious poacher who lived just beyond Stivichall near the Leamington Road; there were roast potatoes and there was cabbage which Julius allowed to cook for rather longer than he ought. Barbara had made an apple tart, of which her husband ate almost half.

'Now don't move a muscle,' said Julius when he had finished, 'or the trick won't work.' And he stood up and opened the cupboard under the stairs. 'This is a magic cupboard,' he said. 'Abracadabra.' He bent his head into the darkness. 'Abracadabra. Come forth, oh bottle!' And he emerged with a bottle of whisky.

'Julius, you are naughty! Wherever did you get it?' said his mother.

One nightcap followed another, until midnight struck.

'Happy Christmas!' cried Julius, and he kissed Barbara and

Tilly and his mother in turn.

'Happy Christmas, dear,' said Mrs Gallagher. She wiped away a drop from her eye which might have been a tear or the rheumy water of age. 'And to you, my dear Barbara,' she said. 'And Happy Christmas to you too, Tilly, it's all nicer to have you than I quite know how to say... Oh, dear me, I better keep quiet and not open my silly old mouth and try to say it when it won't be said, but I did so want to say it because it does make me happy, what with my Julius here and Barbara and now Ruth, and here's you and Daniel now and...'

'Yes, Mother, I think Tilly's got the point.'

Fortunately Mrs Gallagher didn't have far to go to reach her bed because she had vacated her room for Tilly and Daniel. She was going to sleep downstairs. So Barbara made up the couch for her mother-in-law and helped her into it while Julius and Tilly cleared away the supper.

'What a piece of luck that neither of the children woke up,' said Tilly, as she was saying good night to her sister. And as she climbed into bed she thought it was too good to last: the Germans would surely attack tonight.

'It's nice to know it's still possible to have a bit of fun, isn't it?' Barbara said to Julius, when they were alone in their room.

'Yes. Let's hope the Jerries are enjoying their Christmas at home too,' he answered, as he unhooked his wife's dress.

And in church the next morning the minister thanked God for granting them a peaceful Christmas so far. He prayed that the peace would last in the air above their city and that God would bless the Allies with a speedy victory over the Evil of Hitler's armies and establish a real peace; and especially he prayed that on this Christmas Day, in spite of the sorrows inflicted by the war, in each home there would be joy from paying heed to the Christmas message: Christ was born to save us and, he said, as a family man himself he understood the hope offered by a new-born babe in the midst of hard trials and tribulations, whether it be in Galilee all those years ago or now, when their very lives were threatened from all directions...

Tilly didn't quite follow his argument, but in any case she was only half-listening. She was distracted by the back of her Aunt Sarah's head into thinking about the party awaiting them in Earlsdon Avenue. For Aunt Sarah, whose hair had never been notably ornamental, appeared to have had it 'done'; and it was now coiled in the most fashionable way on top of her head. Tilly couldn't help wondering whether it was coincidence that she had chosen the occasion of her nieces' visit to take so bold a step, or whether it belonged to a wider strategy designed to impress on her nieces once and for all the superiority of Earlsdon Avenue.

After church, Julius returned to the house to fetch a basket of presents. He knew that alcohol would not be offered in Earlsdon Avenue and, it being Christmas, he didn't deny himself a nip from the precious bottle. Then he limped hurriedly back through the sparkling, disjointed streets. There was ice on the ground and he wished he had thought to bring a stick.

To the Shearers' dismay, their maid Lucy had demanded two days' leave over Christmas. Her husband was unexpectedly at home and they couldn't even prevail on her to come during lunch. Aunt Sarah therefore opened the door herself.

'Happy Christmas, Julius – again,' she said, for the sight of his basket of presents made her forget for a moment that she had seen him briefly outside church. 'Now hang up your coat and come through into the warm.' As he put down his basket she offered him a coat-hanger and opened the wardrobe door, indicating that he should put his coat inside himself. Then she closed the door, and as she led the way to the drawing-room her hand touched her skirt as if she expected to find a bunch of keys dangling from her waist.

Ruth was the centre of attention. She was sitting on her great-grandfather's bony lap with her mouth open in baffled resignation as everyone admired her and discussed her digestion. On seeing her father, she squirmed and groaned. Old

Mr Shearer's hands dithered about her and his creviced cheeks trembled so that he suddenly seemed very frail. Uncomfortable now, Ruth began to cry, and David said that Barbara would have to take her out. But Julius told him that it wouldn't be necessary; he gathered his daughter into his arms and her humour improved at once. He had expected the party to be wholly family and was surprised to find Mr and Mrs Phelps there too. Mr Phelps, a friend of David's who worked in the City Engineer's department, had a pot belly and incipient jowls, and the lines of his face seemed set in a wince as if he was constantly beleaguered by impatient entrepreneurs. His wife had kind, blue eyes and she wore a silver rose brooch at her throat. As they admired Ruth now, Julius remembered that their son had just been killed when he last saw them in Earlsdon Avenue, and he warmed to them.

At lunch he was seated beside Mrs Phelps, with Sarah on his other side at the end of the table. Mr Phelps sat opposite; beside him was Mrs Gallagher, then Daniel and Tilly, with David at the head. On David's right sat Barbara with Ruth propped on her lap; and old Mr Shearer was between her and Mrs Phelps.

David carved the goose at the sideboard while Barbara dished out the vegetables. As she handed round the first plates to Mrs Phelps and Mrs Gallagher, David turned and cleared his throat loudly. Still holding the long knife and fork, he parted his arms and closed his eyes in a way that commanded silence.

'For what we are about to receive, may the Lord make us truly thankful. Amen.'

'Amen.'

'Happy Christmas,' he said. 'Oh damn.'

A drop of fat had dribbled under his cuff and now he seized a starched napkin and wiped his wrist and the ivory handle of the knife.

'Well, isn't this nice!' declared Sarah. 'What a jolly party we are!'

Everyone murmured their agreement and then Sarah said

that they mustn't wait to start because their food would only get cold.

'Mmm, is this goose? It's not every day one gets goose,' announced Mr Phelps as he put his napkin across his knees and inspected the plate in front of him.

'Some gravy, Mr Phelps?' said Mrs Gallagher, and she prodded the gravy-boat before them on the table.

'Thank you, Mrs Gallagher. How delicious! What a feast you've organized, Mrs Shearer!'

'Well, isn't it Christmas, Mr Phelps?'

Mr Phelps agreed that it was Christmas and poured gravy thickly over his Brussels sprouts and boiled potatoes. When he had tasted his goose and complimented the hostess on her cooking, he addressed himself to Julius: 'I hear you're with Daimler these days?'

'That's right. Brown's Lane, second shadow factory.'

'Hercules engines, isn't it?'

'Yes. Not quite so grand as David at Hawker-Siddeley with his Blenheims and Whitworths and so on. They seem to have a finger in every pie...'

'Nonsense. We all do what we can.'

'Without Coventry,' said old Mr Shearer, 'the country would be on its knees. That's my opinion.' And he looked around the table bullishly.

'That's right. It's Coventry makes all the guns and aeroplanes,' said Mrs Gallagher, with a condescension that might have included the enemy among the beneficiaries.

'They'd be made somewhere else, if not here,' said Julius.

'They wouldn't, though,' said David, tapping his fingers on the polished surface of the table. 'They wouldn't make them as well as us. We know how to do it. We've got the tradition.'

'Don't you think they might learn?' Tilly suggested.

'They might,' said her grandfather. 'But they haven't, have they?'

'And I hope they don't for the moment,' said Barbara. 'It

means people can stay here and work instead of going off to the war.' Instantly realizing that this was tactless, Barbara glanced at Tilly, whose eyes were fixed resolutely on her food. 'I mean it's brave and right going off to fight,' she added, 'but it's nice being at home too, selfishly I mean.'

'That goes without saying,' said Sarah. 'Of course it is.'

'In this war, it doesn't seem to be any safer staying at home,' Mrs Phelps observed.

For a moment everyone was respectfully silent, for though Mrs Phelps had drawn attention to their misfortunes in Coventry, she had actually lost a son in action.

Throughout lunch, conversation turned around the merits of Coventry and its role in the war. Coventry, they felt, was unique both in its capacity for armaments production and also for its resilience in the face of attack from the air. Few factories had closed for more than a week except for Alvis, which was demolished – and they only made superchargers for Merlins; and Barbara told Tilly about the notice outside the wrecked Owen Owen building: *Closed, but not for long*, it said.

It was all extremely dull for Daniel and he began to fidget. Many times Tilly laid her hand on his shoulder. 'Ssh, Daniel,' she whispered. 'Only a little longer.' But his patience was wearing down and he found that Ruth could be gratifyingly alarmed if he pulled faces at her. So he twisted up his features and gaped at her when he thought no one was watching until at last she began to howl.

'Of course she'll cry if you make faces at her like that,' said Tilly.

'You ought to stop him, Tilly. It's too bad! If he's going to sit with us then he must behave himself!' said David.

Daniel was indifferent to the reproofs. They were a cheap price to pay for the pleasure of being taken away by Tilly and Barbara to sit beside the Christmas tree in the drawing-room with Ruth, where he was allowed to play at liberty. He knew that he hadn't really disgraced himself because Tilly wasn't cross with him when they were away from the grown-ups.

'And as for the reconstruction, that's something else we'll have to think about in good time,' David was saying in the dining-room. 'I don't say that it's not a good thing to have people working on plans so soon. But I'd like to know where that Gibson fellow thinks the money's going to come from for the tomfoolery that he calls architecture, planning – whatever it is...' For the radical plans already drawn up by the City Architect were plainly far more costly than the more conservative proposals of the City Engineer.

'I suppose there will be government help,' said Mr Phelps. 'What with us being so much worse hit than anyone else – so far, at any rate.'

'Maybe there will and maybe there won't, Stanley...'

'Well there bloody well should be, that's my opinion if you want to know,' said Mr Shearer.

'Let's hope there is, Dad. But the important thing for us, especially if there is help from the government, is to make sure it's done properly. That young jackanapes can't be allowed to have it all his own way.'

Mr Phelps said, 'You're quite right there. The city must be rebuilt properly.'

'And we must show the world what we're made of in Coventry,' added old Mr Shearer.

'Quite so,' Mrs Phelps agreed. 'And what do you think should be done with the cathedral, Julius?'

'No question about it,' David intruded. 'It should be rebuilt.'

'As was,' opined his father.

'You're asking *me* what *I* think, Mrs Phelps?' said Julius, and he smiled at her with a glitter of teeth. 'Personally, I don't think it should be rebuilt. After the war we're going to need houses in Coventry, not a huge, expensive new cathedral.'

'But you can't just let the cathedral be destroyed!' Mr Shearer insisted.

'It's destroyed already.'

'That's not the point! We've got to show 'em!'

'Show who? What?'

'Show that we've still got spunk in us, boy, show that we can still *do* it! Otherwise they'll stop bringing their industry here and we won't be able to afford your precious houses!'

Mrs Gallagher coughed.

'Begging your pardon, Mrs Gallagher...' Then, turning to Mrs Phelps: 'I may be old, Mrs Phelps, but I speak plainly and always have. I hope you won't take it amiss.'

'Of course not, Mr Shearer. I'm all in favour of plain speaking. But I see Julius is shaking his head. We must let him speak plainly too.'

Julius didn't want to speak plainly. Although he disagreed vehemently with the old man's opinion, it would be wiser now to keep silent; he had shaken his head without thinking. But now he had to say something and he tried to compromise. 'I think we could show them just as well by building houses,' he said. 'Even if we built a new cathedral, I don't see why it should be identical to the old one.'

'Whatever are you saying? That we should have a great hunk of that modern nonsense in the middle of the city?' said David.

Julius scowled. Privately he himself had no great enthusiasm for the new architecture but he had met the young City Architect and admired him; and all of a sudden he found David intensely irritating. 'In any case, what's this about 'our' cathedral? I thought we were all good Methodists,' he said, touching his glass and winking cheekily at his mother.

David saw the wink but chose to ignore it. 'The point of the cathedral is not that it's Anglican or Methodist or anything else. It's symbolic of the city.'

'And would it still be symbolic of the city if the majority of the population weren't Christians?'

'You're being deliberately difficult, Julius.'

'No, he's got a point,' said Mr Phelps unexpectedly. 'It

would be different in that case, I think. But the fact is that we aren't all heathen. We're Christians. I've never been much of a one for theology myself, but it's obvious to me that the cathedral occupies an important place in the heart of an English city.'

'At most, it's symbolic of what the city was,' said Julius. 'And as far as reconstruction goes, speaking for myself I'm interested in what the city is and will be; not in what it was.'

'It will never be anything if you ignore what it was,' said David.

Sarah sighed. She had so hoped to avoid a dispute. 'Well!' she said, 'We will have some lively discussions when the time comes, won't we? Shall we go next door?'

Sitting on the chintz-covered sofa in the drawing-room, Barbara was asking Tilly about her work in London. One hand held Ruth on her lap; the other supported her chin, with the elbow on the back of the sofa. Daniel sprawled between them, drowsily telling Ruth a story. Absorbed in his own invention, he paid no attention to the adults.

'I've been approached about a new job,' said Tilly. 'It's rather mysterious. Apparently it's not in London and it's very hush-hush. I don't know what to do –' she nodded in Daniel's direction – 'I think it might be rather a good job but of course I don't know details. They can't tell you what you're getting into until you get into it. And even then I imagine I'd be working in isolation and wouldn't be allowed to know what I was contributing to anyway...'

'Daniel could always stay with us, if it would help,' said Barbara.

Before Tilly could respond to this or explain her dilemma any further, they were joined by the others from the dining-room. Small strips of marzipan were handed round and, as Christmas presents were exchanged, the current of antagonism ebbed. Daniel was given a clockwork motor car by Julius and Barbara, which he chased about the floor wildly. But David said enough was enough, it was wearing on the grown-ups' nerves, and Daniel began to cry. At this point Barbara said that it was time for them to go – the little ones were tired and they ought to be put to bed for an hour or two.

It was still only three o'clock but the dull grey light outside already hinted at dusk. It looked as if there might be another snowfall. As they walked they could hear the rattle of corrugated iron in the wind and occasionally the flapping of tarpaulins which still hadn't been replaced by something more permanent. It was cold, and they were all eager to get into the snug warmth of Norfolk Street. It wasn't only the children who wanted to sleep: after such a handsome meal they all wanted to put their feet up and have a nap.

*

'Office work of the strictest secrecy' was the only description of the job which Tilly was offered. She assumed it must have some bearing on her work in radio but the nature of the connection was kept from her. In any case, it would be impossible to take it up because of Daniel, but there could be no harm in making one or two more enquiries. After all, Barbara had volunteered to look after Daniel. Perhaps it would be possible; it would be foolish not to follow it up.

At the initial proposal, a lady in the Ministry invited her to think about it and to contact her if she was interested. So she returned and explained her problem: if it weren't for this, she said, she would love to do it; she was impatient to get really involved in a project. And when she mentioned that Barbara lived in Coventry she was advised that, if she accepted, her place of work wouldn't be so far away from Coventry. She would be able to visit relatively often, possibly even once a week.

Tilly had often thought that it couldn't be good for Daniel to be in London and now here was an opportunity to get out. As their routine stood, she saw little enough of him during the week – only breakfast and a bedtime story. It would be much more suitable for him to be with Barbara, Julius and Ruth; if she could visit them at weekends then she wouldn't see much less of him anyway. Besides, the job might not last very long. So she wrote to Barbara asking if she wished her spontaneous invitation to be taken seriously.

Barbara answered that she hadn't thought about it much at the time, but she saw no reason to withdraw her suggestion. She had mentioned it to Julius now and he agreed with her. Certainly it would require some domestic rearrangement and they understood that the responsibility mustn't be taken on thoughtlessly. But they were very fond of Daniel, she said, and would be delighted to accept the challenge. If Tilly would visit them more often, so much the better. Where, exactly, would she be working?

With this dim chance transformed so easily into a genuine option, Tilly returned to the lady at the Ministry and said that she would be delighted to accept the job provided that Daniel didn't object too strongly. Probing for further information, she was told that she would be stationed somewhere near Bletchley.

Tilly arranged it so that Barbara raised the matter first with Daniel. While talking about something different with him, Barbara said what fun it would be if Daniel could only come to live with them. It would be nice for her and Julius in any case, she said, and especially nice for Ruth. What did he think? Would he like to come and be one of their family? Had Daniel's response to this overture been negative or indifferent, Tilly might have abandoned the plan altogether. But, as she had anticipated, he greeted it with enthusiasm. He didn't like his nursery: to leave it in favour of Norfolk Street seemed like the realization of a dream, for he adored Julius and Barbara and Ruth. When it was explained to him that Tilly wouldn't in fact move with him, he became doubtful, but Tilly hastily reassured him that she would see him almost as often as ever.

The difficulty was that she had to go and work in a place that would be very dull for him; there would be no other children, no nursery, nobody like the Misses Cowley to look after him during the day. Meanwhile Barbara wanted to look after him – everyone wanted to look after him, said Tilly with a laugh.

It was March 1942 when Tilly took Daniel to live in Coventry, almost three years since she had brought him to England. Originally he had possessed only his shawl and the few items provided for him by Esther. For this next stage he had a small suitcase full of his own clothes and possessions, the accumulated baggage of his time in London with Tilly. The case contained nothing unusual but Tilly was conscious of omitting some things which belonged to Daniel more strictly than anything he was now taking to Barbara's – his shawl and the things packed by Esther, including her ring. It seemed pointless to hand these over now, for they were useless, and the ring would get lost. Yet these withheld belongings were the only tangible remnants of his past. Tilly wondered if he had any memory now of his family. Certainly he knew of them, but they must surely be unreal to him. Did he secretly imagine a reunion? Even the question seemed misjudged, for it was of the utmost importance that he felt completely at home where he was. But still she wondered: in the end, perhaps his hopes – if he had any – would prove justified.

She told Barbara and Julius that she had never deceived him about his family. She also said that she had never denied that he might meet them.

'Does he ask about them?' said Julius.

'Sometimes.'

'And you tell him they're alive and he'll join up with them?'

'They might be alive.'

'I doubt it.'

For the moment, Daniel would be sharing his room with Mrs

Gallagher. Tilly sat on his cot, the same one in which he had slept at Christmas. She had just finished unpacking his case with Barbara and they had all been laughing together. When he followed Barbara to help her hang out the washing, Daniel was chattering away as if his life depended on it. Tilly could see at once that he would be happy here but – wasn't he even the slightest bit sad?

Suddenly she found she was weeping. She would miss him – she had never doubted that she would – and he would surely miss her: but the merest suspicion that he might not made her bitterly sorry for herself.

The following day Tilly returned to London to clear out of her flat, which she was going to let to an American. Three days later she began her new job at Bletchley Park, working in a disciplined team of girls who systematically intercepted enemy wireless transmissions; it was something to do with breaking codes. Apart from brief but regular visits to Coventry, she stayed there until the end of the war.

Thus it came about that Daniel found a home with Barbara and Julius.

7

I found what happened yesterday at Kate's bedside eerie. It was like seeing in a new acquaintance a tenuous resemblance to an old friend: instead of attending to what is being said, you try to work out how the image of the friend has slipped into this person's features. It's not the pinched mouth, nor the eyelids' curve, nor the twist of hair over the ear – it's not the matrix of the face; perhaps it's the colouring, or the line of the nose? Then, as you watch the shift of the eyes and the flex of the facial planes, you realize that whatever reminds you of your friend nowhere isolates itself into the triviality of a feature. Whatever it is, it is both absent and present, and your effort to identify the yoke that binds them results in defining more precisely what separates them.

It's her unnerving stillness which is the most conspicuous evidence of her misfortune, now that the injuries to her head and leg have healed somewhat. When the external damage was clearly visible I think I behaved as if her internal damage was a subordinate facet of the same thing. I read or talked to her as if she could hear me, as if she were lying still only because of the physical discomfort of moving. Now I can't ignore that the stillness is a separate phenomenon, like the blueness of light that has passed through blue glass: the blue is a phenomenon in itself, not an incidental quality of the light. You asked me before what was the point of talking to her. Whatever flushed response I made then no longer satisfies me. Her awesome silence is an unknown space: it may be an immense universe, cluttered by a million galaxies but sealed from the flaring sparks of our words; or it may be a boundless vacancy, in which every word constitutes a star and every story a firmament. It's hard to keep on talking and you wonder why you bother. Is it vanity? Is it all for the sake of self-respect? Yet she looks so pretty, and through the shroud of her stillness some vitality still draws one forward.

And Mum said, taking the 'closed' view of Kate, the 'brick wall' view, and talking to me without tailoring her words for the benefit of Kate's unconscious, 'I think it's unfair, it's a cruel trick.'

I looked around, half-expecting to see a nurse step out of the gloom with a beadle's officious outrage, but there were only sleek surfaces and the inscrutable eyes of the machines.

'Do you remember all that business in the Seventies?' I said. 'Whether Churchill knew that Coventry was going to be bombed?'

'They just thought he should have done something. If he knew.'

'If he had done anything he would have blown ULTRA, which he knew would save more lives than would be lost in Coventry.'

'He couldn't know that. Anyway, so what? What are you saying?'

'The Machine and the old-fashioned God...'

'There's nobody quite like you for twisting someone's words,' said Mum, with the abrupt rise and fall in her voice which, in her case, indicates the end to a conversation. Then, glancing towards Kate, she crossed her legs and added, 'You may think it's cruel to keep her alive with these machines, but I don't. I simply meant that it was an unfair stroke of fate in the first place.'

You will appreciate what I mean, Jake, when I say that I doubt the unity of Mum's truth here. I rather think she meant at first that preserving Kate's constricted life indefinitely in this way is inflicting on her a cruel indignity. Irritated, by my mosquito-like buzzing, into shame for her own harshness, she dumped the thought on me and scuttered sideways to the comfort of a pious platitude.

No more was said about it. We were silent for a while and then we read Kate a few of her cards, I told her about the panel I put in an exhibition last week and Mum told her about the boredom of marking essays. We described what we were wearing and what the weather was like and finally departed in the distinctive subdued spirits I've come to associate with sitting beside someone in a coma, taunted by the feeling that we might as well have been talking to a brick wall – behaviour which is usually reckoned to be that of an idiot.

Mum had cause to swerve. I knew it would be emotive to her but I couldn't help mentioning the resemblance. Only the previous day I'd been thinking about Tilly going to Bletchley, so perhaps my comparison was already lying like a chrysalis in my mind, waiting for the warm reforming breeze of circumstance to open the image.

You should understand that the 'prior-warning' theory emerged very suddenly, in a book by Group Captain F W Winterbottom, who was responsible in 1940 for the security of ULTRA material. People like us didn't know about ULTRA then, and we weren't equipped to argue. All at once we were presented with the bare facts of ENIGMA, the German coding machines, and ULTRA, the computer-like systems devised by the British to combat ENIGMA. Here, it seemed, was the truth, and Coventry was quickly represented as a martyr to ULTRA. It was ages before we realized that the 'prior-warning' theory was held to be most unlikely. You know that famous picture of Churchill, cigar rammed between his teeth, cane jabbing into the rubble ahead as he strides grimly through the wrecked cathedral pursued by a gaggle of eager aldermen? Suddenly we thought he'd been acting. All his rhetoric about every person doing their bit seemed moulded by cynicism. So, at least, it seemed to Mum.

Julius and Barba didn't discuss it. The idea that Churchill behaved in bad faith was preposterous to them, and they weren't interested in the irony of Tilly having worked at Bletchley. I wonder if Tilly herself had any idea of it, but in any case she was dead by then. And Percy always acted as if the war had never happened. Apart from me, there was no one with whom Mum could share her dislocated rage. You will remember how for a long time we tilted at it, but though you knew that talk of the Raid was likely to provoke her, you were too young to understand why. It must lie across the memory of your childhood like a streak of impurity in a pane of glass: I can't remove it, but I feel bound to try to explain it.

The issue between us wasn't simply whether Churchill had prior knowledge. We both knew that we weren't in a position to know with confidence or not. For my part, I'm quite willing to believe that the old fox knew – he was certainly cunning enough to fool his private secretaries. But then, so what? He had no extra resources to offer. Evacuating the city would have been an unprecedented course of action which no prior knowledge warranted; and it would have seemed like running away, which was unthinkable to him. The best available defence was the operations of R V Jones and No 8 Wing but, tragically, on this occasion the signal they sent out to confuse the radio-navigation systems of the Heinkels had the wrong tone. Even if Churchill did consider taking action which might have jeopardized the secrecy of ULTRA, I have no doubt that he was right to decide against it. Equally, he may never have known.

'If he knew, his decision involved grave responsibilities either way,' I said.

'My grandparents died to save a machine – !'

'They didn't. The machine saved lives.'

'The act of sacrificing them to a machine is inhuman!'

Her grandparents were killed, her father was maimed – these things complicated her distress, but bitterness wasn't its substance (she owes her existence to the same event, after all). Never mind that 555 people were killed (compared with 30,000 in each of the big raids on Hamburg, Dresden, Cologne, etc). It wasn't the result of the decision but its nature that Mum found particularly disturbing: if Churchill *had* known then he *would* have been guilty of a kind of spiritual trespassing. Instead of doing the morally obvious thing, he put his faith in the obscure, transcendent possibilities of something else. He granted to a machine the ultimate power, that of evaluating lives. I said to Mum that this wasn't inhuman at all, he was simply trusting in the highest rationality available.

'Precisely.'

God's seat had been usurped. But though this may be sad, even tragic, in my view it's nothing if not human. Sometimes it may even be necessary. I used to say that we had no right to argue whether he was wrong or inhuman – anything to lay the matter to rest.

I remember a swift exchange even as late as May 1977, when nobody seriously still believed in the 'prior-warning' story. I was working on some glass for a village church in Gloucestershire at the time.

'I don't know why you bother!' said Mum.

'Why shouldn't I?'

'Tell me – why do you think they built the new cathedral?'

'Why do *you* think they did?'

'To give back to God what they gave to the Machine.'

'Or persuade themselves that it was never taken away?'

'In any case, they knew it had to be done.'

'And did they succeed?'

See for yourself.

Nobody minds a stained glass maker being confused. Confusion in a mathematician is unsettling, but it upsets nobody more than the mathematician. In recent months the bats of confusion have plagued us. Once we felt protected, as if they were behind a thick pane of glass: now we see that the glass is fragile. We used to think of Percy as the old one. Now he is dead and we will soon be grandparents.

You can see why it wasn't tactful of me to raise this matter at Kate's bedside. If you can see why I didn't restrain myself, then you are wiser than I. If you would have done otherwise then – congratulations! I shall give you a gilded codpiece for Christmas.

8

Dan was enthusiastic about the expedition to Mr Peabody's studio because Tilly had given him a grey flannel suit for Christmas. Although a little large, it was his first pair of long trousers: he suddenly felt grown-up and was eager to have this new status recorded in a photograph. Ruth had a new yellow pinafore and was allowed to tie matching bows in her hair, which she fancied to be particularly becoming. Her mother said she looked as pretty as a picture. Amy was proudly wearing her sister's old red frock. Everyone was happy, although Barbara wished she had managed to lose a little more weight since John's birth; to her dismay, she found it necessary to stay up rather late the night before, hurriedly putting gussets in the sides of her best blue dress.

It was Sarah who gave them the idea of having their picture taken. One day she unexpectedly said that she would like a photograph of them all to put on her mantelpiece. Although complaining that it was a foolish extravagance, Julius and Barbara agreed when they were alone together later that they ought to have one done. They made an appointment at the new studio in Jordan Well for January 6th, the earliest convenient day in the first new year after the war. Since the death of Barbara's grandfather the previous spring they had been living in Earlsdon Avenue. With Amy, who was already two, and John, who was born in the cold spell two months before, there were now four children including Dan, and, in deference to the needs of the growing family, David and Sarah had agreed simply to exchange houses.

Leaving work punctually at half-past twelve, Julius drove home in his second-hand Model T to pick them up himself. It was strange, he thought, how whenever he used to hear of people settling down, they seemed sad and stupid; he had pitied them, never imagining that he might settle down himself. And now, if he wasn't settled, who was? Yet life with a young family was often bewildering, and his earlier life, when he liked to think of himself as a little wild, seemed comically easy and calm in comparison. To be sure, there was a pattern to his life both at home and at work, but it was often observed more in the breach, existing as a grid on which to sort the surprises and new demands of each day than as a dependable routine.

Mr Peabody welcomed them at the door to his premises. 'Good afternoon, Mr Gallagher. Is this the family then? It's as fine looking a brood as ever I've seen, if I may say so! Come on in, Mrs Gallagher! And what's your name, young man?'

'Dan.'

Mr Peabody was almost completely bald. He had stretchy lips and his hands moved stiffly as he ushered them inside. Barbara entered first with John in her arms, then Dan and the girls, and finally Julius. On the stand where he hung his coat there was a bowler hat.

The walls of the show room were adorned with several pictures of bright-lipped ladies with milky skin. In some of them there was also a man standing at the lady's side with his hand on her shoulder. Behind the desk sat a lady whom Dan took to be Mrs Peabody. She smiled at each of the children in turn and then patted her tightly set hair, as if the movement of her face might have disturbed it. On the edge of her desk stood a notice facing outwards which read: *'Peabody Photographic Enterprises' will also Photograph You in the Location of your Choice.* On the wall behind her hung an imposing picture of the smiling photographer himself.

Mr Peabody gestured towards an open door on which was

written *STUDIO* and begged them to go through. Ruth was
holding Barbara's other hand now and Amy clutched at Julius's
trousers. Nor could Daniel help feeling the strangeness of the
room in which they found themselves but, just as boys who
wore suits didn't cry, so too they didn't hold hands or reveal
themselves to be intimidated. One corner was draped in white
sheets and on the floor was a stool; in the adjacent corner stood
a sofa, with black sheets on the wall behind. On the opposite
side of the room was a jumble of clothes and surprising objects
including a bicycle and numerous walking sticks. But the odd-
est thing of all was the merciless light, which proceeded from a
lamp in the middle of the room, with a shade like a large open
umbrella.

Julius imagined Peabody's leer as nubile models flaunted
themselves before his camera. 'Natty little set-up you've got
here, eh, Mr Peabody?' he said.

Mr Peabody closed the door behind him and, with brisk lat-
eral swings of his elbow, appeared to screw the heel of one
hand into the palm of the other. 'How kind you are, Mr
Gallagher. It's a modest place, but it serves. Please, make yourselves at home.' And he fussed nimbly around them until they
were gathered at the sofa.

Uncertain how to 'make herself at home', Barbara sat down.
Ruth promptly sat beside her and her feet stuck out straight
over the edge of the cushion.

'Good, Mrs Gallagher. How would you like to arrange
yourselves now?' Mr Peabody asked. 'I think that's a good idea
to have you sitting down with the baby on your lap, Mrs
Gallagher – what's the little one's name? John? – looking moth-
erly. There! And then, yes, quite so... What's your name, dear?'

'Woof.'

'Eh?'

Ruth sat further back in the sofa, as if trying to escape from
Mr Peabody's determined good cheer. 'Woof,' she repeated.

'Ruth,' Julius corrected her.

'Ruth, I see. You sit beside your Mummy, dear, that's nice, what a nice yellow frock that is, quite the dainty little miss aren't you? And Mr Gallagher, let's be having you on the sofa too, shall we? What do you think? Yes? Good. With your other daughter on your lap, I think — it is a little girl, is it?' he suddenly asked.

'Daughters generally are girls, I believe, Mr Peabody.'

'Quite so, Mr Gallagher, quite so! Most amusing! And what's your name, dear, if I might ask? Amy? Delightful! Well, Amy, I'm sure you'll be comfortable sitting like that on your father's lap won't you? You look perfectly charming, I must say, you with your hair in bows, Ruth dear, and Amy with your father's hands around you, showing us all your smart shoes. And now, young man,' he said, turning to Dan, 'where are we going to put you? Would you like to stand behind, or sit on one of the arms? Or would you prefer to sit on the floor in front?'

'Not behind,' Dan said at once.

'No, no, I quite see, not behind,' Mr Peabody agreed. 'On the arm then, or with your legs crossed, on the floor?'

Dan thought for a moment. As he imagined the picture, it would look better if he were sitting on an arm rather than on the floor. But if he were to sit on one of the arms he would have to choose between Barbara and Julius. Sitting on the floor, he decided, would be quite acceptable.

While Mr Peabody organized Dan so that his bare legs weren't showing when he sat and so he didn't obscure Ruth's feet, Barbara leaned across and touched Julius's shoulder. Although herself amused by Mr Peabody's quaint mixture of awkwardness and sensitivity towards the children, she was aware that her husband found him repulsive. She smiled gently at Julius now, and then touched her own hair to indicate that a strand of his hair was floating wild. He pressed his hand flat against his head and moved it back over his scalp with a frown. Then his forehead smoothed and he waited for his wife's response: she nodded, and he smiled at her. 'I thought men were supposed to lose their hair and look distinguished,' he said.

'What's that you say, Mr Gallagher?' Mr Peabody asked, stepping back towards the camera.

'I was admiring your baldness, Mr Peabody,' Julius answered; and the children at once began to giggle. 'You lead a carefree life.'

'Quite right, Mr Gallagher. It's a fact not always appreciated. Now children, Mrs Gallagher, are we ready?' And he ducked behind his camera. 'Do not say 'bald', because you'll look like goldfish. Say 'cheese'!'

While they all laughed, Mr Peabody's head disappeared behind his little black hood. 'Good! Very good!' he declared, and the camera clicked. 'Ruth, look at me, not at Dan, if you please! You look as if you're preparing to kick the back of his head!' The camera clicked again. 'Mr Gallagher, perhaps you'd take your hands away from Amy now, and then we'll see what she looks like between her head and her feet... and Ruth, my dear, sit still, I beg you! And see if you can't control your charming giggle just a little! Dan, would you like to close your mouth for a couple of shots? Good, Mrs Gallagher, you are blissfully composed! Immaculate, if I may say so! But I must report that your husband's hair is beginning to – how shall I put it? – beginning to...'

As he chattered, the camera clicked. From time to time he raised his head and inspected the group critically, as if considering whether to pose them more artistically, but he left them as they were. When he was satisfied he lifted his arm like a referee and snapped his fingers. 'That's it!' he announced, as if breaking a spell. 'It wasn't too painful, was it?'

'Not at all, Mr Peabody,' said Barbara.

'Splendid,' he continued. 'Shall we go straight on to the next thing then? Mr and Mrs Gallagher, you'd like some of the two of you alone, isn't that right? Might I suggest you come over to the white corner? Not the stool, perhaps, but the chair over there? Mr Gallagher, would you be so kind?' And he pointed to a simple wooden chair with a fox fur hanging over the back.

While Julius fetched the chair, laying aside the fur, the children rearranged themselves so that Dan was sitting in Barbara's place with John on his lap, carefully supported in the crook of his arm.

'Now be good while Daddy and I have our photograph taken,' said Barbara to the children on the sofa. 'Ruth, hold Amy's hand. And don't fidget.' Then she went to sit on the chair.

Behind her stood Julius, his long fingers reaching towards her collar-bone. His free hand attempted to flatten his hair, then hung by his side. Mr Peabody asked if they were ready and they smiled.

When he had finished they relaxed again. Dan was assiduously rocking John, who had begun to whimper.

'I'm coming now,' said Barbara, and she returned to the sofa and took the baby from Dan. 'There, here's Mummy,' she said, and John was quiet again.

'I'm weally not surpwised he was cwying,' said Ruth. 'Dan was weally wocking him!'

'Weally wocking him,' Amy echoed.

'Rreally Rrocking,' said Julius. 'ARround the Rragged Rrocks the Rragged Rrascal Rran!'

'Awound ve wagged wocks ve wagged...'

'That's enough now,' said Barbara. 'Dan was doing just right.'

It was agreed when they planned the expedition to Mr Peabody that Julius would leave at this stage, having exhausted his lunch hour. But they thought it a pity, while the opportunity was there, not to have some pictures taken of the children: and so Julius had organized a taxi to take his family home. It was worth the little extra, Barbara had said.

These photographs were to be informal and, after Julius's departure, Mr Peabody was confident of taking a delightful series of pictures. With their mother helping to organize them, he only had to make occasional suggestions. He could concentrate on catching the right instant. After photographing them individually and then in groups of two, when Dan took John on his knees he photographed them all together. Then Dan thought there should be a picture of the little ones alone and he laid the baby on Amy's lap and pulled Ruth away.

'Perfectly charming! Perfectly charming!' uttered Mr Peabody. 'And now why don't you sit with them, Mrs Gallagher?'

Barbara did so; then she gathered up John and stood up, for they had surely done enough. But Dan had joined Amy on the sofa. He sat on her feet and she squealed, whereupon Ruth jumped onto the sofa and tried to sit on Dan.

'Children! Children!' cried Barbara.

Mr Peabody continued to photograph them zealously.

'That's enough now!' said Barbara, pulling Ruth away with her free hand. But the commotion hadn't degenerated into a squabble and, as the session ended, she registered the dry eyes all round with relief.

The taxi-driver was waiting in the show room. 'Are we all ready to go then?' he said, smiling at the children as they filed out of the studio.

When they said goodbye to Mr Peabody he gave them each a boiled sweet from a glass jar, except for John who hadn't got any teeth yet – Barbara said thank you, but it wasn't good for him. 'And you'll send the bill to my husband, won't you?' she added on the threshold.

'It's already settled, Mrs Gallagher,' said the lady behind the desk.

'Is it, Miss Simmonds?' said Mr Peabody.

'Mr Gallagher settled up as he was leaving.'

'How very prompt and kind of him!' said Mr Peabody.

Barbara felt herself blush. There was nothing mean about her husband. Even if he didn't like Mr Peabody, in the end he behaved better towards him than a friend might.

At the kerb, glittering in the pale, wintry afternoon sun, a large black car waited to take them home. Dan and Ruth were excited to be going in a taxi. Ruth could only remember once going in one before, while Dan considered himself something of an expert because he had often travelled in one with Tilly. Amy had never been in a taxi, according to Ruth.

The door was open and they were about to climb in when they were accosted from the other side of the street:

'Hoi, Barbara! Barbara! Hoi!'

Barbara stepped back onto the pavement and looked up. Advancing towards her, as if she had been waiting in the scaffolding on the other side of the road, was Rose Evans.

'Rose!' Barbara cried. 'What a treat!'

Since her marriage, Barbara had scarcely seen Rose at all. This was less a result of the change in her own life than in Rose's life, for Rose became a nurse in 1940 and thereafter had visited Coventry infrequently on leave. Nor did she return at the end of the war. Instead, she settled in London, and Barbara had heard that she was engaged to be married – to an ex-RAF man, apparently.

They embraced, taking care not to squash John who was in Barbara's arms. 'Look at you, with all your children!' said Rose, disengaging herself.

'Yes,' said Barbara, slightly pink. 'This is Dan, this is Ruth. That's Amy, and this one's John. This is Rose Evans, an old friend of Mummy's,' she explained to the children.

'So where are you off to so grandly in your taxi?'

'We're just going home. We've been having our picture taken, what with the New Year. But Julius had to go straight back to work.'

'Julius, yes! I haven't seen him for years! How long have you been married now, Barbara? Five, six years?'

'Five.'

'How time flies!'

'You're engaged now yourself, Rose, I hear?'

'I'm getting married in a fortnight. To an airman called Philip Sheen. I'm just going to meet him as it happens.' Rose paused. 'I tell you what, Barbara, why don't you come with me? I'd love you to meet him. He's coming to pick me up in his car by the cathedral, in Bayley Lane, and then we're going on to my parents in Stivichall. We can easily drop you all off.'

Barbara glanced nervously at the taxi-driver, who had turned his back. 'I don't know,' she said. 'The children were looking forward to the taxi ride, and the little ones are rather tired...'

'But you'll still be going in a car,' Rose said to Dan and Ruth. 'Wouldn't you like to go in a brave pilot's car? To be driven by Flight Lieutenant Sheen? And he won't be late,' she added, stroking Amy's curly hair. 'He's never late.'

Barbara was curious to meet Philip Sheen.

'Do you mind awfully?' she asked the taxi-driver.

'It's only half the afternoon I've wasted,' he answered. 'Suit yourself.'

Barbara fished in her bag to give him something for his trouble. He thanked her brusquely.

'Well then, shall we go?' said Rose. 'It's only just round the corner. Sarcastic ape,' she added. 'He's done very nicely out of you, Barbara, I saw what you gave him.'

As they set off up the street, Barbara took Amy's hand. She had to call out to stop the older ones from running ahead.

'We're goin to go in an aewolpane! We're goin to go in an aewolpane!' Ruth chanted.

'No we're not, stupid, we're going in a car but a pilot – that's an aeroplane driver in case you don't know – is going to drive us,' said Daniel, impatiently striding away.

Ruth was unabashed. 'We're goin to go in an aewolpane!' she repeated.

'Slow down, you two! Stop running off!'

When they reached Bayley Lane and found that Mr Sheen wasn't there, Daniel asked if they might go into the ruins to play. Barbara felt it wouldn't be fair to turn down the request. Nor was it in her best interests: they would only grow impatient if they were made to stand around; the ruins were safe and she could keep an eye on them there. Meanwhile, she could chat with Rose.

Dan and Ruth had been among the cathedral's ruins many times, but never before unaccompanied. Barbara was nearby now, but she was outside the walls; although aware of her presence, they couldn't see her. And so, exhilarated by a sense of freedom untainted by loss, they ran up the central path and cut among the tracks trodden through the years over the rubble. Within the high walls they were secure in a private playground: the heaped-up ruins had been provided, it seemed, for their pleasure alone, adjuncts to their own games. The cross of charred beams in the apse was an exotic sculpture, a focus for their swooping and chasing as, arms outstretched, they enacted an air raid.

'Boom! boom!' cried Dan. 'Here I come!' And he ran down a path, gathering momentum, towards Ruth. 'Out of the way or you'll be dead! Watch out! Bombs away! Boom! Boom! Boom!' he cried as he raced up the flat strip in the centre; and then, as he approached the apse: 'Now I'm coming in to land!'

Ruth followed him, laughing and shrieking with excitement. She couldn't run so fast on her short legs, but Dan thought she acquitted herself admirably. 'Well done,' he said. 'Now we'll go bombing down to the other end!' And off they went, Dan in the lead and Ruth losing ground behind him but eagerly repeating, 'Boom! Boom! Boom!'

It was the most satisfactory terrain on which to play this game. They could see the damage wrought by their bombs. The field of action was wide but clearly defined by the walls, enabling them to play on a magnificent scale without the game losing coherence. Their sorties had a beginning and an end; the enemy could be located, and couldn't escape. Secluded, they could nurture their fantasy and mould their triumphs. Outside, if they wanted, there was an appreciative audience.

Through the excitement, Dan was aware of an increasingly urgent need to urinate. When he could ignore it no longer and looked around for somewhere to relieve himself, the sense of privacy which he had been enjoying suddenly vanished and he felt exposed. He could go behind one of the larger mounds, but he would be visible through the window if anyone happened to be passing by. If he went on the other side of the mound so that he was hidden from without, he would still be visible from within. His difficulty wasn't simply fear of being seen as he peed, nor that he knew that this ought strictly to be done in a lavatory. It arose from a sudden, overpowering sense that he ought not to do it in this place. The cathedral was in ruins and so nobody could mind about them playing aeroplanes. But peeing here might make people extremely, if unaccountably, angry.

One of the few pieces of masonry still intact was the font, and the space between it and the wall seemed to be better screened than anywhere else. As he ran towards it, Dan was already pulling at his trouser buttons. He halted with his back to the wall and, with a voluptuous surge of relief, he started to piss towards the base of the font. He heard Ruth call his name. Then he heard a man's voice.

He raised his eyes from the splattering arc and looked over his shoulder. Approaching at a furious half-run was a clergyman in a black cassock. He was shaking his arm and his face was swollen and red, like a radish. 'How dare you? How dare you! Godless brat, I've been watching you!'

Dan tried to stop pissing and tuck his penis back into his trousers, but in his frightened haste he misjudged the manoeuvre and he felt the hot liquid down his right trouser-leg. Shame prickled behind his eyes.

'Vicious little animal! Of all the...! This is the cathedral! That is the font!' the clergyman shouted, and seized Dan by the ear. 'Now I've seen it all! What is your name, boy?'

As he was pulled up roughly towards the man's stomach, Dan caught a sharp whiff of his musty garments. The pain in his ear forced out his tears. 'Dan Flasch!' he cried. 'Ah! Let me go! Dan Flasch!'

'What do you mean, 'Damn Flash'? Are you swearing at me, boy?'

'It's my name! It is! Dan Flasch!'

'This is intolerable! Where's your mother? Who's your father?'

'My mother's in Germany – '

The clergyman yanked on Dan's ear.

Dan howled. He felt as if his whole body was concentrated in his ear, and he raised himself on tiptoe, struggling to follow the direction in which he was being pulled. His eyes were tight shut, and now he opened them and saw the man's sweating face leaning over his own. In terror he tried to recoil, increasing the pain, and he yelled again.

Mr Sheen had just arrived. The uproar burst as Barbara was being introduced: she apologized and hurried away, clutching John to her shoulder; Amy toddled after her. 'What's up? What's the matter?' Barbara called as she drew near.

'Does this wretch belong to you?' said the clergyman, releasing Dan as he turned towards her.

'Yes. What's he done? What have you done, Daniel?'

'I did a wee,' he said, and began to cry, his hand pressed to his ear.

'This is a cathedral, Ma'am, not a public convenience. I suggest you explain the difference to your son, if you love God; and if you don't love Him but respect the community, I still suggest you explain it. If you don't respect our community then I suggest you leave it. Isn't that why we fought the war? Go to Germany, where your son claims he comes from. Not only urinating in the cathedral, but pretending to bomb it! It is an insult! An outrage!' he cried. 'Now take him away from here!'

Barbara took Dan's wrist and led him rapidly away, more rapidly than he could comfortably walk, so that he felt himself being dragged and he had to stumble and half-run to keep up. 'What a thing to do!' said Barbara. 'Whatever possessed you? What a thing to do!' And then, more ominously: 'You just wait until I tell Julius!' She felt her skin smarting from the humiliation before the clergyman, and the anticipated shame before Rose and her fiancé; she herself was shocked by what Daniel had done.

Mr Sheen was leaning on the open door of his car. He was a tall man with shiny black hair and a neatly trimmed moustache. 'Well, well,' he said. 'What was that all about?'

'Dan was found doing what he shouldn't in the cathedral,' answered Barbara, and as she spoke she heard the coyness of her expression, but she couldn't bring herself to state the crime openly. 'I'm so sorry!'

'Dan was doin a wee!' said Ruth, who had been hovering at the fringes of the incident.

'Shut up, Ruth!'

'So this is your eldest?' said Rose. 'Dan?'

'Well, he's not actually ours,' said Barbara, 'but yes, he's the eldest.'

'Don't worry about the accident,' said Rose, looking at his sodden trousers. 'Say hello to Captain Sheen and then hop in and we'll take you all home.'

Although Rose gave no indication of hearing Barbara's disclaimer, Dan had heard it. Rose's smile seemed to mock him. Introducing him to a pilot in the present circumstances was a further taunt. Even Ruth was making fun of him. In a turmoil of humiliation and self-pity, he groaned and began to weep.

'Now stop that!' said Barbara, 'Or the others will all start!'

John and Amy promptly began to cry.

'Stop that, I said!' she cried. 'Get in! Get in the car!' And she pushed in Dan, then Ruth and Amy.

'Barbara, Barbara, it's perfectly all right,' said Rose.

'It is not all right!' she snapped. 'I'm so sorry, Rose. Mr Sheen, I'm so sorry!' And she climbed into the back seat beside the children. 'Now sit still, all of you! And stop grizzling Daniel! How old are you?'

When Rose and Mr Sheen had got into the car and closed their doors, a faint scent of urine was apparent. Mr Sheen discreetly wound his window down.

'How could you?' said Barbara.

'I couldn't help it,' Dan sobbed at last. 'I *had* to go, and then he came and picked me up by the ear and...' The resulting wet leg was beginning to itch. Although he didn't feel that he merited this disgrace, he knew there was no chance of justifying himself. His situation was irredeemable, and again his tears flowed: no pride was left to him for which to hold them back.

On reaching Earlsdon Avenue, Barbara apologized profusely once more to Rose and Mr Sheen and said that she hoped to see them again soon in happier circumstances. Privately, she hoped that she wouldn't see them again for a long while. She was furious with Daniel. Frustrated in her desire to impress, she had responded ineptly to his behaviour and made a fool of herself. But she was also genuinely distressed by his action. While she understood his urgent need to relieve himself and couldn't blame him for that, the fact that a clergyman had been so cross with him somehow nullified her own understanding and rendered Dan automatically in the wrong. She was responsible for him, after all, and so the clergyman's wrath reflected on her; and a clergyman's wrath must be justified – at least, it couldn't be ignored. She felt that she ought to punish him.

Although angry with Dan, Barbara was afraid that the sympathy which she also felt for him would corrupt her self-disgust so that she took it out on him. Alone, she would be able to recover her temper. So she told Dan to wash himself and sent him to bed. When Julius came home, she could explain the situation and he would be able to restore the peace. It wouldn't be the first time he'd done so.

Ruth was told that she was on no account to go into Dan's room. At first she had no desire to because, in his present mood, he wasn't promising company. However, she was curious about him and played with her marbles on the blue linoleum outside his door. Her game wasn't very energetic: from time to time she pushed a marble idly down the passage or aimed at a cluster of stationary ones; or she rolled one at his door. His crying stopped and she heard him muttering. She knew he was aware of her but he sounded as if he didn't care. 'It's not fair!' she heard him shout all of a sudden.

She lay on the floor of the passage, listening to sounds within his room. He wasn't lying on his bed but moving about, banging around: she could hear him opening his drawers and rummaging in the wooden box where he kept his private things. 'It's not it's not it's not fair!' he repeated.

Ruth stood up. Still holding two marbles in one hand, with the other she touched the door handle and pressed her eye to the keyhole. She caught a glimpse of his old brown suitcase open on his bed, and she was afraid.

'Dan, what're you doin?' she said.

'Packing. Stop spying.'

'I'm not! I'm only peepin fwough ve keyhole cos I was wowied,' Ruth answered. 'Whewe are you goin?'

'Away.'

'But where?'

'To find my own mother and father.'

'But you can't! You can't just go and find vem!'

'How do you know? Nobody wants me here.'

'You can't go!' said Ruth, her voice rising with her anxiety. It seemed to her that Dan was already gone for ever, and the prospect of life without him suddenly pierced her like a splinter of glass. 'But you can't, you can't go! It wasn't your fault, Dan!'

'I'm going,' he said obstinately.

Ruth heard the suitcase shutting, she saw his legs stretched out as he sat on it. Then he put on his overcoat and suddenly she burst into tears and ran downstairs, her feet slipping and scrambling in agitation.

'Mummy!' she cried, 'Mummy!' And, entering the kitchen, where Barbara was rolling out some pastry for a steak and kidney pudding, she grabbed at her mother's skirt, dropping her marbles with a clatter. 'Mummy! Dan's runnin away! He's packed his suitcase! Quickly! He says he's goin to find his own mummy and daddy!'

'What? Oh my Lord!' said Barbara. And after wiping her hands on her apron, she pulled it off and dropped it on the floor.

The sound of her stamping feet as she hurried upstairs reminded her that she used to move so lightly up this staircase, and she was filled with a sudden, intense regret. She was appalled both at the mire into which her temper had sucked her and also at the nature of her responsibility.

'Dan!' she called as she ran down the passage. 'Dan!'

When she opened his door she saw him dressed in his overcoat, scarf and flat cap, holding his suitcase in his hand; it had once belonged to Tilly. Kneeling, she put her arms round him, beseeching him.

'Whatever are you doing?' she cried. 'What's all this silliness?'

Dan shuddered. His chest lifted and he breathed very rapidly as he looked at Barbara. 'I want to go and find my own mummy and daddy,' he said.

'But Dan, Dan, you... it's not as simple as that! You can't just run off! This is your home! What would you do, out there in the world, how would you find them? I know you're a big boy now but you're still only eight...!'

'I'll find them if I want to.'

'I'm sure, but... perhaps not for a long time. This is where you belong for now. We'll go and find your parents together, if that's what you want, when the time comes.'

Dan was silent. His cheeks were flushed and the skin under his eyes puckered.

'Is that what you want?' said Barbara softly, trying to hold his eyes steady. But his gaze shifted to her shoulder.

'You said I'm not your son to... to Rose. And I'm not, am I?' His strength was unravelling. His voice faltered and Barbara felt his ribs heave with a sob. 'I couldn't help what I did!' he added plaintively, and his tears at last broke free.

'I know you couldn't, love, I know you couldn't. What I said to Rose, I didn't think, you know you're just the same as our son; you're Ruth's brother, Amy's and John's brother. Think how upset they'd be if you left them like this, never mind horrid old me!'

'Then why were you so angry with me?'

'Because you shouldn't have done it there, Dan dear!'

'I couldn't help it! I *had* to!'

'I know. But the vicar couldn't see that you couldn't help it,' she said, conscious of her specious logic as she avoided admitting to the part played by her own temper.

'He was horrid! He hurt me!'

'Yes, he was horrid. He shouldn't have done that.' Barbara felt as if she had reached firm ground, and she changed the subject now more confidently. 'How about coming downstairs and helping me with some cooking?' she suggested.

Dan nodded, his body bucking with sobs; only then did Barbara remove his cap and help him take off his overcoat and scarf. She was intrigued to know precisely what he had put in his suitcase, but she felt it would be wrong to open it.

The rest of the afternoon proceeded quietly and, by the time Julius got home, John was asleep in his cradle and the others were bathed and gathered in their dressing-gowns in the sitting-room. Ruth had a red dressing-gown with a hood, which had been given to her by Julius's mother.

Julius always enjoyed the time between his return from work and the children's bedtime. Sometimes he would read them a story; more often he would chat with them and play games – he had recently taught Dan to play draughts and halma. Inevitably, today they talked about the photograph session, and the unfortunate sequel was soon revealed to him.

When Ruth and Amy were sent to bed, he intercepted Barbara as she was following them upstairs. 'Dan was really saying he would find his own mother and father?' he said.

Barbara nodded, pressing her lips together tightly. The colour in her face was uneven and her eyelids were sluggish, as if she hadn't slept for two days.

Julius put his hand on hers as it rested on the banister. 'This has got to stop,' he said. 'I'm going to talk to him.'

'Now?'

'Yes.'

She nodded and went upstairs. After tucking in her daughters and saying good night, she went into Dan's room. She longed to do something special for him, but she knew he would be sensitive to anything she did and she was afraid of seeming to intrude. Her position was delicate at the moment. She looked at his suitcase sitting forlornly on the floor but dismissed the idea of unpacking it; she even resisted opening it. Seeing that his bed was very rumpled, she straightened it. Then she decided to fetch clean sheets from the linen cupboard on the landing and make his bed afresh.

'Dan, old chap, I think we ought to have a bit of a chat, you and I,' said Julius. 'Come here and sit beside me on the sofa.'

Leaning back himself, with his leg up on his footstool, Julius looked thoroughly at his ease. His left arm lay along the back of the sofa, ready to rest on Dan's shoulders; his right arm hung loosely in his lap. Only a slight frown betrayed that he was a little nervous. He had long felt that Dan should be told something about his parents, but the difficulty of knowing how much to say and the lack of a suitable moment had made him procrastinate. Was it really his duty to speak? There seemed to be so many new duties these days. Could Dan be expected to understand and cope with such information? Julius had often considered ways of talking about it but now, when it had to be done, he could remember none of the careful euphemisms. When Dan sat beside him he touched his shoulders with his arm, feeling their fragility. He loved the glossy black hair beside him; the white, almost transparent skin of Dan's face and his heavy lower lip. He felt the latent bitterness in the boy which would surely emerge if he were betrayed; and he understood now the drained, hurt look on his wife's face. It was important to be honest, he thought, but it was essential to preserve him from knowledge of the suffering.

'You're not to worry about what happened this afternoon, eh? I would have done the same in your position. Perhaps I'll go and do it. I'd like to see him try and pick me up by the ear.'

Dan smiled wanly at the thought of the clergyman picking up Julius, who was several inches taller, by the ear.

'Perhaps he wouldn't try it. I'd just have to go on peeing until he did. But I'm afraid I wouldn't be able to pee for long enough.'

Dan chuckled.

'Still, he was quite right in a way. It's not a good idea to pee in the cathedral if you can help it. Whether or not it upsets God we can't tell, but it upsets other people, which can be a nuisance. That's all it is. Nobody around here's cross with you.'

'Barba was,' said Dan.

'No, she was upset. People can behave as if they're cross when they're upset. Honestly, Dan, she's not.'

Dan looked into Julius's steady grey eyes.

Julius turned towards the little table beside him and picked up his cigarettes. Before he lit one, he touched one of his straggly eyebrows with it. 'But that's not really what I wanted to talk about,' he said. 'What I want to talk about is much more important. It's about you setting off to find your mum and dad.'

Dan sniffed, looking at his toes. He knew that Julius had been working towards this.

'You know that we would all be very, very sorry indeed to see you go. But that's not the only reason you're here. If it was possible for you to go back to your parents, of course that's where you should go if you want to; we all know that. But I think it's time you were put in the picture a bit more, don't you? Now the war's over, you must wonder why it's not possible for you to go to them, and where they are? Don't you?'

'Yes,' Dan admitted.

'And what do you think the answer is?'

'I think they're probably dead,' said Dan slowly.

'You're a brave chap to say so, and it's as well to be straightforward like that. And now, since you're a sensible fellow I'm going to treat you like a sensible fellow and be straightforward with you. All right?'

Dan nodded, and as he blinked his eyelashes cast tiny shadows on his lower lids.

'Good. Now hold my finger and pull it if you want me to shut up. That's right. Have a practice if you like. Ow! Splendid! Now, as you know, your parents are German and also Jewish. That means that you were born a German, but you're not a German now because you've lived in England almost all your life. You could become a German again, if you liked, but for the moment you're English. And you're still Jewish. Now one of the things that happened in the war was this: as you may know, Hitler didn't like the Jews and he put them in camps, where almost all of them died. When the war ended last year, the ones who survived were released and helped to get back to their families, or what was left of them. We don't know what happened to your parents and your brothers because we don't know for sure which camp they were taken to or even if they were taken to a camp. But you must believe me when I say that we've been trying to find out. Do you believe me?'

'Yes.'

'Good. Well then, it is just possible that they're still alive. Just possible. But the chance is so small that it's hardly big enough to be called a chance. By now, if they were alive, we would have found them or they would have found us. They know where to look for us, after all, even if we don't know exactly where to look for them. I won't say they're definitely dead, that I know they are dead, because I don't actually *know*. But you must assume they are dead, Dan. You must accept that we are your family, and Tilly too, like it or not. We like it, and I hope you do too. There. Now I've finished. And you didn't once pull on my finger.'

Dan pulled now but instead of pulling away he drew himself towards Julius, inviting Julius to hold him in his arms. He seemed to be resting.

'Tilly came and got me,' he said after a moment.

'Yes.'

'She brought me...'

'Yes.'

'Julius, it was lucky Tilly came and got me, wasn't it?'

'Yes, Dan, it was lucky.'

Barbara entered. Julius smiled at her; he was exhausted.

'Would you like me to carry you up to bed, Dan?' he offered, 'Like I used to?'

Dan raised his head and smiled softly.

Julius's foot hurt as he picked up the slight boy. 'My, but you're a heavy brute these days!' he said.

When Dan made to kiss Barbara good night she smiled and said that she was coming upstairs too.

Julius tucked Dan into his clean bed and Barbara sat by him until he was asleep.

9

So, she has woken. The ground mysteriously shifted, the entombing blackness rolled aside; Kate's trapped consciousness is free. It is marvellous news!

Yet for a while we must be patient. They say she is confused, she needs quiet; for the present she remains in the doctors' care and we are discouraged from visiting her. The fires of her memory are dim; we do not know if, deprived of the bracing air, the fibres of her mind have withered. She must be tested, and rested: only then, when her fitness is judged as secure as can be, will she come among us again. Meanwhile our thoughts will run beyond her mere recovery as we look for the unlocking of something new, hopeful that the jolt which nearly killed her has released an unseen bolt on our world.

And what of this, my narrative? My tongue is unhinged, suspended.

Jake, I am embarrassed to talk about Kate now. I feel her watching over me, saying, 'I can speak for myself.' My speculations seem impertinent and I no longer know how to address you...

I recall that night when I sat on your balcony while you and Kate made love indoors. As I stared into the fading darkness a shape appeared in the seemingly blank sky, and even then I wanted to tell you something about myself and Mum, something about yourself. Invited by you after Kate's accident, I began. No doubt I could rewrite it all, constructing different windows through which to look at the past, but I shall let it be;

I'm wary of dismantling and altering windows which already occupy their place. Anticipating whatever follows, however, is like having all the pieces for a new window laid out on my work-bench except for the enclosing lead, which was cast badly and has to be melted down. The picture isn't fixed and if I'm not careful it will scatter: but the movement is liberating and exhilarating. A halo can be removed and a saint becomes a man, and the man – why not? – can be given a yellow robe.

Have you ever read Theophilus's treatise on stained glass? There's no obvious reason why you should have, since you don't make stained glass, but its interest transcends its subject. I first read it when I went to Lisbon a few years ago, after Tilly died. The hotel in which I stayed was on the side of one of the hills facing the sea. From my balcony I could see the tiled roofs and the gardens clogged with refuse descending to the shore; beyond them was the languid, hazy sea. The harbour was some way off to the right: I could just make out the shoulder of land embracing it. It was like looking at a transparency with the light shining on it. I remember watching the ships, thinking of Tilly, distracting myself from time to time with another paragraph of Theophilus. Although he wrote early in the twelfth century, I was surprised to find that much of his technical advice remained pertinent. But some of the respects in which it's out of date are themselves fascinating, and oddly amusing. A sentence I always remember is: 'Do not use yellow glass much in robes except in halos and in those places where gold should be used in painting.' It is curious to see 'halos' in such a context. The author is confident of the relationship between his craft and his readers: if they make stained glass then they will be portraying saints, and if they wish to make good stained glass then they must avoid excessive use of yellow. Note the use of 'should' in 'where gold should be used in painting'. The author is announcing rules which he doesn't expect to be questioned. The techniques of stained glass scarcely changed for centuries but art history tells us that the aesthetics underwent a typical shift. From making images which invited contemplation of the Eternal, craftsmen began to create figures with more concern for their particularity. In the fourteenth and fifteenth centuries, stained glass reveals a discreet foppery, a subtle invitation to the eye to behold what is ephemeral. It displays itself – and, as the years accumulate, this develops into our cult of the individual. This is what we are told: but if you look at figures in medieval stained glass, you will often find that the characterization is very much more acute and attentive than in later glass.

Kate's regained voice will rouse the foot-soldiers of psychology; I'm afraid she will be scarcely audible against the sound of their marching. And when they have formed their squares, still chanting to keep their spirits up, they will stand firm together against all naïve or inconvenient answers. So much for the cult of the individual. The phrase itself is incoherent. Which individual? Or is it the Individual, i.e. not an individual at all but the negation of one, the general idea of the individual? It's astonishing how the Individual can go on gratifying us long after any individuals have been lost from sight.

Tilly's death disturbed me unexpectedly. I don't mean that I wasn't fond of her: I was devoted to her. But not since I was a small child had I seen her as often as our intimate link might have prompted. When she was based at Bletchley she visited us regularly, but after Percy's return she slipped from the frame of our lives. He got a job building railways in Nigeria and she went with him. All her experience, all the groundwork for a career, was thrown away and she went off to be an expatriate. It's impossible for me to believe she was content but, I suppose, she loved Percy; and, after the loneliness and hardship of the war years, the prospect of an utterly new life must have been alluring. We'd see them between postings, when they came to Coventry for a week before hopping off again to Egypt or Venezuela; sometimes they'd join us for Christmas. Percy grew more relentlessly jovial and patronizing: we could see him age but he seemed never to notice that we grew older, as if he expected time to stand still for him in the Old Country. And, though Tilly was always responsive, she seemed to resist the involvement of earlier years. I think she guarded against it, as if it might threaten her decision to be abroad with Percy: so our familiarity with her faded. On the occasions when we visited them we were on Good Behaviour. When Mum went to see them in Jeddah in 1964, she said it was like going to stay with friends of friends. It wasn't that she didn't feel welcome, nor merely that their world was foreign to her: she felt that she was quite alien to them. In my case, of course, it was different. I remember going out to the Middle East a couple of times before then to stay with them. It was on those visits that I discovered the little I know of my background and infancy. In a way, the conditions were ideal. There was so little to do out there in those days, even for a man. As a woman, Tilly was virtually confined to the house, and her friends were wives of other foreign workers. God knows what she did all day when I wasn't there – endless canasta parties – it makes me cry to think of the waste. So, when I was there, nothing was more obvious than to speak of the past. But it was always of the past. I didn't have much else in common with the groomed, slightly bitter expat that Tilly had become.

And then she died, very quickly, of cancer. One day Percy telephoned to say that she'd gone into hospital for some tests after complaining of chest pains. The following week she was flown home; two months later she was dead. We said at the time, perhaps more in an effort to console ourselves, that the release was fortunate. My opinion hasn't changed: for most of the time she was almost unrecognizable because of the drugs they gave her to quell the debilitating pain. To Ruth and John and Amy her death was never very upsetting. It was unlikely to be so, for to them she wasn't a close figure. But grief stupefied me. I suppose I was dimly aware that, having no children of her own, Tilly regarded me as the child she might have had, and the role she had played in my life certainly emphasized this.

Considering that I was ignorant of the extent of that role for a long time, it was probably of greater importance to her than it was to me: in my life, she was replaced by Barba; in her life, my place remained empty. The terms of her will confirmed all this and made me suddenly conscious of things I knew but on which I hadn't reflected. I owed my life to Tilly: it was as simple as that. At considerable risk to herself she had saved me, then taken me into her home without regard for her own tranquillity or expense. Had I ever shown due appreciation for this? Of course not. And I found myself struggling beneath a crushing weight of guilt, appalled at the inadequacy of my love for her. It seemed obscenely unjust that she should die while I lived. One couldn't help resenting that old Percy – though shrinking a little more each year both in body and in mind and himself desperate (but not dying) to join dear Tilly – remained alive for almost two more decades.

Curiously, Mum was always more aware than I was of the possible effects of my background on me. But when Tilly died she still didn't know what to do with me any more than I did. In the end, I announced that I would go on holiday alone. Perhaps she was a little hurt but she agreed that it might be a good idea. So off I went to Lisbon, where I sat for hours on a balcony gazing out to real or imagined ships. I wonder if you remember when I went? You were quite young at the time, about nine. I was only gone for a week, which wasn't so unusual in any case. I'm sure you didn't know the reasons for my trip – at least I hope you didn't – and it was more likely the present I brought you that marks it in your mind than anything else. God knows why I went to Lisbon. In part, I think, it was because I knew nothing whatever about it. Without preconceptions, I was free to do and think and feel as I liked. The blankness of the sea seemed to match my state of mind: my memory retains the image of a ship but I associate no direction with it. It's neither coming in nor going out, just suspended.

I remember dwelling on that day when I was caught pissing

in the ruined cathedral. Despite all that had happened since, both in Coventry and in my own life, it didn't feel remote. My humiliation and Barba's violence were still fresh, though maybe I was grafting subsequent feelings on to the event. Julius's and Barba's gentleness were fresh, too, and so was the force of their revelation to me about myself. I think they knew that life couldn't be quite the same for me afterwards – not worse, nor better, just different. And they were right. I don't mean to exaggerate the immediate impact. I didn't wake up a different person – but in retrospect I saw that I was awakened. For until that day I'd felt that Tilly, not Barba, was my acting mother: I was on a sort of long loan to Barba and Julius but I belonged really to Tilly. That evening I learned that I belonged to nobody. There was a place for me with Barba and Julius. I was welcome and they would always treat me as if I was one of them: but ultimately my destiny was in my own hands, my home wherever I wished to make it. An ironic attitude for me to hold if you consider the fate of my parents.

It will not suddenly become easy now that Kate has woken up. Don't let your fixed ideas and bunched desires blind you to her wishes – as they blinded you to my presence in your flat. You are very good at getting what you want in material terms – you have a responsible and lucrative job which, despite your age, has already brought you a splendid flat and a fast car. I suppose it was partly this talent for concentrating your energies that made you forget I was coming to stay with you. But you won't get anything worth having if you forget Kate in this way. Now that she's conscious, attend to her voice.

Perhaps I ought to have revealed myself that night. Perhaps I was foolishly deferential to you in the circumstances. I'd seen Amy at Percy's funeral and she always makes me feel benevolent. Had I come forward, who knows what might not have happened? Because the more I think about it, the harder I find it to believe that you never knew I was there – even allowing that you somehow managed to miss my messages and weren't forewarned. The door wasn't double-locked, my bag was at the foot of the stairs, I was sitting quite openly on your balcony *all night*! I must assume you didn't realize until later, of course, but then – didn't you suddenly wake up to my presence? And then flee, in a storm of embarrassed recrimination from Kate, the kindling of an argument which exploded again so terribly six weeks later?

Now I'm urging you to listen to me, not yourself. But if only I had listened to myself that night!

No. I will not regret it. It's nonsense to compare the situations.

10

The new Precinct is split at the top by a pair of flaking, dank staircases which lead to the grey and neglected upper level. If you stand facing down the incline and you're persistent – or unkind – enough to scrape away the birdshit and the skin of urban grime with your toe, you will find a picture of a phoenix. I went there recently and was reminded that I too, like a dove, was once bewitched by this trapped bird. It's like rubbing at the filthy glass of an old photograph frame and discovering the clear picture of a child. The subject is flat and dull if you don't recognize who it is but, if you see that it's yourself, then it comes to life as a sudden, intense image of a vanished world. You look at the haircut and you remember your mother briskly trimming your fringe; you look at the shorts and you tremble once again at the peppery touch of the fabric on your infant thighs. It is a window in the screen of time that separates you from your childhood.

*

There were to have been fireworks but Donald Gibson persuaded the committees otherwise. He hurried up to Yorkshire with a friend and the next day they returned triumphantly with a lump of Westmorland stone, in which the friend obligingly carved a phoenix. It was called the Levelling Stone and it was laid with great pomp among the ruins at the culmination of the official Victory Celebrations on June 8th, 1946.

'The idea is that the city will rise again from the ruins, like the bird from the ashes,' Julius explained to Ruth and me.

We stood behind the white tape barriers and listened to edifying speeches which promised a glorious future for the magnificent city we would build. The crowd cheered and clapped and I threw my cap in the air shouting 'Hoorah!' I imagined the huge bird floundering in the wreckage, struggling to its feet and then surging forwards and upwards with one huge, powerful, languid flap of its wings: and I imagined buildings breaking through the ground with a mighty heave, lurching to their full height like bountiful knights come to reward us.

A thin drizzle began. Now the furtively carried umbrellas were pointed at the clouds and opened with smug flourishes. 'June already and weather like this! You'd think we deserved a bit of sunshine, wouldn't you?'

Tin shacks still occupied the wasteland like a freak crop, manured by thick heaps of rubble. Wooden scaffolding clung to the tottering walls like a hideous, rampant creeper, as if a seed from some unearthly jungle had strayed here.

In a room scarcely changed since the Black Prince's time, Gibson's new designs were displayed for all to see. Scandalous! said some – the old street plan had vanished! Brilliant! said others – now there was a splendidly ordered shopping-precinct: released from its ill-fitting past, Coventry could lead the way into the future. From his seat on the City Council David deplored it all, but he was overruled.

Stepping across a ditch into an earth-floored hut, I asked for three pounds of potatoes. Seated on up-ended crates, a group of men barked at each other through the yellowish fug of cigarette smoke. 'Have to have separate access,' said Mr Timms. 'Customers in the front, suppliers in the back. Make it nice while we've got the chance, that's what I say.' And he crushed his cigarette stub against his wooden leg.

In the butcher's, I put my coupons in a fan on the makeshift counter and waited for Mrs Solesbury to finish her conversation with the previous customer. She interrupted herself: 'What's it today, young man?'

'Bacon and sausages please, Mrs Solesbury.'

'Well,' she concluded to the other, wiping her hands on her stained apron, 'it's my view slaughterhouses should be kept away from the shopping centre. Who wants to hear pigs squealing in the back while they're buying their bacon, eh, Dan? Besides, it's not hygienic.'

In a Lyons tea shop in Jordan Well, looking up towards the wrecked cathedral, I overheard: 'I do like them nice ceilings they 'ave in cathedrals. And plenty of stained glass, that's what I like.'

Going into town one Saturday morning with Julius – walking, because Barba needed the car – we had to keep our eyes to the ground to avoid tripping among the pot-holes. 'Why don't you get another car? The Astleys have got two,' I said. The Astleys were our neighbours. Like everyone else, they always talked about cars. 'I think we might get another one,' said Julius, 'All in good time.' And we did.

The local paper said Coventry was a boom-town. With the new decade, it said, we were entering a new phase of prosperity. Julius had been on some committee to do with re-employing those who had worked in munitions factories. Most people found good new jobs, he told us. For it wasn't only builders and builders' merchants who came to Coventry: car designers and investors came too – drawn by the machine tools, the factories, the workers and the way of life which were already there. All it needed was a diversion of energy, a twitch of wires at the head, and a factory which once produced aeroplanes for war was soon producing motor cars for sweet, clean, honourable and substantial profit.

Julius knew how to manage a work force and he rose swiftly in his firm. Our house in Earlsdon Avenue was intact and it benefited from his growing income. The old range was taken away in pieces and replaced by an efficient gas stove; a fridge and new cupboards were installed. Carpets replaced linoleum, comfort and ease overtook the fixed demands of what was 'done' or 'not done' on the scale of domestic priorities. We were sent to school and helped with our homework; if we did well, it was hinted, then... then what? We'd be rich? We'd be famous? Taken to the pictures, perhaps. We used to go to the seaside in Norfolk. One year Barba threw a plate of food at the wall, I forget why. Julius said she could bloody well clear it up herself, he wouldn't be terrorized by her anger. Taking John and Amy, he went off to the beach. Barba cried, and Ruth and I helped her clear up the mess. Sometimes we were sad; more often we were happy. Like innumerable other families, we felt ourselves to be different.

*

We used to charge about over Hearsall Common with other children, arms outstretched, pretending to bomb each other. Then a group would form around the great beech tree, directing imaginary hoses as if it were a burning building. One or two of the smaller ones would get into the hollow trunk, coughing and spluttering, shouting for help. Someone would fight through the flames and smoke and emerge, dragging one of the victims by an arm. At that moment another wave of bombers would appear and everyone scattered and dived for cover. When the attackers had passed, the survivors would slowly stand up, if they weren't wounded. Then: 'You're dead!' – 'No I'm not!' – 'Yes you are!' – 'No! My Dad was in the garden when an incendiary fell!' – 'Well my Dad worked at Alvis, and he says the incendiaries did as much damage as the high explosives!' – 'But I was in the open! You made the incendiary noise just now and I was at least ten yards away, so I can't be killed!' – 'Next time I'll drop a parachute mine!'

Unlike all the older children, Ruth and I couldn't claim experience of the Great Raid, which detracted from our standing. (It counted for little that I had been in London during the Blitz.) Nevertheless, we were well informed about the mechanics and effects of war when we were very young, and our imaginations were sufficiently agile to feel vividly what the Great Raid itself must have been like. It seeped into our memories so that at times it was a surprise to realize that we didn't remember it ourselves, that we hadn't even been there. But, though nurtured on destruction, we knew neither its purpose nor what had been destroyed. Ruins surrounded us, they had always surrounded us, and they continued to surround us throughout our childhood. 'Ruin' meant something different, for it wasn't chained to memory: to us, ashes were ashes, not the dust of cherished objects, contemplated with sadness or bitterness. The adults were reconstituting their world, which was *in* ruins. Our world was constituted of ruins.

Yet we knew that things were not as they ought to be, because everyone spoke either of how they had been or of how they would be. That night scorched the lives of all those who lived among the ruins and our family was branded by it: Barba's parents were killed then; Julius's foot was injured... So much of the conversation we heard as we grew up was connected in some way with November 14th 1940 that we couldn't help wanting to know about it and seek explanations in its events. And gradually we realized that, buried in the familiar ruins, like a seed planted deep in shadow that mysteriously grows into the sun, was a set of circumstances that accounted for Ruth.

'Mum, was I late or was I early?'
'I can't remember, dear. Late, I think. Why?'
'I just wondered.'
I stood in the kitchen doorway holding a basket of peas, watching Ruth wheedling at Barba before joining me with a

bowl. I knew that she was up to something, but I didn't know what. Her mind had always crackled with impulsive deductions but she had recently got very clever at concealing her direction. Distracted by my wildly leaping voice and the clumsiness of my growing body, I couldn't formulate the right questions fast enough.

We took the peas out to the garden and sat on the ground. As we began to shell them, I asked her why she had said it. Instead of answering me she turned to John, who was tearing apart a pod with reckless disregard for the peas inside.

'You do it like this,' she said. 'You take the little stalk bit at the top and pull it gently. Then the string down the side comes off and you can press the two sides apart. It's a bit like opening a zipper.'

Her slim thumbs rested for a moment against the edges of the perfectly opened pod. 'Do you know how long it takes for them to grow?' she asked.

John looked up from her demonstration and frowned, as if he felt there was a trick in the question. He pushed his hair from his eyes, little pieces of pea still clinging to his fingers, and said he didn't know.

'It's like a baby in its mummy's tummy. Except it doesn't have any sort of birthday.'

John's eyes seemed to swell. 'That doesn't mean anything,' he complained.

'Don't you know what it means? Well I'm not going to tell you!'

'Ruth!' Amy objected. 'What's the matter with you?'

'Nothing. It's not my fault you're so stupid!'

Now John's eyes filled with tears and with a sudden squeal he flung his mangled peas at Ruth and went off towards the house, crying loudly.

Amy followed him. 'Now look what you've done!' she shouted, and indignantly tossed her plaits over her shoulder.

Barba came out quickly. What was the matter with us?

Couldn't she leave us alone just for five minutes without us squabbling? 'You are not to get at John, Ruth, I won't have it! You should be helping him. And Dan, you're the eldest, you should be keeping them in order! You two shell those peas on your own, and work out which of you is going to help Nan at the bazaar on Saturday!'

We worked in silence for a while and I thought of Ruth's questions again. Nine months before her birthday, plus a few days, was November 14th.

'When was Julius's foot injured?' I said.

'In the war, silly!'

'But when?'

'In the Raid.'

'I know that, but when exactly? Wasn't it in the morning after the Raid?'

Ruth shrugged. Peas slipped between her fingers into the bowl.

'And when did he come back from leave before the Raid? Wasn't it just the day before?'

'I think so. Why are you so interested suddenly?'

'Ruth, do you think they did it on the night of the Raid?'

'Did what?'

'You know – *it!*'

She contrived to look mildly offended that I imagined a nice girl like her would understand such vulgarity. Then she smiled. 'Maybe.'

The idea enticed us, like a trail of exotic feathers that seems to promise a rare and incandescent discovery.

The Central Methodist Hall had been in use as a temporary library since the destruction of the Gulson Library. It was only recently available again for bazaars and this novelty mitigated my chagrin at having to accompany Nan. My first duty was to carry all the jam made from the blackberries she had gathered in Coundon; the two jars of whisky marmalade she entrusted to nobody but – reluctantly – a buyer. I was also expected to sit beside the old lady and keep her company, which was liable to be embarrassing. She never displayed prices and, if someone asked how much a jar cost she was likely to say, 'Are you talkin' to me or chewin' a brick?' She was a little deaf.

We set up our stalls between Betty Green's cakes and the lucky dip, and sat back in our chairs.

'Dan, run and get me a nice cup of tea, would you? Get it from Mrs Prissington and tell her Elsie's got some. Plenty of milk.'

'Got some what, Nan?'

'Just tell her I've got some.'

Mrs Prissington was a stout lady with a mole on her neck. She sat behind a tea urn near the door.

'Mrs Prissington, my Nan Mrs Gallagher says Elsie's got some, and could she have a nice cup of tea please with plenty of milk?'

'Got some, has she? Well, I'll be jiggered! What a one she is!'

She turned the tap and filled a white mug with grey tea, which I took to Nan.

'Didn't you get a saucer? I need a saucer, Dan,' she said on my return.

I went to find a saucer but Mrs Prissington said there weren't any, they were mugs not cups.

'Same difference,' said Nan. 'What'll I do if I spill?'

'There's more in it than in a cup.'

'Never mind more, I want to keep my frock clean.'

I had to swallow a giggle. Ruth wore frocks.

She put her mug on the table and folded her hands in her lap. Then with a sigh she lifted her chin and considered the view. Stalls ran all round the hall and back-to-back in a line down the centre. Already a surprising number of people were ambling about examining the junk and sorting through piles of cast-off clothes, but they might all have been stall-holders. It always seemed to me that people mostly sold things to each other. By the time the general public arrived anything worthwhile had already gone. Nan sniffed and eyed her own jars proudly.

'Nan,' I said, 'where were you on the night of the Raid?'

'Me? Out in Coundon I was, with Sis, safe as houses out in Coundon.'

'Were Julius and Barba there too?'

'No, they were in Norfolk Street.'

'Was there an air-raid shelter there?'

'We'd fitted out under the stairs.'

'It must have been a bit cramped.'

'I think they managed well enough,' she answered. She glanced at me keenly and I looked away.

I continued after a pause, as if only to keep the conversation going. 'Is it true that Julius only came home from leave that day, and the next day he was in hospital?'

'Here, what are you getting at?'

When I raised my eyes, I saw that instead of scolding me her blue eyes were twinkling with mirth. 'Well, I was thinking, Nan, that maybe without the Raid there wouldn't have been a Ruth.'

A raucous cackle of laughter suddenly burst from her, like the foam from a shaken bottle of Mackeson's Stout.

'What's bitten you, Mrs Gallagher?' said the woman sitting behind the crochet stall opposite us.

'My Dan's put five and five together!' she declared.

Mrs Prissington lumbered over. 'What's that, Elsie?' she said.

Nodding towards me, Nan replied: 'He's tumbled to what my Julius and Barbara were up to the night of the Raid.'

Mrs Prissington's mouth opened wide and her tongue heaved into activity. 'Well, well, well. Is that so Dan? What are you doing thinking about that sort of thing at your age?'

'I think this calls for a nip, Bessy. He's perfectly old enough, aren't you Dan?'

Nan reached into her basket for one of her brown bottles. Attached to the basket's handle by a piece of string was an opener, which she applied with a practised wrench. She took a short pull herself before handing it to Mrs Prissington, who drank furtively before returning it. Then it was offered to me.

I was astonished, and made no move to take it.

'Go on, Dan, what's the point of discoveries if you can't celebrate them? If you're old enough to know about that, then you're old enough to have a tipple. Ain't that so, Bessy?'

Mrs Prissington looked doubtful, but I did as I was told.

If Mrs Prissington knew then everyone must know that Ruth was conceived that night. And suddenly I realized that Ruth was treated differently because of it. She was the child of the Raid and everyone felt that a part of her belonged to them: everyone indulged and protected her. As for Julius and Barba, while I saw that their future, like everyone else's, had been altered by the Raid, I saw that their experience of it was different. The manner in which my discovery was greeted made me feel as if I had joined an exclusive club, and this feeling was reinforced as Nan continued encouraging me to drink from the bottle. I was very pleased with myself and, though I didn't quite know why, I suddenly felt intensely proud of Julius and Barba.

It transpired that the bottle in Nan's basket was one of many and, though the morning passed very cheerfully, when the time came for us to eat our sandwiches I was thankful. I was feeling a little wobbly. If I stood up I was careful to put my hand on the table to steady myself because my legs felt oddly distant. The jam-jars on the table were no longer precisely delineated but seemed to converge and disperse like a thick pane of cloudy coloured glass. I noticed a few people looking at me very strangely; Nan noticed too, and was entertained.

An old man stood before me. Apparently he wanted to buy some jam, for his finger was wagging around in front of his heavy stomach. His hair was grey and his face was puffy; he seemed familiar and, when I managed to control his shifting features, I realized that it was Uncle David. Nan was saying something to him but he ignored her and spoke to me.

His words were unintelligible, but he was plainly angry. This was a shame because we were having such a jolly time. And as he gesticulated on the other side of the table, failing to make himself understood, he seemed not frightening but ridiculous.

'Are you talkin' to me or chewin' a brick?' I said, giggling.

David stepped back. Now I saw that Julius and Barba were there too. They both had red faces as if they were cross, and they were talking at once. I couldn't hear what she was saying because his voice was much louder; I only caught something about the Devil feeding the boy beer. I wanted to stand up and tell them not to be angry, I knew what they'd been up to during the Raid, but my legs wouldn't rise for the occasion and I stayed where I was. Then I saw Ruth. Her hair was tied in bunches like sheaves of corn; her eyes shone with concentrated excitement and her mouth was slightly open.

Pulling on the table, I made a huge effort to get up and tell her the good news. 'Ruth, we've the Germans to thank for you!' I announced, and then my arms refused to support me any longer.

I expected to be caught by the table as I fell across it, but my weight caused it to give way. For an instant I was suspended by the outrage of the surprise, and then I was crashing to the ground in a cascade of jam-jars.

I felt wretched. My head ached, my stomach churned with a foul and heavy sludge. Was this all my punishment? I wondered.

It was a Sunday in the school holidays. Normally I would have got up when I wanted, but at eight o'clock I was woken. 'Come and help me get the breakfast, please, Dan.'

I had to sit and watch them eat the pungent kidneys and the

glutinous eggs. In the back of my spoon I saw my pale and bloated face.

I was taken to church, where I sat between Barba and Julius. (Oh Lord, I am silly. Oh God, please make me good; Oh God, please let me be – don't stop me from being – good. And don't let Julius be too cross with Nan, she was only being kind. Didn't I learn from her that they can overlook things? Or was what they did wrong? Don't tell me it was wrong – I won't believe it.)

'You're to go to David's and apologize. Then invite him and Sarah to lunch,' said Julius.

I walked down the hill towards Spon End in the sunshine, under the bridge, skirting the building sites of Spon Street. It seemed right that I was going to him, but I was afraid: the cost of his forgiveness would be my humiliation.

'Apology accepted, Daniel, we'll say no more about it,' he said.

I caught my breath and looked at Sarah. 'Please will you come to lunch?'

'How kind of you, Dan, that would be very nice.'

They had just got back from church themselves (a different church nowadays). Sarah put her hat on again and they were ready. Their Sunday best did for God and lunch.

'Let's take the car, dear, it's rather hot to walk.'

I couldn't understand why Sarah needed her hat in the car. Whenever we went over a bump it touched the roof and her hands darted up to protect it.

'I'm sure it wasn't your fault, Dan,' she said. 'That Mrs Gallagher will be the disgrace of us all. I must say, I don't blame them for being angry with her.'

'They didn't have to make a scene in public,' said David.

Barba's shame had flared up. Outside the Hall she shouted at her mother-in-law that she wasn't fit to look after children; and would have slapped her if she hadn't been holding on to me and if Julius hadn't been holding her other hand. 'She'd go to

178

hell sooner than be beaten into repentance,' Julius had said in the car. 'But she did it on purpose! He'll have to live with this, not her!' Barba cried.

David continued: 'But whatever their mistakes in the past, I'm sure they do their best.'

When we arrived home, Barba called me into the kitchen. 'You're doing the lunch, Dan. The beef's in the oven. I've written out what you have to do. Any questions, come and ask me, but with a bit of initiative I think you'll manage by yourself.' And she handed me a sheet of paper.

I felt the sweet heave of tears but they didn't surface. As she left the room I sat down and looked at the table. All the ingredients were laid out on it; they seemed to mock me. In Barba's neat handwriting I read: '12.00: peel potatoes. Baste beef. 12.15: peel, core and slice apples for Apple Crumble. 12.25: make mixture for crumble as in recipe book (p.131). Put potatoes on. 12.35: wash cabbage... If you find you have spare time, lay the dining-room table.'

Once I had started, it wasn't as difficult as I expected. The challenge lay in keeping to the schedule, and I worked frantically to keep pace with it. Once or twice Barba came to check on my progress. 'When did you last baste the beef?' she asked, and then did it herself. When it was almost ready, Amy came to lay the table. She kept loitering round me, looking into the saucepans and covertly examining my face as if she wanted to chat but had been told to leave me alone. I was too busy to talk to her anyway.

'So how's the miscreant been getting on?' said David. He beamed at me and looked over my shoulder towards the kitchen, as if he expected it to be a reeking greasy wreck.

Everyone else sat down while Julius and I served the food.

'My potatoes aren't cooked,' said Ruth.

'Nonsense!' said Barba.

John and Amy exchanged grimaces of disgust. Nevertheless, they ate what was in front of them.

Evidently continuing from a conversation begun while I was cooking, Julius turned to me and said: 'David says Spence's designs are the work of a pretentious con-man, Dan. What do you say to that?'

'I – I think they're good designs,' I said. 'They're interesting. I don't think he's a con-man at all.'

'Call them designs?' said David. 'They're a child's doodle!'

I shrugged and sought refuge: 'The Reconstruction Committee didn't think so.'

'Proof, if further proof is necessary, that the world has gone berserk.'

Julius wiped his mouth with his napkin. He leaned back in his chair and raised his chin, as if he was trying to fortify the seriousness of his expression. 'But you'll uphold standards, won't you, David?'

'Someone has to, Julius, someone has to, as well you know!'

'Quite so, even though the cruel might say it's a rearguard action.'

'There's no dishonour in a rearguard action, if fought with courage.'

'David, you should have taken orders, they could do with some firm men like yourself in the Ministry.'

'Too late now, Julius.'

Julius tilted his head. I could see him trying to catch Barba's eye but she was looking elsewhere – at the ceiling, out of the window. Neither of them was fond of the cathedral and they certainly believed that standards should be upheld – but I could see they still both wanted to laugh.

When I brought the apple crumble, David said: 'Ah! The penitent's pudding! How delicious!'

I asked Ruth to pass the water.

'Wouldn't you rather have stout?' she murmured.

'Ruth!' said Julius. And she sat back in her chair, chastened.

At last lunch was over. Sarah thanked me. 'It was a very fine effort,' she said.

'Miscreant's mess, I thought it would be when you asked us, but it turned out to be penitent's pudding,' David remarked obscurely.

As soon as David and Sarah departed, Julius went out too. Nothing was said but I knew he'd gone to see his mother. Normally she lived with us, but after the bazaar she had withdrawn to stay with Sis in Coundon. While Julius was gone we cleared up the meal and, when everything was done and Amy and John had gone out to join some friends on Hearsall Common, we sat down together in the living-room.

Tucking one leg beneath her, Barba sat on the sofa and smoothed her skirt. She smiled as Ruth sat beside her; I perched on the edge of a chair. Her blue eyes turned on me and I saw that her anger had dissipated. My punishment was finished. I settled myself more comfortably. It was almost worth getting into trouble for the intense, almost sensual pleasure of these moments. The matter was now released to the family, as if with a quick-eyed nod permission had been given to break the seal on a coveted tin of toffees.

She reached up, plucking at the grips that secured her severe Sunday bun and, as she shook her head with a tumble of golden hair, she said, 'How are you feeling now, Dan?'

'Much better,' I replied, and it felt as if I was rediscovering the power of speech. 'I was terrible this morning, though.'

'I know. We could see.'

'You were green!' said Ruth.

'I'm still black and blue with bruises from the jam-jars.'

'Serves you right,' she said. But she was still suspicious and wanted proof.

I rolled up my trouser-legs, revealing some small bruises on my shins.

'I always thought your Nan's jam was powerful,' said Barba. 'I don't know why she had to start in with bottles too.'

Ruth suddenly folded one leg beneath her like her mother, but she was leaning forward at the waist, her fingers playing with the hem of her skirt which had ridden up to her knee. 'Why did she start?' she said.

Uncertain how to reply, I looked at Barba. 'Was it anything to do with the remark you made to Ruth?' she said.

My precious jewel of knowledge suddenly seemed dirty, deviously gathered and suggestive of a disloyalty which I didn't feel. I was afraid that Barba would reproach me bitterly if I confronted her with it; or that if, instead, she suppressed her rebuke, it would be out of contempt, as if I wasn't worth it. What had seemed to be an honestly discovered secret appeared in the guise of a vicious accusation. While fearing that my face betrayed me, I was drawn into the lie.

'What do you mean?' I said.

Barba shrugged. 'I must have been mistaken.'

Her steady gaze stifled me, twisting further contortions from my lips as I clumsily tugged at the edges of the truth, struggling to patch the hole. I told her I couldn't remember saying anything to Ruth, that Nan had simply kept on offering me drink...

'I thought I heard you – '

'Dan, you did – !'

I stared at Ruth, aghast at the prospect of her puffing away my feeble tale. Her eyes were wide open, her cheeks flushed at my absurdity. She was sitting up straight now, her shoulders tensed, like a hound waiting to see where the fox breaks from the thicket.

'I didn't!'

'You did!'

'What did I say then?'

'You said we've the Germans to thank for me!'

Ruth knew what I had to say and she was determined to enjoy its revelation. But, as if her cruel slash had severed the fetters on my inventiveness, I suddenly glimpsed an escape from my predicament: I could turn her mask of innocence around and call her bluff.

'Well – ye-es, I know... I discovered... what...' – I looked at Barba complicitly – '... what happened on the night of the Raid...'

Barba's eyebrows puckered hesitantly. She didn't know whether or not to smile.

'I didn't think... I didn't mean to tell you, Ruth. I hoped you'd forgotten,' I said.

'You mean you didn't think I'd understand? You think I'm not old enough?' And she hunched back into the sofa with an indignant sigh.

I said nothing; just smiled, a little coyly perhaps, and spread my hands on my knees. I glanced at Barba. This sudden display of delicacy – did she believe it?

Ruth appeared to believe in my prim concern. It didn't matter that she would discover the truth later: for the moment, her outrage conveniently misled Barba.

'I didn't know you were so protective of Ruth,' said Barba. 'Perhaps she's not as foolish as you think. She's certainly better behaved.'

Ruth shuddered. 'Ugh!' she said, but it lacked conviction: I saw that she had noticed how Barba passed by the opportunity to deny everything.

'Well, I think it's time I did something about the tea,' said Barba, although our bellies were still full from lunch.

Julius returned and the little ones were called in from the Common. Evidently Nan had told Julius of my discovery, but he showed no concern for it. 'It's the fact that she used you to make a scene that infuriates me,' he muttered, and then drank his tea in silence.

After a suitable interval I said I was going to read a book in my room. I left my door open and waited for Ruth to arrive. In a few minutes the door closed with a click and she sat decisively on my bed. As she settled herself against the wall, using my pillow as a cushion, she said: 'Liar. It wasn't me, it was Mum you didn't want to tell, wasn't it?'

I put my knee on a low stool by the window and leaned my forehead against the sash. Dusk was falling and I saw the silhouette of a cat jump onto a wall, then pause before leaping to the branch of a scraggy ash tree and into the yard behind the house.

'I didn't know how to say it. I was embarrassed.'

'Coward.'

'I wasn't being a coward,' I answered.

'Coward,' she repeated.

I was silent, trying to see the cat.

And then again I thought of my discovery, and it made me smile. 'But think of it! Isn't it amazing?' I said, turning to Ruth.

'Yes!'

Ruth held her breath, as if suspending her exclamation. 'But why? Why is it amazing?'

I hadn't considered this question, and was disconcerted to find I had no ready answer.

Her gaze fell to her toes. 'It's a bit horrid too.'

'Why?'

'To think I was an accident.'

'Who says you were an accident?'

'Of course I was. If it wasn't for the Raid, Mum and Dad wouldn't have – you know!'

'Why not? Maybe not then, but another time they would. And anyway, the Raid did happen and they did... They didn't *do* it by accident, did they?'

I remembered what David had said in the car: 'Whatever their mistakes in the past, I'm sure they do their best now.' His words seemed to kill action, to deny Ruth. I remembered his sweaty, aged face peering over my shoulder into the kitchen, and a shiver ran down me at the ugliness. He was wrong, and my sudden conviction of this made me laugh.

'What's so funny?'

'The idea that you're a mistake – it's so stupid! I think it's amazing what happened that night!'

'So do I!' Ruth drew her knees up so she could rest her chin on them, and started pulling at her toes. 'Dad said something really horrid to Nan yesterday, when you were tipsy.'

'What?'

'It was awful.'

'What did he say?'

'I can't tell you. It was too awful.'

'Come on, Ruth! You can't just tell me he said something awful and then not tell me what it was!'

'But it was awful! He swore at her!'

'What did he *say*, Ruth?'

Ruth's voice dropped, as if the words wouldn't taste so bad if she mumbled them. 'He said she was a callousselfishbitch.'

'What?'

'I told you!'

'I didn't hear! You said it too fast!'

'A cal–lous, sel–fish bitch!' she repeated in a whisper.

'That's not swearing!'

Ruth's head jerked up and her eyes reproved me sharply. 'Yes it is!'

'No it's not, it's not really bad. It's just his way of talking to her. He said the same thing about her to us just now, only he put it differently.'

'Liar,' she repeated, but from habit.

*

I had a friend called Jeremy Laffin, an intelligent, pugnacious fellow with a slightly flattened nose which flared like a bulldog's when he was angry. For some reason he was forbidden by his parents to go with us to London for the day to see some of the Festival of Britain exhibition. Having looked forward to his company, I was very disappointed. I urged him to argue – and if necessary to disobey: he said it was useless, there was no point even trying.

'You're not usually so meek,' I answered.

He looked at me with detachment, suggesting that I couldn't be expected to understand, and said, 'It's different for you.'

Jeremy was right in a way that was too obvious to deny; he was also wrong in a way that I neither understood then nor understand even now.

My own family was dead. We didn't know whether they'd been shot beside a nameless ditch or perished in a concentration camp. Perhaps they'd had the good fortune to be murdered in a hurry at home – we didn't know, and we had given up hope of ever finding out. Naturally I used to fantasize about their return, but I never believed in it. They weren't a known quantity that I missed. To have faith in their return would have been to imagine for myself a world utterly different from that in which I was brought up so carefully. Yet I was encouraged to honour them.

Each year I used to be taken to the Yom Kippur service at the Abbey Road synagogue. When I was little Tilly took me, later it was Julius. The dark, spiky interior smelled strange and used to frighten me. Men with long beards and hats chanted in a language I didn't understand. The sound of the ram's horn was haunting and the sonorous utterances were of an unreachable gravity. It was a world altogether foreign to me and to be told that it was my parents' world set them beyond a barrier which I couldn't and didn't want to cross. As I got older and achieved an elementary comprehension of the ideas of atonement and remembrance expressed at those services, I still drew no closer. I think the visits used to be traumatic for Tilly because she had known my family, and her passionate sympathy for me overwhelmed her then. She was moved in a way that I never was – after all, she had faced a change of facts which I was too young to remember being otherwise. Julius was unnerved by the ceremony but, because I was older and no longer helpless, he felt less engaged. He felt less sorry for me than other people but he thought it right that I should remember and honour my parents.

My own early life was different from that of Ruth, Amy and John; we all acknowledged this fact. It lay out of reach of my memory but I had a sense of acquaintance with it, as if I really remembered my family; as if the life I knew I'd shared with them, when viewed through the shaded lens of my imagination, amounted to true memory. My separation from the Gallaghers was open and it embarrassed none of us: I was, in effect, the eldest son. Nor was it ever very interesting to us as children. We – that is, Ruth and I – shared a more exciting secret.

Not that the unusual circumstances of Ruth's conception were exactly secret. They were rarely mentioned openly, but everyone knew them. David spoke of Barba and Julius's 'mistake' because, as he understood the matter, they had committed a sin: yet he wouldn't have presumed to judge them. Though often clumsy and self-righteous, he never believed that forgiveness was his to grant or withhold, nor did he behave as if he did. I'm certain that Barba and Julius recognized this – certain because, in an obscure way, they believed it themselves. In my view their subsequent life together offered no support to the charge of sin but to them it remained at best a vindication; never a justification. They were happy sinners: life didn't allow them to regret what they had done, nor did it wholly uproot their belief that they had sinned.

Too much can be made of 'the communion of souls', but I think it fair to say that our fascination with the remarkable twist in events on November 14th 1940 was like a shared understanding of a joke. It wasn't something we whispered to each other: it hovered beneath the surface of language. As if following the refraction of light through a prism, in the picture we made of the night of the Raid we were able to glimpse it in each other. What we saw there, amid the raging destruction, was level ground and a cornerstone, a creative action without which neither Ruth herself nor her family – my family – could exist. Like a screened candle, it illuminated our world from behind. David's stage had been savagely torn down, yet he continued blindly, heroically, to prop up his disapproval of the action, as if it shouldn't belong. Such a manoeuvre looked preposterous to us, and we laughed: for us to do as he did would have been unthinkable. Jeremy said that I was different, as if my obligations towards Barba and Julius were complicated by my background. But my loyalties weren't divided: like Ruth, I was unequivocal in my support of Barba and Julius. It would have been absurd otherwise.

We wandered in a gaggle round the Festival of Britain exhibition halls, gazing with wonder at the grandiose presentations, the new schemes and machines, the proud engines of hope. And I remember stopping suddenly at a stand, my eye drawn by the words 'Coventry Scheme'. The display belonged to a development company and the words occurred in a bold list of their current projects. When I looked closer I saw in smaller type, 'Completion of the New Precinct'.

A man in a suit with a name tag on his lapel was watching me. He seemed uncertain how to address me but I forestalled his offer of help.

'I thought Coventry were doing it themselves,' I said, 'without commercial development companies.'

'Oh, that was their idea all right, but they couldn't manage it.'

'Why not?'

'Too busy talking about phoenixes. They forgot their precious phoenix was just a picture in the stone. It takes more than that to build a city, as they found out, so they offered up the project and we got the contract. Here, have a look...'

He opened a brochure for me on the Formica-topped desk and I saw a short exposition of the Coventry scheme, together with photographs. At the top was a picture of the Levelling

Stone. During the eight years that had passed since it was laid in 1946, it seemed to have gone rigid. In the phoenix's opaque eyes I saw no trace of the fire I remembered: I saw instead the bullying glare of a lobbyist uttering a slogan.

*

Despite the triumphant rhetoric, the new building was slow and painful. But at least the idea of rebirth was fertile and from beneath its heavy skirts crawled other fledgling revivals. Although her world was further from redemption than that of my elders, Lady Godiva was brought back on civic duty. At every kind of public occasion she was flattered and invoked, as if she was expected to come again – as if she hadn't done enough for the city six hundred years ago. There were Peeping Tom and Leofric too, castles strapped to elephants' backs, emblems and contraptions noisily yoked together, a gaudy hoarding to keep the spirits up among the slumbering ruins – or to screen the ruins from us. And the Miracle Plays. Let me tell you about the Miracle Plays.

Corpus Christi Day, 1954, five o'clock in the afternoon. On the chancel steps of the ruined cathedral of St Michael, Coventry, a sequence from a cycle of medieval Miracle Plays was about to be performed. I had come with a group including my family, a friend of Ruth's called Rosanna and my friend Stephen, whose father was one of the actors – or Players, as they styled themselves. It was Stephen who told me that one of the plays was traditionally performed by the shearmen, which excited me because it was like Shearer and made me persuade the others to come. Collapsible chairs had been put up in rows for the occasion and, after paying our entrance fee, we took our seats in a line about half-way back.

The stage was bare except for the cross of charred beams, a gaunt structure prised from the shadows by the evening sun which fell directly on it. The walls rose behind to the gaping sockets of the windows, where once the eye and the mind focussed together on still images. The shards of tracery at the edges seemed to make the vacancy quiver, like the flicker of recognition in the eyes of a condemned man confronted by his executioner.

The noise grew louder as the seats filled up. We didn't know quite what to expect, for we hadn't watched Miracle Plays before. The publicity emphasized the traditional link with Coventry. I had the impression that anyone who considered themselves a good citizen felt it their duty to attend, although many, I think, feared that it might just be glorified pantomime, more suitable for the children. So the chairs were all occupied, leaving only standing-room for latecomers – but a whole nave of standing-room. Only fourteen years ago they had come here for hymns and sermons, and perhaps the note of intense antic- ipation expressed what Sarah felt when she said she wouldn't feel comfortable watching a play in the cathedral.

Four musicians appeared at the edge of the stage with strange stringed instruments which they gripped between their knees when they sat down. After an unsteady ripple of clapping they began to play. It was a quaint piece of music and the crowd stopped their chatter. The melody kept changing its course, like a snipe, and the harmonies never resolved as I expected them to, but they were very clear. In the final bars Stephen's father, wearing a long false grey beard and an ankle-length robe, walked to the centre of the stage and stared out grimly over the heads of the audience. Stephen leaned across Ruth, who was sitting between us, and said, 'That's my Dad. He's playing Isaiah. It's The Annunciation, the one the shearmen did.' And he nudged Ruth.

Then the drama was played out. I know it by heart now, so I shall give it to you in full.

No – that's a ludicrous idea. I can't throw the book at you like that, it's misleading to quote it verbatim. So many of the images released by the text are beside the point, they suggest another point which will make you recoil (has your old man suddenly got a thing about God and virgins?). I didn't intend this at all, I don't believe in Isaiah's acid-gutted groans about Original Sin, I don't believe in Original Sin at all – who does, nowadays? I do not share his guilt at the sexual act, his hatred of women's sexuality; I loathe his morbid care for purity and his cupidity for grace repels me. This was not Isaiah, this was Stephen's Dad and Stephen's smirks didn't allow us to forget it.

The religious language might prompt a specifically religious interpretation, but it didn't compel me in this way. Not being accustomed to the idiom, I didn't follow every word anyway. What I saw was not an Old Testament prophet but a prophesying shearman. His precise words passed over me: I was enchanted instead by a vagueness that wasn't there, by the broad possibility of a miraculously creative action. It wasn't Adam's so-called sin that tolled within me, nor Jesus's atonement; it wasn't the invocation of Judah. It was a chorus of steel-sprung echoes, slicing across each other from six corners – from the Shearers, Coventry, the Raid, my parents, myself and Ruth.

The particulars of my confusion – both their narrowness and their breadth – are mine, and mine alone. I cannot presume that you will understand them: I certainly can't expect you to share them. But if you see a glimmer in the chamber of my imaginings then perhaps my description of what followed will make it grow – not into a pattern, perhaps, but into melting splashes of colour.

Isaiah had left the stage now. While the musicians played a leisurely cadence a stagehand placed two large cushions at centre-stage-right. A lady came and sat on the ground, leaning back against the cushions. She began to sew diligently and then suddenly looked up, startled by an angel, who greeted her, 'Hail, Mary, full of grace!' Then he told her the substance of Isaiah's prophecy and departed.

Mary turned as the musicians began to play and swiftly put

the smaller of the two cushions under her dress. As the cadence drew to a close she turned back, obviously pregnant.

Joseph entered with a hearty stride but, when he saw his wife's distended belly, he recoiled. His mouth opened wide and then snapped shut; he stamped hard, like a bull pawing the earth, and struck the air with his fist as he shouted:

> *What, I tro that we be all shent!*
> *Say, woman, who hath been here since I went,*
> *To rage with thee?*

In the ensuing argument, where Joseph bitterly accused Mary of betraying him, Joseph's indignant tones and stiff gestures for a moment resembled David's; the actor was unmistakably from Coventry. And I sympathized with Joseph, for though I knew that Mary was 'without sin', as she claimed, how could he know this? Why should he associate any more gravity with the event causing her condition than with, say, a frolic in the shadows beneath the stairs?

Joseph stomped away in fury, but when he reached centrestage-left his legs seemed to buckle and he slumped to the ground, no longer able to support the weight of disappointment. Immediately, an angel appeared behind him:

> *Arise up, Joseph, and go home again*
> *Unto Mary, thy wife, that is so free.*
> *To comfort her look that thou be fain,*
> *Be not aghast.*
> ***Joseph:*** *Now, Lord, I thank thee with heart full sad,*
> *For of these tidings I am so glad*
> *That all my care away is cast;*
> *Wherefore to Mary I will in haste.*

Joseph's faith in Mary was restored and strengthened by remorse for his earlier accusation. Here was recognition that, even though the action remained outside the domain of understood convention, it nevertheless carried due weight and must accordingly be accepted. He had a link with Mary forged on the anvil of the unexpected. He grinned, as if he felt this new bond to be one of happiness, not a constraint. Earlier I had imagined a similarity with David but now, in the deep furrows round his mouth and the way he raised his face to expose his throat, I suddenly saw the swift motion of Julius when he laughed.

Joseph returned to Mary and kneeled before her:

Mercy, Mary, for now I know
Of your good governance and how it doth stand.

Mary told him that forgiveness wasn't hers to grant – but if it were, she would gladly give it. Joseph offered her his hand and she stood up and, while the musicians played again, the stagehand removed the cushion. Then, united again in their mutual trust, they set forth towards Bedlam, or Bethlehem; fresh with the angels' private blessing, they went out into the world's chaos.

I sat in a daze after the last scene. I imagined Joseph and Mary entering Bedlam and in my mind's eye it was a place of devastation, a crazy and desolate place, and I wondered if the people there would help the holy couple? I was moved by the sight of them linking their destiny with this town.

Ruth nudged me. 'What did you think?' she asked, and the roundness of her rich blue eyes told me that she had enjoyed it.

Barba reached across Amy and touched my knee. She said they were going; they wouldn't watch the next play; John and Amy had also had enough. I was disappointed but not surprised. I was certainly going to stay.

'What about you, Ruthie?' said Julius, standing up and speaking over our heads. 'Can you make any sense of that fancy language? You're a lot cleverer than your poor Mum and Dad if you can.'

'I don't really understand it all,' Ruth admitted, and her cheeks went slightly pinker. 'But I'd like to stay and watch all the same.'

There was a rustling in the wide space between the scarred and roofless walls. Many people had stood up and were edging past knees towards the end of their row, determined to leave. Occasionally above the chatter a distant voice could be made out, an exclamation or a laugh. Then everything quietened down again as the musicians began to play.

I don't know why – it seems a bizarre choice to follow the Nativity – but the next play was The Slaughter of the Innocents. I suppose the intention was to give us the flavour of the Cycle, little gobbets of history, instead of observing the proper sequence.

I myself wasn't taken with it and consequently I remember nothing. I was still preoccupied with the first one and couldn't concentrate. For it was only now that the coincidence of the shearmen being responsible for the Nativity struck me: just as Joseph had nothing to do with begetting Jesus but had provided for him like a son, so Julius had given me a home and I felt like his son. The Slaughter impressed Ruth much more, and afterwards she was unusually silent. Years later, when we were living in Germany, she told me that the killing on the stage was equated in her mind with the killing of my brothers.

'That never occurred to me,' I said. 'I felt too involved with the other one to pay much attention.'

'Don't tell me – you identified with Jesus.'

'No. Even then, I realized that you would be my saviour,' I teased her. 'It was the sense of belonging that excited me, I think.'

'But surely you didn't feel that you didn't belong?'

'No, but it provided a context for the belonging. Anyway, if the belonging was complete, how could I ever have married you?'

I followed the rebuilding with a convert's zeal. Greedily I peered through cracked fences in Smithford Street and spied from the steeple of Holy Trinity on the huge building site of the Precinct, willing our new city to rise from the ground, urging the cranes to move heavier loads and the workmen to lay their bricks faster. And now at last the most glorious of all schemes, the cathedral, began to stir.

One evening in May, 1954, David appeared unexpectedly at our house. He seemed to be in a hurry, as if he was on his way somewhere, but when Sarah followed him inside and sat down in the living-room, he also sat. He crossed his legs, uncrossed them and ran his hands up and down his thighs; then he stood up again. 'Well,' he said at last. 'That's it then!' And for the first time he looked directly at Barba and Julius, his red face quivering in agitation, waiting for their reaction.

Julius and Barba waited anxiously for an explanation but he offered none. They were confused because David's behaviour suggested that something terrible had occurred, while if anything ruffled Sarah's composure it was an eddy of amusement. When they looked at her for help she said gently, 'They've given planning permission for the cathedral.'

"Planning permission', they call it!' David burst out, spattering the carpet with saliva. 'Planning permission, my eye! Wrecking permission, more like! 'The City Council of Coventry hereby grants official permission to a pack of fools to muck up the city'!'

'Poor David!' said Barba, putting her hand on his arm, guiding him back in to his chair.

'Have a chair, David, poor you, you'd set so much store by it,' said Julius.

'I should think I did!'

Julius cordially disliked the whole project. 'Of course, I've always said it was a waste of money. The funds should be spent on housing.'

'That's your view, I know, Julius, and you're entitled to it. I happen to think differently. I think there ought to be a cathedral. But a cathedral, not a... not a...! Words fail me, I'm sorry!'

'Well I agree with you, but you mustn't let yourself be upset so,' said Barba. 'Let me get you a cup of tea.'

Barba didn't agree with Julius that nobody was interested in a new cathedral in Coventry, that the whole enterprise was a clumsy display of vanity by those with power, but she was still reluctant to speak about it. There were people better qualified than herself and she had a disconcerting faith that these experts would manage their task much better without her interference. She regarded David as such an 'expert' just because he sat on the City Council. In fact the City Council had no control whatsoever over the building. It was the Reconstruction Committee who set up the competition and judged Basil Spence the winner in 1951, who approved and entered into contracts, while the cathedral Council had the power to examine or veto their decisions. The City Council were only involved with planning permission, which they refused with determination. David considered it a sacred duty to undermine the architect's intentions. Unfortunately for him, his power now proved to be strictly limited. But his conviction remained unshaken.

'I believed... I was foolish enough to believe that they would see sense! I saw the piece of paper: 'Building of a new cathedral... at a total cost not exceeding £985,000...'. That's what it says! Who can describe those doodles as plans for a cathedral? And who are they trying to fool with the cost? They won't lay their wretched foundations with that, or pay their lawyers' fees after the complaints...'

'David, David...' murmured Barba. 'You mustn't take it to heart so.'

'I've done all I can. My conscience is clear, at least.' He sighed, closing his eyes as he sat back in his chair.

Sarah was not expected to hold opinions of her own. It wasn't considered quite lady-like. But now she looked for a moment in my direction and I was astonished to see her wink. She actually winked. I never again saw her do such a thing. Yet it seemed to come naturally to her, as if she had been practising for years. I was jubilant that the scheme was now officially approved. The question of finance seemed a detail and, in the ensuing weeks and months, as the old cathedral's ruins were secured and tidied and the site cleared for the new building, I repeatedly scrutinized the plans. The enormous interior would have no internal columns except the slender stilts tapering down from the fanning roof. Behind the altar would hang a tapestry by Graham Sutherland and it would be the largest tapestry in the world. Facing it at the entrance to the nave would be a great glass screen with saints engraved on it. On one side would be a star-shaped chapel and in the opposite corner a round chapel, like little satellites; in the angles of the building's jagged sides would be seven pairs of tall, narrow stained glass windows. Light would be directed towards the altar so that the windows would be invisible from the nave. I loved the simplicity of the design, I loved the grandeur, and I loved the care taken by the architect to organize the best possible works of art for it. Even the one that caused such embarrassment, the sculpture of St Michael, Patron Saint of Coventry.

On the wireless we heard Big Ben striking in the New Year. Ruth and Amy were sitting on the floor in front of the Christmas tree with a bowl of sugared almonds. Julius held an open bottle of bubbly towards them.

'On your feet, girls, quick quick!'

The liquid splashed and fizzed in their glasses, a mouthful for each.

Everyone else rose to their feet as the glasses were refilled. Tilly was there, a bit plumper, delighted to be with the family, and Percy, benign as ever and eager to please by tipping back the food and drink as if his welcome depended on it; Sis and Dennis; Terry Deakin, a colleague of Julius's, was there with his wife Daphne; Joe Dodds with his new but not so young bride, Belle. ('You should see me dance the polka, you should see my coat tails fly!' she sang earlier to John and he asked her what the polka was.)

'David, you old rake, if only you'd resist!' said Julius.

David smiled at the old joke.

'Sarah, I swear you'll die of thirst. Ladies and gentlemen, your glasses please, quick quick quick! Terry, Daphne, Tilly... Percy, old cock – so sorry, a drop won't harm the trousers... Just a taste I'm afraid Joe, Belle... Mother, where's your glass? Sis, Dennis... Barbara – here, Dan, John. Mother, quick...! Twelve! Oh! Happy New Year everyone!'

'Happy New Year Happy New Year Happy 1955 Happy New Year...!'

Someone hummed a bar of Auld Lang Syne and we all chimed in because it seemed the thing to do – although Sis said it was a daft song. Then Tilly sat down again on the fraying red sofa and I clinked glasses with her. The fire was burning noisily and, with the alcohol and so many people, I felt hot.

'John and Amy, I said you were to go to bed now! Off you go!' said Barba, shooing them away. 'Say good night.'

John was already in his dressing-gown. There was a bell on the pocket which tinkled as he leaned down to kiss Tilly. Then they were gone.

I caught Ruth's eye. So privileged, so important. David's cheeks creased with an indulgent smile and he took a sip of his ginger beer.

'...and so I told Barbara that he ought to go to technical college,' Sarah was saying to Percy. Me at technical college? First I'd heard of it. Poor Percy, he was always being brought up to date on us.

Joe had his hand on Belle's knee and her hand covered his

fingers; privately they eyed each other 'Happy New Year'.

'Julius, is that bottle empty? You only gave me a drop!'

'Mother, you know it's empty!'

'Where's David's? I'll have David's.'

'He hasn't got a glass. Why don't you take a leaf out of his book – make a New Year's resolution for a change?'

Nan sat up straight. 'Lord 'a' mercy! What d'you think I'd want to be like him for?' she muttered.

Terry diverted the conversation. He was always a good guest. 'What'll you drink to for the New Year then, Julius? Let me start the ball rolling. I'll drink to health.'

Everyone raised their glasses in a toast. 'Health, health, health...'

Nan looked round the company obscurely. 'Fat chance for some.'

'I'd better drink to wealth, then,' said Julius. His long-stemmed glass twinkled in the warm light. 'Wealth!'

Tilly followed: 'Peace!'

'Hear, hear!' said David, and tapped his tumbler on the arm of his chair. 'And moderation.'

'Happiness!' said Daphne, raising her glass towards Joe and Belle.

'I'll drink to that!'

Sarah, 'Family!'

Barba, 'Success!'

Percy, 'Freedom!'

'Mother?' said Julius.

Nan rubbed her nose and stared. 'You're asking me? A good bowel movement's all I ask at my age.'

'Oh Mum! Trust you!' said Sis. 'What about the children? We'll drink to children keeping out of trouble, won't we Dennis?'

Everyone laughed, nervously glancing at Ruth and myself. Jim, their son, was supposed to have come along this evening but he was in a police cell, drunk. Their daughter Joan had gone to America four years previously with a man.

'My turn!' said Ruth, pinkness unfurling up her neck. 'The rebuilding of Coventry!'

'Hear, hear! Hear, hear!'

'What about you, Dan?'

Something fluttered in my throat. 'To Jacob Epstein!' I cried and tipped my glass up against my lips.

David cleared his throat. 'Dan, now...'

'Who's Jacob Epstein?' Tilly asked.

David shifted his weight to his other buttock. 'Some artist.' His mouth shut tight, the lower lip pushing against the upper to make an arch.

'The cathedral's architect wanted him to do a sculpture,' I explained, 'but the Reconstruction Committee said no because he's a Jew.'

'You know it's not as simple as that,' said David.

'Yes it is,' said Barba.

I thought, thank you Barba, that's exactly how simple it is: they said no, because he's a Jew. The Reconstruction Committee wouldn't be responsible for such a thing, they wouldn't be skewered on this one, so they referred it to the Cathedral Council. Fine, Jacob Epstein would do the sculpture after all, but the episode had happened, it existed in time.

'How perfectly extraordinary!' Percy declared.

'Incredible!' said Tilly. 'I thought that was what the war was all about!'

'Good Heavens, Tilly! How you over-react!' said David. 'It's a completely different issue. The cathedral's Christian, Epstein's a Jew. Might as well have have one of them lotus-eating Buddhist fellows do it!' The Reconstruction Committee had surrendered everything in their pathetic attempts to be fashionable; the bishop was feckless too – he should have sent the pipsqueak Spence away with a flea in his ear: I heard David say so to Julius.

Sarah was silent.

'But – you wouldn't mind if it was Dan?' said Tilly.

'What's that got to do with it?'

'I'm Jewish.'

'Not really, you're not.'

'Yes I am, really.'

'Where's your little cap and prayer shawl then?'

'I don't have one...'

'There you are then. Now please – let's talk about something else – we're supposed to be celebrating the New Year!'

Everyone shuffled uneasily. I shouldn't have drunk to Jacob Epstein, it was asking for trouble. 'Yes,' I said, 'here's to the New Year!' My glass was empty but I lifted it anyway to encourage the others.

'Just a moment,' said Tilly. Her mouth was twitching and sweat had broken out in little beads across her forehead. 'Let's be clear about this before we think about the New Year. Dan's family weren't practising Jews either, but they suffered because they were Jews. Was it all a ghastly mistake, do you think? Or, had they been practising Jews, what then? Would it not have been a mistake?'

'There you go, running off again, Tilly, trying to trap me in one of your arguments,' said David. 'You always take everything so seriously. You always end up spoiling things.'

'We still haven't drunk to Jacob Epstein yet,' said Ruth.

And so we drank to the man who produced our St Michael.

*

Rosanna Boroman – I'll always remember her strange name. Her dark hair came down to her waist; she had fleshy lips and bright, heavy-lidded eyes that sometimes made her seem fierce. She was a schoolfriend of Ruth's and was often to be found at our house. At first I paid scant attention to her but as she became more familiar my awareness of her changed. I would look to see if she was sitting on her hair and my eye would rest a moment longer on her hip; as she spoke or laughed I would notice the changing shapes of her lips; if she touched her cheek I would sense the softness of the skin beneath her fingertips. My new and persistent desire made me awkward with her. I didn't seriously consider that she might submit to my banal sexual fantasies but a kiss, I thought, wouldn't be misguided. Achieving this was much harder. There never seemed to be a suitable moment: it was almost as if she knew my intention and was determined not to let me try. I couldn't contrive to be alone with her except for one or two occasions when Ruth left the room for a moment, and then her barrage of chatter prevented my approach. In the end I simply put my arm across the door when she tried to follow Ruth into the garden one day. Ruth was just far enough ahead to have turned the corner in the hall and not to realize what was happening. 'I want to kiss you,' I said, and as I put my other hand on her arm I felt elated by the boldness of my action.

Rosanna flinched. 'Let me through!' she said, looking hungrily over my shoulder. In her eyes I saw the stupidity of my behaviour and my hopes crumpled. I removed my arm and tried to apologize. She cut in, 'How could you...?' Then she smiled.

Gradually we overcame our embarrassment. Mistakenly imagining her to be available, I had thought her beautiful: now I saw that she wasn't actually so beautiful. She told nobody about my indiscretion and I didn't repeat it, so that it became a point of mutual confidence. We were often together and, as my desire for her lost its urgency, I was content just to enjoy her company. We became friends.

I was wandering about with Rosanna and Jeremy a couple of days before I left Coventry to go to art school. We went into Woolworths, which had been open now for three years. I bought several new pairs of socks. Then we went back past Broadgate House and entered the Precinct. We climbed the stairs to the upper level and leaned against the rail, looking down at the brick walk-ways and the nicely ordered new shops. People with carrier-bags wandered in and out and a couple of old men sat on a bench facing the incomplete Lower Precinct. There was nobody else on our level. The shops had not been a success and were being used as storage and office space for the shops at ground level. The doors and display windows were unused and dirty, giving the whole circle an air of imminent dereliction. The paint was already chipped in many places.

'Do you feel sad to be going away?' Rosanna asked.

'Yes,' I said. 'I'm excited. But I'll miss everyone, and Coventry.'

'Let's carve our names here,' said Jeremy all of a sudden, and began to scratch at the varnished wood with a pocket-knife.

I was touched. But I was also shocked and he must have seen it in my face. 'What's so wrong?' he said. 'If we don't, other people will.'

'They certainly will as soon as one person's done it,' said Rosanna.

I felt suddenly depressed, not merely because of the vandalism but because of the change it seemed to record. Carving our names would imply the end to one phase and the start of a new one. In so doing, it arbitrarily set limits on the past and the future, and with a hectic confidence that could be born only of uncertainty. How could the change be recorded before it had taken place? But though I disliked what Jeremy had said, I felt the lure of nostalgia as I thought about leaving my friends and my family, afraid of loneliness. Looking downwards I saw the flat face of the Levelling Stone and was suddenly struck by its crude demagoguery. How could they know that the city would rise again like a phoenix? From the concrete island where we stood, we could still see the acres of old ruins. I was eight when the Levelling Stone was laid. I imagined then that the city would lift up, like the bird, before our eyes. Later I realized that this phoenix measured time like adults – in years, not days. But what kind of phoenix took ten years to get to its feet? Fire couldn't reach behind it: the slab was fixed in concrete and it cast no shadow. It was no more a foundation stone than a tombstone.

'Hasn't the phoenix deceived us?' I said.

Jeremy was astonished. 'What do you mean? What's all this?'

He waved expansively at the new shopping complex and the building sites beyond, which made me feel insensitive to our collective good fortune. 'Yes, I suppose so,' I admitted.

'And the cathedral,' said Rosanna. 'They've started on the cathedral.'

It was true: the official foundation stone had recently been laid and I had felt so proud of our city. This was one in the eye for the Foul Fiend! Yet why wasn't the Precinct more exciting? I'd looked forward to it so much and now, as I surveyed it, I was strangely disappointed because it wasn't perfect.

Maybe the cathedral would be perfect.

11

But you must be out of your mind...! You asked her to marry you, she said no, not yet – and you took it as a malicious swipe...! Surely it's not because Tilda and Joe have just paid a visit to a registry office? It's like hoisting the banner of the phoenix over the wreckage of Coventry: it's all very well as a statement of intent, but to presume its accomplishment, to look around you confident of congratulations – don't you see? It's like painting garishly on the church floor the projected patterns and colours of the stained glass windows.

Do you remember that play a couple of years ago about Alan Turing? I went to see it with Luke. I wonder if you know the story? It's been nesting in my mind like a cuckoo, nudging out the rightful tenants as it grows: but now it too has sidled to the edge and is stretching out its fragile wings for flight.

Turing, more than anyone else, was responsible for inventing the principle of computers. More specifically, he developed the mathematics by which ULTRA worked. He was eccentric and impractical, impatient with social conventions and poor at communicating his ideas, but he managed to harness his theories on the Allies' behalf and willingly engendered their most potent single advantage. In a war fought to defend freedom of thought and individual values from the tyranny of generalized convictions, it is apt that this small and independent-spirited man was the purest antithesis of all that Hitler stood for.

After the war, Turing's achievements at Bletchley remained behind the screen of the Official Secrets Act. He was given an

OBE for 'services rendered', but his specific contribution not only to the war effort but also to science remained almost completely unknown. Mathematicians were aware of his theoretical advances but even they were kept ignorant of how far his theories had been put into practice at Bletchley. Forbidden to cite his war work to advance his career and further frustrated by his explicatory incompetence, he failed to secure support for the open realization of what had already partially succeeded in secret, and thus his role in the quick development of the computer after the war was very limited. He was at Manchester University, where he was viewed as an oddball professor with obscure credentials, when the teeth of his destiny caught up with the tail.

One morning, after a visit from a rent-boy, Turing noticed that various things were missing from his house. Homosexuality still being against the law, he did the most foolish thing he could have done in the circumstances – he went to the police. They were more interested in convicting a homosexual than a thief and Turing was soon given a suspended sentence of one year's imprisonment. At the time, a government project was investigating the effects of castration on homosexuals. In this case the offender was spared such a punishment and instead obliged to take a long course of hormones, which, it was hoped, would correct his deviation.

Turing was rendered virtually catatonic for several months by these drugs and his sexual activity magically abated. As he began to recover it emerged, bafflingly, that his sexual orientation hadn't changed. Being an intelligent man, if not always a wise one, he realized that it was best to avoid being found guilty of the same offence again, so he took himself to Helsinki where he wouldn't be jailed for this manifestation of himself. And there, in a city which, at the height of the Cold War, swarmed with spies and seducers, the man who had done so much for the defence of open behaviour and freedom of thought, who was nevertheless responsible for the most closely guarded secret of the war, was allowed to risk whatever secrets he knew for the sake of rigid behaviour and conformity of thought at home.

Soon afterwards he killed himself by eating a poisoned apple.

Turing was condemned for a facet of his character which, like his mathematical genius, was essential to him. He was trapped in an absurdity: while valuing him for his particular contribution, the authorities – and, presumably, society, on whose behalf such authorities are supposed to act – wanted to regulate his particularity.

I sense that you are afraid of time, that your determination to marry Kate so soon is an attempt to retrieve the moment when she fell from the balcony, to dis-occur the event and somehow counterbalance its repercussions, to cancel time. But – and I say this warily, because it would be monstrous of me not to want such a miracle for her too – since each of us is the sum of our emotional and physical engagements, to wish away those which have upset us is an attempt to stunt growth by denying our own specific shape. Yet we love and celebrate people because of the ways in which they are unique, so why should we wish away or pre-empt the development of a loved one? Perfection isn't featureless, nor is love. It is true of all terrible events that we want to undo them, to go back in time and dodge or seize the threat before it strikes, and it seems preposterous that, though we can walk into a room that we left an hour or a week ago and find it unchanged, we can never return to a moment. Indignant that we cannot master time, we dub it an enemy and struggle against it. Valuing things that endure, like gold and the Great Wall of China, we forget how we treasure time: if we could unravel in time all those whom we cherish, it would be the end of love. Time renders things unique and – tautologically – solitary: our feeble efforts to break time's seal, our wily subversions of the individuality conferred by time, are but expressions of our own cosmic loneliness.

It is wonderful that you want to marry Kate – yes, I admit it,

I too would be thrilled if it transpired. But to ask her and assume that she will agree, only two weeks after she has emerged from a coma, is a monolithic imposition. I know you feel protective and strangely chastened by her suffering; after your powerlessness during the last few weeks you want to demonstrate your love. But these things are your concern. You haven't given her time to assess her new circumstances. Her eyesight is still wobbly, she hasn't remembered her fall, her concentration is weak. Give the girl a chance to say she hates you, or she'll soon have reason to. In the grip of your own sentimental idea, you are somehow leaving Kate out and thereby threatening the very values for which you so ardently profess your love.

It is easy to take refuge in smug dismay at the dishonourable treatment of Turing during his lifetime: honouring him now is much harder.

As you guessed, it was Tilda who told me about your disappointment. Incidentally, I'm very glad for you that she's at last taken all her belongings from your flat and moved in properly with Joe. She was here at the weekend while Joe's in Brighton, looking a bit dazed, but cheerful and not baggy-eyed. She was wearing a skirt, an Indian print, if you can believe it. She said, 'I don't know why Jake doesn't relax. After all, Kate's not going to marry anyone else just now. He's as bad as John – Uncle John, not Joe.'

John is rich but he's not happy. He never has been, I don't know why. You've always been alert to time. But afraid of it? That's new. Yet you seem to be afraid of something.

12

Straight black hair parted a little to one side, reaching to her shoulders; an oval face with a wide, lipsticked mouth and a long, almost hooked nose, pale skin and dark eyes with a quick, mocking glance that distanced her from the rest of us: but Janey was beautiful and nobody ignored her. She laughed loudly in the corridors with other people and I saw that they had all made her acquaintance easily.

Stepping out of the main door of the college one afternoon in the early autumn, I was surprised to find her at my side. I must have been distracted because, had I seen her earlier, I would have waited for her to leave first.

But she forestalled me: 'You're Dan Flasch, aren't you?'

'Yes.'

'I've seen you around.'

As we walked, I looked sideways at her. She had strong black eyelashes. They challenged me in some unrecognized way.

'And I've seen you. You're Janey.'

She nodded, but at first said nothing. She seemed to be waiting for me to continue.

'What do you think of the college.?' I asked.

She said, 'Why do you always avoid me? Do I smell?'

'What...!'

'Don't tell me you're shy. That's just being stand-offish. Everyone's the same, you know, really.'

Despite her smile, I was stung. I'd been afraid to approach her because she seemed set apart.

'Not everyone would introduce themselves like that.'

'I don't see why I shouldn't.'

'Because not everyone could do it and get away with it.'

'Get away with it?'

'I didn't hit you.'

'Do you want to hit me?'

'Not really.'

'Why?'

'Well, it sort of cuts against the grain to hit a girl.'

'How charming. But you're attacking me now. I wouldn't say I'd got away with it. Anyway, I don't say things like that to get away with them. Always getting away with it is boring.'

There had been a short rainstorm earlier on. Now the sun was out and the ground was mottled with puddles and scraggy, rotting leaves. A gust of wind met us as we reached the green, bringing down more leaves which rustled around our uneven steps.

Surrounding the green at hip height was a rail. Suddenly Janey put her hands on it and leaned over, tucking her head round so that her knees hunched up to the bar and her feet left the ground. Her light coat fell up her back. She was wearing trousers but, as her buttocks rolled forwards before my eyes, I imagined her naked.

There was a clickety-clink of coins falling from her pocket. I bent down to retrieve them as her feet touched the ground, and she stood up. I quickly had all except a halfpenny, which rolled on its side into a puddle. In the sunlight I saw my face reflected in the shallow water; behind my nose lay the penny.

'Don't be so Jewish! It's only a halfpenny, it doesn't matter.'

I picked up the coin and tossed it at her feet. 'Being Jewish comes naturally to me.'

Her eyes revealed no shame, no hint of embarrassment. They had narrowed with a sudden, glittering hatred.

'I'm surprised you didn't pocket it!'

I walked away.

I was chatting with a couple of people in the college's front lobby when a coin appeared at my feet. I looked up and saw Janey, her feet turned out, with two books clutched against her breasts. She smiled flintily.

'You've dropped some money.'

I picked it up, but when I tried to give it to her she walked away. I wished I'd paid no attention.

It happened again four days later. I kicked it away; she kicked it back.

'You're very careless.'

She turned and I saw her narrow ankles.

Nobody else recognized her actions and I didn't comment on them. I was amused to see that in front of others she said nothing about my being Jewish, as if she didn't want them to know that she was a Jew-hater but at the same time wanted me to believe that she didn't care if they knew. I thought of ripostes to her facile taunts. I could so easily expose her. But I didn't: the affair was between Janey and myself.

This undisguised hatred was new to me and I didn't know how to deal with it. I was too shocked not to care and it was impossible to ignore it because she forced it on my attention. It was categorically different from teasing because I had no inclination to reject the term 'Jew'. Nor was her behaviour intended to win favour with others.

A high grey corridor connected the studios. It had no natural light, only bare bulbs. Footsteps echoed so that there was no escape even from yourself. One day, as I entered at one end, I saw that she had come in simultaneously at the other. It was a small place and such an accident had been sure to occur. She held a paintbrush in one hand which she tapped against the wall as we approached each other. As before, she fixed me with her thin smile and watched me without blinking. Her beautiful face was a canny harbour for her hatred.

She put her hand in her pocket and flicked out a coin. I watched it fall to the floor, half-expecting it to return to her pocket as if it was on a string, for I didn't understand why this was happening. But its descent was unchecked, and my temper suddenly split from its mooring. Snatching the paintbrush from her hand, I gripped her wrist and forced it behind her back and up towards her shoulder-blades. As I pushed her against the bare wall I caught the fresh, private scent of her body, like the springiness in a dew-laden lawn.

I was glad that she didn't cry out.

'Why? Why are you doing this?'

'Jew!'

'And?'

'Mean-minded thieves!'

I pressed up her elbow and she hissed.

'Why?'

'Eee! Let go!'

'No. Why? What's happened to you, Janey? You don't need to hate Jews. Everyone else worships you but you're more interested in your hatred.'

'Don't patronize me with your stupid psychology!'

I pushed up her elbow again so that her cheek was squashed against the cold wall.

'Why do you make me hurt you?'

'You hurt me because you want to. True to type!'

'And like all Goy, true to type, you hate Jews!'

Easing my grip a little, I put my shoulder against the wall and looked into her filmy eyes. 'No, you don't behave true to type. All Goy don't hate Jews like you, any more than all Jews are alike. For your information, I wasn't brought up among Jews. I don't know what Jews are like. But you know, Janey, because you hate them. So tell me why you hate them. Now tell me!'

I made her fingertips grope for the nape of her neck. She screwed up her eyes and bit hard, pulling apart her lips, trying not to scream.

'Tell me!'

'Aa!'

'Tell me!'

'You're breaking my arm!'

'Then tell me! Or are you enjoying it?'

'All right! All right!'

I relaxed a little and allowed a few seconds for the pain to subside before repeating, 'Tell me!'

'The Jews stole everything... They stole *everything! Us!*'

'What? What do you mean?'

Twisting from my unnerved hand, she faced me with grappling eyes.

'Don't you understand, you idiot? I'm Palestinian!'

She seemed to spit the word. Her teeth and her red lips glistened and I thought I felt a speck of saliva land on my cheek. I stepped back.

'I didn't know...'

'And if you did?'

She had slipped away and was striding along the corridor.

'It's got nothing to do with me!'

Nothing to do with me. Could I have said this, Jake?

I said it, and I thought it was true. Had my name been Gallagher, not Flasch, it might have been true. Concealed beneath the coloured mesh of childhood lay a fault-line between myself and the Gallaghers. When cracks were glimpsed, instinct told us how to mend them and we might have continued very well like this for ever had I never met Janey. For she accidentally tapped on the fault-line at such an angle that a fissure silently opened between us and then – it's obvious really: when the centre no longer holds, things are pulled apart by their own momentum.

I spent that Christmas vacation at home, in my bourgeois family's bosom. Yes, I'd heard a thing or two by then about what it was to be bourgeois. In London we all paid dutiful lip-service to socialism and then returned to the conveniently forgotten, conveniently remembered, cosy nests from which we all – except Janey – had sprung.

I was glad to be back home. The first evening, I sank into my family with grateful relish. It was like a capacious cushion, drawing me into itself. John and Amy told stories about school; Barba told how Julius's recent promotion had made him very conscientious about his suits. She wouldn't recognize the glamorous man in the house as her husband, she said, if it weren't for his unbrushed hair. Julius said this was wishful thinking because he didn't have much hair left to brush and anyway I mustn't think all his pay rise was going on suits: we were also going to get a new car.

'And how's Nan?'

Mrs Gallagher was in an old people's home. She had become very difficult in the preceding months and could no longer manage the stairs. One day she announced that she'd had enough of the bother of it all and wanted to go and live in a home, where things would be made nice and easy. At first we thought it was just Nan being grumpy but she wouldn't let up about it until it was settled. She wanted to be put out to grass, she said.

'She keeps them all in order,' Ruth said. 'I went to see her a couple of days ago and she'd got them playing whist.'

'And David and Sarah?'

'He wanders around with his walking-stick,' said John. 'Sometimes when I'm coming home from school I see him and he's standing there making faces, sort of conducting at the cathedral.'

He imitated David's hurt, angry muttering and shook his fist across the table at Ruth, 'And you, you're an oaf! You stand idly by watching all this happening and one day when it's too late you'll wonder why the world has turned into butter!'

'Now you mustn't laugh,' said Barba. 'He finds retirement

very difficult.'

I thought of David striding around in his Sunday best, brandishing his stick at the building-sites and buttonholing labourers and passers-by. I giggled, although I was ashamed to do so.

When at last I stopped, my stomach ached. I groaned, then wiped my streaming eyes. The others were all looking at me with puzzled amusement.

'Pleased to be home, Dan?' said Julius.

'I'm sorry, I didn't mean to laugh at David, I just got the giggles.'

'Don't they giggle much in London?'

'Not much.'

'Why not? Are they all too busy being arty?' said Amy.

'Yes. Or getting at me for being Jewish, which isn't always easy to laugh at,' I said thoughtlessly.

They were stunned, as if they'd never heard that I was Jewish. Then they all asked me at once what I meant.

'Not everyone,' I said hastily. 'It's just one girl. She hates Jews and she's always trying to bait me, throwing coins on the floor at me and so on. She's Palestinian.'

'How dare she?' said Barba.

'But why doesn't anyone stop her?' said Ruth.

'No one else realizes.'

'You shouldn't take any notice. You should report it if it happens again,' said Barba.

'Who to?'

'I'd swipe the little minx if I were you!' said Julius.

Amy laughed, nervously brushing her mouth with her sleeve.

Later, as everyone else was going to bed, Julius took me aside and poured me a whisky. 'Has it been giving you a lot of trouble, Dan, this... anti-Semitism?'

'Not really. It's just one girl, and I try to avoid her.'

He said, of course, reporting her wouldn't get her to stop thinking her thoughts but it would at least oblige her to stop bothering me. She shouldn't be allowed to bait me, he insisted; she shouldn't get away with it.

'They can't chain her up.'

'No, but they can try and teach her a lesson in manners, at least.'

'I don't think she's very interested in manners, Julius.'

'Well she ought to be! It's all very well teaching people to paint, but if they can't teach them manners first, then what's it all for?'

Julius knew that his remarks were unsatisfactory. There was no trenchant argument, no triumphantly delivered solution. Our conversation just tailed off. Julius didn't know how I should respond, he didn't even know how to respond himself. We finished our whiskies and he patted me on the shoulder. 'Sleep well, old boy.' He advised me as if I was being bullied at school, but I don't think he even convinced himself with this refuge. All the Gallaghers could only see it in this light: and how should they see it otherwise?

It wasn't the Gallaghers' problem, it was Dan Flasch's problem. And in considering it I was confronted by a self that was unfamiliar. The secure perspective of the Gallaghers and Coventry in which I had stood was suddenly shaken out of its joints and I found myself the solitary observer of unfamiliar stars at a scarcely noticed attic window, a window that turned out on closer inspection to be a prism, my Jewishness. And why, after this bizarre glimpse, couldn't I revert to the comfortable lines and shadows of the old perspective? I could have ignored Janey. Perhaps, were I stronger, I would have done so.

Throughout the vacation I kept on thinking about her. Fiddling about in my room with paints, sketching cranes and ruins in the city, turning the pages of my books, I wondered about her. She was attractive – but there was more to my curiosity than sexual fantasy. It had never seemed to matter to anyone that I was Jewish. Now, by attaching such importance to it, Janey seemed to grant me a strange power which I didn't understand and which perhaps she had misplaced. Palestine, Israel, what were they to me? Nothing had driven me to think about them before – but did I now secretly want to tell her that it wasn't my fault? To persuade her that she was unreasonable to hate me purely because I was Jewish? From this distance it seems impossibly naïve – so much so that I'm inclined to think that my real motive was a desire to get into her knickers. But I was naïve; and, back then, the likelihood of getting into her knickers was exceedingly remote. But in whatever relation I stood or imagined standing to her, it was as a Jew.

I may have implied that the other students at our college were stupid, or very slow to catch on to the conflict between Janey and myself. I'm sure this wasn't the case. Because of Janey's behaviour they knew that I was Jewish and they knew that she was Palestinian because she told them so. Under no circumstances would they have sided openly with Janey against me – they were liberal art students with well-oiled consciences and all the appropriate responses to Jews in the wake of the Holocaust. Likewise, under no circumstances would they have sided openly with me against Janey – they were liberal art students, after all, with well-oiled consciences and all the appropriate responses to a race (and a beautiful girl) which had been ejected from its homeland. It looked very much as if the survivors of the one outrage had been the perpetrators of the other, but they didn't feel able to condemn the Jews for kicking out the Palestinians; nor were they able to condemn the Palestinians for their dislike of the Jews. It was all very inconvenient for their consciences. They couldn't admit to wishing me elsewhere, and Janey was far too beautiful to wish elsewhere... Whatever were they to do?

Keep quiet! was the accepted solution. They didn't talk about Janey to me and, presumably, they didn't talk about me to Janey. Whatever the nature of the dispute, it was one in which they wanted no part. So the halfpennies still rolled along corridors in the new term and everyone smiled awkwardly as I kicked them back. If the insults hadn't hurt I might have wondered if I wasn't imagining them, for nobody else seemed to hear them. Every encounter was like walking through a plate-glass window. Meanwhile, it seemed, people were friendly with Janey. I watched her in groups and saw that we had plenty of friends in common – for others she was good company, evidently.

I was walking with a long-necked fellow called Neville Ritchie along one of those corridors one day when she paid her most dramatic tribute so far to my race. She emerged from a studio as we were passing and, seeing me, as if on reflex, she spat. Uncharacteristically, she withdrew at once. Perhaps she hadn't seen Neville at first; perhaps she was dismayed at what she had done.

'Well, that's the nearest anyone's come to kissing her,' said Neville.

I felt the gob of saliva slip down my cheek towards my lip and hurriedly wiped it away, first with my sleeve and then with my handkerchief. 'It didn't feel like a kiss to me.'

'No, it didn't look like one either,' he said, regretting his flippancy.

'Neville, is she going to back off?'

'She's got it in for you, Dan.'

'I'd noticed. It's getting very irritating.'

'She was brought up in Tel Aviv, in quite a rich family, I think. They left when she was ten. They thought they'd go back soon but they never did, and they lost everything except what they took then – the clothes they were wearing and their front-door keys.'

'I'm very sorry to hear about it. I didn't take it. I lost my mother and my father and my brother and my other brother and my grandfather and my grandmother – and I never had any front-door keys.'

I had never revealed this to anyone at college – very few people even in Coventry knew the whole story – and it felt strange saying these words now, hearing myself say them. Why was I saying them? I certainly didn't want sympathy. I was exasperated.

'Can you tell me why I don't go in there and thrash her?'

Neville couldn't tell me, he didn't know what to say. It was unfair of me to burden him with this information and, attempting to deflate it, I added, 'Not that I ever knew them. I was taken away when I was one, just before the war, by a friend of my mother's, and brought up very happily in Coventry. They are my family.'

I have a vague memory of Neville stammering, his head straining forward like a chicken; I don't remember what he said. I realized, however, that what I'd told him constituted a news item and that everyone would know it within a few hours. Everyone except, perhaps, for Janey. But in the weeks that followed her abuse ceased. If we passed in the entrance or the lobby, she still looked at me intently but the rage in her eyes was calmed: whatever she had been told had impressed her. She seemed to have found something in me to respect and this forged a strange bond. There was a fierce intimacy in her eyes which I sensed was reserved for me, even though I didn't know what to make of it. Among the other boys she was an object of desire but she preserved a cool, humorous detachment which ensured that she was also popular among the girls. But to me, who could never attain her, she shimmered with the heat of her agitated nerves. I unsettled her. Having stopped abusing me, she didn't know how to behave towards me.

Late in January there was a heavy snowfall. In the morning it lay across the green like a pristine white rug. At first the light was pale and watery; then, as the sky cleared to a brilliant blue, the whiteness hurt the eyes as if the millions of tiny crystals had grazed the retina itself. By the time I went out there with a couple of others, a tangle of trails was already stamped into the snow but it was still crisp underfoot and the air was sharp. Several of our fellow students were already hurling snowballs. We bent clumsily in our coats and hurriedly grabbed handfuls of snow ourselves. Soon there must have been at least twenty of us, shouting and floundering about, ducking and compacting our little bombs of snow. With all the extra clothes people were wearing and the awkwardness of movement caused by the snow, it was hard to be sure of everyone's identity. Turning as you were struck on the neck, you might not recognize the bent figure at whom you were aiming a few yards away. After a furious exchange in one direction, when the snow slipped down your sleeves and collar and the waistband of your trousers, you would suddenly be attacked from another direction; you ran a few yards, threw a snowball here, there, and were struck by a few strays, then you were embroiled in a new confrontation. And all the time it didn't matter who your adversary was. You might or might not recognize them: whoever it was, it was the Enemy.

Suddenly I realized I was fighting Janey. I don't know which of us threw a missile first nor who was the first to recognize the other. We were still laughing and behaving as before, as if we were fighting the Enemy and not the individual, but our game soon acquired an edge. Our fire was reserved for each other; we paid no attention to snowballs from other hands. We drew rapidly closer and I could see her eyes glinting as she aimed and the red flush of heat in her cheeks. When I scooped up handfuls of snow I could see her body move accordingly, darting out of my line and trying to catch me off balance. But in the end it was she who slipped onto her rump and, as my arm was drawn back to throw, she covered her face with her hands and turned her head away.

I halted.

Janey lay a yard away, almost at my feet. When she realized I wasn't going to throw the snow she sat up, leaning back on her hands. For the first time our eyes met steadily. I saw no malice in hers. They were like those of a surprised cat; then they narrowed. She sniffed and her nose twitched in the cold. I approached her and dropped the snowball onto her head and, as it crumbled over her face, she closed her eyes and tilted up her chin. Her pink tongue licked the melting flakes from her lips; she smiled.

'Hey, Dan! Are you coming for a coffee?'

I looked up and saw Neville. My hands were cold, my gloves stiff with ice. I nodded and walked towards him. From the corner of my eye I saw Janey stand up and shake herself.

'The canteen or the café?' he asked.

The café was opposite the college's main entrance. Janey had run ahead to join a couple who were always in the café.

'The café,' I said.

For a moment we just listened to the crunch of the snow. Then, 'Aren't you going to thank me for rescuing you?' said Neville.

'Oh, yes. Yes. It was all right though. She's relaxed a bit towards me.'

'I suppose she must get tired of keeping up an attitude like that.'

I shrugged. It didn't seem to me that Janey had simply dropped her attitude towards me but that it had changed – into what, I wasn't sure.

We paused just inside the door, rubbing our hands and enjoying the sudden fug. Several tables were occupied by men eating their lunch. Janey was sitting in the far corner, where there were still two empty chairs. She saw me and her eyes flicked around the room, then back to the empty chairs, before returning to me. Ignoring Neville's anxious whisper, I went forward and we sat down. Besides us, there was Roderick, with fat cheeks and a thin crop of blond hair; Lorna, his girlfriend, whose sallow, earnest face compensated for Roderick's ruddy exuberance, and Thomas Singleton. His beard made him look older, which he was; he was in the third year, while Lorna and

Roderick were in the second year. I had been in this café often, and with these people: but – as they all knew – never with Janey. Lorna glanced uncertainly at us. I sensed Neville give a little shrug of helplessness. Roderick beamed genially, while Thomas fingered his beard and stared intently at a book in front of him on the table.

'What's that you're reading, Thomas?' I said.

'Sartre.'

Everybody was reading Sartre.

'Don't you ever read for fun? A detective story or something?' said Janey.

'This is fun.'

'Fun?'

'I don't understand how people can concentrate on detective stories,' said Lorna. 'They're so boring.'

'No, they're not,' said Janey. 'You only say they're boring because you want us to think your mind is pure and sophisticated.'

'That's a contradiction in terms,' said Thomas.

'Damn you, you know what I mean!'

'How can I, when you don't define your terms?'

'When you don't even know yourself,' said Lorna.

Janey sat back, pressing her palms against the edge of the Formica table. 'Why are you attacking me all of a sudden? I only said I don't believe that anyone is incapable of enjoying a detective story!'

'Perhaps we're all mad geniuses,' said Neville.

'Don't flatter yourself, Nev,' I said. 'Anyway, it's not good manners to call yourself a genius.'

'Or anyone else,' said Janey. 'It's a bit callow.'

Missing her irony, Neville blushed with shame. He looked as if she'd disparaged his manhood.

'Who wants what?' said Roderick, and he called over Beryl, the beefy waitress. Janey, Neville and I asked for coffee; the others shared a pot of tea.

Lorna and Janey were still arguing about detective stories. I was no connoisseur but I had certainly enjoyed the few I'd read and so, though it wasn't clear that anyone arguing against them had actually read any, I found myself agreeing with Janey.

'They have no art,' said Thomas.

'Do you mean art or skill?' said Roderick.

'Oh, I don't deny their skill,' said Thomas. 'But they address nothing beyond themselves.'

'Oh God!' said Janey. 'You're going to say something about the Eternal Verities soon. I can feel it in the air, like the smell from a baby's nappies.'

'Nonsense, Janey, you know perfectly well – all art should have some moral purpose!'

'Pié Jesu,' I intoned.

Neville said I was being difficult – I couldn't deny that all good art had a serious intent. I answered that he was confusing art with missionary work.

'I don't believe this! You think that all art is immoral?' said Thomas.

'He didn't say that,' said Janey, glancing at me for an instant. 'It's you who's dragging morality into it all the time.'

'Any art that's not trivial must be *engagé!*'

'The man speaks French!' said Janey. '*Engagé avec quoi?*'

'With things that matter,' said Lorna.

I laughed. 'Things that matter to the reader or viewer, or to the writer/artist?'

'Part of the artist's role, surely, is to pinpoint the things that do matter?'

'I hate the idea of the artist having a role,' I said, 'either as a preacher or anything else. It reduces all art to a social function. What's interesting is not the artist's so-called role but what an artist actually does.'

'All good artists shock,' said Janey.

'That's so naïve!' said Thomas.

'By showing the world in an unusual – a shocking – way,

they provoke a response that is moral. That's where morality comes into art.'

'I think no one should be allowed to pick up a paintbrush or a pen until they've read *Das Kapital*,' said Thomas.

'Perhaps you should write a play, Thomas, about dead artists sitting around in Hell, discussing *Das Kapital* with *les autres* and repainting their pictures,' said Roderick.

'Maybe you're right, Thomas,' said Janey: 'Since I'd rather read detective stories than *Das Kapital*, which I wouldn't understand a page of anyway, I'd better give up art...'

'It amazes me that you, of all people, should be so hostile...'

'Shut up and stop preaching at me, Thomas! Go away and paint a picture!'

Lorna looked at her watch. 'Oh my! It's two o' clock!'

Everyone exclaimed over the classes they were about to be late for and stood up with a noisy scrape of chairs, except for Janey and I. We didn't look at each other; we didn't move, as if we each held a key to the other and couldn't move until we were released.

'Haven't you got a life class, Dan?' said Neville.

'Yes,' I said, but still I didn't move.

He shrugged and followed the others out.

Janey faced me. By remaining here she seemed to be permitting me to look at her directly, such as she never had before, even inviting me to do so. Her black hair was damp from the snow. She had pushed it behind her ear and it hung straight to her shoulders, slightly lopsided and lank. Her eyes were like discs of flecked jet and, in the warmth, the bud of colour in her cheeks had flowered into a soft pink that I wanted to touch. Her lips, usually vermilion, were pale now and set in an oddly childish grimace. For a moment she looked afraid; then her face was taut with concentration, as if she found our uncertainty towards each other exciting.

'Not spitting?'

Her mouth flickered with a readiness to smile but she still

wasn't sure whether it was timely.

'You spat at me,' I persisted. 'Don't you remember?'

She nodded and I touched my cheekbone.

'It hit me here and then trickled down to just near my lip.'

She continued watching me in unnerving silence.

'So now you've stayed here with me deliberately. What's up? Is there something you wanted to say?'

Suddenly she looked down. One hand passed across her face. 'I don't know why...'

'Of course you know why you did it! I know why! We both know why!'

'Yes, yes...'

'But you've stopped.'

'Yes!'

'But you haven't stopped being Palestinian any more than I've stopped being Jewish.'

'Listen,' she said, with an echo of her former ferocity, 'don't expect me to like Jews. I'm Palestinian!'

'I don't care a damn whether you're Palestinian or Abyssinian. And you suddenly seem to care far less that I'm Jewish. Which suits me fine.'

Janey drew in her breath. I watched her carefully. She seemed to be wrestling with something that she wanted to say but which was very difficult to admit. She looked at me and drew in her breath again, then apparently decided not to speak.

'Do you want some more coffee?' I said.

At last she smiled and it was a normal, thoughtless smile. I called Beryl. Janey ran her fingers through her hair, and we waited for the coffee in silence.

Her hand curved round the hot mug and she began again:

'Someone pointed out to me that if I felt no guilt for what happened to the Jews in the war because I wasn't responsible and I suffered at their hands afterwards, then I shouldn't expect you to feel guilty for what the Jews did – do – to the Palestinians. It was wrong of me to try and make you suffer as if you were responsible.'

I had expected some confession of this sort and, though surprised by its articulate statement, I was sceptical. I responded in the only way that felt appropriate: with irony.

'A miracle of logic!' I said.

'You can believe it or not – that's up to you.'

'Who was the inspiration for this jewel?'

'Neville.'

'Neville!'

Aware that at last she had caught me off guard, Janey smiled. Her lips parted in a dazzle of white teeth. Then she continued:

'He came to me one day and said, did I realize that your family had all been wiped out and that you hadn't been brought up among Jews, let alone among Israelis? He thought it was the first bit that should matter but I have to tell you that it's the second part that's more important to me...'

'Why do you have to tell me? Why are you telling me all this?'

'Because I think I owe you some sort of explanation...'

'You mean that by considering me an honorary Goy you can avoid the inconvenience of hating me while continuing to hate the Jews.'

'Don't get clever with me!'

'But isn't that what you mean?'

'No!'

'It is! You reserve the right to hate Israelis. Since I'm not an Israeli, it doesn't matter to you. But I am a Jew!'

'Do you want me to hate you?'

'No.'

'Well, then!'

'What do you mean 'well, then'? You think I should be grateful for your little dance of reason? You think I should thank you for your mercy?'

'No!'

'You hated me because I was a Jew. Now you've decided

that I'm not a proper Jew and stopped hating me. I'm sorry, I don't accept that. Either you hate me or you don't.'

'This is ridiculous! Don't you understand? I'm trying to tell you that I don't hate you!'

'My family died purely because they were Jews. That makes me *absolutely* Jewish. Do you understand?'

'Yes! Yes! Stop shouting, I can't bear it when you shout!'

I looked round quickly. One or two heads were turned in our direction, suddenly alert at the whiff of dispute.

'Why should I care what you can or can't bear?'

'Pardon?'

'Why should I care what you can or can't bear?'

Janey looked into her cup, avoiding my eyes, as if ashamed to be seen drinking such ordinary tea from such an ugly cup.

'No reason. I said it without thinking,' she said.

Ignorant as I was of Palestinian politics, I knew enough to realize that it couldn't have been easy for Janey to say what she had said. She had almost apologized to me and, however doubtful I was of the value of such an apology, I admired the courage required to make it. I felt sorry for her all of a sudden, which was a new sensation.

'Actually, of course I care,' I said. 'I wouldn't be sitting here if I didn't, would I?'

'We've both skipped class,' she agreed.

We fell silent but neither of us made any effort to leave. Our conversation was so full of unresolved questions and uneasy half-truths that we were reluctant to drop it, but we didn't know how to resume. Any thread that we followed was likely to lead to conflict. It was clear, however, that we wanted to find out whether it was possible to be together without conflict.

'How about making up for the lost life-class and drawing each other?' I suggested.

'What? Here?' said Janey, sitting up straight. She looked round the dismal interior with a frown, as if seeing it for the

first time, the film of grease over the cheap, varnished pan-
elling, the fluorescent light.

'No. I haven't got my sketch-book anyway. How about
going back to my digs?'

'To your digs? Where...?'

'Only five minutes' walk.'

Janey stared at me and swallowed hard. Two hours ago such
a proposal would have been unthinkable.

'Thank you... All right,' she said, and smiled with her head
a little to one side.

We went briefly into college to collect our bags and then set
off together into the snow.

I shared with two other students the first floor of a late
Victorian semi-detached. We each had our own bedroom and
there was a bathroom and a small kitchen. Our landlady, Mrs
Croucher, lived downstairs; she was a widow. We saw her
often, either hovering at the door or when she came to clean
our rooms. She told us many times how she only started letting
out rooms to students after her husband's death eight years previously, 'to make ends meet': she wouldn't do it if she weren't
obliged by circumstances, she said. Nevertheless, we felt quite
welcome because she derived vicarious pleasure from our activities and vigorously delighted in criticizing them. She would
complain about banging not because she disliked the noise or
was anxious about the walls but because she was curious to
know what we were doing. She would come half-way up the
stairs, leaning heavily on the banister and call: 'What you up to
Danny-boy? What's all that banging for? Hanging up pictures
are you? You want to get yourself a proper hammer, no use
forever using the heel of that poor shoe.' By now she would be
standing squarely in the middle of the room, hands braced on
her hips. 'Here, you go and look in my kitchen, there's one
under the sink.' And off I would go to find the hammer – what
else could I do? – and by the time I returned she'd have the bed
pulled out with a chair wedged against the wall behind, herself

perilously installed on the chair and eagerly awaiting my arrival so she could smash a hole in the wall herself. And then only with the utmost difficulty, or cunning, could we get rid of her. She would volunteer to bang in more nails, clean the top of the pelmet 'while she was there', tidy up 'that blamed heap of canvasses...'. But she had a weakness.

A few doors along on the corner was a sweet shop which sold a virulent strain of acid drops. And before entering my digs I told Janey that I must go and buy some.

'Oh, that's a good idea,' she said.

So I bought two bags. 'My landlady likes them,' I explained. 'It's an unspoken bargain: if you give her some, she keeps out of the way.'

We stamped our feet outside the door to get rid of the snow and, as I hung up our damp coats in the hall, Janey complained loudly of the cold. 'There's a heater in my room,' I said, fearing that Mrs Croucher would interpret this as a reflection on her housekeeping. But Mrs Croucher didn't appear, so she wasn't there. All the acid drops were for us.

My room was brightly illumined by the snow outside. Deprived of the usual murk, my pictures seemed naked. They glared from the walls in a shameless parade of their inadequacies. While I fumbled with the heater, Janey studied them. At last the match found the gas and, with a little 'pop', the heater came to life. I pulled up my solitary armchair and offered it to Janey.

'Have you got any coffee?' she said as she sat.

While I boiled the kettle in the kitchen I thought of Janey examining my room. She had said nothing about the lame sketches and palsied daubs that I'd hung up with such vanity; I sweated with shame for them. It wouldn't have mattered so much if they had been lying in a dusty pile under the bed, for then, if she chose to pull one out, though it wouldn't improve the picture I could at least have demonstrated that I knew it was bad by saying that it was terrible, that I was embarrassed for her to see it. By flaunting my shortcomings, I'd set myself up to be laughed at.

I nudged the door with my knee and paused on the threshold with the two mugs, watching her. With her feet slightly apart she was standing in front of the heater warming her hands. So intent was she on the photograph on the mantelpiece, she seemed not to have noticed me enter. Bent forward at the waist, her cheek bulging with an acid drop, she seemed about to devour the picture.

'Here's the coffee,' I said.

She turned abruptly. 'Who's the photo of?'

'My family.'

'Your family?'

'My foster-family.'

'Ah!'

I gave her one of the mugs and she sat down again. 'Tell me about them,' she said. 'I'll draw you first, and you can tell me about them as I draw.' And she reached into her bag and pulled out her sketch-pad, a pencil and an eraser.

'And when I draw you, you'll tell me about your family, is that it?'

'Have an acid drop,' said Janey, 'and stand in the middle of the room.'

I did as she said. As her eyes roved up and down me the taste spread warmly down my throat.

'How did you come to be with them?' she prompted.

As I began to speak I saw her eyes dilate and then narrow to a squint. At first I was tentative but as I watched her I felt a looseness pervade me which made the words tumble from my mouth as if she was pulling them from me. Her right eye kept closing, so that her cheek squeezed up and her mouth was crooked, then she would relax and peer at my knees and torso, my head, my shoulders... I couldn't always tell precisely where she was looking. It felt as if I was being shifted and dismantled, transposed and reassembled by her dark eyes: but she was observing me, not judging me, I thought. From time to time she would turn over a sheet of her pad and tell me to move – to sit or kneel or to raise my arm – and she would begin a new drawing. She never interrupted my narrative with a comment or a question, she just let me speak. Only when I came to a halt did she look at me with focussed, steady eyes. 'It must have been strange for you when I started attacking you for being Jewish,' she said.

I laughed uneasily.

'But you *are* Jewish.'

'I realize that.'

Janey laid down her pencil and pad on the floor and put another acid drop between her lips. She sucked it into her mouth and smiled. 'Now it's my turn,' she said, and stood up.

'Or my turn, depending on which way you look at it.'

She glanced at me, her eyes bare with surprise, and quickly looked down. I was a little taller and, as she bowed her head, I could see the top of her hair gleaming in the snow's light. She was wearing a long blue woollen skirt and a cardigan over a loose man's shirt. It was a shame to be drawing her in her clothes.

'My father was from an old family in Haifa,' said Janey as I began to draw. 'They had a lot of orange groves outside the city and they used to grow all sorts of other fruit too. I remember it very well. Me and my brothers and sister used to go out there sometimes and help pick fruit. It was hot and there was a special smell and it was so beautiful. Sometimes when it was very hot we used to go up into the hills and you could see the haze over the land to the Mediterranean. Our house was big, with a big courtyard and a fountain where we used to paddle...' Her voice was soft but slightly strained, as if she was trying to find a suitable tone for her story. But it eluded her and I was irritated by the practised nostalgia which made her words seem empty. I concentrated instead on drawing her, trying to capture the slimness of her body beneath the bulky clothes. Her neck was difficult because, although I knew it was very straight and clear, one tendon seemed to shimmer in the glancing light: either I drew it as I knew it to be and it became flat and plastic; or I drew what I could see, and then it acquired an ugly scroll of muscle up the side. Suddenly her voice was harder: '...and so we left, thinking it was a scare, thinking we'd be back in a week or two. We each took one bag and went to stay with cousins in Beirut. I was ten. I remember worrying about the pet rabbits we kept but my mother said the neighbours would look after them. I still sometimes wonder about those rabbits.'

Deciding to concentrate more on her face, I turned another page and began a new sketch. She was watching me closely, with a slight frown, as if disconcerted by my lack of reaction. But she hadn't responded to my story and I had no desire to comment yet on hers. Besides, she hadn't finished it. 'So what brought you to England?' I said.

I drew a line for her jaw and quickly marked a little patch of shadow beside her nose. Her mouth was still. 'I mean, how come you didn't stay in Beirut? Did your parents have particular contacts here?'

'My mother's English,' she said.

I lifted my pencil, startled by this revelation.

'There's no need to look so amazed. How else do you think I speak English? My mother worked there under the British Mandate and met my father. So coming to England wasn't very difficult.'

I hadn't considered her English. Had I paused to wonder I might have guessed that one parent was English but she gave the impression of being so wholly Palestinian that it would have been churlish to question it. She seemed devious and suddenly rather absurd. Perhaps it had been traumatic leaving Palestine, but the idea that her subsequent life was especially difficult as a result had a flimsy foundation; it was an insult to real Palestinians, I suspected. Maybe the family had suffered, maybe they missed their country very much, but at least they were able

to settle in England and become English. Become English?
They *were* English!

Janey was still talking but I was scarcely listening. My pencil
had diverted from her head and, without consciously deciding
to do so, I was drawing her without clothes, imagining the
planes of her breasts and her belly, attempting to judge the
curves of her hips and thighs. As I stared I could sense the
smoothness of her skin and her firm flesh against mine; I could
see the angles of her legs inside the skirt and, as my pencil stole
towards her genitals, I felt myself becoming aroused. I shifted
in my chair. There was a distinct bulge which I quickly
screened by holding the pad upright on my thighs. I tried to
look at her with the same detachment as before but I was afraid
I was blushing. She had stopped talking now and was watching
me as if making some sort of appraisal. Had she been watching
my trousers at that critical moment? The more anxious I
became, the more excited I grew: swiftly I turned the page,
intending to draw her clothed again – but I didn't, I drew her
naked. She seemed not to realize. I smiled, trying to reassure
her, and she returned my smile obliquely.

Suddenly there was a hefty knock on the door and Mrs
Croucher entered.

'Goodness me, what a surprise! Mrs Croucher!' I cried, but
I couldn't get up without revealing my furtive arousal.

'I heard voices, Danny-boy, and I thought I'd come up
because you never know, these days...' Without explaining
what it was that you never knew, she peered at Janey.

'This is Janey, another student at college. Janey, this is Mrs
Croucher, my landlady.'

'Pleased to meet you, Miss,' said Mrs Croucher with a nod.
'I'm not nosey-parkering – I'm a lady, Miss. But if a lady hears
voices in her house, she can't be too careful, that's what I say.'

'Of course, Mrs Croucher,' said Janey. 'Dan and I were just
drawing each other.'

'Were you now? Let's have a look, Dan. He's so clever with

his hands, is my Danny-boy!' she added to Janey.

In these circumstances I subsided fast, but the prospect of Mrs Croucher looking at my drawings induced a feeling like panic. 'There's some acid drops there, Mrs Croucher!'

'Let's have a look at your drawings, Dan!'

'Some acid drops! There!' I pointed frantically towards the brown paper packet on the floor.

Mrs Croucher's red face turned greedily towards them and then she slowly bent down, extending her pudgy hand. But as soon as she had them she swivelled with unexpected speed and plucked the pad from my knee.

I smiled helplessly. If I tried to stop her looking, I would fail and she would certainly show it to Janey; if I allowed her to proceed, it would still be embarrassing but she might not show it to Janey.

She flipped to my appalling nudes almost immediately, as if she knew what she was looking for. 'Well, Danny-boy, you are a one for surprises!' she said.

I hoped she would leave the matter there but she wanted a response from me and was clearly prepared to wait, or push me further.

'It's an exercise we have to do at college,' I said. 'An exercise of the imagination.'

Mrs Croucher didn't believe what I said but it wasn't the truth she was interested in so much as the quality of the lie. Now she nodded thoughtfully, choosing just how much mischief to make. 'I didn't think, in this weather, that you'd be posing starkers,' she said. Then she added, 'Cheerio, nice to meet you, Miss,' and left with the acid drops, closing the door behind her.

'You devious, devious monster!' said Janey.

She was advancing slowly towards me, her expression so contorted by intensity that I wondered for a moment if her outrage wasn't feigned. Her eyes gouged mine; her teeth were bared in a snarl that might, conceivably, have resolved into a grin.

'It's all right, you can have the drawings! Look, I'll tear them up at once!' I cried, and tore out the offending pages.

'I thought you were hiding something,' she said, oblivious of the pages I held towards her. And she raised her hand.

It wasn't until she actually struck my face that I understood that she was serious and then my anger was ignited by the self-righteousness of hers. I seized her wrist harshly. 'Don't talk to me about hiding things! You pretend you're Palestinian but your mother's English!'

As I pushed her backwards she tried to hit me with her other hand, but she couldn't get any swing. 'I'm Palestinian!'

'You poor baby!'

Now she was against the wall. I could smell her and I felt her hip hard against my prick which was rearing again insistently.

Janey was still. 'I thought you were hiding something,' she said.

Suddenly I realized that she wasn't trying to move away from me. Her hip was pressing against me and her face, however it seemed to challenge me, was only six inches from mine.

We assaulted each other. To this day, though I remember the ferocity of our sex, I don't understand quite how it happened. Would it have occurred if I hadn't made those drawings or if they hadn't been discovered (not that Janey ever looked at them herself)? And what if I hadn't had a packet of French letters tucked into my sock-drawer? I had no sound reason to be prepared: I just lived in hope that I would get lucky. Perhaps we would have carried on regardless.

And – get lucky? How lucky was I? Certainly they thought I was lucky at college, where not only were they amazed by our about-face (so were we), but also Janey was considered a most impressive conquest. But... lucky?

I remember lying on the bed afterwards and my eyes fell on the photograph on the mantelpiece. I felt a dizzying sense of distance from them. All this had happened simply because I was a Jew: I was sharing my bed with Janey only because I existed.

*

It is June 1960. I'm leaning against the barrier to Platform 7 at Euston. I am tall, with large feet and large hands and a peak of black hair. Sometimes it falls across my right eye and I jerk my head to flick it away with the hectic assurance of a second-year art student. There's not much flesh on my face: my eyes are deep, my nose prominent; only my mouth gives an impression of regularity, for my lips are full and my teeth white and straight. My hands are crossed on my forearms. On the little finger of my left hand is a ring with a miniature, stylized Star of David.

Tilly had given me my mother's ring when I stayed with her in Jeddah at Christmas. I didn't even know of its existence. We were sitting on the balcony talking over cocktails when the rasping voices of the *muezzins* called the Faithful to prayer and we fell silent and listened. Then she said, 'I have something of yours.' Placing her glass on the low inlaid table, she stood up and went into the cool interior of the flat where Percy was snoozing.

I had been telling her about Janey. Predictably, perhaps, the affair had come to an end after just a few months. Although it still mystified me how it had ever happened, I was aware that it had affected me beyond the mere loss of my virginity.

We didn't fight. On the contrary, we grew bored with each other. As I got to know her better she seemed less exotic and more English; she became rather dull to me. She talked about 'being true to yourself', as if everyone had only one dimension. Ironically, she insisted now that my consciousness of being Jewish constrained my 'real self'. But by that stage it scarcely mattered. I had accommodated the original reflection she showed me into my image of myself and it seemed to justify a creeping sense of solitude. While she chased after images of peace and violence to justify her own experience of dispossession, she pointed out a heritage to me, the Holocaust, a single image of violence that underwrote a world of dispossession. I thought Tilly would think my involvement with Janey was foolish, but she didn't. 'Emotional experience can stunt growth,' she said, 'But you can't grow without it. If you're lucky, and wise, it enables you to grow.'

The last hour before darkness on a warm, lazy day always promises to last for ever. As the sun smears itself across the sky you can still feel it on your skin and there seems to be no good reason for everything not staying as it is. When Tilly returned she held a little box towards me and, for a moment, she was no longer the ruminative Tilly I knew with her brittle carapace: she was offering something to me with fragile simplicity – and twenty years had dropped from her.

'It was going to be a birthday present,' she said, 'But – it's not mine to give. It's yours anyway.'

Mounted on a plain gold ring were three little oblong emeralds.

'My mother's?'

'Yes.'

'How...?'

Tilly bent over the table and took a cigarette from the little mother-of-pearl box. Standing by the parapet, she lit it and looked out over the basking city. Then she told me how she had come by it.

When she had finished I said, 'It's a shame I can't wear it.'

'You could always wear another one, a sort of token replacement. Why don't you have one made? And send me the bill – that can be my present. Haven't you got a friend who could make you one?'

The Coventry train has just come in. My hands are not crossed on my forearms: my forearms are resting on the barrier, and I am fiddling with the ring that was made for me by a friend of Janey's. A crowd has spilled from the Coventry train and at last it has yielded Ruth.

She was struggling with a large suitcase. She needed both hands to lift it: her right hip was braced against the case and her torso lurched away to balance the weight. Over her left elbow was a wire-handled shopping-bag which repeatedly slipped to her wrist, trapping a fold of her yellow skirt and impeding her legs. Every few paces she had to stop, put down her baggage and shake her strained arms. In the distance I twice saw someone speak to her, presumably offering help, but she shook her head and continued alone. But when she paused, I also saw her look round quickly as she patted the blonde hair piled on her head, as if seeking a porter or a trolley. Then she saw me, whereupon she dropped the case and waited with tightly folded arms for me to relieve her. There was nothing pathetic in her action, for there was no request: she was simply stating that I would carry the case. Meanwhile she grinned and her face shone pink in the heat from her exertions.

'What on earth have you got this for?' I said when we had greeted each other. It was Julius's big leather suitcase with steel-reinforced corners. 'And what have you got inside? It weighs a ton!'

'I've got lots of stuff from home. And I wanted a choice of clothes. I don't know what the weather will be like.'

'Ruth, it's June!'

'It may be June but last week I had to wear winter clothes.'

'So you've brought your winter clothes with you, although it's boiling hot? Shouldn't you have brought your gumboots too, and a fur coat and a few pots and pans just to be on the safe side?'

Ruth disdained to answer me. A sudden gust fluttered the wisps of hair against her exposed neck. Her trim nose twitched and she touched her throat as if to check that her blouse was buttoned. An observer would certainly have thought that I was complaining about carrying the pretty, dainty lady's suitcase, and in a way, of course, they would have been right: but Ruth deserved no sympathy. She had come to London for three interviews for her university entrance, two on Tuesday and one on Friday; they didn't require a ball-gown. And she was staying with me. That morning I had changed the sheets on my bed for her and tidied my room; I'd even bought some flowers. As for me, I was going to sleep on the sofa in Mrs Croucher's sitting-room. Mrs Croucher had been delighted when I asked if Ruth might come and stay and, for a consideration, she had helped me prepare for her. I had taken trouble to make Ruth's visit pleasant and was indignant that she felt it necessary to bring so much with her.

The suitcase was opened in the middle of my bedroom and Ruth laid her clothes on my bed. I might complain about the quantity but I liked having them, as I liked having her. They were light and airy beside the hardware which was spreading out across the floor.

Among her clothes, Ruth had brought the old kettle which Julius had tried to foist on me when I'd last been at home, an old kitchen knife, some glasses, a few local newspapers with the latest about the new cathedral and lots of other useless things. Her suitcase was like the junk cupboard in an ironmonger's shop. There was even a mousetrap for Mrs Croucher because I'd once said that there were mice in the house.

'Mrs Croucher has a mousetrap that could catch a bison! No sane mice come here after the carnage last Christmas!'

Everything I'd resisted bringing from home over the last two years had arrived now with Ruth.

In the shopping-bag were parcels of food lovingly prepared by Barba. Did she think I starved in London, or that I'd starve Ruth? There were pork pies and oranges, some banana bread, half a pound of butter wrapped in greaseproof paper, some ham, a turnip; even a whole roast chicken, dismembered and wrapped in tinfoil. I could see Barba, so generous and thoughtful, grimacing as she pulled the bird from the oven in a puff of smoke, trying to keep the oven-gloves out of the fat: she would set it aside to cool for half an hour before removing it to the chopping-board, and then hack-snip-hack-snip, the hunks of meat would fall away from the blade in rivulets of juice and each one would be wrapped separately in tinfoil because it was easier to deal with there than in London. I refused to eat any. I couldn't bear the smell of summer roasting in Earlsdon Avenue invading my room, the little piece of lemon that fell to the floor and the thought of the slippery wishbones left to dry on the kitchen window-sill at home.

Ruth knew I wouldn't have brought all this myself but she attributed it to male laziness; she thought I'd be glad to have it all delivered like this. 'In any case, they kept on loading me down with more stuff. It was easier to bring it all than to argue.'

After all her effort it would have been harsh to complain but I couldn't conceal my dismay. There was a worn mortice-block with a note attached in Julius's writing, 'Thought this might be useful for making picture-frames'. How did he think I usually managed? I couldn't throw it away because he'd be offended if he discovered. And even if he didn't, it still felt wrong to throw it away. I felt miserably ungrateful and depressed. A fly was buzzing against the lower half of the window, not realizing that the top half was open. Grabbing one of the newspapers that arrived with Ruth, I swatted it.

The notion that I might have achieved a degree of independence from Earlsdon Avenue seemed to surprise Ruth but she wasn't hurt. She could see that what she had brought imposed on me: there was nowhere to put it all and in this context everything seemed degraded. The mousetrap was no longer The Mousetrap, it was just a clumsy old mousetrap; the knife was no longer The Old Kitchen Knife, it was just a blunt knife for which I'd have to buy a new whetstone if it was to be useful; the food was excessive and inconvenient and the chief motive for eating it was not to waste it.

Mark and Derek, the other two lodgers at Mrs Croucher's,

thought Ruth was marvellous. So did my other friends whom she met. They all said later how relaxed and friendly she was. I myself was surprised to see how easily she mixed with them, how ready she was to laugh. In the college canteen I even introduced her to Janey, who said, 'You're a real free spirit, Ruth, you could teach Dan a thing or two.' I tried not to show it but I was furious: in my eyes, Ruth was possessed by Coventry; she even spoke with a Midlands accent. I was proud of her and pleased that she got on with my friends, but I was taken aback by the idea of her being 'a free spirit'.

I'm afraid I condescended disgracefully to Ruth when she stayed with me over her interviews. That she didn't notice, or didn't mind, is no redemption. In my defence I can only say that it was really the first time I'd ever been with her away from Coventry. Having no clear idea of how she would seem among my friends in London, I was stupidly surprised to see that she was admired: then I was possessive. Eager to display my independence to her, I was startled to see through the eyes of other people that she too had independence.

When she arrived in the early autumn to take up her place at Imperial to read physics, it quickly became apparent that our positions would be reversed. Though nobody's fool, Ruth was good company; she was gregarious and people sought her out. While my social life contracted a little more each year, Ruth's expanded, so that I was amazed that she had time for any work. She was always with different people, always mentioning new names; I couldn't understand what drove her.

It was then that I began making stained glass. I used to go and watch a craftsman in Whitechapel and after I left college I became informally apprenticed to him. I had no money but I was happy. Ruth's reckless hurtling about entertained me: when I saw her she would gasp a few stories at me, then rush off and I'd settle down again to my glass and my strange tools, my lead and my colours; or to my girlfriend. Yes, I led a narrow life but I wasn't utterly single-minded. I wasn't going to deny myself pleasure. Although Ruth used to complain that I was a hermit, I must have had some appeal for I was rarely without a girlfriend then. They were curious about me, perhaps, and the Sixties allowed people to indulge their curiosity that way. Or look at it differently and say that I took advantage of their curiosity. And Ruth – each time I saw Ruth her skirt was a little shorter, and I wondered how far her curiosity was taking her.

I discovered some time in the late spring of 1962.

I was living in an unfurnished flat over a bookie's in Stepney at the time. There was a bath and a loo, but otherwise only a cooker was provided. Being penniless, I'd only bought a mattress and a smelly paraffin heater to improve my comfort. Instead of chairs I made do with some large pieces of foam rubber I'd found on a builder's skip. Perhaps there was one chair, I can't remember. There were a couple of aluminium saucepans, some chipped plates and some cutlery; I had my own frying-pan. Barba and Julius never came there, I'm happy to say: they would have been appalled. I lived on the floor, like a dog, and I rather enjoyed it.

One evening I was shifting around some pieces of glass, playing with shapes and blocking off bits with pieces of grey card when the bell rang. I went downstairs, wondering who would come all the way to Stepney to visit me unannounced, afraid some splinter was about to enter my cocoon.

'Ruth! What a surprise! Come in!' I said and kissed her. She didn't lean towards me to be hugged. Her face was gaunt and toneless and her eyes were scared. A drab mac reached to her ankles.

I followed her up the bare stairs. 'Are you all right, Ruthie? You look ill. What's up? You should have come to me before if something was wrong.'

I had two rooms, a living-room where I lived and a play-room where I played. She walked into the play-room and stopped to look intently around her, as if absorbing all my strange objects into her memory. Still saying nothing and avoiding my eyes, she went into the living-room where she sat down, without a glance around her, in the middle of the floor.

'What is it, Ruthie?'

Now she looked up and smiled grimly, as if at some private joke.

'What is it, Ruthie?'

'Stop saying that!' she cried all of a sudden. 'What is it Ruthie, what is it Ruthie, I'm not your bloody baby sister!'

'What?'

'Stop treating me like that!'

'Oh dear, I...'

'Oh, Dan!' she said, and covered her face with her hands. There was a blue ribbon in her hair. The bow had tightened into a hard knot and the ends hung towards her right ear. I touched her shoulder and she surrendered her tears to my hug.

'What is it?' I murmured after a minute or two.

She disengaged herself and confronted me. Her lungs filled sharply and she said, 'I'm pregnant.'

'Oh God! Who...? Or – '

'Yes, I do know who it was. But – '

'But.'

'But.'

'Well, we're agreed on that then.'

She sighed and her lips gave way to a thin smile. 'I don't know what to do, Dan.'

'No,' I said.

'It's like killing myself, Dan!'

'Does he know?'

'He can't understand. How can I expect him to?' she said. 'He says I should get rid of it – 'get rid of' – as if it's a germ. In any case, I don't love him and he doesn't love me, although he pretends he does if he wants something from me, namely getting me into bed. I'm only twenty, I don't want a baby! Especially a fatherless baby! I can't believe I could have been such a fool!'

'Not foolish. Unlucky,' I said.

'Foolish and unlucky.'

'How long?'

'I should have had my period ten days ago. I'm usually pretty regular.'

'Is it definite? I'm sorry, I don't know much about...'

'Yes. I don't know what to do,' she repeated.

Nor did I. 'To start with, take off your coat. There may not be much here, but it's warm and I have a bottle of wine. And if you don't mind waiting for an hour, I'll have some baked potatoes.'

We talked for a long time that evening, about Barba and Julius and about our childhood. And gently, deviously, I persuaded her: by the time she went to sleep under Julius's old army blanket, she agreed that she must get rid of her baby.

I bullied her into having an abortion.

A fortnight later, when it was done, Ruth and I went home. She was weak and very miserable. Harry, her lover, had produced some money but she resisted any further involvement with him. She said the pain was excruciating, it was like having broken glass scraped around inside her, he couldn't possibly understand. For some reason she believed he was hopeless despite his declared wish to help. I don't know why she thought my understanding was any better but it seemed I was acceptable while he was not. I thought she ought to get out of London and rest, although I knew that telling Barba and Julius the true cause of her exhaustion was out of the question. So I rang and said that Ruth was a bit poorly and low with 'female complaints'. That was enough to ensure that I wasn't questioned any further. Since I hadn't been in Coventry for some time, I said that it suited me very well to accompany her home and stay for a few days.

We didn't talk much on the train. Although the idea of going to Coventry was for Ruth to rest, we both knew that home would impose its own particular strain and Ruth seemed to want to conserve her energy. She sat by the window with a closed book in her lap, watching the skedaddling countryside. Barba would certainly ask Ruth about her 'female complaint' and Ruth was prepared to say that it was a severe attack of cystitis. It didn't matter that I knew only dimly what cystitis was because Barba wouldn't speak to me about it, nor would she expect Ruth and me to have discussed it. Ruth assured me, moreover, that Barba wouldn't press her for details: it would not be a difficult fiction to maintain unless she suffered unexpected complications.

It was a year since I'd spent so long in Coventry. That was over Nan's funeral. She had died a few days after the ceremonial opening of the new cathedral, which I hadn't attended. She died in her sleep and we were all gently relieved because her mind had been rapidly fraying. I went into the cathedral then and saw the tapestry for the first time. I was so astonished by the lurid green that it was a while before I took in the design itself. In the centre was the colossal figure of Christ, seated, his skirt forming an oval like a huge egg. His head and feet and hands were depicted with surprising precision, in sedate contrast to the four lesser figures. Each of these – a calf, a lion, an eagle, a man apparently climbing out of a window – was in a separate box-like web of lines, and flashed with reds and yellows. I recall thinking that it was all very calm for a Last Judgement before realizing that it was actually Christ in Glory. And then I thought, I should have guessed they'd plump for Christ in Glory. The conceit! I was glad poor Nan wasn't important enough to be buried here. She wouldn't have liked.

It wasn't that I didn't like coming home but it was subdued now and, after a short time, I usually felt overfed and puffy. Amy was already at Bristol University and John started at Manchester in the autumn. Being there alone I would feel oppressed by the attention I received. Ruth used to go frequently. She would turn up in a rush of good spirits and overwhelm them with news of London. Then she would turn the house upside-down in search of something she absolutely had to have: nobody was ever sure what she was looking for and it almost seemed as if she was going through the attic just for the fun of replaying her past, as if by touching all these old objects she was recharging her cells. After a day of sorting through cardboard boxes of toys and children's books, through chests-of-drawers and cupboards full of long-discarded clothes and old magazines, she would say that she hadn't found what she was hoping to find; but she would have got an old vase instead which used to sit on the window-sill over the stairs, or a plastic duck, which she took back to London with her the next day, apparently happy.

All children reach a stage when they think they can hoodwink their parents. They say they're going outside to put the rubbish out late at night – and they do, but they also have a cigarette; they say they're going to the cinema with friends but they go to the pub instead; they say they're going to play tennis but they spend all the time necking with their adolescent lover. It's so easy to tell only half the truth: parents, it seems, will believe anything. And then they catch you out because you told a cynical or disrespectful lie, and they don't like that. They are angry and hurt because you're not quite playing the game. Gradually you realize that they had their suspicions of what you were up to all along – they were young once, too, incredible though it may seem. But though they suspected you, they didn't question your account of yourself; they didn't mind only knowing half the truth. With excitement and dismay you understand that they no longer feel altogether responsible for you. If you want their help they will probably give it but you're not answerable to them any more. While remaining within their sphere of commitments, you are your own centre now with your own commitments rippling outwards, embracing, amongst others, your parents.

For the first two days Ruth spent most of the time in bed. Then she sat downstairs in the living-room, reading or just listening to the radio. She didn't go out much, she didn't explore the attics and she wasn't very talkative. I'm sure that Barba and Julius realized she was troubled by more than cystitis but they didn't press her to confide. They could see that she was relieved to be at home in peace and they were content to let her rest. They gave her space. I remember Ruth sitting on the straight armchair by the fire, her face partially obscured by one of the wings. Her legs were crossed beneath a long brown skirt and she was wearing ankle-boots of some kind. I could see her hand fiddling in her pocket with her cigarettes, nervous about bringing them out because Julius had given up and they didn't know she smoked. Eventually she said, 'Do you mind if I smoke?'

Barba said, 'There's an ashtray on the mantelpiece.'

The following day Ruth and I went for a walk in the afternoon and she referred back to this exchange. 'It's silly, isn't it? I've just had an abortion but I'm afraid they'll think I'm naughty if I smoke.'

'I suppose it's strange when parents treat one as an adult. It's something you have to get used to.'

'So do they, probably.'

'Yes, it can't be easy. Or maybe it just happens and usually nobody notices.'

'But I can't tell them about my abortion.'

I turned to her as we walked, aghast at the idea. 'Don't tell them, Ruthie! Never tell them!'

She was surprised by my vehemence and reassured me. 'Of course I won't, Dan! Don't worry!'

But it wasn't enough. 'Promise me, Ruth! Touch my ring and say you promise!'

I held my hand towards her so that she could touch the stone. It was a childish, foolish, melodramatic gesture which I should have despised. But it seemed so intensely important that she never tell Barba and Julius that I had to record her promise without delay, to formalize it – and what else was there but my ring?

Instead of laughing outright, Ruth uttered a faint, breathy titter and stepped back – but her middle finger brushed against my ring and she said, 'All right! I promise! I won't tell them!'

I think we both expected each other suddenly to be facetious. But we were silent and, as the silence endured, it seemed to endow Ruth's strange promise with gravity.

As we approached the cathedral, she said, 'Why do you always come here, Dan?'

'To the cathedral? Do I?'

'Yes, always. You know you do.'

'I don't know, I've never thought about it.'

'Well think about it. Anyway, I don't believe you've never thought about it.'

'A new cathedral!' I answered. 'Who wouldn't get excited about a new cathedral?'

'Most people, for a start.'

We were entering the perimeter of the old cathedral under the bell-tower, which had miraculously survived like a finger pointing to the sky. The reddish walls had long been secure. The interior was like a courtyard with benches facing each other at intervals down each side.

'Do you remember the ruins?' I said.

'Yes, and the day when you got caught peeing,' Ruth replied with a laugh.

'Sometimes it feels as if I remember the bombing itself. I can see the incendiaries showering through the lead roof and blazing against the oak ceiling below. I can see the wardens hurrying around with their pathetic buckets of sand and water, exhausted as much by the steps as the heat. I can see the blaze spreading through the fire trap and the first beams cracking; the tension as they wait for the fire brigade and the hopelessness when they arrive and there's no water. Standing there and watching it burn.

'I'm sorry, Ruth, I can't explain why I come here. Perhaps in some vague way it has something to do with why I'm here at all...'

'And why *I'm* here!'

'Yes, and you too. But it's not just that.'

We came to the chancel, where the first incendiary had fallen on the roof high above – to the altar with the Cross of Charred Beams – and turned left down the steps, already beneath the soaring canopy of the new cathedral's porch. In front of us was the west end of the nave, a colossal glass screen suspended on wires angled from the roof. Just inside the entrance there were three notices on separate boards:–

Please give as much as you can.
The work of the cathedral
can only be maintained if
every visitor gives generously

Photography
Permits available at Information Desk
Flash and tripod by special permission only before 4.00pm

We depend on your contributions to maintain the
cathedral and its ministry
Please give generously

In front of the Baptistry window on the right was another notice:

<u>*The Baptistry Window*</u>
The glass of the window was designed by John Piper
and Patrick Reyntiens.
The window symbolizes the Glory of God flooding into
the world. Beneath it is the font, fashioned from a rough

boulder from a hillside in Bethlehem.

Our steps rang out loudly as we walked up the middle of the building. We weren't the only people there, but the sound of others was muffled in the huge space and they seemed small as they looked at the various works of art.

The Tablets of the Word
On these eight tablets are texts from the bible
describing the work and the person of Jesus Christ. The
primitive origins of the texts are suggested by the
irregular carving of the letters, which were incised by
Ralph Beyer.

This crucifix came from Czechoslovakia as the gift of its
maker Jindrich Severa.

The middle of the nave is always open for prayer. Please
be free to sit or kneel here.

to view the BOOK of REMEMBRANCE please ask the
VERGER.

When we were near the altar we turned round and paused so that we could see the stained glass windows. They were set in the jagged angles of the walls so that, except for their light, they were invisible from the west end. But it was late afternoon now and the light they shed was dull. There were five of them on each side, attenuated strips from the floor to the ceiling. The colours in each pair were different.

'They symbolize the Ages of Man,' I said.

'What?'

'Green represents youth,' I explained, pointing to the first pair. 'Red is passion. Then the jumble of light and dark in the next one is the mixed experience of middle age. Then the purple and blue is supposed to be old age, with a few bits of silver and gold for wisdom. The last pair, the gold ones near the altar, are the afterlife.'

'Who says the afterlife is gold? How come they're so sure there is an afterlife?'

'Ruth, it's a cathedral, for Christ's sake, you've got to start somewhere!'

Ruth shrugged. 'And what about the colours? Who says this one 'symbolizes' this and that one something else?'

'Well, it's just the artists. That's what the colours symbolize for them.'

'Rubbish. Someone sat down and made up a lot of pretentious twaddle.'

'You're a cynic, Ruth.'

'I'm not! The poor fellow had to justify his choice of colours, whatever they were. He could have put a completely different sequence of colours in there and used the same story, or a different story with the same title, the Ages of Man. Incidentally, I thought there were seven ages, not five?'

'As I said, you're a cynic.'

Warning mind the steps.

Going round behind the High Altar into the Lady Chapel, the bottom of the tapestry became visible:

<u>*The Lady Chapel*</u>
Above the Altar hangs the tapestry designed by
Graham Sutherland and woven by Felletin in France. It
depicts Christ seated in Glory, worshipped by the four
living creatures depicted in the fourth chapter of the
Revelation of St John, The Eagle, The Lion, the Calf, the
Man.
Opposite the Tapestry is the Cross surmounting the
High Altar, made of Gilded Silver by Geoffrey Clark. Its

form recalls the charred cross above the altar in the
ruined sanctuary of the old cathedral. In the centre is a
smaller cross formed of three medieval iron nails from the
wooden roof of the old church.

At Christ's feet, obscured from the nave by the Altar, was a crucifixion scene.

'I love this tapestry,' I said, 'except for the subject.'

Passing the Chapels of Christ the Servant and Christ in Gethsemane, we came to a car.

Daimler 1898

Model	: *Phaeton*	*Made in*	*Coventry*
Reg no	: *FRW 767*	*Engine Size*	*6 hp*
Reg. Origin	: *Coventry*	*No of Cylinders*	*Two*

Please do not cross over the chains.

To illustrate the close ties between the cathedral &
industry in the city, this car is an example of Coventry's
Heritage. It is one of the many fine models that can be
seen in the museum of British Road Transport a few minutes
walk from here.

Then we returned to the nave, and I was suddenly struck by the single factor common to all the little plaques with messages on them. Some were administrative, telling you the hours of services or coffee-mornings; some were admonitory – give generously, mind the step; most were explanatory – they described something that you could see perfectly well behind, and told you how to interpret it: but whatever the nature of the text, the script was always the same, so that a strange and ignorant eye might be forgiven for taking them all to be spiritually equivalent.

<u>*The Plumbline and the City*</u>
by Clarke FitzGerald, the gift of Christ Church,
Cincinnati, USA.
A plumb line is used to see whether the upright
members of a building are accurate, or whether they are out or true.
So God judges the city, are the hearts of the people
upright or crooked, true or false?
The sculpture is based on Amos 7.7,8

'I don't know why everyone goes on about this place being so new,' said Ruth.

'What on earth do you mean?' I asked.

'Well, I mean the materials are all new, the bricks and concrete and what-have-you, but in the end it's still a cathedral.'

'Yes, it's a modification of the traditional Gothic structure...'

'It's just the same old dish served up with a different sauce. A sauce that smothers everything.'

Ruth's assurance jolted me. It challenged me to consider whether I too hadn't been prevented from seeing what lay beneath the surface. But didn't her idea echo my own unease with the script? At the same time, I felt that there was something magnificently valiant in this adoption of form, not just an assertion of right but a heroic act of faith in the possibility of right.

<u>*Your Gifts*</u>
for the work of INTERNATIONAL RECONCILIATION

As we were leaving I looked up at the ranks of wispy saints and angels engraved on the glass. Against the afternoon light they seemed to be volatile creatures of the air itself. Presiding above them was St Michael, with the slain dragon at his feet. He stood guard with his lance, watching in both directions at once like some ancient heretic as the citizens passed to and fro beneath.

13

Well, I am delighted! I'm very happy for both of you, I must say. I've always thought how lovely Kate is and I'm proud that she will be my daughter-in-law. If I urged you to be circumspect before, it was because I had misgivings about her recovery. I thought she shouldn't be called upon to make a decision without being in full control. But now, though her memory of the days immediately preceding her fall remains patchy, her recovery seems assured. I've seen for myself that she is just as capable of taking responsibility as she ever was. You must have a party to celebrate your engagement. If you tell me what you'd like, I'll supply the drink. Your flat would be the best place for it, if Kate can endure the grim proximity of the balcony.

After you told me the good news, I had a thought: assuming you have children, will they ever know about Kate's fall? How will it and its repercussions seem to them in, say, twenty years from now? I suppose it occurred to me because I'd been wondering what you made of Mum's and my past; and not only you, but also Tilda and Joe – what will this child of theirs know of its antecedents? For example: you don't have to be a sophisticated mathematician to connect Tilda's failure to appear at home on the day of Percy's funeral and her absence from your flat that night with her getting pregnant. (Is this an undignified thought for a soon-to-be grandfather?) She was otherwise occupied, shall we say, if not preoccupied, and never telephoned; had she done so then Mum would have come to Percy's funeral and instead of staying at your flat that night I

254

would have gone with her to an hotel.

Since you haven't told me otherwise, I've accepted that my hunch linking my presence on your balcony to your argument with Kate is correct... Will Tilda's baby ever have an inkling of these associations? They are utterly unproveable; in themselves, they hold no value whatsoever. But I believe such things nevertheless find their images in people, just as the clouds and the air and the seasons all affect the colours on the choirboy's surplice, the glance of a beam on a pillar, the swift shimmer of a pattern low on a high, shadowed wall. Or take another point: Joe is more Jewish than you, but you are much more sympathetic towards Zionism than he is. Perhaps, knowing my indifference, you are determined in some way to compensate for me. It will be a difficult thing for Kate to understand but she probably knows this better than I do already. As for her background, I know practically nothing of it. I look forward to hearing more.

I wonder if the favour with which you look on Zionism is a reaction to an indifference you perceive in me towards my parents? It's never occurred to me before – because I'm not indifferent to my parents. Awareness of them, and of them as Jews, tones my consciousness. And there is an aspect to this which I think we kept from you at the time, but which you ought to know.

While we were in Germany, Mum encouraged me to try and find out more about my own family. I think she was interested partly from curiosity but also because she sometimes liked to emphasize that we came from totally unconnected families, as if to disguise our closeness as children now that we were married. It was quite possible that we should find people who knew my parents, after all. I went to Hamburg but the street in which they lived was gone. I went to Berlin and only when I got there did I discover that their address was deep in East Berlin. It might be possible to find out something now but I didn't pursue it then. Not knowing how to proceed with my inquiry, I read a book about pre-war Hamburg and learned that it was the centre of German communism (such as it was). Many of the communists were Jews and, while most perished and a few emigrated, a tiny handful continued in spite of extraordinary odds to work actively against Hitler for years into the war. Here was a tale of astounding, unsung courage, and I quickly convinced myself that my parents and grandparents belonged to it. Suddenly everything fitted. Why didn't they emigrate when they could? Not because their apprehension of danger was dim but because they felt obliged to fight for their cause. Why did the Macksteins come and join them? Because they were communists too, who insisted on being at the suicidal centre of the battle against Hitler. They had volunteered their lives in a desperate struggle, which at last was won; and they, perhaps, were justified. I worked myself into a state of such frenzied admiration that it was some weeks before I remembered that I hadn't a wisp of evidence for it all. Certainly other Jews had behaved with what, in other circumstances, one might deem insane bravery. Then I looked at myself: was I so brave? And why did they risk my brothers' lives? Why weren't they sent away too – as surely they could have been – to Switzerland, if not to England? If my parents were involved in such dangerous activities, wouldn't they have let my grandmother take the children away?

Mum suggested I try Basle. I didn't go there but it wasn't difficult tracing my grandfather's company. I wrote explaining who I was and that, while I knew Herr Mackstein had died in the Holocaust, I was anxious to find out anything more about him. Was it true that he was a communist, for example? Within two weeks I received a polite but cool reply from an elderly man who in his youth had worked as a clerk for my grandfather. He said that he had no further information regarding his death; and no, Herr Mackstein had certainly never been a communist. Herr Mackstein was a traditional man.

I wish my fantasies were true, but I'm afraid they are not.

I've no reason to doubt that, like millions of others around that time, they died cold, starved and dreadfully savaged because they were Jews. It's more likely that they were hostile to communism.

How could I be indifferent?

Then again, your Zionism may have nothing to do with me. It may be 'purely political', though I doubt the phrase has any meaning. In any case, since you care about it, I wish you luck.

And I wish you both happiness.

Yet still I wonder how you will present your Zionism to your children and how conscious they will be of their diluted Jewishness? And I wonder how you will tell them your parents' story? And your own story? Will they ever know about the strange hiatus in Kate's life or think back to how it happened?

I'm speaking as if everything is clear now about Mum and me, but of course it isn't. There is still a little more to be told. There always is.

14

There is a chapel at Vence with windows designed by Matisse. He was convalescing after an operation when one of the Dominican sisters asked him to criticize her designs for the glass in the chapel which was about to be rebuilt. I hope the nun wasn't too distressed by what happened: Monsieur Matisse jettisoned her work and did the job himself.

Large green cactus-shapes climb behind the altar against a background of blue, which is suspended in front of a vivid yellow. Matisse rejected the first ten greens; it took the factory which produced them several years to pay for his certainty as they slowly sold off their stocks of green glass. In the main hall are two larger windows where tulip-shapes of yellow and green rise against blue. The pieces of glass are unusually large, but the design is successful because the colours and the intervals are so perfectly judged. In what is otherwise an indifferent building these distinctively 'Matisse' windows are magnificent. But something else, which he didn't plan, makes them particularly remarkable. If you come up close to the main windows you suddenly realize that the blue and the green are transparent. Paul Bony, who interpreted the designs in glass, played an unexpected trick by allowing us to make contact with the outside. He has emphasized it by white-aciding the inside of the yellow so that it is translucent, not transparent. With the yellow he invites you and then blocks you. With the darker colours he takes you unawares and propels you where you never expected to go. He has given you the outside, knowing that you are bound to it, but he has given it in such a way that you must react.

You've been reading a story about your family and in at least one respect it's just like any other story: it doesn't seem to affect you very much. But you may be starting to feel uneasy because you know that it will soon reach a point where you must be born and, so far, absolutely nothing's being done about it. The story seems to be unprepared for you. Imagine watching two people through the Matisse-Bony window as they walk along a riverbank, one on each side: you can see that their paths stop but there is a bridge with a boat tied to it. You can't control them, you can't make them see what's coming. What are these people like (before your appearance)? Could they turn round and walk back again? They still haven't noticed that their way forward is blocked, they haven't noticed the bridge or the boat and the longer they remain blind the more abrupt their meeting must be. Are you startled now to see them turn and idly saunter back? Then suddenly they see each other. Unable to make themselves heard above the sound of the river, they signal frantically. Ignoring the bridge, they strip off their clothes – you rub your hands, they think they're unobserved! – and dive. Together they swim downstream and the boat bobs clumsily in their wake. You knew that something had to happen, and from your vantage point you thought you could see how it must be achieved. But they managed it differently, without you.

While I was in Coventry with Ruth that week I had made some inquiries about renting a small studio. There were still watchmakers' topshops around then, with their rows of gleaming windows. While many of the larger ones might be converted for a different use and the smallest weren't much more than an elaborate shed in someone's back garden, it occurred to me that I might find a suitable one for a cheap rent before it was pulled down. So I wandered round Chapelfields and Earlsdon, peering over fences and walls and, whenever I saw one that seemed possible, I knocked on the door and asked the owners if they would consider letting their topshop as a studio. Some people seemed appalled by the idea of having an artist on the premises. Others said the place was already in use, for chickens, as a tool shed, a workshop; or it was going to be annexed properly to the house. But several agreed to think about it, they'd have to ask the husband, but a few extra quid certainly wouldn't be unwelcome and it couldn't do any harm having the place looked after. In each case I said I'd call back after giving them time to think it over. Then, completely without forethought, I went along to the art college and asked if they had any teaching vacancies. They hadn't and I was relieved. Why, I wondered, had I even asked? Teaching had always seemed like opting out.

Impoverished and very unsure of what the future held for me, I went back to London, where I spent a lot of time preparing glass that other people had designed or repairing imitation Tiffany lampshades. Then a letter arrived from the Coventry College of Art and Technology announcing that they had a vacant post for a teacher in mixed media. They suggested I might like to apply. I hurried up to Coventry for a couple of interviews and, though I still had no clear idea of what might be expected of me, I was offered the job. Ludicrously impressed by my own achievement and by the meagre financial security, I accepted at once. The same afternoon I rented a two-room topshop in Craven Street, which could be reached up steps from Hearsall Lane.

Again I returned to London, this time to fetch my possessions. Ruth helped me pack up. She couldn't understand why I wanted to leave. Although she too had no job and no money, except her small allowance from Julius, she said that my going back to Coventry was like tying a mouldy sack over my head. She was glamorous; in her eyes London still gleamed with promises. But as I climbed into the hired van she cried and her mascara smudged, so that I reached through the window with my handkerchief and dabbed at her tears.

It was raining when I arrived in Coventry and the studio leaked. A thin trickle of water ran down one of the walls and the plaster crumbled where I touched it. Going up the steps with a few unwieldy pieces of glass, I tripped on a loose brick. Somehow I managed to protect the glass but I twisted my ankle painfully. Hobbling back and forth between the van and the studio, I thought I must be mad to have left London.

I was living with Barba and Julius. A week later, as we sat down to supper, the telephone rang. Barba answered. She had grown much larger recently and the way in which she held the receiver to her ear, with her elbow raised almost to the level of her shoulder, exaggerated the thickness of her arm and revealed that she no longer had any waist. 'Barbara Gallagher here,' she announced. Then she turned towards Julius with panicky eyes. 'We'll be over right away, Sarah,' she said. 'Stay where you are and don't try to move him.'

David had had a massive stroke. Two hours later he was dead.

About fifty people, most of whom were Methodists, came back to the house after the funeral to express their condolences to Sarah and guzzle the cakes that Barba and Amy had made. Tilly and Percy were there too. Sarah had been sitting next to her sister May in church and I remember seeing them talking together outside before the service. May was a widow. Her husband had been killed in the Great War, less than a year after their wedding. She lived on her own in Nottingham and we rarely saw her. I don't know when they agreed on it – it might have been at the funeral or long ago. In any case, we were all surprised afterwards: when Mrs Phelps expressed the hope that Sarah would quickly get used to living on her own, Sarah answered, 'Dear me, no, I shan't be living on my own, I'm going to live with May. I'm sure I shall be very comfortable there, thank you very much.'

Barba and Julius tried to dissuade her. She would be lonely, they said, away from Coventry and her friends – and away from them. I think they were offended that she could get up and leave like that. Whatever their differences over the years, they were fond of Sarah and David. Having just lost David, they were reluctant to lose Sarah as well and they were taken aback to learn that the reverse was not true. But Sarah had decided. And what about the house in Norfolk Street?

'What about it?' she said. 'Dan can live there.'

At breakfast the following morning, Julius declared that everyone ought to go and see my studio. I could surely use the extra pairs of hands to help me fix it up. He would join the work party too, he said. Barba sniffed and went glowering into the kitchen.

'He can't go, it's bad for his leg,' she said to me when I took through some dirty plates.

Julius caught up with me outside the front door as I was loading a sack of plaster into the back of the car. 'Let me give you a hand there, Dan, old chap,' he said. He picked up one end and together we heaved it in. 'Look, about this work party, I think I'd better cry off, Mum's feeling a bit low.'

Julius was a crafty fellow.

So it was just the four of us in the studio: myself, Ruth, Amy and John. It was strange. Suddenly everything had changed for me. I had a job, a place to live, even a separate place to work. Although I hadn't been a student for two or three years, I had seemed like one because of my limited means. Now I could be genuinely independent – and I was choosing to settle in Coventry. I was no longer just a brother, I was behaving and being treated as an adult. Ruth was excited about my studio. She worked hard all morning patching up the plaster, until her hair was thick with dust and her overalls stiffened by drips, but she was eager to continue. While Amy was still busy white-washing the other walls, Ruth went outside to find John, whom I'd sent up to the roof to inspect the tiles. Her idea was to get him to take over making the glass-racks from me so that we could begin fixing the mullions over the windows for the easel. Through the windows, Amy and I could see her looking up from the foot of the ladder and we couldn't help overhearing what was said:

'Hey, John, what are you doing?'

'Smoking.'

'Have you finished doing the tiles yet?'

'No.'

'How long is it going to take? I wish you'd buck up, we need you inside.'

'I'm staying here.'

'Whatever do you mean – staying there?'

'Why don't you come on up?'

Ruth frowned, suddenly confused. Her voice was carefully steady. 'John, what are you smoking?'

'Pot, Ruthie.'

'John!' She looked round quickly towards the house, then towards us. Despite the fine layer of plaster covering her, she still managed to look fiercely indignant. 'Come down!' she commanded.

'Come up!'

'Come down and help Dan!'

'Why should I help Dan? Everyone else is helping him!'

'John, unless you come down here this minute I shall come up and drag you down!'

'God, Ruthie, you're bossy! What right have you...?'

But from Ruth's poise at the foot of the ladder it was clear that he was moving in spite of his protests. Presently we saw him shifting awkwardly down the ladder, like an old man, concentrating on each step until at the second rung he lost his footing and slipped.

He sat on the ground giggling. His broad shoulders trembled, his face was red and puffy and his mouth was slack. He looked ridiculous. Ruth slapped him.

'Here, what was that for, Ruthie?'

'Get up and come inside!'

'God, you're a bore! Who do you think you are?'

He stumbled after her into the studio.

'Hi, everyone!' he said. 'I've been making big brother a nest, but now I've finished and I'm ready...'

'Sit down and shut up!' said Amy. 'You would go and have to make an exhibition of yourself! You'll ruin it for Dan! Why d'you have to go and smoke on the *roof?*'

Ruth stared at Amy in consternation. 'Why do you have to smoke *at all?*' she said to John.

'Doesn't look to me as if I've ruined anything,' said John. 'Dan Freeloading Flasch rides joyfully on...'

Ruth sprang at him, both arms raised to strike.

'John, you don't know what you're saying!' said Amy, as she struggled to pull Ruth away.

But the terrible thing is that he did know what he was saying, for at that moment Tilly entered and said, 'Hey, what's going on here?'

And he replied immediately, 'We were having a barney about guilt.'

I laughed. I couldn't help it. It was funny. I was impressed.

Ruth and Amy had quickly retreated from John, furious both with him and now also with Tilly for catching them in this disarray. I'd taken no part in the dispute myself because there was nothing for me to say. They accepted this but when I laughed they froze, as if suddenly afraid that I was laughing at them. Even if I could provide an explanation, now was not a suitable moment. I flicked my hand out impatiently towards John. 'Speaking of guilt, John, would you mind getting up? I'd like to offer my chair to Tilly,' I said.

He wasn't as stoned as he'd been pretending. 'Excuse me,' he said as he jumped to his feet. 'Of course, it's nice to do things properly.'

Tilly remained on the threshold of the shambles. She looked bemused, aware that she had interrupted something: wondering whether to ask what it was all about and then deciding against it. For an instant I thought that one of the others was going to tell her and I began to chatter as I conducted her round the studio, showing her what we had done that morning and what I was going to do to improve it.

I do not deny that John's words hurt me. It was like ramming a window down on the back of my neck and inviting people to throw stones. I don't know – and will never know – whether or not he meant what he said and, without this knowledge, how can I start to forgive? I don't entirely understand forgiveness. 'Forgive and forget' sounds like a sanctimonious piety: does one ever entirely forget such a thing? Yet the memory has weakened until it's just another aspect of the generative light within me, which I imagine to be free of malice. Perhaps this is forgiveness. And John must have undergone a similar process, for I've never seen that colour in him since.

Although never formally adopted, I was confident of my position in my foster family: yet John could scarcely have said anything more likely to wound. And while Ruth and Amy might be upset by his reference to the fact that I wasn't their brother, they couldn't deny its truth. 'The causal chain' is a misleading phrase, for it implies that an event depends on a particular linear sequence, which might have been cut or diverted in some way so that the event itself would never have occurred. That may be so in some cases: if you cut through a tangled skein with a good pair of shears, it may fall apart. But you may have countless loose ends bound together in an indissoluble knot. I do not claim that John's remark directly influenced what happened a few weeks later, but it pleases me to reflect that it may have worked to my advantage.

The next day, John returned to Manchester in the morning. In the afternoon Tilly and Percy returned to London, whence they would leave for Bahrain. Ruth and Amy stayed two days longer than they had originally intended and they helped me in my studio. I didn't consciously associate their extension with John's remark – none of us ever referred to it again – but I remember being very grateful.

Two weeks later, Julius and Barba took Sarah to Nottingham. After almost fifty years of married life in Coventry she was leaving with only two suitcases, a stool and three boxes. The stool was a wedding gift from her sister which had always stood in front of her dressing-table. Its seat was embroidered with the legend *dulce et decorum est pro patria mori* in flamboyant purple letters around a scene depicting St George and St Michael; it was all very faded now and hard to make out. One of the boxes was an elaborate Victorian needlework box. The other two were cardboard (one contained some pieces of Jubilee and Coronation china, the other was filled with photographs and a few books). 'An old lady doesn't need much,' she said, when I asked her if that was really all. After helping them load up, I watched the car pull away, sighing and grunting, from the kerb. The engine coughed once or twice; the blue exhaust coiled up and then settled. As they turned the corner out of my sight, I wondered how Sarah could treat her attachment to Coventry so blithely. I had attempted to say something of the sort to her and she answered that she'd never been very attached, it was David who had always been devoted to Coventry. With everything new, she said, she didn't feel at home anywhere any more. But it puzzled me why her sister, whom she'd seen so rarely over the last two decades, and Nottingham, should have a greater hold over her than us and Coventry.

I remember thinking as I watched them depart, the house behind me is mine now.

I turned and it was in front of me. I knew it was mine only temporarily but, as evanescence is a glimpse of infinity, so the temporary can glide into the unforeseen, and I was excited.

You know the house. It is a cottage really. Downstairs there are two rooms and a kitchen, plus a spacious cupboard under the stairs. Upstairs there is a bathroom, two very small bedrooms and a larger one at the front from whose window can be seen the cathedral to the left, lurking behind Arthur Ling's tower-block in the city's centre, and, to the right, the roofs of Earlsdon. A covered alley runs alongside the house to a small garden at the back, which once contained a potting-shed (formerly a privy) and a bed of marigolds, pansies and nasturtiums which David had reared with such zeal that they seemed artificial. Stepping inside, I had the peculiar sensation of trespassing on the house's past, on David's and Sarah's recent life together, on Barba and Julius's life there, and on his parents'. I moved the chairs from the positions they'd occupied for years and put the lacy antimacassars in a drawer; I rolled up the imitation Axminster and stored it under the stairs with the copper relief pictures. I found a presentation edition of George Eliot and put it on one of the shelves vacated by Sarah's china and I hung up a print of Coventry's three spires. But soon I began to feel uncomfortable, despite the familiarity. For not only did the house and its contents not belong to me but also the choices that determined their character were not mine: I felt like a grave-robber, as if by shifting what was settled I was threatening the secure bonds of time.

Unnerved, hoping perhaps to nourish my wan resolve, I returned to my studio.

Sitting on the steps above Hearsall Lane, with her chin on her knees and her hands clasped over her ankles, was Ruth. She smiled when she saw me and said, 'I was restless. So I came to see how you were getting on.'

I bent down and kissed her soft upturned cheek hello. Then I stepped back and said, 'What a lovely surprise! I've just been looking at my new house. I'm like a hermit crab, aren't I? But my new shell doesn't feel quite empty yet, so I came up here for air.'

'You must make it your own. I'll come and help you.'

'That would be... That would be terribly nice, actually.'

I offered my hand and, as I pulled her up towards me, she kissed me lightly on the lips. When I asked her later what she meant by this, she said she was just saying hello. I looked lonely, she said, and she felt sorry for me. I've asked again many times since then and she always insists that nothing more was intended. Except once, when I asked if she hadn't been missing me, and she replied, 'Of course I was missing you.'

How often in our lives we had walked from Earlsdon Avenue to Norfolk Street via Hearsall Lane. Now, however, having just come up that way, I felt inclined to follow the parallel route.

'I'm afraid Barba and Julius are taking Sarah to Nottingham,' I said as we walked past my studio through the garden.

Ruth shrugged. 'I didn't especially want to see them anyway. I feel a bit uncomfortable with them nowadays. It's their stability, I think... I find it a bit repellent.'

'Repellent?'

'Perhaps I just feel detached... A bit envious...'

As we emerged from the narrow alley into Craven Street we were greeted by a sharp gust of wind, then a low growl burgeoned suddenly into a bark of thunder. Although it had been overcast, there had been no previous warning of a storm. Now the sky was filling with banks of grim, grey clouds, and, as we linked arms and hurried downhill, the wind lashed towards us, chasing shadows around the street. When we rejoined the old familiar route at Spon End there was a fierce gushing, like the amplified echo of the sea, and the rain swept over us in a torrent. Headlights and windscreen-wipers came on. Water was very soon spraying out from beneath the cars' wheels and, all around us, people were splashing through the juddering puddles, scurrying with bent shoulders and squeezed-up faces towards shelter.

Seeing a dry doorway, I hesitated, but Ruth pulled me on. 'We might as well keep going,' she cried, and rain flowed down her cheeks and neck. 'It's not far and it might be ages if we wait for it to stop.'

And so we kept going through the rain, as if drawn by a trail invisible to everyone but ourselves.

We slammed the door behind us and stood facing each other in the sitting-room, dripping.

'Take off your wet things,' I said. 'I'll get some towels.'

Two months later Mum was pregnant. Careless? We married. Then you were born.

15

An engagement party: what a happy occasion!

So many people were gathered there to congratulate you both. It was a good atmosphere, I thought. There were people of diverse ages from all walks of life spreading through your flat as if on a current of spring air. Celebrating Kate's recovery added an edge of exhilaration: it seemed to lift a burden and affirm something inside us all. It was good to see Kate's family and I was pleased that all of our lot were there too. Tilda is beginning to look quite heavy now, while Joe, proud and attentive at her side, is thinner than ever despite his new suit. Unshaven – and apparently shoeless – Luke displayed a constant, effortless joviality which astonished Mum and me. He used to be so shy. I was glad that Amy and John came too, and the cousins, although I wish those boys hadn't been so intent on getting pickled. Karen is going to be quite a beauty.

For as long as I am conscious I will remember Kate as she was in that moment when I approached her: blue silk taut across her thigh and stomach, she is half-sitting on the table, half-leaning on her left arm which is braced by her glinting metal crutch. She notices me while she's talking with someone else, smiles and finishes what she's saying. Then she touches her right ear with the middle finger of her right hand, as if pushing back her hair which hasn't yet grown back so far. And then I strip my joker:

'Just think,' I say cheerfully, the disarmingly waggish, presumptive father-in-law, 'last time we were together in this flat

I sat out all night on the balcony and you didn't even know I was there!'

'Oh dear, I'm afraid I don't remember!' she said.

'Well, you wouldn't – because you didn't know I was there,' I repeated.

Then lightly, discreetly insistent, you intervened. 'It's a bit much asking Kate to remember things she never knew, Dad. She's got back pretty much everything now, though – haven't you, Kate, love?'

'Not the fall, I haven't got the fall, or any of that afternoon. Apart from that – well, I'll never know, will I?'

'I suppose not,' I agreed.

Other people were pressing around, all eager to talk with Kate, and you touched my arm and said, 'There's something I want to show you, Dad.'

You steered me to the balcony where we stood in darkness by the parapet, the chilly wind scourging our faces as we surveyed the view. Although cold, the night was clear and it seemed as if the whole city was exposed to us. Raising your arm, you pointed a long, luminous finger towards the river. 'In your description of the view from here, how come you didn't mention Canary Wharf? It's the tallest building in Europe,' you said. And then, 'Dad, please don't speak of that night again to Kate.'

Switching from the lit grid of the tower block – so tall that the single light on its pointed summit seemed like a star – I was unprepared for the fierce, peremptory glare of your black eyes. 'I beg your pardon?'

'You see, it wasn't Kate.'

I didn't understand what you meant at first, Jake. Never, in all the time since that night, had I doubted that it was Kate who was with you.

'It wasn't Kate,' you said again.

'Who was it?' I asked stupidly.

You uttered a name, which I'm glad to say I can't recall, and then continued. You said you'd meant to tell me before but I trapped you with my assumptions like a bubble in glass. You were so busy with your deceptions that you'd simply forgotten I was coming – wasn't that it? And when you realized later on, not wanting to be caught at it, you got the hell out. But you were ashamed and a few days later you told Kate. You argued... Is this right? I don't know. It doesn't matter.

All this time you never breathed a clue to me. Perhaps you didn't read my pages, perhaps even this final clutch will be stuffed unseen into the bin... But no, you say you've kept up with me. Although – wouldn't it have been better if you'd never begun to follow me through my fond and frangible misapprehensions? I thought I knew the way things stood between you but I was so wide of the mark, so ridiculously wide! Clues may have dappled my path like slivers of light through trees but my understanding was fixed and I saw nothing but the inside of my own foolish head.

I went on, trying to be benign, 'Yet here we are...' And when you looked perplexed, I added, 'You're a fool, but she still agreed to marry you.'

'But she doesn't know, Dad. I mean she did, but she doesn't now.'

I hadn't anticipated another surprise. Even in retrospect your answer is like a huge, unseen hand suddenly grabbing me from behind. 'What? She doesn't remember?' I said.

'No.'

'But you must tell her!'

'Why?'

'Because it's wrong, it's a lie!'

'In a way. But...'

'You can't get married on a lie!'

'I don't see it that way. If she remembers then there would be a problem, which I believe we could solve. But she doesn't remember, so the original problem has been dissolved.'

'Jake, this is unbelievable! You have to tell her!'

'It was reading that stuff of yours which made me think that I didn't have to. You know, finding your own way from the past to the future, from one side of the glass to the other, all that stuff. Trusting events... I find it incredible to hear you telling me what to think now.'

'But Jake, that was a story, that was me sitting at a desk: this is a marriage, this is Kate's life and yours! I didn't know...!'

'And if you had done? If you'd known the truth about Kate and me when you started writing, would it have made any difference to what you wrote?'

'Damn it, it doesn't matter! You can't take fantasy into real life like this. You can't just pretend it didn't happen!'

'I'm not pretending that she didn't fall. That would be daft. And, as for my betrayal of her, I'm not 'just pretending', because in a way it *didn't happen*: it's wiped clean from her memory.'

'You have no right to play with her like this...'

'I'm not playing!'

'You are trespassing!'

'Eh? I'm taking a risk, Dad, that's all. And I want to take it. You can try to stop me, if you want, by going on at Kate about the night you were on this balcony, so that her memory is jogged. Or, now I've told you, you could stop me by simply passing on to her what I've said. But, if you keep the secret, her memory need never be jogged. I assumed – from what you'd written and from what I know of you anyway – I assumed that, even though you might be uneasy about it, you wouldn't stop me taking that risk.'

'It's wrong.'

Driving back to Coventry with Mum yesterday, I couldn't think. Your new information cuts through everything I've written, as if I've been working on a huge window without seeing a hairline fracture running from top to bottom. We chatted desultorily about the party as I drove, and Mum dozed for a bit. I wasn't good company. My mind kept reverting to those silly plaques in the cathedral and I was very dispirited. Even the glorious tapestry repelled me. In that position at the east end of a cathedral there is usually a window, an image on glass illuminated from behind. But they have blocked the light there – as they have blocked all light coming from that direction, as if they are afraid of a confrontation with light in their cathedral – and in its place is set a monolithic image. I felt tricked out of my imagined glass and grounded, like Zebedee, in sand.

Suddenly a pebble hit the windscreen, thrown up by a lorry in front, and I realized that for a few instants I'd been staring at the windscreen as if it was a blank wall, utterly oblivious of the road. The glass didn't shatter, but it was like waking to a glimpse of disaster. My hands tingled as I clenched them round the steering wheel. Somehow I had continued in a straight line and escaped an accident. I glanced at Mum and was amazed to see that she was still asleep. 'Safety Glass' they call it, which seems like a contradiction in terms. I smiled at my luck. Then I thought of the transparent West Window where St Michael stands sentinel, and I thought again of you, hoping to span the void by a deception.

Why not say that it's Time, not Kate, that you are cheating? Why not say that this is being alive to what happens? A voice echoes insistently in the cloisters of my mind, declaring that you should tell her.

But another voice whispers from beyond: *Why should I deny you a miracle?*